OF SEA AND SOUL

THE KERRIGAN CHRONICLES, BOOK III

Also by Annie Daylon

Castles in the Sand

Maggie of the Marshes

Passages: A Collection of Short Stories

The Many-Colored Invisible Hats of Brenda-Louise

At the Heart of the Missing

Of Sea and Seed, The Kerrigan Chronicles, Book I

Of Sea and Sand, The Kerrigan Chronicles, Book II

Praise for
The Kerrigan Chronicles

Daylon's talent is apparent in this engrossing opening to a projected series . . . Intriguing characterizations . . . surprising level of suspense . . . a page-turner.
Publishers Weekly

. . . story of family secrets, deprivation, atonement, sins, and guilt. . . . memorable characters who have met life's challenges with strength and stoicism . . . The pages are so well rendered that the reader forgets time and tasks to be done.
Lynne Legrow, Amazon Top Reviewer and Award-Winning Blogger of Fictionophile

. . . recommend books 1 & 2 of the series to anyone interested in historical fiction . . . loved the paranormal element . . . Kathleen is a ghost, telling her story, a literal voiceover for the reader, and I think that was an incredibly creative idea as a narration. Goodreads Reviewer

With insight, wit, and great understanding of the all-too-human emotions of guilt and desire, Daylon draws the reader into a timeless story of yearning and loss.
Paul Butler, author of *The Good Doctor*

Haunting, exhilarating, mysterious. These characters will long fill my mind and soul . . . Amazon Reviewer

With the skill of a poet, Daylon weaves the tale of a Newfoundland outport family in the early 20th century. Her mastery of the written word brings the reader into the lives of her characters as they deal with the truths and tragedies of everyday life . . .
Ron Young, Founding Editor, *Downhome* Magazine

. . . loved the storyline of these chronicles . . .I read every word, every paragraph and I must say Daylon has a unique descriptive mind! Email Reviewer

A longing for the sea, and from the sea...lives out of control since birth, torn by land and by sea . . . souls steadily whipped by the rhetoric of religion. Pounding rhythms. Exciting narrative. Darrell Duke, author of *Thursday's Storm*

I am very impressed with your wonderful prose. It reminds me a bit of Annie Proulx . . . I'm two-score of pages into your novel and in love with your voice. That to me is what makes a read enjoyable. Email Reviewer

. . . you will draw in the scent of the land and the sea, your ear attuned to authentic Newfoundland voices. The old-world characters are compelling in their secretive lives and in acts of love gone wrong.

Nellie P. Strowbridge, author of *Ghost of the Southern Cross*

OF SEA AND SOUL

THE KERRIGAN CHRONICLES, BOOK III

A novel by
Annie Daylon

McRAC Books
British Columbia, Canada

Published by **McRAC Books**, British Columbia, Canada

ISBN-978-1-7771814-3-7 (paperback)
ISBN-978-1-7771814-4-4 (ebook)
McRAC Books Trade Paperback Edition
First Printing: October 2025
Printed in the United States of America

Cover Photo: Wreck of the SS *Ethie* at Martin's Point, Gros Morne National Park, Newfoundland. Shutterstock, EWY Media
Newfoundland map design: Brian Rodda, www.roddawrites.com
Map photo © @FilipBjorkman

. . . for love of Newfoundland, for its greatest generation, for its invincible soul

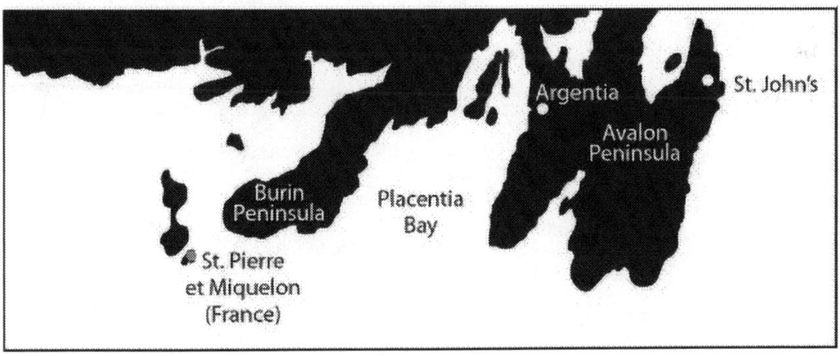

CAST OF CHARACTERS

Kathleen Kerrigan: ghost, matriarch doomed to an afterlife of repeated telling of her story in atonement for mortal sin
Clara Caulins: daughter of Kathleen, woman at cutting edge of social change, rum runner, wife, adulterer
Kate Kerrigan: granddaughter of Kathleen, daughter to Kevin
Dulcie Mullins: family friend, landlady of the Bakeapple Boarding House
Patrick McMurty: Clara's lover
Robert Caulins: British gentleman, rum runner, husband of Clara
Izzie Thompson: boarding house resident, friend of Kate
Peter McGraw: resident of Southeast, Placentia, friend of Kate

Deceased
Alphonse Kerrigan: Kathleen's husband, murdered
Jimmy Kerrigan: Kathleen's baby boy, murdered
Mavis Kerrigan: Kevin's wife, died in tidal wave
Jimmy, Marie, Johnny, Joseph Kerrigan: Kevin's children, died in tidal wave
Kevin Kerrigan: Son of Kathleen, widower, Merchant Marine

Kathleen

Since then, at an uncertain hour,
That agony returns:
And till my ghastly tale is told,
This heart within me burns.

The Rime of the Ancient Mariner
Samuel Taylor Coleridge

CHAPTER 1

IT IS VIGILANT, THE SEA.

The North Atlantic pools into trenches, swirls around sea stacks, and rambles through clefts and knolls. It fingers shorelines, shaping everything, its power unmistakable; the sea owns both the island of Newfoundland and the lives of its people. At times, the Atlantic shifts from calm to bluster, hammering vessels off course and splintering them against the island's own sculpted cliffs. Once regaining composure, it smiles as its harbours welcome dories and schooners and coastal boats filled with fisher folk who build houses and stages and docks along the shore. My Irish ancestors, fleeing famine, accept this opportunity and settle on the shore of a quiet harbour in Placentia Bay.

It takes one hundred years to develop this community. Originally called Little Placentia, it grows to a multi-schooner fishing settlement with a general store, post office, and a beacon of light on Point Latine. To make a clear distinction between it and the community of Placentia across the Gut, its name is changed to Argentia, *argentum* being the Latin for silver, the silver mine in the area being the genesis for the name, the mandate for the change coming from the parish priest, the Roman collar having that much sway.

This is the Argentia of 1904 and this it continues to be until 1940 when war comes and Argentia becomes part of the lands leased to the United States who would transform it into a military base. The residents are too shocked to object, not that it would have done any good anyway. Their fate is ordained, their homes on a chopping block.

Stilled at first, they stumble, then stand to meet the challenge of giving all for the good of all. No surprise, this sacrifice. For all time, Newfoundland's outport dwellers have held within their hearts the capacity for greatness. It lies not in the form of visible wealth, for that has long been disavowed by the acceptance of struggle as a part of daily life. It lies instead in resilience. A community felled, its people rise. This despite their having no home to go to, no place to sleep but in barns with animals, and no air to breathe that isn't laced with the stench of diesel.

In 1941, the American flag is raised and military might demolishes the community. Argentia sinks to misery as houses and businesses and docks and outbuildings and crops are razed to transform the place into an American military base. Excavators remove tons of bog to turn peat into runways. An onslaught during which the tumble of tide onto the coast of Argentia is muted, the comfort in its daily rhythm obscured by rumble and roar. The men work in two shifts, ten hours each. The only lull from the ruckus occurs four hours each day, mandatory stillness to allow bulldozers and trucks to rest.

Houses for the displaced are being cobbled together in the nearby community of Freshwater. Winter is approaching, one that will prove to be the coldest on record with between three and twelve feet of snow. The pressure to build before the short, dark days set in has everyone harried, everything hurried, and town planning ignored.

Ironically, despite the building of this American base at this time, the United States is *not* at war. Not yet. A persistent faction of American citizens and politicians insist on isolationism, not wanting to participate in Europe's war. Not this time. Not after the sacrifices of the Great War. The arrival of American military personnel in Newfoundland is a friendly invasion, but an invasion nonetheless, building bases for a just-in-case scenario, a scenario that shows up on an unconcerned Sunday morning, December 7, 1941, when the Japanese bomb Pearl Harbor in Hawaii, blowing ships and seclusion out of the water and forcing the Americans to join the Allies. Maybe they should have been more vigilant? Not a judgment there. How on earth could it be? I haven't always kept a proper eye out, have I? Certainly not in my living years.

My baby Jimmy met evil. I suspected nothing. My adult son Kevin met evil. I could do nothing. As ghost, I have revisited scenes depicting the blue-lipped corpse of my baby Jimmy and the bullet-ridden corpse of my son Kevin. And now, my useless phantom gaze rests upon those who are left behind—my Clara and my Kate. Just a sigh, I am, an apparition adrift in a cloud, waiting for a whisper of wind to usher me in. It comes soon enough, that wind, not a whisper but a shout that bounces me from comfort of cloud into the scene to announce myself.

I am Kathleen Kerrigan—mother to Kevin, Clara, and Jimmy; grandmother to Kate. Kathleen Kerrigan, who is long dead, yet still here. I am a ghost whose penance for mortal sin is to observe and to narrate the story of my own downfall. The events of my life appear to me in chronological order, and I tell them to all and sundry from beginning to end, then start again. Over and over and over, *ad infinitum*. For the want of a *mea culpa*, no respite, no heaven in sight.

Do I know what's coming? No, for knowing the end would eliminate the torment, and what God would call that penance? Occasionally, I glimpse what is to come—a mere hiccup that quickly rights itself. I want to hold, enfold, and interact in these sequential scenes from my living world. But there is none of that; there is only observation. And no sighing or whining can gain me admittance to the living world. Still, ever vigilant, I keep an eye out for a sign of a crack in the wall between living and dead.

Meanwhile, I must carry on with the telling, in sequential order, to the end. I have no choice but to rejoin the story where I left it, on a hillside in Placentia Bay.

On this day, in the fall of 1941, my daughter Clara and my granddaughter Kate have walked from Freshwater to Jerseyside Hill. Their pace is brisk, the air around them tinged with uncertainty. At the top of the hill, Kate pauses to observe the scene below—the pontoon bridge across the Gut—and Clara steps up beside her. From a distance I witness that all is not well between the two, Kate's forward lean and Clara's folded arms suggesting confrontation. Suddenly, a young man arrives on the scene, speaking Kate's name. The intruder is named Peter, here by chance, his second encounter with Kate. The first occurred at the hospital in Argentia a while back, a time when young Kate had a head injury.

Kate steps aside to exchange pleasantries with him, all the while glowering at Clara.

Clara pulls her shoulders back but doesn't hold the stance; her spine curves as if under heft. How long can she uphold her saddle of secrets?

As for the reason for the confrontation? The answer will come. Truth has a way of creeping or shrieking to the surface of every situation, despite efforts to contain it.-

I will watch both Clara and Kate at close range.

Vigilant. If possible, if necessary, vigilante.

KATE

CHAPTER 2

UNTIL YESTERDAY, FIFTEEN-YEAR-OLD KATE KERRIGAN knew who'd knit her. She was the third child of Mavis and Kevin Kerrigan, just minutes older than her twin brother Joey, born in early spring when Daddy was on a sealing ship, rocked in a cradle carved by Daddy's very own hands. No qualms about her beginning. It was bedrock. Until yesterday.

Yesterday, Kate was alone on the schooner, cleaning chores to do. When the edge of her dust rag caught the corner of a hatbox on the shelf beside Clara's bunk, the hatbox tumbled, losing its lid and spilling its contents—a bundle of letters—onto the bed. Kate sighed. Another chore. She dropped her dust rag. For a moment she stared at the box. Familiar, that hatbox. Where had she seen it before? Oh, yes. Long ago in Argentia, in the closet in Clara's bedroom when curiosity had dared Kate to lift the lid, but conscience had cautioned her to stop there. To venture beyond a glimpse would be a sin, a black mark on her soul that would necessitate a visit to the black box of the confessional. Deterred, she had closed the lid of the hatbox, returned it to its place on the shelf, and straightened the painting that she had knocked askew with her elbow. The painting of a schooner.

Now *on* a schooner—the *Elizabeth J*—hatbox in hand, she picked up the bundle and scrutinized the top letter. Addressed to Clara. Mavis Kerrigan's name was in the upper left corner. *Mommy wrote these? To Aunt Clara?* She sat on her haunches as she slipped the first letter from its envelope and unfolded it. She raised the letter to her line of sight, vacillated, and lowered it again. *Should I do this?* Why was she even posing the question when she already knew the answer? The letter was in front of her eyes again in a heartbeat.

Dear Clara, Mavis had written in cursive. *I know your heart is broken. I want you to know that all is well with your little one. The hardest thing in the world to lose a child but perhaps in the long run it's all for the best. You know that Kevin and I will take good care of your daughter, your Kate.*

Kate fell back, banging her head on the opposite bunk, then dropping to the deck. In shock, she lay there, rendered immobile, while the schooner swayed and sighed, slats groaning. When she could move, Kate slid her hand into her pocket, searching for her small white stone, her souvenir of time on the Burin Peninsula, and of the tidal wave. She found it, she clutched it in her fist then slid it to her fingers, rubbing it like a rosary bead. Not enough to soothe, that action, so she whispered a "Hail Mary." Her breathing slowed. She returned the stone to her pocket. In slow motion, she sat up, reached for the letters.

Hands shaking, she counted them. Twenty-five letters. *Twenty-five.* Betrayal numbed Kate. *Is this real? Who the hell am I?* Without hesitation, she opened every letter, read every word, and dissected every line. All the while, heart racing, she kept an ear and an eye on the hatch. If it squeaked open, if footsteps sounded . . . Truth be told, a part of her wished that someone would dare show up and tell her no. She pinched her lips tight. *No, my arse.* So as the schooner swayed, the lamp flickered, and lumber creaked, she clutched the letters to her heart and sat for a long time while her well-ordered cabinet of memory opened its doors.

Kate was three. Nobody knew the water was coming that day. Yes, the ground had jiggled, but Mommy had prayed it away. Later, the kitchen had returned to cozy: Mommy at the Singer pumping pedals, Jimmy at the stove inserting splits, Marie at the oven withdrawing loaves, and baby Johnny in his highchair, banging his spoon to make his presence known. Kate and her twin Joey hovered by the oven, inhaling the aroma of fresh bread, their mouths watering at the thought of a slab slathered with butter and sticky with molasses. Later still, at supper when sleepiness had Kate nodding her head, Mommy had carried her upstairs.

As years passed, Kate would summon these *before* images often, mostly out of fear, fear that neglect would rip old memories into ribbons like it peeled paint from abandoned houses. These were the memories that she could and did share with Daddy, the good memories. She didn't tell Daddy that she remembered the tidal wave. She wanted to tell Daddy about the monsters that haunted her nights, roiling giant green waves that stifled her breath and salted her tongue. In her dreams, she would stretch her arms to her drowning mother Mavis, but Mommy was always just out of reach. Panic would spurt and Kate's gut would churn like a riptide, dragging her down, down into the memory of being swept away and the miracle of being spat back. She pondered, looking for reason for her survival, but couldn't find a why in any of it. For years, Kate kept the nightmares contained until they owned her, until night after night she was hurtled into wakefulness by violent green walls of water.

When Kate was ten and fresh from another nightmare, she decided she would have to tell. She flung on her clothes and scurried to the kitchen. At the door, met by a rush of heat from the stove, Kate stopped to watch Daddy stoke the fire with splits from the wood box. When flames leapt, he used the lifter to scoot the stove lid back in place. He straightened his back then, or tried to, but Kate could see that Daddy's spine was curved like tall grasses bent by high wind. She kept her gaze on him, waiting for her fright to fade. But the nightmare lingered. With her right hand, she gripped the door jamb until her fingers turned white. She used her left hand to pry her fingers from the frame. She soundlessly turned away. She could not, would not, pile worry on Daddy.

But on that same morning she knew had to tell somebody, or she'd burst. When the clack of the latch on the door marked Daddy's leaving the house, she sidled up to Mrs. Dulcie Mullins, her long-time trusted caregiver. Surely, she could tell Mrs. Mullins. "I dreamed a bad dream," she began.

Mrs. Mullins sat. "I got ears on me."

A relieved Kate poured herself into a chair and emptied her soul of fear, telling all—the green, the roar, the reaching for Mommy.

Mrs. Mullins listened, not butting in once. When Kate ran out of words and let out a sigh, a gentle hand landed on her shoulder. "Sure, you're hag-rode, child," Mrs. Mullins said, her tone hushed, her eyes travelling from Kate's face to the corners of the kitchen ceiling. A puzzled Kate looked up. Nothing there. *What is Mrs. Mullins looking for?* Kate held the question at bay, waiting for some explanation. None came. When Mrs. Mullins folded her arms protectively around herself, Kate mirrored the action.

"The Old Hag don't mind who she hurts while they're sleeping," said Mrs. Mullins. "Heard tell that reciting the Lord's Prayer backward will beckon her but why in the name of Jesus, Mary, and Holy Saint Joseph would anyone want to do that, I ask you?" With that she planted one hand on her hip and threw the other up like she was tossing feed to chickens. "Enough." She crossed herself.

"But I didn't beckon anyone, Mrs. Mullins. I was dreaming about the monster wave," Kate had said. "I couldn't move a muscle."

"You'd best just put all that tidal wave stuff out of your head, child," said Mrs. Mullins, her eyes wandering, one hand rubbing the side of her apron, the other spooning sugar into the teapot. Kate pointed a finger at the blunder, but she needn't have bothered because Mrs. Mullins was on it already. "Dear Father in heaven," said Mrs. Mullins. "What am I after doing at all?" As the sugar streamed back to its bowl, wayward granules danced onto the tablecloth. Mrs. Mullins slid her palm across the table and sugar snowed to the floor. She reached for the kettle. Hot water poured into the teapot and steam rose like morning mist. "A swish and a rinse and all will be right as rain." She smiled as she put the kettle down. "Time for you to be off to school."

"But . . ."

"That's it, missy. Off you go." A single clap of Mrs. Mullins' hands and the conversation was shut down like the lid of a coffin. Kate, shoulders drooping, shoved her reader and scribbler into her book bag. Where was her pencil? Mrs. Mullins, hands on her hips, waiting, was not to be trifled with. Kate could borrow a pencil at school. She headed out.

Mrs. Mullins wanted Kate to forget. Nanny wanted Kate to forget. So did Aunt Clara. But, for Kate there was no forgetting the tidal wave, useless to try. With no one to tell her troubles to, her thoughts nagged and churned and stuck to her like her shadow, sometimes creeping and long, sometimes just a circle underfoot. Even on foggy days, she felt its presence. Insecurity about the sea led her to keep an eye on the sea, and she often stood on tiptoes at the window staring at its swell, attempting to guess its next move. Could she outwit it? When the sight of the sea vanished with the fall of night, she tuned her ear to the sound of waves, waiting for a change from whisper to rumble or, heaven forbid, from whisper to suck which was what happened on the Burin when the sea scraped away from shore, pulling and pulling until it formed a high wall. Then it thundered back in, latching onto piers and rocks and houses and taking them, tumbling them, sinking them.

When Kate was thirteen, she was rushed to the hospital in Argentia to get stitches for a cut on her head. There she met Peter McGraw who innocently asked about the tidal wave, and she had answered. No drama in her words to him, just plain talk about the monster that had taken her family. "Brave," Peter described her. But was she? She didn't feel brave. She had been at the whim of the sea, which hauled her out and threw her back.

After Peter left the hospital that day, Daddy and Aunt Clara assured Kate that they were more than willing to listen to anything she had to say about the tidal wave, anything at any time. But flashes of fright in their eyes betrayed their offers and Kate would not, could not fuel their fear with horror stories, not now, not ever. Easy, that choice, cinched like a sailor's knot. Kate had nodded at them and turned away, quiet so she could revisit the relief she had felt when the stranger reacted calmly to her memories. Peter's eyes had held no alarm, had spoken only interest. Such a pleasant surprise. Would she be able to find similar reactions in other strangers? Perhaps. There were few strangers in her world.

And now Kate was fifteen. The bulldozers had come. For the second time, her home was destroyed. And Kate, sitting on the schooner and staring at letters, realized that she didn't know who had knit her after all. What would she do with all these letters?

In the end, she left the cache intact. Almost. Clara wouldn't notice one missing letter, would she? The first one? Despite being able to recite every line of that letter, she feared it would disappear if she left it where she found it. She also feared that her memory of the letter would recede into doubt. Concrete evidence, that's what she needed. The lining of her coat had a hole, an invisible pocket, useless until now.

The rise and fall of the schooner intensified and the lamp went out. The wind rose, singing through the rigging. No light through any crevice in the schooner. How much time had passed? Kate didn't know, didn't care. She lay crumpled like a discarded rose petal, arms hugging herself, letting the darkness flow over her. Mommy was not her mommy. How had Kate not known? *Wise beyond her years*, her father had always said of her. A derisive snort erupted from her, startling her. Surely there were clues about her heritage. Must have been clues. Why hadn't she noticed them?

Derailed, Kate wished she had never seen the letters, wished she had not rifled through the letters, wished she could reclaim her ignorance about the letters. Too late for that. She sighed and searched her soul for evidence of guilt for the theft of one letter. Nothing. Not a snippet. What she wanted, deep in the soul of her, was to know who the hell she was. The one thing she did know was that Mavis was not her mother. But Clara was? Why were they keeping secrets? Was there any rhyme or reason?

The questions would haunt and harden into quest.

CHAPTER 3

It was an autumn day in 1941 when Kate walked with Clara over the Jerseyside Hill toward the pontoon bridge in the Placentia Gut. The letter Kate had pilfered from the hatbox on the schooner now lived in her right-hand coat pocket, Kate's fingers constantly toying with it. Should she just wrench it out, confront Clara with it?

But no. Instead, from her other pocket, she pulled her long-treasured white stone, her tiny souvenir of the Burin. Why she flung it over the Jerseyside Hill she didn't know. Only knew that every click and clatter of its fall punched holes in her gut. *Damn.* She huffed out a breath and faced Clara. "Did you ever meet my mother Mavis?" When Clara's expression turned to stone, Kate spit another line. "Thought that if you never met her, you might perhaps have written a letter or two."

"Kate? Kate Kerrigan?" A male voice. *Damn! Whoever the hell he is, he better take wing.* Kate swung around. Stopped dead when she recognized him. *Not now.*

Peter McGraw's appearance on Jerseyside Hill at this moment aborted Kate's plans and sent her into a sulk, a stomach-clenching, mind-churning ill-temper, rife with condemnation. She pressed her lips together, hampering accusations from leaping at Clara, at Peter too, a victim of proximity, himself in a state of prattle. What in God's name was he on about? A dance? Did he just ask her to a dance? Kate brushed at a fly that had had the effrontery to land on the lapel of her coat. She walked with Peter for a bit. "Would you mind going on ahead, Peter?" she said, startled at the civil tone that came out of her. "I need to talk to my aunt." A look of befuddlement crossed Peter's face. He brushed his hair from his eyes, folded his arms, and then dropped them to his sides. With a sigh, he patted his back pocket. Checking for his wallet perhaps? Money was God to some. Peter's look switched to one of contentment. Perhaps money was God to Peter.

"I'll catch up," Kate said. Peter smiled and tapped his back pocket again before he went on his way. Easy enough, putting him off. Did she want to spend time with Peter? The dance had appeal but there were more pressing concerns. Kate fingered the stolen letter in her pocket, the letter from Mavis to Clara. She let out a long sigh as she looked back at Clara who was now perched on a boulder on Jerseyside Hill. "Are you coming?" prompted Kate. Clara stood and stumbled into motion, no fervour in her footfall. Kate ploughed toward the pontoon bridge, feet stamping, thoughts seething.

Clara caught up to within a foot of her and held that distance. Kate stopped. A jittery silence spanned the gap between them. Kate stared at the path, caught sight of an earthworm grappling with gravel. Clara's next step, if she were to take it, would crush the creature. Kate placed a hand on Clara's arm, stooped and rescued the wiggler. Barely there, the feeling of it between her fingers. She sighed as she set it in a swath of grass. Remaining crouched, she stared as the creature stalled, then slithered away.

Now what? Should she stand face-to-face with Clara and demand to know everything? Kate hedged, wanting to sit with the comfort of not knowing for a while longer. Life had dealt her harsh blows: loss of home and family on the Burin, loss of home and father in Argentia. But was Kevin really her father? *Not if Clara is my mother.* Another clout, that thought. Why hadn't it occurred to her before? It was not like she could ask Kevin Kerrigan anything; he was away at war. No telling if he would ever come back. If she were to challenge Clara now, she could lose whatever family she had left. She was living in close quarters on the schooner with Clara and Kathleen. Kathleen was still Nanny, wasn't she? And she would be living with these two women in a house on a hill in Freshwater for God knows how long. How much calamity could Kate abide? Was she ready for a harrowing journey to her own soul? She shuddered. She stood.

"What happened to Peter?" Clara asked.

"I sent him on ahead," said Kate.

"Seems a fine young man." Clara turned her eyes to the sea as if looking at something, God only knew what. "I might head to St. John's soon," Clara said.

Kate shrugged. She clomped along the path onto the pontoon bridge, Clara at her heels. The ocean toyed with the pontoons, creating a slight sway. A calm breeze. A salt scent. Kate glared at the water, knowing full well that the ocean could rise and rage at any time and, if the old salts were to be believed, it would do that very thing to this very bridge. Kate had always been quick to denounce the sea. Was it any wonder? The tidal wave took her family and made the sea her enemy. Today, with Clara, she had held back, choosing not to condemn. Not so unlike the sea herself, was she? She could flare up, if she had a like to. But was she ready? There was no curfew on confrontation. To do it now would mean the end of Kate's life as she knew it. Could she hold off on knowing Clara's secrets for now?

"Isn't this something?" said Clara. Her voice had lost its edge, as if she had detected a weakness, a way out. "Did you ever imagine," Clara continued, "you'd be looking at Jerseyside Hill while standing in the middle of Placentia Gut?"

The breeze picked up, slid by Kate's face, played with her hair. On another day, she may have been in awe of standing on a bridge in the middle of the Gut. Not this day. "Did you say you are going to town?" Kate asked.

Clara nodded.

Kate lowered her head to hide her smile. An opportunity for gain existed here, one that she warmed to immediately. A new dress for the dance. If she were to accept Peter's invitation, she would need a new dress. Money was tight. So what? Before long, Kate could have, would have a fancy frock. From her core came a whisper of impropriety. She dismissed it. She'd already stolen the letter, hadn't she? *In for a penny, in for a pound.*

Suited her fine to sanction vengeance, which slithered in and glommed onto her soul like smoke. The wind gusted, flinging strands of hair over her eyes. With a flick of her hand, Kate shifted a bobby pin, jamming it in to keep unruly locks out of the way of the wind. Easy. In the breath that followed, Kate put a pin in the idea of rattling Clara. *Don't show all your teeth until you can bite.*

But that wouldn't be the end of it. Kate would probe until she unearthed Clara's secrets, enough of them to fill a sideboard no doubt. Vigilant, she would shadow Clara, observe Clara, and gather details about Clara by treading softly through Clara's life, ahead of her, beside her, behind her. Kate would have eyes on anyone who neared Clara. Kate would discover who her own father was. When the time was right, when she was ready, when Clara did not expect it, Kate would challenge Clara.

For now? Kate spun on her heel, and with quickened step, closed the gap between herself and Peter. A glimpse over her shoulder brought satisfaction—Clara was following, a plodding pace, but following, nonetheless.

CHAPTER 4

Days later, Clara made a trip to St. John's and returned with a package for Kate. Despite Kate's determination to remain stoic around Clara, the second Clara presented the gift to her, Kate smiled, an uncontrollable lip-parting, cheek-raising grin. Could this be her new dress? She tugged the twine, tore at the brown paper, and removed the lid. Slowly she pulled out the contents. A blue suit. Sagging with disappointment, she stared at it. Nice enough, with a square-shouldered jacket, patch pockets, and a tailored skirt. "But I can't wear this to the dance," she said.

"What dance?" Nanny and Clara said simultaneously.

"The dance in Argentia. Peter asked me to go. He's got a car—"

"A car? You're only fifteen, child," Nanny said. "Besides there'll be plenty of time for dances. Wartime or peace time, there'll always be dances."

"Nanny's right," said Clara. "There'll be singing and dancing regardless of the state of the world. People need singing and dancing."

"Not fair," muttered Kate. She dared not say anything else but was determined to see Peter, dance or no dance. She would sneak around if she had to.

Later that day, she put her ear to the wheelhouse where Clara and Kathleen were deep in discussion, the topic being Kate, the concern being Kate as passenger in Peter's prized possession, his car. Kate rebuked herself. *How stunned was I to mention that he has a car?* She shook her head, returned to her eavesdropping. After Nanny muttered something about keeping enemies close, Kate heard not another discernible word, just murmurs, followed by silence. Footsteps sounded and a startled Kate scarpered to her bunk where she feigned reading.

"Your book is upside down, Kate," Kathleen said.

A sheepish Kate dropped the book and looked into the faces of Clara and Nanny. She was about to explain herself, but Nanny dismissed the attempt with a wave of her hand. "Never mind that now. We think," she said, "both Clara and I, that you should be inviting this young Peter to the schooner on a Sunday, sooner than later. The days are shortening, and darkness is a devil if the fog sets in. Not for dinner, either. Just a get-to-know-you cup of tea and a milk lunch biscuit. Would that satisfy you for now, Kate?"

Kate grinned.

On the appointed Sunday Kathleen, Clara, and Kate piled into the dory, Kathleen elbowing Clara away from the oars. At first Clara resisted the takeover but Kathleen would brook no argument. She was old, she wasn't dead. Kate kept her peace. No sense squabbling with Nanny.

At shore, they clambered from the dory and waited. And waited. With morning turning into afternoon, Clara announced that the time lag was jabbing at her last nerve. She was heading back toward the dory, Kate and Nanny in tow, when Peter showed up, easy to spot in his shiny navy-blue car. "Almost as big as the schooner," Kate whispered to no one in particular.

Peter stepped from the vehicle. "Sorry to be late," he said, removing his cap. He brushed his free hand through his shock of brown hair. "Took the b'ys for a ride last night and had a time getting rid of them. Awful mess in the back seat this morning." He slowly shook his head. "Had to take a shovel to it. And a bucket. But she's grand now."

"It's a beauty." Kate's voice, this time at full volume. A shiver of excitement ran through her. Imagine having Peter as a boyfriend, riding around in this gleaming navy-blue car. "Guess you were a bit of a hero with the b'ys last night," said Kate.

Peter beamed at her. He waved a hand toward the vehicle as if making introductions. "I bought this motorcar for a song. It was in pieces in a meadow for months, its owner having nary click nor clue how to right things. Glad to rid himself of it."

"Kate's right. It is a beauty," said Clara. "But I doubt you'll be offering the b'ys a ride again any time soon."

Peter shrugged. "Hard not to, missus, when you got a 1934 Nash Ambassador, and they barely got boots."

"That's nice of you," Clara said.

Clara's courteous tone slid pleasantly through Kate, even had Kate forgetting her anger, just for an instant. *Is Clara being sincere with Peter?* Kate cautioned herself against having kind feelings here. She needed to keep her wrath alive, to keep her distance until she was ready to confront. Finding fault with Clara was Kate's mission and it riled her to no end that, right now, there was no fault to be had.

"Did you do all the work on the car by yourself?" Kathleen asked.

Peter responded with a laugh and a shake of his head. "Needed my brother's help for that, missus. Me and Nate had at it every free minute, piecing the engine together, assembling the frame, filling holes with lead. No end to the sanding and painting." He brushed a hand on a lacquered fender, then picked off a bit of dust. "When we were done, we showed it to the former owner. He couldn't believe it was the same car."

Nanny nodded. Kate smiled. Hard work always impressed Nanny.

All out of words it seemed, Peter cleared his throat, patted his back pocket, and then looked to the sky. Kate followed his gaze to a widening ribbon of feathered clouds. "Well, would ye like a ride before the wind hauls that front in?" he said.

They tumbled in, headed off, down Jerseyside Hill, across the pontoon bridge into the peninsula of Placentia where the car churned up dust as it grumbled on dirt roads, skirted potholes, and crunched pea gravel. Kate hugged the side door, head spinning with memories of another car ride with Father Mahony at the wheel. A panicked trip to the hospital in Argentia with blood squirting from a gash in her skull that day. While in the waiting room with a bloodied towel to her head, she looked up at a young man who introduced himself as Peter McGraw. He sat. They talked. Now she sighed, contented, as the memory slid away. She eased into the drive, her eyes on the very same Peter as he coaxed the car through its gears.

"What work do you do on the base?" Kathleen asked him, her voice raised above the rumble.

"Right now, I'm a messenger boy to the runway workers. The Public Works Department is housed on the *Richard Peck* for the time being. They allowed me a bunk on that ship to keep me handy so I can go for this, go for that." He was heading back toward the bridge when he added, "Not a bad start, a gofer. Got me a car and a bit of money in my pocket. More to come, I'll see to that."

Before Kate knew it, they were back at the pontoon bridge and over it, into Jerseyside, up the hill, at the pier, into the dory, four of them this time and Peter at the oars with no complaint from Nanny. Aboard the schooner, with kettle stormed and biscuits plated, Peter looked pleased. "Nice to have a cup of tea in peace," he said. "First time I entered the mess hall on the base, I was terrified. Hungry, yes. But didn't know where to go, what to do. Hundreds of men lined up. Never worried about my size my whole life. Always able for hard work. Suddenly I was aware of being five foot six and a hundred thirty pounds. Fish bait, I was. Thought they were sizing me up. Just then I heard a familiar voice. 'Pete! You just come right up here and stand by me.' I looked up, saw Charlie, a buddy from the *Richard Peck*, and I hurried toward him. Charlie leaned in and whispered. 'If anybody around here gives you a hard time, you just let me know and I will take care of it for you.' I eased up a bit then. Charlie is six foot eight." Peter smiled. "Sorry if I'm going on a bit much."

"Not at all," said Nanny while Clara smiled.

Easy to see that the gathering was drawing to a close. Of note to Kate was that Peter saw it too, that it was he who moved toward the conclusion.

"You mentioned a typewriter, Kate?" he said.

"Yes, the typewriter," Clara cut in. "Given to us at a brief stint in a Placentia boarding house. It's over there." Peter dragged the typewriter from the indicated corner and parked it on the top of the table. Clara pushed plates and cups and the Purity biscuit box aside. Peter toyed with the typewriter and gave a brisk nod. He would take it, repair it, and return it.

Peter rowed back to shore, Kate in the dory with him, the typewriter tucked beneath the centre thwart. Clara and Nanny watched from the schooner. As Kate traded places with Peter at the oars, he leaned, their lips brushed, and he was gone, lugging the typewriter with him. Kate sat, steadying the oars, and wondering. That was it? Her first kiss? What was the big deal about kissing? She sighed. He'd be coming back. Perhaps a second kiss would be better. She waved at Peter and maneuvered back to the schooner.

CLARA

CHAPTER 5

Just weeks after their Sunday drive, on a December day, a fit of wind and a whip of ocean slammed the pontoon bridge to smithereens, scattering sections of it up and down the coastline. Clara met the news of obliteration with a shrug.

"Good thing Peter took us for a ride across it while we had the chance," said Kate, a huff in her tone as she wiped dishes.

"We walked the pontoon bridge well before that," said Clara, then bit her tongue. She must learn to pause before responding. She should keep her mouth shut here if she wanted to sidestep a tussle with Kate. Had Kate read the letters from Mavis? Perhaps. Clara had checked to see if the letters were still hidden, and they were. How many were there supposed to be? Twenty? Twenty-five? Clara couldn't quite recall. Were any missing?

"The drive was better." Kate stiffened, nose in the air.

Clara ignored the cheek in Kate's voice. She had no intention of allowing Kate's cauldron of issues, whatever they were, to boil over, not now while they were in the middle of a hectic move. "Yes, the drive was nice," she acquiesced. "And we all knew the bridge was a goner. Just a matter of time. The old salts were right on that, Kate."

At that, Kate's posture eased up, thank goodness. There was enough turmoil around here with the transfer from schooner to house. Clara, Kathleen, and Kate had moved into the two completed rooms—kitchen and dining room—of their house on the hill in Freshwater. They were on an island in a sea of construction surrounded by mud and ice and snow. But this was their new home, and they were determined to make the best of it. Clara headed to the dining room table and perched in front of her Remington typewriter. A practice session.

Now is the time for all good men to come to the aid of their party.

She typed and retyped that sentence until the pounding and clacking became a steady rhythm. Kate bumped the table as she brushed past Clara. Clara stopped typing.

"Your fingers are moving fast," said Kate. "Are you actually creating sentences or are you just hitting keys?"

Clara heard a taunt, discounted it. "Sentences. Or more accurately, one sentence. I'm grateful for your friend Peter for repairing this thing and getting me some ribbons." Clara tugged the paper from the machine and displayed her handiwork.

Kate leaned in. "Why this sentence over and over?"

"It has all the letters of the alphabet in it."

Taking the paper in her hand, Kate looked even closer, then sniffed. "The z is missing. And the q. And the x." She passed the paper to Clara.

"They're right . . ." Clara blinked. "Oh." Kate was correct.

"Try 'The quick brown fox jumps over the lazy dog,'" said Kate. "We used that one at school for cursive writing practice."

"Of course. Thanks, Kate. I don't know how I overlooked that."

"Huh." Kate loomed, arms folded. "Sometimes we can't see what's staring us right in the face." No mistaking the scorn in her voice.

Clara flinched and, although sorely tempted, did not bite back. Instead, she stood and offered Kate her chair. "That's enough practice for me, for now, but you can learn to type too, if you wish."

"You suppose I could?" An upturn in Kate's tone. She sat and poked away at the keyboard.

Clara took a deep breath and let it out slowly. Clearly, she had chosen the right path. "Absolutely," she said. "In fact, that was my plan. It's a valuable skill, typing, one that might help you get a job in the not-too-distant future. Let's just get some tea, shall we? It's freezing in here."

The expression on Kate's face transformed from sour to shine. "The hole in the wall might have something to do with that," she said.

Clara caught the twinkle in Kate's eye and laughed aloud. "I might miss a few letters, but I noticed the hole in the wall. Maybe I'd better make enough tea for the construction workers."

"Not a bad idea." Kate poked at the keyboard while Clara boiled the kettle and warmed the teapot.

The season of Christmas was upon them, and houses were still under construction. Some were halted, frozen in time like the ground beneath them. People did what they could to get on with the season. Help came when the priest informed all that the Holy Rosary Parish would have its first Mass in Freshwater: Midnight Mass on Christmas Eve.

Despite the bitter cold in this winter of snowfall upon snowfall windswept into banks, the familiar warmth of Christmas coursed through Clara as she and Kathleen and Kate headed to Midnight Mass, the still night interrupted only by the crunch of their footsteps.

"It's not really a church, is it?" said Kate, expelling a cloud of vapour with every breath.

"Too costly to build both a church and a recreation hall so they built the hall to serve as both," said Kathleen, who slid on a patch of ice and stuck both arms out to regain her balance. In the process, she dropped her purse which Kate scooped up. All three looped arms then, fighting the forces of nature together.

"I think they're planning to use the recreation hall for events that could raise money for the building of a church," Clara said.

"So, praying Mass in the morning and dancing jigs at night?" said Kate said with a chuckle.

To Clara, the chuckle was a peace offering. *Lovely.* "Some folks think of it as blessed in the morning and befouled at night," she said. "God and Satan sharing space."

When both Kathleen and Kate laughed, contentment seeped, joining all three souls. They were united now. Church or hall, Clara didn't care. When they got themselves in and seated, as the Mass progressed, she felt the magic she had always associated with Christmas Eve, every Christmas Eve of her whole life. The Gospel itself seemed especially apt this year as Father Mahony read from Luke: "At that time, there went forth a decree from Caesar Augustus that the census of the whole world should be taken." People could relate to there being no room "at the inn." Sure, with the upheaval of the last year, many of them had slept wherever they could lay their heads, including in barns on beds of hay. On this night, they could cling to their God and welcome the chant of joy, The Gloria. *Gloria in excelsis Deo.* Glory to God in the highest. *Laudamus Te.* We praise You. *Benedicimus Te.* We bless You. *Adoramus Te.* We adore You. *Glorificamus Te.* We glorify You. Clara felt her spirit rise with each turn of Latin phrase.

When they got back to their house on the hill, Clara was still aglow. With tea and slices of rum fruit cake on the table, while Clara was removing the tea strainer from her cup, Kate garnered attention by clearing her throat.

Clara waited.

"Well," began Kate and then hedged.

"Well, what?" Clara

"Well, since schools won't open in Freshwater until May next year, I have to say I'm worried about my education. Any ideas?"

"Good question," said Kathleen. "I hear some are going elsewhere to school. Lots of schools in St. John's. What do you think, Clara?"

The very thought of Kate leaving, of losing Kate again, shook Clara. She dropped the strainer and a blob of tea leaves landed on her slice of cake. She immediately set about cleaning it up, all the while busying her mind with objections. "St. John's? Where on earth would she stay?"

"Mrs. Mullins lives in St. John's now, doesn't she?" said Kate, excitement in her voice. "Maybe she has room for me."

Clara carted the tea leaves to the garbage, dropped the strainer into the sink, and muttered her way back to the table. "The streets of St. John's will be littered with uniforms, most of them American, now that Pearl Harbor has been bombed and the United States has made their presence known in this war. You're fifteen. Too young to be out and about in town with the likes of that going on." She turned to Kathleen, her mother, her pillar. "Isn't that true, Mom?"

"Don't have to go to St. John's to see military uniforms, Clara. They're filling the streets here too, in case you haven't noticed. Fifteen or not, Kate must finish school, and the Freshwater school is not even open."

Clara leaned on the table to keep from crumbling. Plopping into a chair, hand over heart, she stared at her mother, then at Kate. Literally and figuratively, Clara didn't have a leg to stand on here. They were right, the both of them.

Clara turned to Kate. "You okay with moving to St. John's?"

"I certainly am," said Kate, her eyes and tone defiant.

"No need to be uppity. I may not like the whole idea but I can see the need for it, the sense of it," said Clara, her objections fading into a hollow feeling that was all too familiar. Kate was slipping away again. "I'll contact Dulcie then," she said.

"Merry Christmas," said Kate, raising her teacup.

"Merry Christmas," said Kathleen, mirroring Kate's action.

Two teacups hovered, waiting. Clara sighed as she raised her cup to meet theirs. "Yes," she said, "Merry Christmas."

KATHLEEN

CHAPTER 6

It is chaotic, the sea.

The North Atlantic brims with vessels—submarines and destroyers and cargo ships from Allies and Axis. The sea embraces the lot, heaving them to crests, catching them in troughs, like coins in a game of pitch-and-toss. After a time, perhaps bored with the steady rhythm, the ocean churns into a frenzy, escalating to killer, playing for keeps. A relentless state of turmoil exists on the water, all of it far, far away. Always far, far away. The people of my island cling to this "far-away" certainty. Despite the incoming flood of military bases and uniforms and arsenals, the violence of war will *not* reach our shores. But a gargantuan swell in a North Atlantic storm changes things in February of 1942 when it heaves two vessels—the *Pollux*, a supply ship, and the *Truxton*, a destroyer—into jagged cliffs forty miles from the newly-formed naval base at Argentia, Newfoundland. Breakers bash ships against rocks, smashing them to smithereens, creating corpses and making heroes out of American sailors en route with supplies to Argentia. Future generations postulate that if the ships had used new radar technology instead of old-school charting, the lot of it could have been avoided. Hindsight with its should-haves and could-haves always knows the right way of things. The past is what it is. And during this frenzied bit of it, men from Newfoundland outport communities rise, fighting blinding snow, sleet, and hostile wind, to haul sailors up over the cliffs and lug them along to meagre homes where women wash them and feed them and warm them by the fire. The United States military claims the corpses and transports them to Argentia for burial, a temporary resting place for the duration of the war. After this event, thoughts about war being far away fall away.

The year forges on, slowing at times, sticking in places where people stop and stare, dazed as wartime incidents on home soil increase in frequency until they are falling like rain: all harbours blockaded after attempts to torpedo them; more fires, more sinkings, more deaths of the innocent and the not. People reel from the shock of it until it all becomes commonplace, this chaos washing the island. All ears tune to radio reports, all eyes to daily papers, eager for news of battles and bombings and for boosts of hope from the gravelled voice of Prime Minister Winston Churchill.

At the beginning of this embattled year, I, the ghost of Kathleen, am perched in a plume of pipe smoke on a juddering train bound for St. John's. This train compartment is clogged with military men whose duffel bags and bedrolls are crammed on overhead racks. Over their shoulders or hanging from racks are ditty bags stuffed with toothbrushes and soap and needles and thread, all courtesy of St. John's school children doing their bit for the war effort. The floor is littered with papers and cigarette butts that polished black boots kick under seats or lodge between slats. Some military wear caps, some wear grimaces, some wear smiles, some wear exhaustion in the form of sleep. Chatter is constant, voice upon voice until there is only a steady buzz like radio static sporadically cloaked by a blast from the train whistle or a screech from the rails.

As train noises fade, people noises resurface. A grey-haired civilian lugging a basket of apples limps along the aisle, jostling through the sea of uniforms, stopping now and then to give an apple and take a nickel. My coil of smoke melds with cigarette plumes into a grey haze blurring the image of my granddaughter, Kate, who sits up ahead on an aisle side of a wooden bench, suitcase pressed to lap, pocketbook hugged to heart. I wish I could make my spirit known to her, perhaps slide in like pipe smoke, creating a scratchy throat or a bitter taste, something simple to indicate my presence. But that's not going to happen, and I am left to pulse with concern about the presence of my granddaughter among this muddled throng. What if an unruly uniform accosts her? But I must not borrow trouble. What could I do about it anyway? The train whistles, a forlorn call. My state exactly, forlorn. But I have no call, no warning cry. I can only observe as my granddaughter navigates these troublesome years.

War is here. Until it isn't.

KATE

CHAPTER 7

WHEN A UNIFORMED ELBOW KNOCKED Kate's felt hat off kilter, she released her grip on her handbag long enough to adjust her hat and nod at his apology. Despite the chaos around her, she shrank into aloneness, head teeming with memories of home, more accurately loss of same, not once but twice. In each case, she started over, a coastal boat taking her from the ruin of Burin to the town of Argentia, and now a train taking her from the shambles of Argentia to the city of St. John's.

A bright light on the horizon was the thought of seeing Mrs. Dulcie Mullins, longtime friend and caregiver. Mrs. Mullins had tended to Kate while Kate's grief-laden father, Kevin, eked out a living by inshore jigging or onshore building. She had cared for the solitary child, Clara, when Nanny was "off with the fairies," as Mrs. Mullins called Nanny's stay at the mental hospital. And she had cared for Nanny herself, when Nanny's baby Jimmy Kerrigan died. In addition to that, Mrs. Dulcie Mullins comforted the entire community by baking biscuits and visiting the sick. It came as no surprise to Kate to learn that Mrs. Mullins had been hired to run a boarding house in St. John's.

As thoughts of Mrs. Mullins sifted, as the train car rocked, Kate's head dropped, her eyes drooped, and she drifted. The slowing of the train registered but she was reluctant to move from her comfort. The train continued to reduce speed, hissing and screeching to a halt. She jerked upright. Suitcase in one hand, handbag in the other, she catapulted from her seat and slid into the aisle. There she blinked, realizing that there was no need for heart-pounding hurry. She was wedged in a line of passengers, inching their way to the exit. When she finally stepped onto the platform at Riverhead Station on the west end of Water Street where the Waterford River met St. John's Harbour, the wind and cold greeted her, prompting her to set down her suitcase, don her gloves, and secure her hat. Retrieving her case, she stood and looked beyond the bit of snow that lingered from the last storm toward the bowl of the harbour, expecting a glimpse of fishing boats. What she saw were warships, battle grey, some of them listing, some peppered with holes, some with bows smashed in. She distinguished a few schooners among the lot. They too were painted grey. Necessary for stealth at sea, she supposed. And with that, she was instantly disabused of any notion that she was escaping the up-close evidence of war by leaving Argentia. Nanny had been right about that. The confusion of war was everywhere.

With a sigh, Kate turned toward the city, tramping past shops that looked closed but were not, as demonstrated when a bell clanged, a door banged, and a stout woman toting a brown-papered parcel secured with twine popped into the street. A collision ensued, couldn't be helped. "Excuse me, missus," said Kate. Undeterred and with not a word, the woman scampered away. Kate looked at the small sign above the shop door. Were shopkeepers deliberately concealing their shops? She shrugged and was about to take another step when a *splat* alerted her to the white blotch that landed on the well-shovelled cobblestones in front of her. She looked up. Seagulls were always dropping unwelcome blessings. She was grateful this one had avoided her hat and coat. She moved on.

The streets were a jumble of traffic, no sense to any of it. As with colonial tradition, cars and carts drove on the left side of the road. Military, Canadian and American, drove on the right. There were buses too, empty buses. As she stopped at the side of a street, waiting for an opening to cross, she mused, "Why on earth are there no passengers on any of the buses?"

"I'll tell you why."

Kate jumped. Had she stated that question aloud? She turned to look up at the gaunt face of the woman beside her. Black hair in a victory roll, red lipstick, and a plume of smoke from a half-smoked cigarette. "Because, me darling, those buses are from Canada where they drive on the right-hand side of the road. Here they are driving on the left which means that the doors on the buses open into the street. Who would want to take the risk of walking off a bus into the heart of that mess of traffic? Cobblestone chaos, I tell you." She dropped her cigarette and stomped it out. A lull in the stream of vehicles cued her to dash across the street. "Watch out for the streetcars too," she called over her shoulder. Kate lurched forward, managing to cross without getting clipped by an approaching streetcar. She looked behind her, wondering if city life had any rhyme or reason to it all. Cars swarming like gulls? Some on the right, some on the left. *Pick a side, please!* Streetcars amid this mess?

"Watch where you're going, miss." This from the gravelly voice of a passerby. Kate turned around in time to sidestep a telephone pole. Why was the base of the pole painted white? Shrugging, she took a deep breath and moved on.

It wasn't far to her destination, a taxing walk up a steep hill in a city poured into the side of a cliff. The wind, Newfoundland's chronic tormentor, scudded clouds across the sun, taunting, teasing in a struggle for dominance. Occasionally, rays of sun knifed between buildings, supplying welcoming patches of warmth.

Kate hugged the buildings as she walked, casting glances upward to check for seagulls and clouds. It would be a losing battle for the sun today. She placed her steps carefully, avoiding threatening patches of ice, pulling up the lapels of her woollen coat, and breathing into her knit-and-purl grey woollen scarf. Lattices of sticky tape on display windows caught her eye. She winced, knowing this was preparation for incoming bombs, that the tape would prevent exploding glass and flying shards. Evidence of war was everywhere, including city streets besieged with men in uniform. Kate threaded her way through droves of sailors and soldiers and airmen.

The sign beside the front door read "Bakeapple Boarding House," black letters on white, newly painted. She smiled at the name which instantly conjured memories of picking cloudy golden bakeapples on the barrens back home, berries from which Mrs. Mullins would make pies and jam. Comforted by the memory, she stepped back to look at the house. Time and squall had had its way with the three-storied, wood-framed flat top that had breaches in its clapboards and blisters in its paint. A small stoop, a couple of steps from the street to the door, no front yard at all. Built on the slant of a hill, it looked tilted when Kate stood in front of it. But she was standing straight, wasn't she? She bent one knee and nodded. Then she stepped up, knocked on the door. There was no response, so she reached for the doorknob. The door swung open. She jerked back and stared at the greeter, a thin young man, boy really, no taller than herself, wearing a sports jacket, polka-dotted bow tie, black-rimmed spectacles, hair cropped close. It was the tie that did it—reminded Kate of Joseph R. Smallwood, the little man with the daily radio program, *The Barrelman*, in which he told stories of Newfoundland culture and heritage. She'd listened to him many times. She'd seen his picture in *The Daily News*. The greeter at Dulcie's door held a copy of that very newspaper and, with an expression of annoyance, looked Kate up and down. His eyes sparked as he pulled himself to his full height and adjusted his glasses. "Well, Dulcie will likely take you in. An honest and clean place this. Five dollars a week. Up front. All meals supplied. Bed sheets changed on Tuesday morning."

Who in the name of heaven was he? Sure spoke his mind. And with that squeak of a voice, he sounded for all the world like a woman, a strong one at that, strong enough to poke holes in Kate's resolve. Should she even be here? Should she ask for Mrs. Mullins? Perhaps she should pay first. She put down her suitcase and mined her pocketbook for money. Suddenly, the door swung wide, and Mrs. Mullins emerged, smiling, arms open. "Some grand to see you, Kate. You got yourself here ahead of the weather, thank goodness. Another big snow coming." She turned to the young man at the door. "No money need come from this one, Izzie," she said. He gave Kate another scan, then shrugged and turned away.

"Come in, come in out of the cold. Give us a hug."

Kate welcomed that hug like a leaky punt welcomes the shoreline.

Familiar territory, an embrace from Mrs. Dulcie Mullins. Kate would be happy here. "Wonderful to see you, Mrs. Mullins Thanks so much for having me."

"No thanks needed, me darlin', and you might as well call me Dulcie like everyone else around here. As for Izzie Thompson, don't you be minding her at all. She, and yes it's a *she*, dresses like a man so she can get near double the pay as an office worker at the biscuit factory. Calls herself Isaac. Can you imagine? Her with a bow tie and spectacles and looking like the Barrelman himself. What all this nonsense is about men getting paid more than women for the same job I'll never know."

Kate was smiling as she retrieved her suitcase. Izzie managed to earn a man's wages. An urge to applaud flitted through Kate. Another urge, that of feeling suddenly grown up, struck her. *Mrs. Mullins wants me to call her Dulcie.* Kate didn't dwell on that feeling; Dulcie was still on about Izzie and Kate wasn't going to miss a word. "No, you don't have to worry a snippet about Izzie," said Dulcie. "Helps out around here when she can. Finest kind, Izzie."

Finest kind, indeed. Kate was intrigued. Once inside, she peeked around the door. Perhaps she could catch sight of Izzie again. But no, no sign. Later, maybe.

"How was your trip?" asked Dulcie.

"Train was fine. But there are so many uniforms around town. Had to be careful not to slam into people. And telephone poles. Why on earth are the base of them painted white?"

"They painted the poles and car fenders too, to keep people from banging into them."

Kate must have looked puzzled because Dulcie added, "Because of the blackouts. No light allowed at night. An enemy bomber might fly over."

Kate nodded.

"And yes," Dulcie continued, "the streets here are full of young men, strangers the lot of them. All our own young men are gone to war, every one of them had their smiling pictures published in *The Evening Telegram* before heading off. God only knows what they will have to deal with across the pond, but I doubt if any of them will be grinning when they get back. *If* they get back."

Kate wiped her feet on the thick mat and shadowed Dulcie down a dark, drawn-out corridor with open rooms lining the right and an oak staircase climbing the left, the house buzzing with chatter and creaks and thumps that could be doors closing or feet treading, perhaps a book dropping.

Dulcie entered the first room, a large sitting room, comfortable enough, not overly ornate, four maroon chesterfields, the same number of wingback armchairs each with its own floor lamp. A black cane with a curved ivory handle leaned against a floor model radio. The occupant of the chair beside the radio was hidden behind an open newspaper, only his left hand visible. "Is that you, Reggie?" said Dulcie. The newspaper dropped, and a clean-shaven, stout face leaned forward, dark eyes glinting with what Kate read as curiosity. He offered a welcoming smile. "Would you keep an eye on Kate's suitcase?" asked Dulcie. "We'll be back for it in a minute." Reggie gave a brisk nod. "The news is coming," he said, tilting his head toward the radio and then sinking back in his chair.

Kate shrugged. What she had read as curiosity wasn't that at all. And the smile? A pretence. *So much for first impressions.* Reggie was clearly annoyed at the interruption.

"Oh, for heaven's sake, Reggie, we won't be long," said Dulcie. With that Reggie snapped back into position and they slid by. "Don't mind Reggie," Dulcie said as if reading Kate's reaction. "A bit short with people but 'tis no wonder. Lost his wife when she slipped on the ice and got crushed by a hay wagon. Nearly lost his leg trying to save her. Works at the railway, on the night shift with the flashlight checking for spies. They say spies are all over the place now, but I doubt our Reggie will catch any of them. Can barely manage without that cane of his."

"I'm not put out at all, Dulcie. Doubt I'll have much to do with him anyway."

"You're right about that, but everybody crosses paths here. Reggie rarely leaves that wingback chair, loves that wingback chair. Says he's prone to colds. The chair keeps the chill out of his ears. Smart fella too, knows his way around, always talking directions, north on this street, west on that, and so forth and so on. All I ever knew was up the street and down the street and over the lane."

Kate slipped into the familiar comfort of Dulcie's nattering. More comfort came with the aroma of salt beef. Hunger panged. Boiled supper. Perhaps beans and dumplings? Through an archway and into the dining room now. The table, rectangular, clad in a flowered tablecloth, its plump oak legs protruding, had twelve mismatched chairs, and was already set for supper. Dulcie didn't pause, just continued to the kitchen. "This is the heart of the place," she was saying as they entered the large butter-coloured room. A steady drip from the faucet had Dulcie approaching the sink and turning the handle to thwart the plop. She tightened with all her might but to little effect. "Need some plumbing done, I guess." With that she breezed around the room, opening cupboard doors, stirring the pot on the coal stove, a cauldron, filled with beans. Kate knew that the cooking had been long and slow, the navy beans soaked overnight and the salt beef she had smelled earlier would give them flavour worth the wait. That along with the homemade bread on another counter . . . her mouth watered. "There's barely a breath between this house and the one next door," Dulcie said pointing at the low-set window. "It's a fire lane and a person could squeeze through, make an escape, if needed."

"Through that back door?" Kate asked.

Dulcie nodded. "That door leads to the porch which I use as a pantry and then out into the back yard." Dulcie looked around and wiped her hands on her apron. "Nice to have a yard. Every house needs a place to hang the laundry. And now I'll take you to your room."

They retraced their steps. Kate ignored Reggie as she grabbed her suitcase and joined Dulcie on the staircase.

"How are Kathleen and Clara, God love 'em?" asked Dulcie, as she retrieved a key from her apron. Without waiting for a response, she added, "Now you be keeping your room locked at all times. People come and go with the wind, many of them blown in from the bay. Some passing through, some for treatment at the hospital, some to work. Best kind, for the most, but you never know what vermin might be hove in off the streets when you got your back turned. A few ne'er-do-wells among the military too, no doubt—soldiers, sailors and airmen everywhere in case you haven't noticed. Needs my head on a swivel, I do." She stopped at a corner room on the second floor, unlocked the door, and swung it open. "Here you are, me darlin'. You just go right in."

Kate stepped across the threshold onto a hand-woven mat and blinked at her surroundings. Fading floral wallpaper formed a noteworthy backdrop, drawing focus to the quilt on the single bed, a quilt whose pink-and-green patchwork cheerfulness lifted Kate, allowing her to feel the rightness in being here. She glimpsed the iron headboard that stood, fence-like, against the wall but shrugged away its attempt at severity and turned to the burnished brass floor lamp. Perfect for reading. Perched on a small bedside table was a pink-and-white flowered jug with matching basin. Plenty of storage in the tall oak dresser. An icy breeze from the open window billowed the lace curtains and brushed through her hair. As Kate turned toward it, Dulcie rushed past her, removed the block of wood used to prop the window, and with a bit of a tug, closed the window. "A bit cold to have the window up, but I wanted it to smell fresh for you. There," she said, and she clapped her hands. "How's that?"

"Wonderful," said Kate. Almost said "magical" but wonderful would do. "Thank you." She stared in awe at Dulcie who after negotiating a steep flight of stairs wasn't even winded. This despite her heft, her teapot shape still evident, sagging a bit. "You're looking wonderful too, Mrs. Mullins. Oh, I mean Dulcie."

Dulcie poked strands of silver hair under her woven head scarf. Her smile crinkled her face and sparked a twinkle in her eyes. She straightened her back. "Not doing bad, long as I got me liniment to keep the arthritis at back. Aging is not for the faint of heart. I finds me hip . . . " she rubbed her hip, then brushed her hand through the air. "I'm better off than most, I suppose." She headed toward the door. "There's a couple of coat hooks behind the door. I'm right delighted to have you here, but

I got to get back to me kitchen. Supper coming up in a bit. Beans and dumplings." She was still nattering as she closed the door and clomped down the stairs.

Kate smiled. "Beans and dumplings." She was suddenly gut-foundered.

The sound of a captain's bell, a single clang, marked the call to supper and Kate was through her door and at the top of the stairs before she remembered Dulcie's warning. She retraced her steps and locked her room, then scurried over the stairs and joined the parcel of people emerging from rooms and parlour, a jumble of footsteps and chatter and laughter.

Beside the entry to the dining room stood a little girl staring at the tall clock in the hallway. "Excuse me, lady," the girl said.

Kate paused, letting people slide by. "Me?"

"I'm Teresa," said the child. "Can you tell me if there is a grandfather hidden inside this clock?"

"Hello, Teresa. I'm Kate. No grandfather." Kate smiled at the curious face with its confusion of freckles. "It's just what they call the clock."

"What's that thing called?" Teresa pointed at the pendulum. Before Kate could respond, a wispy-haired, rail-thin woman scooted past. "Let's go, Teresa." She grabbed the child by the hand and hurried off.

Kate shrugged and entered the dining room. Izzie was already seated at the far side of the table. "Over here," said Izzie, jumping to her feet and patting the back of the chair beside her. Kate joined Izzie, the two watching other boarders make their way in. The last to enter was Reggie, his approach distinguished by the tap of his cane which he hung on the back of his chair before plopping down. Kate had noticed his stout face earlier and was surprised that the rest of him was lean, muscular even. Pinned between his left arm and his chest was the newspaper he had been reading. He tucked it behind him. Dulcie showed up, a pitcher of water in hand. As she rounded the table and poured, she introduced Kate.

"I've known this one most of her life. Kate from Argentia, she is. Or was before the military made a base out of it and moved all the people to Freshwater. Kate's here to go to the Academy of Our Lady of Mercy on

Military Road. No school in Freshwater yet. Now ye all can do a go round and introduce yourselves."

"Welcome, Kate, I'm Dominic." His voice grated like a saw blade on cast iron. A short man–Kate saw that as he entered–burly, with large hands, dark circles under his eyes and no sign of a neck whatsoever. "I'm a longshoreman. Strong as an ox but too old for battle apparently."

"You did your time in the Great War, Dominic b'y," said the dark-haired man at Dominic's elbow who gave his name–Jeremiah. "Too many men off to the war fields. Too many women stepping into work forces. Children evacuated, separated from families, fleeing bombs. There's no rhyme nor reason to any of it." He was long-limbed, like Ichabod Crane to Kate's eye, all knees and elbows, and pulled in his spidery limbs as he sat. He nodded as if satisfied with having his say. He picked up his fork and waited, statue still.

"You're right on all of it," replied Dominic who received a grunt in response.

Reggie spoke up next. "We've already met." He adjusted his tie, raised his head and an eyebrow as he uttered his name. "Listening to the news, I can't help but wonder if God and the Devil are in cahoots when 'Thou Shalt Not Kill' is suddenly eliminated from the Ten Commandments. Alongside this insanity of a license to murder is the civility of accounting for the dead. Bodies are probed, tags removed and transported from the front lines to the Red Cross at the rear as identification and to notify families. Madness, I tell you."

The lady next to Reggie patted his hand. "Can't get too broken up over things, Reggie. Madness it is but might as well try to empty the ocean with a teaspoon as to stop all the goings-on." She turned to look at Kate. "I'm Penny and beside me here is my husband, Mick. We comes in from the bay when the fishing season is done and works at the biscuit factory on the assembly line for the winter months."

Izzie nudged Kate. "Don't worry about remembering all the people. Reggie has been here for a while, but most will be here and gone in a heartbeat." Kate nodded and tuned in to the next person.

"Wait a minute," said Dulcie who hurried into the kitchen and then back with a cauldron of beans which she planted on the table. "I don't want to miss a word," she explained as she ladled beans onto plates. "I'm ready. Keep talking. Who's next?"

Next was a door-to-door salesman, nondescript, there for the night, and beside him a squat woman with grey hair, crepe face, and rouged cheekbones. "I'm Granny Grace," she said. "Just call me Granny." She turned to Dulcie. "Where's me special teacup?" she asked.

"I'll get it in a minute, Granny, although I'm not sure I wants to open that cupboard again. There was a mouse at the back of it this morning."

"No, dear. You mean mice, don't you?" said Granny. "Those little critters tend to have friends." This she followed with a wink.

Dulcie chortled. "God love ya for bringing the laughter. Later I'll have at the critters. Now I'll get your teacup."

"Check it for mouse droppings before you brings it in," Granny called. Kate grinned as she eyed Granny. Not a tooth left in the woman's head but well able for talking. Needlework too, by the look of the knitting bag she had carried in with her, a strand of wool trailing behind her. "Granny is one of our regulars," Dulcie explained as she scooped up the wandering wool and discreetly tucked it into the knitting bag. Then she approached Kate's chair and leaned. "Nothing special about her teacup," she whispered into Kate's ear, "except for the whisky."

With a nod, Kate turned to the next guest, the inquisitive child who had asked about the clock. Seated beside her was the thin lady who had grabbed her hand. "I'm Rosemary," said the lady, "and this is my daughter, Teresa." Stiff-backed, Rosemary looked down her long nose at the table, and added, "My husband is a businessman."

"I thought you said Daddy was a bigamist man," said Teresa whose reward for the remark was an elbow to the ribs. "Ouch." Teresa placed a hand over the hurt. Tears sprang to her eyes. Rosemary shrank, folding into her chair, face red as the chunk of salt beef that had just clunked onto her plate.

Around the table eyes widened, hands flew to mouths, heads dropped to hide smiles. Kate squirmed. Not a humourous situation, this. She turned to the little girl. “Teresa,” Kate said,” I didn’t get a chance to answer your question about the clock. A grandfather clock has a weight called a pendulum that sways back and forth, tick-tocking to keep the time.

“Oh,” said Teresa, wiping away a single tear.

“If it is not set right, the clock will run too fast or too slow.”

Teresa nodded.

The room still silent, Kate continued. “It’s called a grandfather clock because of an old song with the same name.”

“I knows that song,” Granny piped in. Waving her butter knife like a baton, she conducted her own singing.

“*My grandfather’s clock was too large for the shelf*
So it stood ninety years on the floor;
It was taller by half than the old man himself,
Though it weighed not a pennyweight more.
It was–”

The baton stopped in midair. A baffled look crossed her face. Shrugging, she said, “I forgets the rest of it.” But her efforts earned her applause, and she grinned as she speared a chunk of salt beef.

During the handclapping, Kate glanced at Rosemary who mouthed the words, “Thank you.” Satisfied that she had helped, and that the situation was over, Kate smiled. But it wasn’t over at all for Rosemary, who loudly cleared her throat. When all eyes glommed onto her again, she straightened her back. “I suppose I could just let you all assume what you wants,” she said, “but there’s no need for me to be all airs and graces. Truth is, the man showed his true self,” she said. “He had the nerve to try to come back, expecting me to feed him three meals a day and scrub his dirty laundry.” She sniffed, disdain dripping from her like wax from a candle. “Was it Shakespeare who said, ‘Fool me once, shame on you. Fool me twice, shame on me?’” She shrugged briskly. “Anyway, Teresa and I were there, now we’re here. And that is that.” After a smile at her daughter, Rosemary picked up her fork.

Kate’s breath caught in her lungs. Around the table, hands were frozen in mid-air, forks and knives held hostage. As the moment thawed and, one by one, the boarders turned their attention to their meal, the occasional scrape and tap of cutlery rose to a full-on rattle and clang. At the height of the crescendo, conversation erupted, first a comment about the delicious beans and homemade bread, then inevitably, about war.

Still in awe of the revelation made by Rosemary, Kate stayed out of the talk for a while. Would there be gossip in the aftermath of Rosemary's reveal? She doubted it. Nothing could diminish the power of that moment, the strength of that woman, the respect she had earned in a single moment. A lot to be said for raw truth.

CHAPTER 8

AT FIRST, DULCIE WOULD HAVE none of the idea of Kate working for her keep, but Kate was well able and well determined. School came first, of course, and despite her anxiety over newness and nuns, Kate took kindly to the shiny linoleum corridors and rows of wooden desks and the sense of routine that had been sorely missing during the months of upheaval in Argentia. One Saturday morning, after a few weeks at the boarding house, after a few guidelines from Dulcie, Kate gathered the tools of the trade—apron, keys, dust mop, rags—and headed upstairs. She tapped on doors, voiced "housekeeping" in a tone that was audible without being offensive, and waited. When met with silence, she jangled the ring of keys before jabbing the room key into the lock, a deliberate attempt to give the occupant more time to respond. Halfway through her first Saturday morning maid service, she reached Izzie's room. When there was no response to her call, no reaction to the key clatter, Kate twisted the knob and nudged the door open. With dust mop in hand and dust rags spilling from apron pockets, she entered. Sunlight greeted her, a swath of it wrapping her, warming her and she was grateful that Izzie had left the curtains wide. Her eyes adjusted to the brightness, and she scanned the walls, no, not walls really but shelves, floor to ceiling shelves, each one stuffed with books. "Oh." Kate was spellbound, always loving books, always owning some, but never imagining making a library in her own room. But she could, couldn't she? "A room without books is like—"

"A body without a soul," finished a voice from the direction of the bed.

Kate dropped her mop and looked into the twinkling eyes of Izzie who was propped on pillows, a smile on her face, a book in her hand.

"Sorry." Kate took a step back. "The sun was in my eyes, and I didn't see you there. Thought you were at work."

"Day off," said Izzie, closing the book and setting it aside into the path of a sunbeam. The book's ornamental gilt lettering and floral decorations caught light, capturing Kate's attention. There was no author's name on the green cloth cover of *Leaves of Grass*, but Kate didn't need one. "Walt Whitman."

"You know it?"

"Whatever satisfies the soul is truth." Kate pointed at the book.

"You do know it." Izzie reclaimed the book, riffled its pages, and returned it to the sunbeam. She stared directly at Kate. "So, what is the truth that satisfies your soul?"

Kate stumbled for words and found only one. "What?" she said.

"Exactly. What is your truth?"

A baffled Kate considered the question and came up blank. "Hard to know," she said. "Been taught that it's sinful to consider your own needs, and I do my best to tiptoe around things that might land me in the confession box. Religion is all about sacrificing self, not satisfying it."

"But," Izzie continued, "you certainly are wondering about things: who you are and where you fit in."

"You say that because?"

"Because you have used two quotes about soul in less than a minute."

"You're observant."

"Not really. It's like looking into a mirror."

Kate nodded. "Oh, I see."

Izzie tilted her head. "I was craving a bit of company. Take a load off." She indicated toward the room's solo chair—oak, rail-back, armless, its sole occupant a fading red cushion.

With friendship beckoning like a welcome invitation, Kate contemplated her situation. Should she sit? Maybe she could have a good friend here, one around her own age. Shrugging, she denied herself that satisfaction. Sinful to engage in socializing when she'd promised Dulcie, a saint of a woman, that she would zip through the cleaning. "Don't know that I can," said Kate, picking up the mop. "Work to do."

"Well then, do two things at once," said Izzie. "Mop while we chat." Her tone took on a lighthearted air. "Did you see that new boarder at breakfast this morning? Some pious, that one, carrying her little bottle of holy water, praying for the Lord to bless her porridge, and then thanking Him for answering her."

Kate appreciated the attempt at humour but stifled the urge to snicker. "Oh, I don't know about that." She busied herself, sliding the dust mop in arcs in the middle of the room.

Izzie kept on. "Never seen the like in my life. Why would God be talking to her when He has Himself an allotment of priests for that very purpose?"

Head down, Kate smiled. She stopped the mop and raised her head. "I have to tell you that I'm not long on gossip," she said.

Izzie let out a sigh. "I'm with you on that," she said, "but—" The light faded from her face. "I'm just a long way from home, that's all," she said, her tone sombre. Then she went back to reading.

Kate glanced at Izzie's alarm clock, watching the second hand, listening to its steady tick. Two lonely people here. Where's the sin in putting aside work for a few minutes? Happiness and holiness are not enemies. Even the saintly Dulcie would see the reason in that. What harm would a little more time here do? Most of the boarders had downed the morning feed of bacon and eggs and toast and porridge, had scanned *The Evening Telegram* and *The Daily News,* and had gone out for the day. Dulcie would be in the kitchen, cleaning up one meal and cutting up vegetables for the next. Kate had time. She put down her mop and picked up the chair which she placed beside the bed. "So you're from Halifax. What brought you from Canada to Newfoundland?"

"A new start."

"Oh?"

"I had a boyfriend. He died. Then another. He died too."

"Really? What happened?"

When Izzie winced, Kate chided herself. "Sorry, Izzie. Too many questions. None of my business really."

Izzie offered a weak smile. "Not to worry. It's just that I can't talk about details . . . not yet anyway." She paused. "For now, suffice to say, I'm not interested in dating. I'm only nineteen, but I'm ready to give up on boys altogether."

"Can't say that I'd blame you."

"What about you, Kate?"

"Boys, you mean?"

Izzie shook her head. "You're making a new start too, aren't you? Dulcie said you had to leave your home."

"Oh." Kate nodded. "Sure did." *Not once but twice.* Kate opted to tell Izzie about the more recent of the two. Not about the Burin. Not yet. It was just too much. "War ousted us from our homes. Argentia is a military base now. I was living in Freshwater with Nanny and Aunt Clara but there is no school there yet and I want an education. So, I was there and now I'm here."

"Dulcie mentioned that bit. A hard adjustment?"

Kate let out a loaded sigh. "I'm young. I can adjust. At least that's what they tell me." She hunched her shoulders and dropped them again. "It feels like a dream. How can all this be real? I'm grateful for Dulcie." Warmth filtered through her.

"Dulcie took care of you when you were little, didn't she?"

Kate nodded. "Yes," she said. "I'm lucky to have her still, and young enough to tolerate the disruption caused by war. All the upheaval is apparently harder for older folks like my nanny."

An unruffled silence fell. *Enough said for now.* Kate slowly uncoiled herself from the chair and picked up her waiting dust mop. Ease accompanied her as she finished her tasks and retraced her steps to the door.

"You may borrow any of my books, Kate." A gentle offering.

Kate smiled. "Thanks, Izzie." She parked her mop in the hallway and reached back to pull the door closed. "Okay if I stop by later today?" she asked. "For a book, I mean."

"Anytime." She sat up. "Kate?"

Wide-eyed, Kate waited.

"Is Kate a nickname? For Katherine, perhaps?"

"Yes and no. It's a nickname for Kathleen. And what about you? Izzie is short for . . .?"

"Isabel."

Kate tilted her head. "Lovely name."

"Thank you." Izzie grinned.

Reluctant to leave, Kate scrutinized Izzie. Was there a reason to linger? She stepped forward, a sigh flowing from her. "Would love to talk more." She paused, wistful for a moment, then retraced her steps and reclaimed her cleaning tools. "Another time, Izzie," she said, the truth of the phrase singing to her. There would indeed be more time spent with Izzie. "Right now, though, I must work. Can't disappoint Dulcie."

"You are lucky to have a guardian angel like Dulcie."

Kate shrugged. "I can use all the angels I can get."

"I'm glad you visited," said Izzie.

"Me too," said Kate.

"I know. It shows."

CLARA

CHAPTER 9

On the heels of Kate's leaving Freshwater came the unkindest weather on record, a winter of boisterous winds and bitter cold and banks of snow the height of a schooner's mast. Clara ached for a hint of spring—a sprig of green, a song from a robin, a ray of warmth from the sun. Eventually, the long shadow of construction with its mud and dust and stench of sludge, gave way to shoots and leaves and fields of flowers. Never had Clara felt such appreciation for buttercups and dandelions and scent of clover mixed with sea salt. Never had she beamed so at sparrows as they chirped and flitted and gathered twigs and feathers and pebbles. They were building new homes too.

All this newness filled her up, but still she ached for Kate. Clara yearned to know how Kate was doing in St. John's, at school, in the boarding house under Dulcie's care. Today, Clara was heading to St. John's, a scheduled train trip. Perhaps she would see Kate. Perhaps. Hope glimmered but fear of disappointment quashed it. Even if Clara showed up at the boarding house, Kate might ignore her, just as she ignored the frequent letters Clara had written. Perhaps Kate just needed some time. Clara could offer time. She could endure being ignored if it meant that she could eventually have a good sit-down with Kate, tea and truth on the table. Ultimately, the *when* of that would be up to Kate. Clara sighed her attention away from Kate and onto Patrick, another person Clara hadn't seen in a while. Patrick was meeting her at the train station.

On the day she moved to Freshwater, Clara had stumbled upon Patrick, who was temporarily living on the USS *Richard Peck*, the steamship that ferried workers to Argentia and then stayed, serving as a barracks. After that, Clara had managed an occasional meeting with Patrick on her schooner. She cringed at the thought of other trysts—in a shed of all places, a Freshwater lean-to, a storage shack, the two of them on top of the red door built by her husband Robert and her brother Kevin, a coat button digging into her back, leaving an imprint. Not exactly a "Princess and the Pea" fairytale. Her face burned at the memory. *What kind of woman am I at all?* The depth of her guilt had her frequently searching the faces of the community, looking for evidence of judgement, but not a wayward glance came her way. She reasoned that her secret was safe. Couldn't say the same for her soul. Black as a coal bucket, that.

Thoughts of Patrick had her hankering for him. Despite her having lived in the Freshwater house for six months, he had yet to put a foot inside the door. Illicit, their encounters, and secrets must be kept. Still, she could imagine him showing up in the guise of a burly construction worker, sod cap lowered, pea coat collar raised, shoulder seams straining at the breadth of him. She could picture herself dancing with him on the naval base where there were dances galore, just as there were every Saturday night on every military base everywhere, she supposed. If not dances, then entertainment of some kind. The military went all out to keep up morale. How tongues would wag at the sight of her and Patrick at an Argentia dance: *and her a married woman whose husband is away fighting the good fight.* She managed to dismiss the guilt, but she couldn't stop the longing.

Her thoughts fell across her mother. Had she ever longed for her husband the way Clara longed for Patrick? A shattered man, Alphonse Kerrigan, warped by the atrocities of the Great War. Clara knew first-hand the sins of her father. She shuddered. No point in unearthing that hell. Her mother had stayed with her husband after he killed their son Jimmy, even though the event broke her, landing her in the mental hospital. Kathleen eventually came back to herself. She may very well have loved her husband but, in the end, she murdered him to save her granddaughter. Would Clara have the strength to kill if she were in her mother's shoes?

No need to think about that because she would never need to know, now would she? Her husband, Robert, would never have hurt Kate. Anyway, he was gone home to England. As for her lover, he would cause her no grief; she was certain of that.

Today, Clara would come close to her dream of having Patrick here. Not in her bed, not in her house, but here as in at the train station. Yes, the plan was to spend a night at the Newfoundland Hotel but if anyone asked, she was off to visit Dulcie in St. John's. It wasn't yet time to walk to the station, but Clara had her tiny suitcase packed and sitting on the floor beside the kitchen table.

Time dragged during the wait, and Clara clacked away at the typewriter until its hammers jammed, bundled like twigs fighting for position at the typing line. Darn. A bother, but a blessing too. She had to fix it, but she prided herself in typing so fast that the machine couldn't keep up. She painstakingly separated the hammers, letting each fall to its home, and then hit the carriage return. *Swoosh.* It was back in place. Fingers poised, she paused. Unexpected, the opening creak of the front door and its instant closing slam. Clara lurched to her feet. *Patrick?* She couldn't be seen with Patrick. *Why the hell is he here?* His arrival at her house was not in their plan. She rushed to the porch. He bolted past, his boots clunking on the hallway floor.

"Mom will be furious if you get dirt on this floor," she said and then wondered why she said it.

Patrick marched into the kitchen. "Is Kathleen here?"

"No. Mom is in Dunville helping old Missus—" She sniffed. "Why do you smell of smoke?"

"You ready to go?"

She followed him to the kitchen, holding her nose. No mistaking the smell of smoke and gasoline that trailed him. She coughed. "What in heaven's name have you been at? Why are you here? We're supposed to meet at the train station."

He turned to face her. "I'm here for you. We must go."

"What are those black streaks on your face?" she demanded. "And why are you in such a hurry to be off?"

"I need you out of there," he said. "There's a fire in the harbour on the base. The USS *Prairie* could go up."

What was he saying? "So? The *Prairie* is just a supply ship," she said.

"It's more than that." He wiped his face with the sleeve of his coat. "Are you ready?"

She grabbed a tea towel and stepped toward him, wiping smudges from his jawline.

"Hold still," she said sternly, gripping his chin with one hand, stabbing at splotches with the other. The instant she touched him she changed her tone. "We have some time before the train leaves." Back in longing mode now, she pondered the idea of him and her, here, in the house alone. "Mom won't be back for an hour or two."

"Where are your things?" he barked.

Slighted, Clara pointed to her suitcase. She tossed the tea towel to the counter and reached for her coat that clung to its hook, as stubborn as herself. One, two, three attempts to remove it. When success came, she dawdled, poking an arm through one sleeve, then the other sleeve. Where were those buttons again?

"Get a move on, Clara."

Satisfied that she had dallied enough to annoy, Clara took her smug self out the door. Instantly her nose twitched. "Is that smoke coming from the *Prairie*?"

Patrick didn't answer. He hustled her into a military truck, the presence of which he explained before she could question it. "Borrowed from the motor pool. I can leave it at the station." Soon enough they were there, at the train station, Clara insisting on boarding ahead of him. Heaven forbid she be seen with a man. But she needn't have worried, as there was a scarcity of people on the platform. *Odd, that. It's usually overcrowded.* She boarded ahead of Patrick. It was only when she had settled into her seat that Patrick entered, strolled nonchalantly down the aisle of her car, and approached her. "May I sit here, missus?" he asked her with a wicked twinkle in his eye.

She rolled her eyes. "Of course, sir," she said, glancing around the nearly empty carriage. Relief was instant, enhanced seconds later when the train kicked into motion, whistling as it juddered out of the station. Patrick jumped into conversation. "You'll get to see that Kate you're always on about."

"She won't want to see me."

"You two have a falling out?"

Clara sighed toward the window, toward framed images of trees and rocks and shore flashing past. Pictures there and then gone in an instant. Not to be seen again. "She may never want to see me again."

"Perhaps you're wrong," Patrick said, his voice quiet as to be barely heard above the clack of the rails. "Do you know where she lives?"

She turned back to him. "Of course I do."

"Well then, let's give it a try. We'll be in St. John's overnight. We'll stop by the boarding house today." He rested his hand on hers. "I'm here for you, you know that."

Clara smiled but something niggled. What was it? How did Patrick know that Kate was at a boarding house? "How do you know where Kate is living?"

"Your parish priest must have mentioned."

"Father Mahony? Why would you be chatting with Father Mahony?"

Patrick shrugged. "We're old friends."

On top of those words and from the back of the train came a spontaneous burst of laughter. Clara had no clue as to who laughed or what the trigger was, but that didn't matter: the timing was exquisite. Sporting a grin, she waved a hand toward the sound. "See? Even he, whoever he was, knew enough to laugh at that. You and the priest old friends? Not a chance!"

"It's true and you know it."

"Excuse me?"

"Don't you remember how you and I met?"

The words stole the grin right off her face. She shifted in her seat, a flush of embarrassment filling her. "I remember the confessional, if that's what you mean."

"Before the confessional. Who was I talking to?"

Clara nodded. "Oh, God. The priest."

"At the time, Father Mahony was trying to be helpful. First met him after a stint with His Majesty."

"His Majesty?"

"The penitentiary."

Clara stifled a gasp and, needing time between shock and response, said nothing. The rocking of the train ticked off the seconds. When her words came, her voice was calm. "You were in His Majesty's Penitentiary? When? What for?"

"Times were tough."

"That's not an answer." She took a different tack. "So, how did you meet Father Mahony? He was no inmate; I guarantee you that."

"The good priest did prison visitations. He said Mass and tried to convert the lot of us Protestants."

"Protestants. Heaven help me." Clara made the sign of the cross.

Patrick laughed. "What? A criminal is permissible, but a Protestant is a problem?"

"I'm beginning to wonder if I'm a magnet for Protestants. My husband . . ." Guilt moved in. Clara moved on. "Lots of Catholics spend time with His Majesty. They don't mind tampering with the law, but they'll take time in hell over hobnobbing with Protestants."

"Well," Patrick replied, his tone tinged with humour, "with all your mingling, I'd say hell has a place reserved for you."

"Hush yourself before I heave you off this train. Now, tell me more about the priest."

"Fair enough. A long time ago Father Mahony offered to help me get back on my feet. I took him up on that. Went to see him. Not once but twice. The first time . . ." He paused. "1915, I believe. A long time ago."

Clara cast her mind back. "I was only six then." Memory flooded and she giggled. "That was the year I stowed away in the dory. I stumbled on Kevin's oilskins and went right over the gunwale."

Patrick's face split into a grin. "We have something in common. I got into a skiff with some intoxicated fellas back then. Whether they shoved me out or I jumped out, I don't remember, but I sobered up quick when pierced with cold. A brutal swim to shore where I crawled in over rocks, waterlogged and stinking of seaweed. Your brother fished you out, I assume?"

"Yes, he did. Bless his heart." She sighed. "Years ago. Seems like yesterday." She tucked the memory away and turned to him. "And the second time you came to Argentia, that was in 1925, wasn't it?

"I'm glad you remember when we met." Clara tilted her head. "How did the priest help you then? Job? Money?"

"A little of each. He put me up at the rectory."

Clara balked. "You stayed at the rectory? We're committing adultery, breaking one of the Ten Commandments in case you don't know, and you stayed at the priest's house?"

"He arranged for a job interview in St. John's. I was on my way to the Coastal Boat when I saw you. I missed the boat and had to spend another night or two with him." He reached, thumb and forefinger poised as pincers, and tweaked her cheek. "It was worth it."

Clara brushed his hand away. "Tell me more. What was the job?"

"What job?"

"The job the priest got you?"

"Some menial thing. Nothing really."

"But it must have helped you. That and the rum running and working as a chauffeur for the higher-ups in St. John's."

Patrick shrugged. "Not much fun being at the beck and call of the wealthy. In the background. A shadow." He blew out a sigh. "But you already know about all that. And now I work on the base. Enough said."

Yes, she already knew. *Why am I being so inquisitive?* Somewhere inside her there was a reason, something she couldn't pinpoint. Silent now, Clara, leaned her head against the window, her eyes blurring as images of stunted fir trees flew past. The rhythm of the train rocked her, somewhat comforting, she thought, until another question cropped up. She turned again to Patrick "You didn't tell anyone you were going to St. John's with me, did you?"

"You worry too much." He planted a kiss on her forehead.

"You didn't, did you? I have to know."

"Of course, I didn't," said Patrick and then kissed her again.

Clara pulled back slightly. "Why all the fuss about the *Prairie*?"

"It is a floating machine shop, Clara. It's so huge that the destroyers tied to it look like model toys."

"So?"

"Clara, you're not hearing me. There's a fire on the *Prairie*, and it has three destroyers tied to it. There are tons of explosives on those destroyers. Enough to take out the base. I couldn't tell you the whole story. You wouldn't have come with me."

"Dear heaven! Thank the Lord Mom and Kate aren't there," she said. "But what about the neighbours? We headed out without warning anyone else?"

"I'm here for *you*, Clara. The best I can do is always for you."

Clara's attempt at a smile didn't take. His words stalled in her craw, then burned slowly through her gut like indigestion. Why couldn't she just be flattered and leave it at that? Because her thoughts turned to Argentia, and fear gripped and held for the rest of the journey. Would Argentia and Freshwater be there to return to?

The train slowed and hissed, screeching to a stop at Waterford Station. Clara prepared to elbow her way off but there was no need, no crowds to negotiate. She wondered if the absence of military on the train had anything to do with the fire on the base. Probably. No way of knowing.

Once off the train and out of the station, Clara headed straight for the boarding house, Patrick on her heels. At the door, Patrick stood back as Clara knocked. The door was answered by Kate whose bright smile faded at the sight of Clara. She briskly abandoned the door. "Dulcie," she called. "Someone here to see you."

Crestfallen, Clara turned to Patrick. "I told you," she said and then wondered at the sudden glimmer in his eyes.

"She's the image of you," said Patrick.

"So I'm told."

"Your mother too."

"What?"

"I imagine your mother looked the same when she was younger."

"Oh," said Clara, the word followed by a fluttering at the edge of her. A caution? Once again, like on the train, she couldn't name it. But concern fell away when Dulcie showed up. Clara quickly introduced Patrick as a friend of Father Mahony's, in town shopping on the priest's behalf. A feeble explanation, Clara knew, but she had been so focused on Kate that hadn't even considered what to say about Patrick. *What in heaven's name is Dulcie going to think?* Clara needn't have worried. Without batting an eye, Dulcie escorted the two of them through the front door and into the front room—the parlour Dulcie called it now, like she'd been a townie all her life. Tea was served and chat began, Patrick sitting silent, eyes shifting from Clara to Dulcie, as Clara talked of the goings on in Argentia and Freshwater. Lots to say about houses and clotheslines and lack of electricity, not a mention of fires and boats and explosions. She, like all citizens, was bound to secrecy. Not a legal thing, but a moral one. One didn't spread rumours in wartime. Besides, Clara's mind was pre-occupied with a monologue, a series of unanswered questions. *How does Patrick know so much about the fire? Why the soot on his face? Is he somehow involved?* Unspoken questions. Here, in the parlour at Dulcie's, she looked askance at Patrick who contributed nothing to the conversation other than a nod or a smile or a thank you. After a short time, he rose to leave, "Off to visit old buddies while I'm in town." *Who is he off to visit?*

When Clara accompanied Patrick to the door to wave goodbye, Dulcie stepped up behind her. As Clara closed the door, Dulcie put a hand on Clara's shoulder. "What are ya at, Clara?" she whispered.

Great. Dulcie's going to lay into me about Patrick. Clara jerked her shoulder and Dulcie withdrew her hand. Still, Dulcie stood her ground. Arms crossed, she repeated, "What are ya at, Clara?" She tilted her head. "You're a married woman with a husband at war."

"Not your concern, Dulcie."

Dulcie threw her hands up and trundled off, muttering. Clara pretended she didn't hear. No point in contesting Dulcie's dyed-in-the-wool beliefs. Not when Dulcie was right.

After a couple of hours, Clara left the boarding house, her plan being an overnight tryst at the Newfoundland Hotel and a train back home the next day. For all her earlier longing and despite her enjoyment of past encounters with Patrick at the Newfoundland Hotel, this night with Patrick was uneventful. Clara just went through the motions, her sole concern being her estrangement from Kate.

All the way home she pondered the fire at the base. When she walked into her house, Kathleen greeted her with a hug. "Some time we've had here. The USS *Prairie* caught fire."

"So the danger was real?"

"Terrifying, it was. Went on for hours." Kathleen's voice was a whisper, like she was telling secrets. Clara understood. Tight-lipped was the way she should be. Nevertheless, Kathleen continued. "If they didn't get that fire under control the whole place would have gone up. An explosion to be felt seventy miles away. All of us goners." Kathleen took a deep breath. "At least you're back. You're safe." With a wave of her hand, she dismissed the topic. "How are Kate and Dulcie?"

"Fine," Clara replied. "Dulcie's doing awfully well for herself, really taking to life in town. She loves meeting people, and running the boarding house suits her to a tee. Must admit that Kate's better off there for now." Kathleen nodded. Clara did not mention that Kate had rejected her, and Kathleen did not ask. Not another word about the fire was shared. A few days later, however, a report appeared in the local newspaper. Apparently, there were funerals for two American sailors after the fire. The USS *Prairie* was to be sent to the States for repairs, then come back to Argentia.

The incident slid away. Summer slid in.

CHAPTER 10

WHEN DIESEL TRUCKS, A COMMON rumble in the light of day, thundered in the black of night, Clara lurched into wakefulness. For seconds, she lay in limbo, blinking. When reality insinuated itself, she exhaled a heartbroken "Oh." She had known the trucks were coming. Everybody did.

The powers that be, having ousted the living souls from Argentia, were now moving the dead, a process that involved disinterring three cemeteries—Mount Rosary, Point Roache, and Pond Head—and reinterring the bodies in Freshwater. All under the veil of darkness, an attempt to lessen the trauma for the relatives of the deceased.

Clara's need to stand vigil with her mother surpassed any reluctance to lose the warmth of the bed. She jumped up, slipped into her chenille housecoat, and stumbled down the hall to the front room, tying her belt tight along the way. At the threshold, she paused. There, beside the window, in the glow of a single flickering candle set on the sill, stood Kathleen. Grief filled the room, the weight of it pushing at Clara until she leaned into the door jamb.

"The ground is well-thawed," said Kathleen without turning around. "They're getting a start on the job of digging. Digging up and replanting bodies. The dead exiled, just like the living."

Clara said not a word as stepped up to the window and put a trembling arm through Kathleen's.

"You cold?" said Kathleen, squeezing Clara's arm. "No help from the candle, I'm afraid. The candle's for hope, not heat."

"I know," said Clara. "And I'm fine. Have to say I'm glad it's just you and me. No need for Kate to bear witness to this."

"She'll hear about it soon enough." Kathleen let out a sigh. "A few nights back, I looked through the window at shadows of horses hauling coffins and I thought I was seeing things. The next day, the truth came. It wasn't my imagination at all. People had taken it upon themselves to move their relatives' graves. Can't blame them for not waiting. Nobody wants their loved ones heaved into a mass grave."

Clara squeezed Kathleen's arm. "But they have to move them, Mom," she said. "They can't be putting airfields on top of one hundred fifty years of remains."

"Yer brother Jimmy is in that pile of bodies somewhere." Kathleen placed a hand over her heart. "No peace in his short life and no peace in death." Her voice broke. "So long ago, still the grief is raw. It just shows up, no warning, eats away at the soul."

"Some things you have to just let be, Mom. The bodies of Jimmy and his father."

Kathleen stiffened. "I know you don't like to think it, but Alphonse was your father too. And don't be mentioning him to me anyway, Clara. If I saw the likes of him dug up, I'd knock him down again. But Jimmy? My baby? Heaven forbid I be asked to identify his remains."

"You know darn well you don't need to concern yourself over that. There would be nothing to identify; Jimmy died a long time ago."

"A long time . . . and just yesterday." The night wind sighed its way under the front door. The candle flame wavered, then righted itself. "Heaven help the poor people who have to identify the newly dead," Kathleen said.

The trucks struggled in the sludge, roared their way through it, and continued to climb toward the new graveyard at the top of the hill in Freshwater. "Just bits and pieces of people," said Clara, a glum undertone to her voice. "The new grave in the shape of a cross. What about the old headstones? I heard if there's anything left of them, they'll be lined up on the one grave."

"His name was Jimmy," Kathleen began, her voice quiet and firm.

Clara's innards soured. Not now. Not a story now. Not when they were locked into the murk, the muck, the racket. A thump on the door thwarted the protest in her throat. Clara turned toward the sound. The knock came again, and again. "You wait here, Mom," she said.

"Get the kerosene lamp so you can see your way to the door." Kathleen pointed towards a shelf, her arm a black-on-black shadow. Taking the lamp, lighting it, and turning up the flame, Clara approached the door and opened it a crack. She raised the lamp.

At the sight of Patrick, she widened her eyes and tilted her head toward the window where Kathleen stood. He caught the warning. "Sorry for the disturbance, missus," he said, loud enough for his voice to bounce into the room behind her. "Just stopping by houses that have candles in the windows. Letting you know that all is as it should be. Good night."

Clara nodded, grateful, and closed the door. "Just one of the workers checking in," she said, extinguishing the lamp to hide the tremor rising in her body. She took her time returning the lamp to its shelf, time to breathe, time to clear her throat. "There's no end to the destruction," she said, steering conversation away from the knock at the door. "We bury the departed and time buries our sorrow. War digs up the bodies and wakes up our torment. No peace for souls, living or dead."

Kathleen gazed at Clara, through Clara, her eyes like polished pennies in the glow of the candle. "His name was Jimmy, and he was not like you at all."

Clara's body slackened. Kathleen, deep inside the memory of her lost baby, had paid no heed to the late-night caller. Clara needn't have concerned herself. She let out a slow breath. Was there anything new to be learned about Jimmy here? She waited.

Kathleen reached a hand to Clara's hair and stroked it. "You with your brown hair and brown eyes. Jimmy had golden hair, curls flowing through it, eyes as blue as the ice on a glacier. He was born during the Great War and died shortly after it. An innocent, a lamb who happened to be there when the wolf emerged. Your father was a kind man once, but after the war he railed about the world being against him. War had triggered the wolf in Alphonse. Sometimes I wondered if killing had just become part and parcel of him. I knew he'd gone off himself, but never suspected he'd kill my Jimmy. Not until it was too late." Kathleen looked toward the door and then back at Clara. "You never know when the wolf will show up, standing beside you, or knocking at your door."

Clara jerked upright. What did Kathleen know about the man at the door? If there was anything, Clara would not glean it now, for Kathleen turned away, toward the candle in the window. "When are we having the root cellar built?" she asked, her voice eerie, creeping through Clara, shivering through Clara.

"Oh, I'll see to that, Mom," replied Clara. "You'll have a place to put your vegetables."

"There's more than vegetables can go into a good cellar."

Clara could not pinpoint meaning in those words. She asked no questions, offered no response at all. Both remained at the window until the noise in the night fell away, leaving nothing but the whisper of waves to shore.

KATE

CHAPTER 11

PARKED ON THE CHESTERFIELD NEAR the front window in the parlour with books fanned out beside her, Kate picked a title, thumbed through, and tossed it aside. She selected another book, riffled the pages, and read the last few. "God damn it," she muttered.

"You're some crooked today."

Caught with curse words dangling, Kate cringed at the sight of Dulcie, who stood in the doorway, leaning comfortably against the jamb. *How long has she been there?* "Sorry about the swearing," Kate muttered as she lowered her head to hide her flushed face.

"Pfft." Dulcie scooped up the books and set them on a side table. "Don't trouble yourself over it," she said. She plopped down on the chesterfield. "But I would like to know what's under it."

Baffled, Kate blinked. "Meaning?"

"What ails you, child?"

"Oh," Kate said. She waved her hand toward the books. "All fiction. Every last one stuffed with conflict. The world has enough troubles. I don't have the strength for imaginary ones." She sniffed. "The truth of it, Dulcie, is that I've been scanning the beginnings of books, then skipping to the end."

"You think the way out of troubles is to skirt them altogether?"

"I don't know." Kate sighed, loud and long. "In Argentia, all the graveyards were dug up, all the bodies moved to Freshwater. Nanny must have been beside herself, her own baby Jimmy among the disturbed dead." She dragged her sleeve across her face. The graveyard issue, although genuinely troubling, was not the root of Kate's worries. Kate couldn't talk about the cache of letters she had uncovered on the *Elizabeth J*, couldn't tell Dulcie that Mavis had written to Clara repeatedly. There was no one she could talk to about that. Not yet. But she could talk about war. War belonged to everybody. "War is a torment. Three graveyards . . ."

"We are all reeling from the shock of the bodies being moved." Dulcie placed a hand over her heart. "And who'd have thought that a passenger ferry like the *Caribou* would be torpedoed by a U-boat on its way here from Nova Scotia?"

Relieved, Kate glommed onto the subject of the ferry boat. Anything to allow her to sidestep her personal conflict. "I heard there was an escort mine sweeper that *trailed* the ferry rather than *lead* it. How did that happen?"

"I don't know. One hundred thirty-six souls lost." Dulcie shook her head. "We can only pray for them." She made the sign of the cross, then placed a gentle hand on Kate's shoulder. "Now, child, you can't spend all your time in torment, a young girl like yourself."

"But I do." Kate's eyes flooded. "I never expected war at our doorstep in Argentia. It destroyed everything and displaced every living soul. And now? U-boats on the coast and war planes in the skies and blackout blinds on every window in the boarding house." At that instant, the windows rattled, punctuating her concerns. "Damn Atlantic wind. No stopping it. I'm chilled to the bone." She wrapped her arms around herself. "Everything feels like a threat. At night when the wind slams from the northeast, all the lights shake. Fear in everything."

"I'll get you something to rid you of the chill." Dulcie bolted to the kitchen and returned with a quilt. "Had this warming by the stove." She wrapped it around Kate.

"You're an angel, Dulcie," said Kate, eyes filling with tears.

Dulcie offered a handkerchief from her apron. "We just have to take things as they comes. We're all worried, Kate."

"And no way out."

"Do you believe that? You think your nanny would agree with you?"

Kate shook her head. "Nanny is as strong as a church pillar. She would say that the way out is through," said Kate.

"That sounds like your nanny all right," said Dulcie.

"Yes, it does, doesn't it?" Kate sat silently for a few seconds, then nodded. "Well, I suppose you're right; I'll just have to take things as they come." She stretched, stood, and folded the quilt. "Thanks, Dulcie." She passed Dulcie the quilt and reclaimed her books. "I've Latin homework to do," she said and headed toward the foot of the stairs.

"Take a walk in the sunshine, Kate," Dulcie called after her. "After you finish your Latin. A rare day it is with the sky as blue as the cloak on the Virgin Mary. Good for what ails you."

Without comment or commitment, Kate made her way up the stairs, her ear still tuned to Dulcie's voice. "Well, that's that," Dulcie said. "Now, where was I when the boat turned over?" Kate couldn't help but smile. Dulcie would be back at work in the kitchen in seconds, moving on, calmly doing what had to be done.

Having translated a chapter on the Punic Wars, Kate paused to consider the use of this study to her life. Was there any?

A tap on her door. She lifted her head. "Yes?"

Izzie's voice. "A visitor in the parlour for you, Kate."

"For me? Who is it?" Footsteps, Izzie's footsteps, sounded, then faded. *Darn it.* Kate would have to find out for herself. She hurried over the stairs and charged through the door of the parlour. An abrupt halt, eyes wide. "Peter? What on earth are you doing here?"

Peter jumped to his feet, cap in hand. "Hi, Kate. Hope you don't mind my stopping by."

"Of course not. Just surprised is all. What are you doing in St. John's?"

"In town to buy shoe leather for my father." Fingers of both hands tapped his cap, rotating it in a complete circle.

"Shoe leather?" said Kate.

"Father makes all our shoes." He cleared his throat. "Thought I'd pay you a visit."

"Oh." Kate remembered her manners. "Good to see you. Can I get you a drop of tea?"

"Got any of them Purity biscuits we had on the schooner?"

Kate smiled. "Certainly do. Please make yourself at home while I fetch them."

In minutes, with tea and biscuits on a tray, Kate returned.

"How is your family doing?" Peter asked as they settled in.

"All right, I guess. Nanny is pretty upset about the graves being moved."

"Can't say that I'd blame her. I was there during the excavation. Was shocked out of my boots at a young military man who picked up a huge bone and snapped it over his knee." Peter made the sign of the cross. "It was a human bone, a thigh bone. Not an ounce of respect for the dead, some people." He let out a relieved sigh. "Good to say that out loud. You're the only one I've told."

"And you're the only one I ever felt comfortable with, talking about the tidal wave," Kate said, her response liquid and true. "Don't worry, I won't repeat your story." That was a promise, tamper-proof. Telling would only cause pain to the families who had already suffered enough. He smiled and she moved on, still on the topic of war, and talk about the sinking of the *Caribou.*

At the mention of the ferry boat, Peter hunched his shoulders and dropped his head. A concerned Kate leaned forward. "Peter?" she said gently, then paused.

At a quarter-hour chime from the clock in the hall, Peter looked up. "Remember the friend I told you about?" he asked, his voice a stifled whisper, "the tall sailor who helped me in the mess hall?"

"Charlie?" said Kate.

"You remembered." Peter looked pleased. He straightened, then sighed. "Charlie died," he said, his tone calm now, his gaze steady.

Kate waited for more words, connecting words.

"He went home to Alabama for his father's funeral and was returning to Newfoundland on the *Caribou.* And that was the end of it for him."

Kate softened. "I'm so sorry, Peter."

"So am I. A great friend, he was."

His wistfulness elicited a gentle smile from Kate. She reached to touch his hand. "You'll be coming back to visit again, won't you?" she asked.

Peter's eyes lit up. "Be delighted to." He stood. "I'll try some letters too, if that's okay. Not much for writing, really, but I'm learning."

"A grand idea," said Kate, trying not to flinch at the mention of letters. She did not want to discourage his learning. This was the young man she first talked to about the tidal wave. This could be someone she could talk to about other things. *But letters? Not if I can help it.*

Peter's grin couldn't have been any wider. "Thank you for the tea and biscuits." He patted his wallet. "I've got to be heading out. The day is getting on. Wouldn't do to get caught in fog and dark. Rain coming too. Long drive on a dirt road. Won't get any shorter if I land up to my axles in mud." He moved toward the door. Kate followed. He was still talking. "Oh, I've done that before, trying to drive a big old truck to the mess hall on the base." When he reached the door, he stood still and stopped talking. "Don't mind me rambling on." He patted his wallet again. "Goodbye, Kate."

After she closed the door behind him, she heard a singsong voice behind her. "Kate's got a boyfriend."

"Well, Izzie," Kate said, "he's a boy and he's my friend, so I guess I do." The two headed upstairs. "And what about you? Any new prospects on the horizon?"

"Ouch."

Kate stopped dead. "I'm so sorry, Izzie. I forgot about the men in Nova Scotia."

"Don't worry about it. Serves me right, teasing you like that. But I got more to think about than landing a husband. Once a man gets a ring on your finger, he's a millstone. A woman can barely move with the weight of it. Just so you know," said Izzie, "that Peter of yours is all about money. Money is first with him and always will be. Mark my words. If he has a choice, it'll be wallet before woman every time."

Kate didn't respond. But Izzie had a point. Kate had noticed the attention Peter paid to his wallet. What was that well-known expression about money? The root of all evil?

The two continued up the stairs, each to her own room. Once on her own, Kate pulled out a fresh scribbler and a sharpened pencil and wrote the date. Below that she penned the remembered phrase about money: *The love of money is the root of all evil.* Would Peter fall into the mistake of loving money too much?

KATHLEEN

CHAPTER 12

It is covert, the sea.

The North Atlantic steals in and out of capes and coves, sculpting caverns, smoothing stones, pulverizing rocks into sand. In its depths sit mountains and valleys, some taller, deeper than those on shore, some undetected or neglected by humans for eons. The sea exemplifies stealth, its blue ripple, whitecaps, and black calm concealing both elements of nature and machines of war. The Atlantic betrays nothing, a perfect veil for lurking U-boats.

On days, and there are many, when warm air sweeps the cold Atlantic, fog forms and rolls, offering a shield to coastal cities and towns like St. John's and Argentia. Ideal camouflage. But what obscures our homes also obscures our enemies. Traitors exist in fog, traitors conspire in fog, and, at times, traitors are caught despite fog. When military patrols inform civilian lighthouse keepers near the base at Argentia to ignore the sound of guns at night, the response is a nod. No reason requested. None necessary. Whisper has it that when traitors are caught, they are shot and land in a plot on Boot Hill.

Ashore, under heavy fog and behind blackout blinds, mentions of the particulars of war are shushed, confined like closet skeletons. A survival skill. Loose lips sink ships.

Ashore, under hefty scrutiny and behind closed doors, secrets of the particulars of people are cloistered. Another survival skill.

The phantom Kathleen, me, unearths nuggets of truth at every telling, carrying them forward into the next passage, inserting them like puzzle pieces into the frame of my life. The living Kathleen conceals all about assaults upon her and reprisals by her. My daughter Clara keeps her childhood in the dark, in essence hiding the truth about the origin of her daughter. Clara manages to maintain the illusion of marriage while indulging in an affair. Kate, having scraped the top layer of earth from one of Clara's secrets, holds the information close, all the while seething under cold calm.

Indeed, a troubled time on a small island which, although not on the front lines of war, is strategically located, a gateway to North America. Strange as it may seem, war offers blessings to the impoverished nation of Newfoundland for along with the invasion of military comes an influx of money. The proof of the boon in December of 1942 lies in the busy shops along the harbour St. John's which are decked like the halls of song. Wreaths, shaped from dropped fir branches festooned with red ribbons, adorn the doors of even the smallest shops. Joy resounds in carols sung by all, military and citizens.

The war itself is hidden in plain view, beneath sea, beneath secrets, beneath song.

CLARA

CHAPTER 13

THE HOLIDAY SEASON BLINKED AHEAD, but Clara couldn't find a glint of joy in herself. Yes, she and Mom would be together for Christmas, but Kate hadn't shown a glimmer of interest in coming home and, in fact, hadn't contacted Clara at all. It was Dulcie who sparked hope when she sent a letter inviting Clara to the boarding house for a pre-Christmas visit. "I'm sure Dulcie means for both of us to come, Mom," Clara said.

"And I'm sure she doesn't," Kathleen said, without a second's hesitation. "Not born yesterday, that woman, and she knows there's a barrier between you and Kate. If Dulcie wants to topple walls like Joshua at Jericho, more power to her. I'll be grand here by myself."

"Oh." Clara shrugged. "Makes sense." This clarity had Clara fired up, ready to go. She wanted to be there *yesterday*. "You think I can get on the train this afternoon?"

"Not anxious, are you? Well, I wouldn't aim for the train today. Always loaded with troops. But Father Mahony's driving to town in the morning. Guaranteed he'll give you a lift."

"Good enough then." Clara grabbed her coat and headed to the rectory.

All in all, not a bad day for a car trip, thought Clara as they headed out at the break of dawn. Kind of Father Mahony to take her, no reluctance in him. Bumpy roads, icy potholes, and a light snowfall, enough of which had landed to dress the fir trees along the way. At the slightest cue from the wind, branches released sprays of snow which floated like dust and then slid across the windshield. The ride was long, but the day was bright, and Clara was enjoying the prospect of escaping her cold draughty house for a short time. The presence of a warm fire, the absence of a heavy sweater, small things, joyous things.

So lost in pleasant thoughts was she that she almost forgot about the good Father beside her. *Where are my manners?* "I'm grateful for the ride, Father. So, what spurred you to make this trip today?"

"You're most welcome for the lift." Father Mahony let out an elongated sigh. "The curate spurred me. Not in a good way. Can't believe they sent me a curate who collected parish dues from the people and then absconded with the money. And here I thought he was a wonderful young man. Now I have no choice but to report him to the archbishop."

A wide-eyed Clara had no words. Why was the parish priest telling her this? Imagine if she were to drop this tidbit at the corner store. No end to the gossip. She cleared her throat. "I guess things, and people, are not always what they seem, Father," she said gingerly.

"No, my child, they are not. Needs eyes in the back of my head, I do. I'd best be keeping this stuff to meself. God forgive me for the mention of it."

"I won't tell a soul, Father." An easy promise. Clara Kerrigan was schooled in the art of sealed lips. Still her mind danced with doubts about the whole thing. *Shouldn't our parish priest, shouldn't* every *parish priest, all of whom had God on their side, be clever enough to pierce deceit, to halt it in its tracks?*

Silence swept in, a reprieve. Clara pressed her lips tight. There was not another word she could drum up that would be fitting in this conversation. Father Mahony had a few words, however. "You know, perhaps I told you so that you would tell others. Already had one parishioner at my door this week looking for a receipt for church dues he'd paid to the curate. Of course, I had no record of it, not a slip of paper anywhere. Don't need any more visits like that."

"I guess not," said Clara who made no offering to seed a rumour. Indeed, she would keep herself at a safe remove from all of it.

Father Mahony dropped Clara off at the Bakeapple Boarding House on Brazil Square, walking with her to the front door. Dulcie grinned in greeting, offering the obligatory cup of tea to the priest who turned her down, got back in his car, and drove off.

"Where's he off to in such a hurry?" Apparently, Dulcie didn't need a response because she immediately shifted her attention to Clara. "Come in, come in!"

"Great to see you, Dulcie!" Clara stepped across the threshold, removed her overshoes, and set them aside. She embraced Dulcie who then held Clara at arm's length.

"Hold still till I have a gander. Haven't seen hide nor hair of you in a dog's age."

"Are you keeping well, Dulcie?"

"Indeed I am. Workin' every hour God gives me and lovin' it."

Clara caught a whiff of baking and inhaled the scents of cinnamon and nutmeg and cloves. "Mmm, Christmas."

"Does smell grand, doesn't it?" said Dulcie. "I got a good start on me fruit cakes yesterday, one light, one dark. Used up all the molasses and cinnamon and whatever else I could find. Will have to go to the shops. I'm still dusted with flour, me and my kitchen too."

Clara glanced around, taking in the hallway, front room, and staircase, seeing everything, seeing nothing, not caring about any of it. "The place looks wonderful," she commented, a mandate of courtesy. *Where is Kate?* Clara peered behind Dulcie, eager to get to the point of her visit. "Where's Kate?"

"Here I am," came a chilled response from the landing at the top of the stairs. Kate trudged down the staircase and leaned against the newel post, arms crossed, eyes flashing fury. Clara recoiled like she'd been slapped, ready to collapse right here at the door. She struggled against gravity and won, just barely. "Lovely to see you, Kate," she managed.

Kate glared.

"And it's lovely to have you here, Clara," Dulcie offered against the brittle void. "When Kate told me about the state of your house in Freshwater, I thought you could use a break. We'll have a grand time. Keep the kettle dancing from dawn to dark. Are you working on the base yet?"

"Not yet." As the answer popped out, relief slid through Clara. *God bless you, Dulcie, for moving things along.* "It's crossed my mind that I could sell the schooner. Did you know that the military are buying local schooners to use for target practice?" Clara removed her coat and Dulcie put out her hands to take it, dutifully hanging it in the closet.

"You don't say?" Dulcie perked up, clearly interested. "Isn't that heartbreaking for folks, sending beloved schooners to that fate?" She put an arm in Clara's and led her toward the front room. "Let's have a sit down and you can tell us more."

A few steps, a comfortable seat, and a cup of tea later, Clara continued. "Yes, Dulcie, it's upsetting for fishermen to lose their schooners but harder for them to risk their lives at sea. There's perfectly good work, safer work, available on the base. I'm pretty sure I will follow suit, sell the schooner, seek a job. Not likely to have doors barred in my face, there's so much office work to be had. Interviews next week, so I'll have to return home with Father Mahony tomorrow afternoon if I want to apply."

"Sounds sensible enough to me. As for today, we'll go shopping downtown, if you're up for it."

Clara nodded.

"Lovely. It's not far and it's downhill, easy to walk there. It's the climb with the parcels on the way back that's the trouble. Might be some light snow today, but if the wind holds off, we'll be fine. Let me show you to your room and you can get comfortable." She headed toward the stairs. "Kate, have you seen Izzie? Is she going to the big dance tonight?"

Kate trailed after them. "Yes. She has a date."

"What big dance is that, Kate?" asked Clara, determined to get into the conversation.

Before Kate could offer a word, however, Dulcie paused at the foot of the stairs, spun around, and spewed the information. "The Uncle Tim's Barn Dance Show! It's broadcast on VOCM radio and it will be grand." Her face beaming with enthusiasm, Dulcie brought her hands together in a single clap. "It's on many a Saturday night, starts at 10:30. People will be packed in together. Probably will be hard for them to find room to breathe."

"It's held at the Knights of Columbus Hostel, only for military and their guests," added Kate.

"But we can listen to the whole thing," said Dulcie as she started up the stairs. "The radio will be at the ready."

Clara followed her up the staircase. "Here we are," said Dulcie, stopping at a door and inserting its key. "I put you in the room next to Kate. The bathroom is at the end of the hall." Dulcie stepped back. "If you need anything, anything at all, just speak your mind. Just know that you are as welcome as rain in a drought. Dinner at one o'clock. Hope you're up for a bit of salt beef and cabbage. Boiled dinner usually goes down well here. Now, if you'll excuse me, I got to get back to work." She pivots toward the stairs.

"Boiled dinner will be fine . . ." Clara said, her voice trailing off when she realized that Dulcie was no longer within earshot. She smiled at Kate who was lingering at the door. "Things seem a bit hectic around here, Kate."

"The usual confusion," said Kate, shrugging.

Clara paused, expecting Kate to head downstairs. Kate stayed. Clara coughed to clear the hesitation from her throat. "I don't . . . well, I . . ."

With a wave of the hand, Kate shut her down. "You can keep your secrets," she said. "I'm not ready for any of it." Then Kate stepped forward and Clara raised her arms, expecting, perhaps just hoping, for an embrace. Kate abruptly stopped. She sniffed as she bent to pick up Clara's suitcase. "I'll help you unpack." She strode into the room and deposited the suitcase on the bed. "What do you think of the room?" Kate spread her hands wide.

"Charming," said Clara, although she had not taken her eyes off Kate. *You can keep your secrets. Not ready for any of it.* As the weight of the Kate's words sank in, Clara leaned into the door jamb. Even if Kate were ready, Clara could not, would not ever, reveal everything. The thought made her head spin. She pulled away from the door frame but struggled to maintain her balance, so she leaned again.

"What's the matter?" Kate asked, keeping her distance.

Clara shook her head, took a deep breath, and stood erect. She stepped, away from the doorway, away from the cusp of a faint, toward Kate. "I'm fine, absolutely fine. Just all in from the trip."

"You have a lie down. We still have two hours until dinner." Kate reached, placed her fingers lightly on Clara's arm. "Can I get you anything? Some tea maybe."

"Yes, maybe a drop of tea would be just the thing." Clara saw concern in Kate's eyes and felt comfort in Kate's touch. *Perhaps it will all work out.* But then Kate withdrew her hand. "I'll go down to steep the tea," she said.

When Kate left, Clara plopped onto the bed whose springs bounced in response. Dizziness snatched her again, so she pushed at her suitcase, which thumped to the floor. Without removing her shoes, she fell supine onto the quilt and then curled herself into a ball. Minutes later, Kate's footsteps crossed the threshold into the room, crossed the floor to the side of bed. A soft slide of a tray onto the bedside table, a welcome aroma of tea and homemade bread. Clara feigned sleep, made no movement. With a delicate touch, Kate removed Clara's shoes and covered her with a blanket. A shrouded Clara resisted the urge to open her eyes and pour out her heart. Long, slow breaths, that's all she needed to do. Finally, receding footsteps. The door clicked into place. Stillness filled the room. The clock in the hallway chimed the hour. And she drifted. Off to sleep and dreaming of a day, nearly seventeen years ago when she, a banished sinner, a terrified girl, felt the rip of pain in her loins.

Clara awoke with a start, heart pounding. She looked around. Was Kate here? No. Clara was alone. Her fears subsided. At some point truth would come to the fore. How much did Kate know? How much was Clara willing to tell? *Not ready for any of it.* Kate would not confront her on this visit. When, Clara wondered, when would that shoe drop?

That afternoon, the Bakeapple Boarding House on Brazil Square emptied a quartet of women into the street—Clara paired with Dulcie, Kate with Izzie—all taking their good, sweet time on the narrow pathway. Wouldn't pay to barrel headlong down the hill to Water Street; the rutted and littered route required eye-to-ground scrutiny. Clara's foot took a bump from an empty beer bottle—an apparent fugitive from a pile beside a stoop. She gave it a kick and it came to rest amid a clump of cigarette butts encircling a telephone pole whose base was painted white. Odd-looking, the white paint, she thought, but cars had bizarre paint jobs too, their headlights black, their bumpers and fenders outlined in white. All for pedestrian safety during blackout regulations. She wondered how many injuries had occurred before the white-paint-safety-measure showed up. Broken noses from slamming into poles? Lost limbs from stepping into the paths of cars? Lost lives too, probably. She shuddered. Unpleasant thoughts. She shoved them down.

At Water Street, they crossed to the south side, giggling as they zig-zagged through the clatter of streetcars and cluster of uniforms toward the Arcade building with its brick exterior, dormer windows above and picture windows at street level. There, Dulcie paused to catch her breath. "Could get trampled to death if you're not careful. So busy downtown these days."

Clara nodded. War had made St. John's a boomtown, bringing military and money, taking a well-needed broom to cobwebs of poverty.

Kate and Izzie eyed the window displays, taking note of ladies' suits with shoulder pads and buttoned pockets.

"Classy," said Kate.

"Practical," said Izzie.

"I like the blue one," they both said in concert and giggled.

Their delight was contagious and took Clara back in time, to the first occasion she had shopped in St. John's. She had been on a quest for a dress for a ball at the Newfoundland Hotel and was quite taken with her choice—a black chiffon chemise with a dropped waist. Shapeless really. Quite the departure from the slim-belted waistlines, boxy shoulders and close-fitting styles the girls were admiring.

Dulcie nodded toward Kate and Izzie. "They seem to be enjoying themselves."

"Yes. They surely do." Clara relished every second of watching Kate sharing a joyful moment with a friend. Thoughts of Kate's early childhood panged: Kate was only three when she lost her 'siblings' to the sea. Clara wondered if Kate had shared joyful moments with them. Of course she had. But she was so young. Did she remember them? Maybe, someday, Clara would ask.

A brisk day when the wind picked up and Clara curled her fingers inside her fur muff which kept hands toasty and money close. She eyed both sides of the street and glimpsed a barber shop, its display window highlighting a barber as he curled a steaming towel onto the face of a customer. "That looks like a good idea, warm and inviting," she said to Dulcie, pointing toward the shop.

Dulcie smiled in agreement. "Let's get in off the street before we freeze our arses," she said, steering the lot of them through the door of the Arcade, the first of a series of stores in an afternoon of browsing.

Clara's only purchase that afternoon was a planned one—blue satin fabric and decorative braid. She would create a new dress for the holiday season. *Maybe I'll wear it at a private celebration with Patrick.* That thought stirred longing; perhaps she should have asked Patrick to meet her in St. John's. She knew that he had scheduled a trip in and that he would have changed the dates to match up with hers. But she discarded the idea the instant it occurred. There was no way that she would divide her time between Patrick and Kate. This was Kate's weekend. Kate was first. Would always be first.

They entered a tiny tea house and sat at a booth beside the window. Clara shrugged off her coat. "Your new hat is lovely, Kate," she said, a safe offering.

Smiling, Kate touched the brim of her newly purchased hat, then the hat pin, a white faux pearl with gold leaves at its base. "Is the pin in the right place?"

"Perfect," said Izzie.

"Grand," said Dulcie.

Clara nodded in agreement. Striking, that hat whose hue picked up the brown of Kate's eyes and framed the curve of her face. Clara beamed at

Kate while conversation swirled. When Clara's gaze fell toward the window, she flinched. Was that Patrick, standing there, across the street, leaning on a lamp post, looking for all the world like he was waiting for her? Just as he had in the past. Clara blinked. Was she dreaming?

"Why, Clara, are you after hearing me at all?" A gentle nudge from Dulcie.

Clara tuned in. "Sorry. What were you saying?"

"I was late getting to the making of my fruitcakes this year. Got a grand start yesterday, as I told you. Should be buying ingredients today, I suppose. But I must say I'm enjoying the break from the lot of it. Bless Rosemary's heart for handling the supper today. I should get out and about more often."

"What's not to enjoy?" said Clara. "This is a lovely spot." She looked through the window again. No Patrick. She must have been daydreaming. She scanned the tearoom, catching sight of a variety of teacups. "Oh," she said. "Before we head back to the boarding house, Dulcie, I must tell you that I'd like to buy a tea caddy. Not for myself, mind you, but for Mom. The corner of her old one is cracked, and the darn thing is snowing tea leaves. Must have gotten damaged in the move. A perfect opportunity to get her a gift for Christmas."

"Oh, I know just the thing. Admiring it the other day. Antique, mahogany, it is, divided into thirds. The two slats can be removed if you want to use it for something larger than tea. At Bowring's down the street. Kathleen will love it. We'll head there next."

Clara turned to Izzie. "Now, Izzie, tell me about this dance you are going to tonight. And Kate's going too?"

"I-I . . ." began Izzie.

"What Izzie is stumbling to say is that she has a date, and I don't," Kate said pointedly.

Izzie's eyes glinted gratitude. She eased back into her chair as Kate continued. "It's a couple's affair, Canadian and American military men and their dates. I'm a bit young for all that. Anyway, I'm run ragged. Would much rather listen to the program on the radio tonight, with Dulcie."

"Good thinking for a young thing like yerself," said Dulcie.

Pride in her daughter's wisdom burst through Clara like a flower in bloom, yet she said nothing. Kate would likely resent words of admiration from Clara, maybe even seek out military suitors to spite Clara. After a hesitant smile, Clara turned feigned attention to the tea leaves at the bottom of her cup.

Izzie leaned toward her. "This place has someone who reads tea leaves. We can have her stop by the table, if you wish," she said, her eyes shining, a bit of mischief in them.

"Oh, no thank you," said Clara. "Not me." Heaven forbid something leak through her well-honed veneer.

A grinning Kate downed the rest of her tea. "I'm not beyond the idea. Let's ask for the reader." She held her cup up to signal the waitress who threaded her way to them and informed them that the reader was not available today. Izzie sighed. "Sorry, Kate."

Kate hunched, then lowered her shoulders. Clearly a mild disappointment for her, yet one that gouged Clara who grappled with, and resisted, an urge to wrap her daughter in comforting words. *Better to keep the peace than rekindle her anger.* Clara opted to breathe life back into earlier conversation. "I think that the radio show sounds like a great idea, Kate. The three of us can make cocoa, curl up, and tune in. What time is the program—10:30, is it?"

"Yes," said Kate, her demeanour brightening. Clara smiled.

"I'm almost tempted to stay home," said Izzie. "Bone-chilling cold tonight, I hear. A good reason to toast one's buns beside the fire instead of risking life and limb on icy hills."

"Ha!" said Kate. "You can't wait to be jitterbugging over on Harvey Road with the rest of them."

"True enough."

Later that evening, after Izzie had gone off to meet her young sailor from the state of New York, Clara and Kate and their host Dulcie sat in the parlour, huddled around the radio, close to the fire, while boarding house guests re-angled chesterfields and squeezed into them or grabbed a chair from the dining room and filled every available space. Clara smiled at the orderly arc of seats around the radio. Clearly, a practised event, this gathering around the radio on a winter's evening. Soon the fire was toasty, and the people were cozy, and the aroma of steaming cocoa filled the room. At one point, Kate set aside her cup, stoked the fire, and added a log. She claimed the wingback chair, usually occupied by Reggie who was working at the railway tonight. "Cold and crisp out there," she said. "The streets are sheets of ice. Hope Izzie doesn't take a spill." She retrieved her cocoa and, just as Clara was about to warn her that the beverage was too hot to drink, Kate blew across the top. Clara was close enough to see the ripples slip across the milky brown. She leaned back. There was no need to warn Kate, sensible Kate. The music from the radio, the glow from the fire, and the warmth of the cocoa eased through Clara. The next thing she knew someone was gently shaking her shoulder, rousing her from sleep. The someone was Kate who whispered in her ear.

"Aunt Clara, it's after ten. You drifted off."

Clara yawned. "Oh, yes, the radio show."

"Doesn't start until 10:30," said Kate. "You've had a long day; maybe you should skip the program and get some sleep. Izzie will tell us all about the dance tomorrow. Dulcie's turned in already. She's probably hard asleep by now."

Clara looked around the room. A few chairs were vacant, abandoned at odd angles, no effort made to return them to their original spot. The chesterfields were still stuffed with eager people who spoke in whispers, perhaps out of sensitivity for the needs of a slumbering few. That was kind of them, Clara thought as sleepiness overwhelmed her. Apparently, Kate had a point. "You going to bed too?" Clara asked.

"Indeed, I am," said Kate.

Clara pulled herself from the chair. She wrapped her knitted shawl over her shoulders and followed Kate to the stairs. Kate raised the kerosene lamp she was carrying in her left hand. The glow of the flame created an arc on the wall, one that moved and flickered with each tiny movement from Kate. As Clara trudged along behind, staring at that glow, following the shadow of her flesh and blood, she felt full in the moment. She let out a sigh. Must have been a loud one because Kate stopped in her tracks. She turned, her face haloed in light. "I heard that. Everything all right, Aunt Clara? For now, anyway?"

Clara looked into Kate's bright eyes. "I must tell you, Kate, that I really appreciate all you do and bring into my life."

Kate smiled, a soft smile. She opened her mouth. Clara hoped for a positive reply. Just then, from the top of the stairs a voice rang out. "Can't ye do your compliments in the light of day? Such a commotion. A woman needs her sleep."

"And her hard liquor," whispered Kate.

Clara leaned in. "What hard liquor?"

"Granny Grace has a special teacup for a special drink." Kate and Clara snickered.

"Sorry, Granny," called Kate who then put her fingers to her lips. "Ssh." Clara nodded and they tiptoed to their rooms.

CHAPTER 14

Content that, in time things would work out with Kate, Clara drifted easily into sleep that night. She floated in dreams, which at first were pleasant. Ocean and gulls and sky, blue sky with puffy white clouds. Searching, she was, for someone or something but the clouds blackened and the sky aback of them darkened and she was stumbling through the murk. A deep breath jolted her awake. She coughed. *Smoke? Do I smell smoke?* Jumping from the bed, she ran to the hallway. No sign of smoke. Back in her room, she threw open the blackout curtains. Instantly, she was chilled from a draught clawing through cracks in the casing. The window-pane, layered with frost, had a strange glow at its centre A swipe at the rime with the sleeve of her flannel gown did no good at all so she scraped her nails across it several times. As soon as she could see, she gasped. It was supposed to be a clear night, with a bite of cold that would add fog to every breath. And it was supposed to be black, wartime black, when a glint of light through a single curtain would signal the blackout warden to pound on your door.

But the sky was alight with a column of fire producing a spiral of smoke that obscured the stars. The shock of the sight locked Clara in place, her fingers gripping the windowsill. Couldn't be far off, this fire, its smoke scorching her throat and its flames roaring in her ears. Not until she heard the shriek and clang of fire engines did Clara burst into motion. She grabbed her robe and tore from the room to awaken Kate and Dulcie. Together, the three roused all the boarders. They gathered in the parlour, earlier warm and joy-filled, now cold and silent. "There were screams on the Barn Dance show and then the radio went dead," someone said. No one knew what was going on. With no sign of Izzie, Kate hurried to her friend's room. "Izzie's not here!"

"Dear Father in heaven. She's still at the dance." Dulcie crossed herself repeatedly. "It must be the Knights of Columbus Hostel that's on fire."

"We must get outside and see what is happening!" Clara, along with Dulcie and Kate, stumbled into the hallway, grabbed coats and boots, and headed for the door.

Kate let out a wail that was lost as the scream of a siren split the night. She darted forward, but Dulcie and Clara each grabbed an arm and held her back. "What about Izzie? Izzie is there," Kate cried.

"We know," said Clara. "But we mustn't be in the way."

Kate struggled to get loose.

"You can't just go—"

"Like hell I can't!" Kate broke away and tore off.

"We can't let her take off like that," said Dulcie. "We have to go with her."

"Yes, you're right. Button up your coat. We'll walk together. It's slippery and we are not taking off like demons."

"But we have to catch up to her."

"We will find her when we get there."

The two started off, Clara still holding the lamp. A car approached, crossing from the left side of the road to the right. It crept along beside them. *Who is he and what does he want?* Clara switched sides with Dulcie so that she, not Dulcie, was nearer the vehicle. The car stopped. The window opened, just a crack. "And where do you think you're going in the middle of the night?"

Clara's concern for safety was swallowed by relief. "Patrick! What are you doing here?"

Patrick raised his hand, beckoning to them. "Get into the car. You'll freeze to death out there." He slid across the bench seat and opened the door. Clara turned the lamp down to a mere glow and got in. When Dulcie hesitated, Clara urged her on. "Dulcie, this is Patrick, you remember? Get in." Without a word, Dulcie obliged.

"You told me you were coming to visit Dulcie this weekend," said Patrick. "I had to come to town this morning after all. When all the commotion started, I thought I would check on you."

Something niggled at Clara. *Did I tell him I was coming to St. John's?* She shook her head. Not important. "We are beside ourselves. The Knights of Columbus Hostel is on fire and our Kate just took off, looking for her friend Izzie who had a date there with some young soldier."

"Sailor," interjected Dulcie through chattering teeth.

Clara put an arm around Dulcie and pulled her close. "We need to find Kate. She heard the news and just took off. The poor girl is out of her mind with the worry about her friend." Clara swallowed. "We were going to listen to the show on the radio but were too tired. I had just settled in for the night when I awoke to the smell of smoke and—"

Patrick patted her arm. "Sssh. Everything's going to be fine. Don't worry. I'll take you there, and we'll find Kate and her friend."

Soothed, Clara eased herself into the seat. She was remembering now, remembering when she stood on the shore in Argentia, waiting for her brother to come on the coastal boat with his one surviving child after the tsunami, not knowing if the child was Kate or one of her 'siblings.' A dark time, equal to the day Kate was born, the day she gave her up. Now she wondered. Who had the right to make such decisions? To rip a child from the arms of its mother? Was there a God? Clara blinked and tears flooded her cheeks. *Not the time to be selfish. Time to think about Kate and Izzie.*

She sucked in a deep breath and coughed as acrid smoke assaulted her nostrils and throat. The fire was close, too close. She pivoted her head toward Patrick. Remarkably unruffled for a man driving into drama. Not a calm-water captain, then, Patrick. Passion gushed through her, followed by another bout of self-retribution. *Not the time for this either.* Patrick returned her glance and reached across to pat her arm again. This time she caught a whiff of the sleeve of his woollen coat. A distinctive odour, like creosote. *What has he been doing?* She dismissed the thought. By this time, they must all reek of smoke which permeated the air and the car and every porous surface. Clara detected another odour too, like that of pork chops hissing in a cast iron frying pan on a red-hot stove. She could not for a second allow herself to contemplate meaning there. Instead, she looked to the skies, to the towering ribbon of flames in the blackness. The German planes could find this old city easily tonight. Blackout blinds seemed suddenly pointless.

When they could not get any closer to the fire, Patrick parked the car and they got out. Around them, engines roared and water gushed and screams of agony cut the air. In a huddle they stood, shivering, watching, and afraid to move on ground that was iced over by water spurting from fire hoses. Amid chaos and spray, the building teetered, on the point of collapse. More screaming and pounding erupted from its interior. Dulcie covered her ears. "I can't bear it."

Clara cast her eyes over the crowd. "Where's Kate? I have to find her. I just have to find her."

"No," said Patrick. "I'll do that. You stay here with Dulcie. I'll find her."

"You've only seen her the one time. You barely know what she looks like!"

"As if I'd ever forget that face." He slipped into the crowd.

Clara and Dulcie huddled together, trembling. The crowd's roar downgraded to a mumble. The building yielded. Still the swish of water, the hiss of flames, the choke and billow of smoke.

"Maybe we had better go to the car," Dulcie whispered.

Clara shook her head. "Not going no place."

Dulcie tugged at Clara but to no avail. Looping an arm in Clara's, Dulcie capitulated. She stood firm.

The smoke continued, a thick fog. Every breath scorched Clara's throat. She was about to give up hope when a figure emerged, close to them. Izzie. And not far behind her, Kate.

"Thank God!" Clara rushed forward, embracing both Izzie and Kate. Then she held them both at arms' length. "Are you all right?"

"We're fine." Kate's contribution.

"And your boyfriend?" This was directed at Izzie who let out a wail.

"He pushed her through a window and got trampled," said Kate.

"Sweet Heart of Jesus." Clara looked past Kate and Izzie. There was no sign of Patrick and, since there was no way of maneuvering a car in the jumble of people and traffic on the street, Clara saw no need to wait for him, no need to mention him. He was perfectly capable of taking care of himself. She cast Dulcie a knowing look. "We're walking back." Kate and Clara supported Izzie and the four scrambled up slippery hills, amid shocked onlookers, toward the boarding house. Clara would see Patrick back in Argentia. Hopefully.

In the morning, Clara sat in the parlour with all the boarders who gathered around the radio, craving news about the fire that had killed ninety-nine people.

"No hope for any of those poor souls rammed up against doors trying to get out," remarked Granny nursing her teacup.

"The doors opened inward, for God's sake," said Reggie.

At this point, Rosemary ordered Teresa to leave the parlour. "You can do some colouring upstairs, Teresa." As soon as Teresa rounded the landing on the staircase, Rosemary spoke again. "Why were the emergency exits locked?"

Clara listened to all the talk and tutting about the absence of safety regulations, the presence of spies in the city, and the possibility of arson. She made no comment. Kate was safe in the chair beside her. Izzie was safe in her room. Dulcie was safe in the kitchen at work. When all voices fell silent, Clara sipped her tea and stared into the fireplace with its tiny flames and soothing crackle. So welcoming. But last night? Fire had created a funeral pyre. Her eyes clouded over, tears forming of their own accord. She eased from her chair and headed to the stairs, leaning into the banister for support as she climbed. She needed to lie down for a bit.

That afternoon, when a car pulled up outside the door at the appointed time, Clara was more than ready to go home. She would take Kate home too if she could, but Kate would never leave her friend Izzie to cope with such a loss on her own. Did Clara even have the right to ask Kate to go? She shook her head.

When Clara opened the door to the boarding house, expecting to see Father Mahony on the stoop, she was met instead by Patrick. "Father Mahony sends his apologies, but he's staying behind to help with the funerals."

Clara nodded. "Hard for him to leave, I suppose."

Patrick peered behind her, into the parlour.

"They're all upstairs, napping, exhausted," said Clara.

"You were a strong woman in the dark of night," he said.

"I was just grateful that my Kate did not perish. Thank you for what you did." Clara was leaning on the door frame, an attempt to keep herself upright. There was a time when she believed that Patrick was Kate's father, a time when she was too naïve to know that she was already pregnant when she met him.

Patrick smiled at her now. "Don't worry. I'll always watch over you and Kate. I'm here for you, always."

Clara closed her eyes. A slide of relief, the release of a burden. She grabbed her suitcase from beside the doormat. A glance at her shoes showed soot. She cringed. "I've already said my goodbyes. Let's be off then." Outside she used a gloved hand to rub the tops of her shoes and stamped her feet to rid the soles of cinders.

As he was helping her into the car, Patrick whispered in her ear. "Kate is the face and eyes of you. She is your child, isn't she? Mine too, I assume." He paused, perhaps waiting for an answer, an answer that Clara did not want to give. She hesitated.

"Don't worry," he continued. "Your secret is safe with me. And so is your Kate, our Kate." He closed the door and walked around to the driver's side of the car. "I'm here for you," he said when he was perched behind the wheel.

Clara sat devotedly, safe and sound, comfortable with his supportive words, knowing that the truth would shatter his belief about Kate, and maybe even terminate his interest in Clara. Still, in the face of that, Clara managed to utter the words she was avoiding. "Kate is my child, Patrick, but she is not yours," she said. He looked at her, disbelief in his eyes.

"It's true," she whispered.

His brows lifted and a question came. "Whose then?"

In an overlong moment of nothingness, Clara pondered. *Should I tell him?* She shifted uneasily, weariness encroaching like a fog. *Perhaps he will just let the question dangle.* She willed him to start the car. He did not.

"Whose, then?" he asked again, determination in his clipped tone. "Whose, Clara?" He reached across, grabbed her shoulder, shook her. "Who is Kate's father?"

"Alphonse." The word dropped like the clop of an axe. Long-buried shame rose to the surface, burning into her face. As Patrick's slackened hand fell from her shoulder, she slouched into her seat, willing herself to fade into oblivion. *What the hell have I gone and done?*

"Alphonse? Your own father?" he said, a surprised whisper.

Drained, Clara nodded. Out of the corner of her eye, she watched as Patrick bit his lip and clutched the steering wheel. She stiffened, bracing for more questions. But there were none; there was only silence laced with an uncertainty that put the fear of God into the heart of her. *What if he tells her?* "You can't tell Kate. You can't tell anyone," she said, her voice shaking.

No words from Patrick.

Clara's whole body started to quiver. "You won't tell her, will you?" She wrapped her arms around herself. "I'm begging you, Patrick. Please."

Eventually, Patrick turned to her and smiled, a controlled smile. He let out a long sigh. "You don't have to worry, Clara. I'm here for you, just for you," he said. "Always."

He started the car.

CHAPTER 15

DURING THE LONG SILENT, RIDE home, a shaken Clara belittled herself for letting the secret slip. No going back. She would have to resign herself to it. She trusted Patrick, didn't she?

The next day, as she sat in her Freshwater kitchen, teacup in hand, her whole self in shock, she was barely able to lift a finger. That was the state of her on both the Monday and Tuesday after the tragic fire, after the dismal drive, the best she could do. On Wednesday morning, when Kathleen left a copy of *The Evening Telegram* beside her own teacup, Clara, heart hammering, reached a feeble hand for the newspaper, but Kathleen snatched it, rolled it, and stuffed it into the stove. "You don't need to be seein' none of that, Clara. You need to move as far away from that as possible."

Clara remained silent.

"Ya got to count your blessings, Clara. Kate wasn't hurt. Izzie wasn't hurt."

"Izzie's eyebrows were singed off," Clara offered in a frail voice, distant even to her own ear.

"They'll grow back," Kathleen said without hesitation. "As for you, you need to go back to the concerns of daily living. What about that job on the base you were on about?"

Clara said nothing. *Always right about everything, my mother.* Clara had made no bones about wanting work, needing work, and getting work if there was work to be had. She heaved a sigh, pushed herself out of her chair, and moved forward, one beleaguered step at a time.

Days later, Clara lined up for hours for a job interview. The men in the line glared and taunted. "What are ya doing here?" one of them cried. "We needs these jobs to feed our families."

An incensed Clara sprang back to her determined self, strode up to him, and launched a tirade. "My husband is away at war. In the merchant marine. I lost my home. No money coming in. I have mouths to feed, too." She stood her ground waiting for the next words to fall from his face, but he dropped his head and dug a hole in the ground with the toe of his boot. Clara reclaimed her place in line.

At her interview, Clara assured the officer that she could type and file. Hired. She acquired a job as a filing clerk in the Public Works Department and gradually became used to the day-to-day, punching-a-clock routine. As was protocol on the base, Clara carried a pass displaying her photograph, fingerprints, and signature—nobody got onto the base without identification. Clara worked quietly and, although privy to snippets of conversation, all related to war, she stayed quiet outside of work, repeating nothing. The only thing she puzzled aloud about was the time zone on the base which was set a half-hour ahead of the rest of the island. Hers was not to query though, so she just set her watch to base time and lived by it all hours.

The workaday world of typing and filing was a source of gratitude for Clara. The fire at the Knights of Columbus had emptied her of lust for travel, for excitement. She scoffed at the idea of heading out to sea, itself a war zone, and dismissed thoughts of shopping in the city. Yes, she missed Kate, loved Kate, but needed to focus on the here and now, on finishing her Freshwater house in which she found purpose, security, even solace.

Among frequent visitors to Freshwater were Kate's friend Peter and Clara's lover Patrick (the latter only when Kathleen wasn't around). Both men were helpful with the build, both could handle a hammer, a saw, or a paint brush.

With their coupling covert, Clara and Patrick planned trysts carefully. When Clara experienced an occasional thought about her husband, the lack of communication from Robert, she met it with a shrug. Why should she be concerned? She could support herself. Money in the bank. She could satisfy herself. Patrick in the wings.

By mid-February, Clara had shoved the shock of the December fire in St. John's into the past, letting the memory cool, fizzle, darken. She had moved on.

The last thing she expected when she glanced through the window of her office at the end of an Argentia workday was the sight of a blaze at the Bachelor Officer Quarters. In an instant, the memory of the Knights of Columbus fire roared from its hiding place. Her brow broke out in sweat, her breath came in gasps, and her ears rang with screams of sirens and victims. Again, the smell of wood smoke and sizzling meat and lingering creosote on Patrick's wool coat. Overcome now, she gripped the window ledge, locked her eyes on the flames. When a skulking shadow appeared in the foreground, the fiery background gave it shape, the shape of a man who glanced over his shoulder as he fled the scene. Clara's mouth dropped open. *Patrick.* The harder she tried to stifle the recognition, the harder it sprang back. She'd know that form anywhere. She had folded her own body into that very form many times. *What is Patrick doing here?*

Clara was frozen to the spot, head spinning. When a panicked yell to evacuate reached her ears, her body jumped, an automatic response to training drills. Before she knew it, she was outside, a safe distance from danger, cringing as whisky bottles popped and ammo cracked above the roar of flames. Her thoughts were still on Patrick, on the suspicion that was creeping in around her lover. *Three fires. Patrick at all three. First in Freshwater, when he'd come to fetch her, smelling of smoke with soot on his face. Then in the car in St. John's–smoke and creosote. And now this?*

In short order, young Peter approached and offered her a ride home in his 1934 Nash, young Peter who talked all the while behind the wheel, on and on about how terrible it was for the young men in the BOQ. Clara didn't utter a syllable.

Once home, Clara sat on her bed in her room, staring into the full flame of the kerosene lamp on the night table. Terrible, Peter had said. Terrible was an understatement. Could Patrick be responsible for the terrible? Could she ask him about it? Perhaps. Would she ask tonight? She perked an ear toward the door.

"Mom won't be home," she had told him when she'd seen him the day before. "She's on an overnight vigil for an ailing senior." No mention that the prospect of having the house to herself had Clara practically sweeping her mother through the door. If Kathleen had suspected anything, she didn't say, or perhaps Clara chose not to see. All she wanted to see was Patrick. She had told him that there was no need to knock. "Just open the door and walk right in."

When the front door finally whined open and distinctly clacked shut, her heartbeat doubled its pace. Should she talk to him? A shuffling sound of his removing his boots, individual thumps as those boots hit the floor. Footsteps thudded. A floorboard creaked. She winced. A source of bother, that creak. One would think a new house would be free of squeaks and groans but perhaps with the necessary quickness of the build, the carpenters had made mistakes and chosen to leave well enough alone.

The door to Clara's bedroom stood ajar and the shape of his shadow filled the space, confirming all her suspicions about the shape she had seen earlier. She shivered. Patrick strode across the room, no resistance from floorboards here, his arrival announced fully not by word from him but by whine from bedsprings as he plopped beside her on the bed, his left thigh touching her right. Yes, she had expected him. Yes, she wanted him. A planned meeting, this one, all about lust, nothing about conversation, and yet?

Should she confront him now, now when she was searing with new memories of fire and sirens and screams and explosions of bottles and ammo? "Patrick, were you there, at the fire?" Her voice was hoarse, a whisper, but safe enough, she reasoned. A simple question. No hint of accusation in it.

His immediate response was a shudder that rumbled from his thigh into and through her body. Lengthy seconds passed as he slid a stiffened hand from her thigh to her neck and wrapped his fingers around her throat. The thud of her heart grew louder, faster. *What is he doing?* His fingers slackened from taut to tender and he gently turned her head toward him. Lightheaded with relief, she raised her chin, or did he raise it for her? Didn't matter. When their eyes met, his caught in the light of the flame from the lamp and glowed brilliant blue. She fixed her gaze on his and detected an image rippling across those blue eyes. Clara tilted her head. There he was, her blue-eyed baby brother Jimmy, his little face smiling at her. A sense of loss flickered in Clara. She blinked. The focus was lost, the picture gone.

"Everyone was there," he said.

Oh. An answer to the question she'd all but forgotten she'd asked. "Yes, I suppose everyone was." She waited.

"You shouldn't trouble yourself, Clara."

Did she detect a ring of command in his voice? "Whatever do you mean?" A cautious step.

"You've had your share of worries," he said, his voice slow, low, calm. "You are a beautiful woman, the face and eyes of your mother. You were a beautiful child, left in the care of a father who had lost his way. In the end you lost your own child, your beautiful Kate, who is the face and eyes of you. You've had more than your share of worries."

Unbidden tears sprang from Clara. *More than my share.* Alongside the pain of that certainty, alongside the burning of her eyes and aching of her heart, floated a morsel of comfort. She longed for more assurance. "You won't tell Kate, will you? About Alphonse, I mean?"

Patrick shook his head. "I want you to know that I am here for you," he continued. "And I am here for Kate. Here to guard you against men like your father, Alphonse. Petty acts of war hold no interest for me so there's no need to trouble yourself about my comings and goings, Clara. I am where I am to be where you are. War will leave. I will not. I am here for you, Clara. Forever."

Clara let doubt dissipate slowly, like mist. A wisp of something lingered, a feeling of being trapped. It niggled for a few seconds. Would she contemplate it?

In the end, she leaned into Patrick, folded into Patrick, and dismissed the feeling.

CHAPTER 16

Days later, Kathleen came through the back door, grocery bag in one hand, a letter in the other. "It's from Robert," was all she said as she handed the envelope to Clara.

Clara's eyes widened. She toyed with the letter, a fat one, many pages.

"Knowin' is better than wonderin'." With those words, Kathleen busied herself in the pantry putting away tinned goods. Clara sat at the kitchen table and set the letter down on the oilcloth. She stared at it. She picked it up. She put it down. Then repeated the action. Impatience kicked in. She ripped off the end of the envelope, pulled out the letter, and unfolded it. Her fingers trembled.

Dear Clara,

I have been trying, for a long time, to convince myself that this letter is unnecessary, that all could be revealed when I saw you. But that would be unfair, to say the least. I need to let you know that, yes, I will return, and no, I will not stay.

I failed you. I lied to you. Both in what I said, and in what I did not say. I was already married when I met you, Clara. My wife, Elizabeth–or Elsheva to use her Jewish name–was never accepted by my family. Shameful that I stood silent while my relatives berated her heritage, more so that I did not follow her when she took our three children and left. Instead, I escaped to the sea, met you, and through some skewed hope of redeeming myself, married you. A selfish idea, unfit for a sound mind.

Clara's eyes brimmed, the lines in the letter swirling and curling into meaningless clouds. She dropped the letter. She maneuvered her way to the dishtowel rack and stood there, hovering helplessly between the rack and the stove. Still at first, then shaking, low vibrations making their way through her body. The urge to cry accompanied them. Did she even have the right to cry over this? Herself a full-fledged adulteress. When Clara let out a whimper, Kathleen turned from the sink. Clara grabbed onto the towel rack and locked her fingers around it to hold herself upright.

"Clara," said Kathleen, her face awash with concern. "What is he after telling you, child?"

Clara shook her head. She pointed a shaky finger at the letter. She offered not a word when Kathleen picked up the letter. Clara remained rigid, fingers stiffening around the metal rack. Kathleen rushed to her, pried Clara's fingers off the rack, and led her to her chair. "Shall I read it to you?" asked Kathleen.

Clara heard the question. She could not formulate a response. Kathleen retrieved the letter and read it aloud. She began at the beginning, speaking in a monotone. Clara didn't look up until Kathleen got to the part where Clara had stopped reading.

> *When I discovered that my Jewish wife and children were in Germany, I set out to help them. They are safe.*
>
> *You and your mother need to know that Kevin helped me. Without him, I would not have succeeded. It breaks my heart to tell you that Kevin gave his life for my family. His chance at redemption, he told me. He couldn't save his own family, so he wanted to help mine.*
>
> *I have mementos from Kevin, messages from Kevin and, although in the long run I belong here, I will eventually, likely at war's end, return to Newfoundland to deliver them.*
>
> *Perhaps by that time, you will find it in your heart to forgive me.*
>
> *Robert*
>
> *P.S. One last lie I must dispel: you will by now have guessed the schooner is named after my wife, not my mother, as I told you before. Please do whatever you wish with the* Elizabeth J.

When Kathleen was done, she folded the letter, returned it to its envelope, and stood. "It's time to make dinner," she said.

What the hell? Shocked, Clara shook her head. Perhaps Kathleen didn't understand what she had just read aloud. Perhaps Clara herself had misheard it. "He said Kevin is dead, Mom!"

Kathleen paused. She took a deep breath. She nodded. "I expected as much. He would have died here if he stayed. Told you as much when he left."

There was no more talk from Kathleen, just the rattle of pots and pans and the steady slosh of water as she poured a pot of navy beans into a colander. Softened by their overnight soak, the beans were ready for the next step, the stove. There was no sign of softening in Kathleen. A jagged thought entered Clara's head. "We have to tell Kate," she said.

"No," said Kathleen, "we do not. The child does not need more tragedy in her life. The news will keep."

Clara opened her mouth and closed it again. How much had time and tragedy had hardened Kathleen that she could just slide past the death of her son like that? Clara herself was overcome, first with the shock of the letter, and then with the loss of Kevin. The latter took priority, and she recalled her last encounter with him. He was angry, rightfully so, as he had just discovered that his beloved Mavis was not Kate's mother, that Clara was. Such a dark secret, such raw hurt on his face, and now, no chance to mend things. Crushed, Clara folded her arms on the table and dropped her head. *Whatever is the point of everything? Is there any purpose to living and dying at all?*

Late that night, Clara heard sobs coming from her mother's bedroom. Knowing that her mother wanted, needed to be alone, Clara covered her ears with a pillow as she waited for the sounds of anguish to stop. It was almost dawn before silence came. Clara drifted.

Betrayed by Robert, bereft over Kevin, Clara trudged through the house in a stupor, steering clear of Kathleen whose daily routine of washing and cooking and cleaning continued without as much as a hiccup. Annoyed by that, but not deterred, Clara allowed herself one full day of lethargy. Before dusk on the second day, Clara no longer owned the schooner. She had scoffed at the postscript in Robert's letter telling her to do what she wanted with it. *As if I need his permission.* But undeniably, his betrayal clinched her decision, that and the glare of the name *Elizabeth J* on the hull of the boat. *His wife's name.* Not an ounce of sentimentality left in her about the schooner now. Let the military shoot the hell out of it. A fitting end to it.

In the days that followed, Clara found that she didn't miss the schooner at all. Privately owned boats couldn't sail near the naval station for security reasons and wouldn't sail the waters of the coastline for safety reasons. With her crew gone to war, with U-boats skulking the shore, the schooner was a deadweight. Useless. Even before the deciding letter from Robert. The days she had spent aboard with Robert were gone. Now? Robert be damned. Clara turned her focus to Kate.

Should she tell Kate about Kevin? Kathleen said no to that idea. Was Kathleen right? Usually. Was she right this time when she said that the news would keep? Clara sighed in affirmation.

What about Patrick? All this time, keeping him in the shadows. Could she bring him into the light now? Should she? When Kathleen exited the house, when her mystery man showed up, Clara hemmed and hawed. He sat on the daybed in the kitchen, waiting, arms folded.

"I'm not married, never was," she announced and then hurried to sit beside him.

"Oh?" he said, a slight tilt of the head, a raise of the eyebrows.

She blurted an explanation, a mutter of words, the gist of which was "bigamist."

"Robert? A bigamist?" A smile spread across his face. "But this is great news," he said, taking her hand.

"However could you think that?"

"Because now it's you and me, out in the open."

"But how the hell would I explain it? How can I tell anyone that I was never married at all? That my so-called husband is a bigamist?"

"I'm here for you, Clara," Patrick uttered.

Clara trembled, no comfort for her at all in Patrick's words.

"I'm sorry, Patrick," she said. "There would be nothing but shame in flaunting our relationship. And I can't bring any more shame into this family."

"So we maintain our secrecy then?"

Clara shook her head slowly. "I don't think I can do this at all anymore, Patrick."

His smirk surprised her. "But I'm here for *you.* I told you that many times."

Clara was silent.

"What I'm telling you, Clara, is that you don't have much choice." His voice carried an air of triumph. "Either we continue, or I announce Kate's parentage to all and sundry."

Clara jerked her head up, stared into the vicious glint in his eyes. "You wouldn't," she said.

He stood and angled for the door. Halfway there, he stopped, turned. "I would. I'm here for *you,* Clara. Whatever it takes." He strode toward her, placed a hand on her back, and bent to kiss her cheek. When she shrank from the gesture, he jolted upright. "Give it some thought, Clara." He huffed his way to the door, hesitated again, cast a backward glance at Clara who was too shocked by the threat to offer a word.

KATE

CHAPTER 17

On Pancake Tuesday, Kate was in the kitchen, at the table helping young Teresa clean an assortment of objects: pennies, dimes, medals, pencils, string, and nails. These objects would be hidden inside pancakes that Dulcie and Rosemary were frying in two huge cast iron pans.

"Where on earth did the idea of Pancake Tuesday come from?" Kate asked.

"Feast before famine," said Rosemary as she blobbed butter into a sizzling pan. When a column of steam rose to the ceiling, she stepped aside long enough to prop open the lone kitchen window above the sink and then took up her station at the stove once again.

"Feast? Famine? What does that mean?" Teresa asked.

Dulcie turned to her, one arm wrapped around her old yellow mixing bowl, the other clutching a wooden spoon. "The idea," said Dulcie as she vigorously stirred batter, "was to use up foods like eggs and butter and flour before the sacrifices of forty days of Lent."

"But what about all this stuff?" asked Teresa, spreading her hands wide to include the myriad of items on the table.

"Your turn, Rosemary," said Dulcie. "I'll handle the stove for a minute."

At the table now, Rosemary pointed at each item in turn. "If you get a penny in a pancake, you'll be poor, a dime you'll be rich. A medal means nun or priest, a pencil is for teacher, a string for fisherman, and a nail for carpenter."

"Oh. Like fortune telling, then?" said Teresa.

"You're a smart cookie," said Kate.

"Not cookies. Pancakes!" Teresa laughed.

Rosemary echoed the laugh then tilted her head. "Where's the thimble?"

"A thimble is for tailor, right, Mom?" said Teresa.

"Yes, or seamstress," said Rosemary. "Same thing. Teresa, run to the Singer, open the top drawer on the right, and get the thimble." While Teresa was gone, Rosemary suddenly pulled her wedding ring from her finger and placed it on the table.

Kate shot her an inquisitive glance.

Rosemary caught the look and shrugged. "My idiot husband had the nerve to ask for that thing back. I told him I'd lost it down the outhouse. He'll not likely hunt for it there." She grinned. Kate nodded. The ring stayed put.

At the pancake feast, Kate pricked her top pancake with the tines of her fork until its surface was dotted with tiny holes. Nothing hidden in it. But, in the bottom pancake, clearly visible, no stabbing necessary, was Rosemary's wedding ring. Kate picked it up, cleaned it up, and, despite Rosemary's earlier joke about the ring, attempted to pass it back to its owner.

"You keep it," said Rosemary with a wave of her hand.

Kate winced. Barely a visible reaction, she thought, but Rosemary noticed and acquiesced, taking the ring back, and placing it on her finger. It didn't stay there long. Rosemary stared at that gold band, shuddered, then pulled it off and pocketed it in her apron.

The next day, Ash Wednesday, Kate attended church services at the Cathedral where the priest marked people's forehead with ash to remind them of their insignificance. *Memento hominis pulvis es, et in pulverem reverteris.* Catholic school had drilled the translation into Kate: "Remember man thou art but dust and unto dust thou shalt return." Resentment squirmed through Kate as she went through this annual ritual. It seemed that the aim of all the so-called higher-ups was to keep the Kates of the world entrenched in insignificance: the Cathedral dominated the skyline of the city of St. John's; the citizens of St. John's looked down upon citizens from the bay; the merchants from the bay practically spat on the fishermen. Tiered systems everywhere, and women, apparently the least significant of all, were clamped underfoot. Kate sighed her way through the service and then sighed her way home, all the while pondering the idea of making an information-gathering trip to Freshwater. In the last few months, in conversations with Izzie, she had come to terms with facing Clara, with unravelling truth. Yes, Clara had given her up, but wasn't Clara a victim here? No longer satisfied with mulling over this, Kate needed to know.

In the front of the boarding house, Kate met up with Teresa and a group of her friends. "Hi, Kate," Teresa grinned impishly. "You're number eleven."

"Eleven what?" said Kate, grateful for any distraction.

Teresa's friends scampered like timid mice. Teresa looked at them, then back at Kate. "Me and my friends are counting Catholics," she said. "Ye all have soot on your foreheads."

"Counting Catholics? Why in heaven's name are ye doing that?"

"Just for fun," she replied and ran off to join the others.

Amusement flooded Kate like sunshine, and she grinned her way toward the kitchen to start her cleaning rounds. A cross breeze met her as she entered, courtesy of Izzie who was pushing through the back door. A pleasant surprise, seeing Izzie who, since the Knights of Columbus Hostel fire, spent most of her time in her room.

"I'm all in." Izzie put her mop and pail in a corner. "Just cleaned the cellar steps. Dulcie likes everything spic and span, and I like to help occasionally." She let out a sigh and pulled out two chairs. As she plopped into one, she pointed to the other. "Have a seat, Katie girl. You doing okay?"

Katie girl. Lovely phrase. Kate liked Izzie. "I just ran into Teresa on the stoop."

"And?"

"She and her friends are making a game of counting Catholics today." Kate pointed at the sooty cross on her forehead.

Izzie laughed out loud. "Thanks," she said, still giggling.

"For what?"

"For laughter."

Kate shrugged. "Teresa made me smile. I'm just passing it along."

"Well, I hardly laugh at all these days, too busy trying to keep a low profile. Can't handle the pitying looks I've been getting since the fire."

"I think the people here mean well, Izzie."

Izzie stiffened. "I'm sure they do." She tapped her fingers on the table. "What about you? Are you going to Freshwater soon?"

"Yes," Kate replied, but did not dwell. "Izzie," she said gently, "I remember that for years after the tidal wave, people stared, whispered, and asked me about the tragedy."

Izzie stilled her fingers. "Then you understand. People keep asking me about the fire. All their questions only serve to keep my nerves on edge."

A hunger to help gnawed at Kate. "I could field questions for you, Izzie," she said tentatively.

A single tear slipped from the corner of Izzie's eye. "And just how could you do that?" she asked, her voice strong at first, then trailing to a whisper.

"I could mention to Dulcie that any questions about you should come through me, better yet through Dulcie or me. We could allay concerns and stay the gossip, giving you the freedom to get on with things."

Izzie wiped her eyes with the edge of her apron. "That might allow me to get myself sorted," she said and sighed, a deep sigh, a clear signal of relief.

"You're not alone," said Kate. "Whatever you need, I'll help."

"Thank you, Kate." Her eyes welled up again.

Kate reached to Izzie, touched her hand, and met her glance. "I'll go find Dulcie."

Before Kate could move, Izzie gripped her hand. "Three men Kate. Can you believe that? Three strikes. I think the universe is sending me a message. Not hard to decode it either."

What is this? Kate felt her face flush. Surely there must be something she could say here, something light to diffuse whatever this was. Kate searched for humour but words failed her. She wrenched her hand from

Izzie's grasp. Awkwardness propelled her to her feet. "I'm off. Gotta find Dulcie, tell her about her idea."

"Thanks again, Kate," Izzie said, a mild disappointment in her tone. She smiled, eyes shining.

Confusion clung to Kate, accompanying her to and through the door. "You're welcome," she called as she ran toward the stairs.

CLARA

CHAPTER 18

CLARA GLANCED AT THE CALENDAR and flipped its page. It was July already, the first Sunday in July. The morning sun beckoned, and she stepped outside into the wind which teased dust into swirls and made a mop out of her carefully placed pin curls. She caught herself smiling, unsure if her contentment came because of the wind or despite it. She didn't question the feeling, just strolled in the lull beneath cheerful sun, alongside glistening sea. An abrupt thought—*the calm before the storm*—had her glancing upward. No evidence of a front moving in.

Back at the house, as the sun climbed, Clara put a pot roast in the oven and cleaned while it cooked. A sharp knock at the door, the red door built by Robert and Kevin for the old house in Argentia, the same door smuggled by Clara and Kathleen into their new house in Freshwater, had Clara stopping in her tracks. *Who is here?* A come-from-away, a stranger, no doubt. *Locals don't knock.* With dust rag dangling from apron pocket, she pulled open the door. Standing there, was Kate. Clara hoped against hope that her own eyes were not playing tricks. She blinked. At second glance, still Kate. The very idea that Kate would knock meant trouble. Clara pushed through her disquiet to reach for a hug. Kate shrank back. A rejected Clara dropped her arms and braced herself for a verbal onslaught. It didn't come.

In a haze, Clara noticed Peter who stepped up behind Kate, said his hellos, and announced that he was dropping Kate off on his way to Argentia.

Thinking that Peter might serve as a buffer between herself and Kate, Clara invited him in. He declined. "I'm meeting with one of the b'ys." To Kate he said, "I'll pick you up on my way back to St. John's tomorrow." He waved and left.

"You're only here until tomorrow?" Clara said. It was then that she noticed Kate had only a large purse, no suitcase.

Kate nodded.

"Well, come on in." Clara was on eggshells, knowing that Kate's presence had purpose, certain she herself was at the core of that purpose. When would Kate light into her?

Not now. Not when Kathleen entered and the hugs and smiles between grandmother and granddaughter filled the room. It was Kathleen who chatted with Kate, who wrapped her arm around Kate's waist as the two walked down the hall, leaving Clara standing alone, forlorn.

There was nothing Clara could do but wait. She puttered with the plant—Joseph's Coat—on the windowsill, snipping a couple of withered red and green leaves, adding water, wiping up water she slopped when she couldn't stop her hand from trembling. All the while, she kept watch on the hallway. Muffled voices from Kathleen's room, no other sound or sign of movement. The aroma of roast beef caught her off guard. She had almost forgotten about dinner. *Good. Something to do.* She checked the roast, readied the table, and steeped the tea. The opening click of the door in the hallway signalled Clara to carve the roast and plate the food. No words were spoken as Kathleen and Kate approached the table. When they were seated, Clara served the steaming plates and took her place. Kate locked her gaze on Clara. "I'm ready now," she said. "Ready to hear whatever secrets you've been holding." She paused there.

A nervous Clara managed a nod.

A stoic Kathleen shook her head. "First, we eat," she said, then folded her hands and started to pray. "Bless us, O Lord, and these Thy gifts which we are about to receive from Thy bounty through Christ, Our Lord, Amen."

"Amen," echoed Clara and Kate. Then began the dragging of time, an agony to Clara, this scraping of plates and the scrutiny from Kate. As soon as the plates were emptied, Clara cleared the table and clumped the dishes into the sink. In her haste to regain her seat, she stumbled, managed to grab the chair and then slide into it. She heaved a deep breath and waited.

Stirring her tea, Kate looked at Kathleen who offered a nod of approval. "Okay, then," said Kate. "Dulcie told me lots of stories about you, Nanny. About the loss of Jimmy, about the trouble it brought. About you, Aunt Clara, being left to your own devices and getting yourself in a predicament through no fault of your own. She wouldn't say much more about that predicament though. Just went on about some things you hang out in the wind and some things you don't. Not another word out of her. So, I figured that if I want to open the door to my past, I should ask the right person." Kate pulled an envelope from her pocket and slowly opened it. With steady hands, she pulled out a letter, unfolded it. She parted her lips to read.

Once again, Kathleen interrupted, this time reaching for Kate's hand, the one holding the letter, and gently pulled that hand down to rest on the table. A quizzical look came from Kate. Clara, who was poised to get to, to get through, this dreaded conversation, jumped from her chair. *What the hell?*

"Sit down, Clara," said Kathleen, her tone allowing for no argument. Clara obliged. Kathleen continued. "Before you say any more, Kate, you need to know we got a letter too, one about Kevin."

"What about him?" Kate was trembling now.

Clara clutched her hands to her heart. "Jesus, Mary, and Joseph, Mom! What are you doing?"

"Stop it, Clara." Kate held a hand up, palm toward Clara. She turned to her grandmother. "Out with it, Nanny. What about Dad?"

"Kevin's gone and there's nothing to be done about it. May the Good Lord rest his soul."

In the silence, Clara sat stunned, staring at her daughter. Kathleen might just as well have pounded Kate with a sledgehammer.

Kate wheezed out a question. "What are you talking about?"

"Clara will explain it," Kathleen said, and excused herself from the table.

"Mom!" Clara called to no avail. She stared after Kathleen. The gall of her mother to drop a bomb like that and then burden Clara with mopping the mess.

Kate grabbed Clara's arm. "Tell me what's going on!"

Clara looked into Kate's confused eyes. There was no running away for Clara, no following Kathleen out of the room. Kate, Clara's daughter, was waiting and this conversation was long overdue.

"Are you going to tell me or what?" Kate's tone indicating not a question, but a demand.

When Clara reached out a hand, an attempt to console, Kate withdrew completely, leaned back, and folded her arms.

"Good enough then," sighed Clara. "We got a letter. Kevin died in Europe."

"Letter from who?"

"The powers that be," lied Clara. "Official notification." Another black mark on her soul, this lie. But a necessary one.

A single sob came from Kate.

Again Clara reached out a hand.

Again Kate pulled away. "When did you get this letter?" she stammered.

"February." Clara didn't have it in her to tell another lie.

"February? And you waited until July to tell me?"

"Your grandmother would have none of it."

"Nanny? Never mind Nanny. What about you? He was your brother. My father, or so I thought." She was sobbing now. "But he was my uncle, wasn't he? My Uncle Kevin." Kate wiped her eyes with the heels of her hands. She looked up. "Because you are my mother."

Cornered, secrets staring her in the face, Clara's mind raced. Desire to escape engulfed her. The red door caught her eye. A fleeting thought, the idea of running through it. Was she so stupid as to think that the opening and closing of a door would stop the secrets, stunt the pain? Heat flushed her cheeks, and she whispered, "Yes." A single word, dropped, it just sat there, no relief with its release. The truth hit, echoed.

"Is Robert my father?" asked Kate.

This question landed with a jolt. Clara hadn't thought that far ahead.

"No, Robert is not your father."

"Then who?"

The name Alphonse entered Clara's mind. Yes, she had spoken that name when questioned by Patrick but this time she halted it at her lips. She could not, would not, plunge that stiletto into Kate's already gaping wound. As for Patrick, she would have to continue to see him lest he carry out his threat. She would just have to hope that he would never tell Kate the truth. So, for now, perhaps forever, Clara had no answer. The shaking of her head was ever so slight.

A chasm of silence fell between Clara and Kate. Slowly, like a battered warrior, Kate stood, retreated to the other side of the house, leaving the letter from Mavis on the table.

Kathleen returned to the kitchen. "That's it now," she said. "The knot of lies has been mauled. Only a matter of time, I suppose, before it decays altogether."

Clara shuddered. "All these years, I thought I'd be happy telling her that I was her mother. Far from it. But at least the deed is done. As for her father . . . I can never tell her that. It was hard enough for her to hear about the death of Kevin today. Knowing the name of her father would shroud her in shame; she'd never be able to raise her head again." Clara looked down the darkened hallway, her eyes stopping eyeing at the closed door of Kate's room. "She won't learn the rest of it from me."

"Perhaps the rest of it needn't come at all," said Kathleen, "but I'll have a word with her." She headed down the hall, determination in her step.

Clara's spirit rose. Kathleen, if anyone, could heal the rift between Clara and Kate. A few chosen words, a story or two could calm Kate. After a long couple of minutes, the pair returned to the kitchen and Kathleen guided Kate into a chair. Clara began to breathe easy. She sat silent, waiting, eyeing Kate who was eyeing Nanny. *Tell her, Mom. Tell her.*

"Her name was Kathleen, just like you," Nanny began, the familiar opening sending hope-filled shivers down Clara's spine. "Brown eyes, brown hair, just like you," Nanny said. "But no longer young like you. A mother of three, Kathleen. She loved her children, her Kevin, her Clara, her Jimmy. But love and loss often tread the same path."

Kate touched her fingers to her lips, a shushing motion. Nanny eyed her, questioning, waiting. Kate exhaled slowly and dropped both hands to her lap, lacing her fingers tight. Nanny continued. "One day, Kathleen came in from the clothesline to find baby Jimmy lying stone still on the daybed in the kitchen, his body cold, his skin blue." Nanny shook her head. "Kevin blamed Kathleen for the death."

Nanny sighed, a cavity in the storytelling which Kate filled with a question. "Why did Kevin blame Kathleen?"

Nanny put a hand up, palm out. "Patience, child. While Kathleen was washing the little body for burial, Kevin was watching. Shortly after that, at sixteen, he up and left home."

"So Kevin just assumed that Kathleen had killed Jimmy?"

Nanny nodded. "When he returned years later, he wouldn't trust Kathleen to care for his three-year-old Kate. So certain was he that Kathleen had killed Jimmy." Nanny reached for Kate's hand and held tight. "Things are not always what they seem, Kate. Assuming something doesn't make it true."

Clara was relieved that Kate allowed for the grip of Nanny's hand, but concerned as Kate's eyes searched Nanny's face. *Is she wondering where her nanny is going with this story?* Clara was wondering the same thing herself.

Kate pulled away from Nanny's grip, glanced at her watch, and pinched her lower lip with her teeth. "Why are you telling me this?" The question was abrupt, like the pop of a balloon. Clara winced, then resumed her stillness. No need for disruption from her. *Things are going well, as long as Kate is willing to listen.*

"Kevin was quick to assume that Kathleen was a killer based on what he saw." Nanny dropped her voice to a whisper. "Are you being quick in your assumptions about Clara?"

And there it was. Clara's heart pounded. Kate's glance at the door told Clara that Kate wasn't taking kindly to that answer. *Is she going to leave?* Clara didn't think so. Kate might walk out on Clara, but Nanny? Different thing entirely. Kate would not want to cut ties with Nanny. That thought alone kept Clara glued to her chair.

Kate traced a flower pattern on the oil cloth with her fingers. "Did Dad, I mean Kevin, learn the truth about Jimmy?"

"Yes," said Nanny, reaching for Kate's hand again, holding it tight. "And Kathleen was some glad as it gave her time with her granddaughter." A moment of quiet, then Nanny continued. "Things are not always what they seem, Kate."

"You said that already," said Kate, her voice strident. She pulled away, straightened her back, then suddenly doubled over as if rammed with pain. "Dear God. Kevin lied too." Interminable seconds passed before Kate unfolded slowly. When she was again eye to eye with Nanny, she dredged up another question. "Why did Kevin let me think he was my dad?"

"Truth of it is that he didn't know he wasn't."

A gasp fell out of Kate. "What do you mean, he didn't know?" Kate flung her hands up. "How could he not know?"

"Kevin was at sea with a sealing party, gone for months. Clara showed up in Burin and Mavis took her in. Upon Kevin's return, he expected one newborn but there were two. Mavis told him she had had twins."

Clara watched as Kate sat with this astounding round of information, this pre-meditated ruse to fool Kevin. Mavis who was her mother but not her mother. Kevin who was her father but not her father. Joey who was her twin but not her twin.

"Were Joey and I even born on the same day?" Kate asked.

"A day apart, I believe."

A stunned Kate stopped talking. Once again she fled to the bedroom.

Clara found her voice. "Aren't you going to go after her, Mom?"

Kathleen sighed. "No point," she said. "The state she's in, I could talk till the cows come home but she'd never let in a word of it. Not the time to tell her any more about it."

Clara lowered her head into her hands. She felt a light touch on her shoulder. "Let her stew for a bit," said Kathleen, as she reclaimed her seat at the table. "I'll talk to her tomorrow."

"She's leaving in the morning."

"Is that so? Well, then I guess at some point I'll have to go to St. John's. Long time since I visited Dulcie." She picked up the teacups from the table and headed for the sink. "It will be all right, Clara. The child needs to sit with things a while."

Clara nodded.

"Let's just focus on what we can do," added Kathleen. "Come on, me darlin'. Brooding won't make it better."

A numb Clara focused on picking up the sugar bowl and returning it to its shelf. What else could she do? Nothing, other than waking, sleeping, and walking through daily chores. She was certainly useless when it came to knowing what to do about Kate. More waiting, she guessed.

The next morning, Peter's motorcar rumbled up to the house, lingered, stuttering, and then roared.

Kate was gone.

KATHLEEN

CHAPTER 19

It is fretful, the sea.

The North Atlantic is agitated from battles in its depths, on its shores, in the skies. The sea is a receptacle for the spillage of war, all of which, like the blood of my son Kevin, seeps into soil and flows home to the sea which is the mother of creation. The ghost of me is soothed by the notion that the soul of my Kevin intermingles with the soul of the sea, the souls in the sea.

The North Atlantic is a worry of ships now, every wave spitting troops ashore, more than twelve thousand American military in Argentia in 1943. Most new arrivals are disoriented young men, likely assuming they are on their way to the warm climes of Argentina in South America, not the cold climate of Argentia on a small island in the North Atlantic where they are cut by wind and blinded by fog. Their isolation and melancholy are punctuated with barbs of rain and bombardments of snow. All of this with the rage of war hanging over them.

While these friendly invaders fret about their fate, Newfoundland parents fret about their daughters, wagging their fingers at girls besotted. Any port in a storm, the parents say, with a scathing look at some American in uniform. A waste of breath when young girls' heads are turned, and ears are closed.

I myself am a quivering suggestion of a presence, the air surrounding me rife with uncertain faces and undefined fate. This is the case, not only in Argentia, but also in St. John's where an underlying dread dances on every nerve. The Knights of Columbus fire in December is rumoured an act of arson, committed by spies. Spies are everywhere, apparently. Is it safe to set foot out of the house? Even a stroll to church on a Sunday morning is cause for trepidation. And in school? Every Thursday morning at ten o'clock there is air raid practice. The sirens scream, exciting at first to children but then gist and fright set in, causing little heads to twitch at the slightest sound. Fear and worry are reinforced in the dark when the windows are covered with boards or with blackout curtains conjured from canvas sails. The girls help with masking the windows but only the boys are allowed out with their fathers to check those windows. Are all the drapes closed? They knock on doors of houses where slivers of light shine through. Air raid drills occur; bundles of splits, doused in kerosene, are tossed into the streets and the occupants of houses run with buckets of water or a stirrup pump to extinguish them.

The events of night merge with the updates of day. Radio and newspapers report the state of war in the world, doling out truth measure by measure, all with caution attached. *Loose lips sink ships.* The ghostly me shivers when news of sinking ships and dying men elicit images of the living me and the dying Alphonse in a dory in the dark, him slumped over the oars, me hovering above him, dripping knife in hand, while the child Kate sleeps low in the stern. In spearing Alphonse to spare Kate, I crossed a line. Only onward now and that meant pushing the limp body overboard, rowing back to shore, putting Kate to bed, and then washing and washing and washing my hands. *Out damned spot.* But the stain on my soul is permanent.

Because of that blemish, my granddaughter Kate is here and for her presence I am grateful. Her whole life has been spent on a faltering track. Uncertainty enfolded her when she was given away as a newborn, given away again as a three-year-old when her family was swept away by a tidal wave. A worrying thing for a ghost now, watching her beloved granddaughter traipsing around the city core, not the accepted thing for a girl. It is only boys who can beat the path at all hours without accounting for themselves, boys who collect cigarette butts littering the streets and smoke them to their last. No worry planted in boys about falling ill to the ever-present threat of tuberculosis or about staying away from the doors of houses displaying ribbons to mark the presence of diphtheria. No effort to stop boys who spend a lifetime roaming chaotic streets and sliding icy hills. There's more danger in that now than there was before the war because of the wartime confusion of cars and convoys. Still boys bang about, collecting aluminum cans and scrap metal to aid the war effort while girls stay at home, knitting socks and making fruitcakes to send to soldiers. Defined roles, defied by Kate.

I watch as Kate spits on the ground and then instantly looks around to see if anyone takes notice. With an insubstantial sigh, I acquiesce to the fact that Kate will choose her own path, perhaps not too far from that of her mother. Clara spat when angry. Rebels, both of them. Not much a ghost can do in this time of worldwide worry.

Still, I stick close to Kate.

KATE

CHAPTER 20

WITH EARLY SNOW CRUNCHING ON cobblestones beneath her feet, Kate walked and walked. No destination, just tramping around downtown St. John's in her newfangled boots while she worried things through. She kicked her foot high, a brief glance at a black boot. They were fine boots, created by Peter and his father on one of their boot lasts. A family of all trades, apparently. Carpentry, fishing, shoemaking, boatbuilding, ice hauling, nothing the McGraw bunch wouldn't tackle. A gift from Peter out of the blue and at a time when the world was in a supply shortage, the boots were a clear symbol of Peter's burgeoning interest in her. Should she accept such gifts? Would he think her enamoured of him? She wasn't, not really. But she loved these boots. Kate squirmed in her wool coat, tightened her belt against the wind, and shelved concerns about selfishness. She would not entertain guilt over taking gifts.

There was only one thing that troubled her, drove her to distraction, and it had nothing to do with Peter. It had everything to do with the unidentified leaf on her family tree. *Who is my father?* The thought was a nagging constant, causing her to scrutinize every man she passed on the street, examining him for cut of hair and colour of eyes and fit of suit. Could it be this one? What about that one? An obsession, this, which she could brush aside for morsels of time but overall, she kept on it, or it on her, pushing her forward on a relentless journey into a puzzle with no defining edges. Where would Clara have met the man in question? When? And how old would Clara have been? She must have been around the same age that

Kate was now. *Dear God.* Kate's heart raced and her resolve cracked. She stopped in her tracks. Perhaps she should not have read Mavis's letters. Perhaps she should not have confronted Clara. But she had. And she did. And that was that. No changing it. She stumbled forward again, picking up her pace, letting her thoughts ramble.

Yes, Clara was her mother. An inkling of truth there, but it wasn't enough for Kate's starved soul. She craved wholeness. If she didn't belong in her known version of her past, where did she belong? To whom? And what about Clara, lying all those years? Both Clara and Nanny kept the news of Kevin's death from her. How dare they? Her Uncle Kevin, whom she thought all her life was her father. Exactly where had he died? How? When? Had there been a funeral? Could there be a funeral without a body? How could they have kept her in the dark about all of this?

Lowering her head, Kate tramped along, her anger festering. To hell with Clara. And Freshwater. And Argentia too. St. John's was the place for Kate to be, Dulcie welcoming, Peter visiting, Izzie offering friendship. It was Izzie who reassured Kate that flinging open the door to her past was the right thing. But was it? Kate hurtled forward, veered right to avoid a passerby, and smacked into a telephone pole. She rebounded and landed on her backside, handbag released, her face heated.

"Are you all right there, young lady?" A smooth voice, warm and deep, melted through her like chocolate.

Kate blinked up at an older man in a pea jacket and woollen cap. Her embarrassment dissipated as she encountered all kinds of kindness in his blue eyes, in the crinkles around his blue eyes. Curious. There was familiarity there, but she couldn't place it. Had she seen him before? There was something else too. Was the kindness a mask? Perhaps it was his tight, thin lips that told her he could be demanding. His left hand clutched a newspaper that he tucked under his arm, then extended a hand to help her. A quick tug, and in no time at all she was upright, then leaning in, close enough to inhale the scent of shaving cream. He loosened his hand. Kate took the cue and withdrew hers. Then, newspaper still under his arm, he bent to sweep a wandering lipstick, compact, and a handkerchief back into her handbag, which he passed it to her. He glanced around the ground. "I'm pretty sure that's everything," he said.

"Thank you, thank you, thank you," she said. How childish was she at all. Too many thankyous. "Just wasn't watching where I was off to." She fell silent then but did not avert her eyes from his face. She waited for his next words.

"I'm a friend of your aunt's, Clara Caulins, from Argentia," he said.

Disappointment bit Kate. That wasn't what she wanted to hear now at all. Was nothing in the world just her own? "I thought you looked familiar."

He nodded. "I'm Patrick," he said.

"So, Clara's a friend, is she?" Kate's thoughts whirred, paused, and hope flared like a struck match. Could this man be her father? She studied him, then blinked at the intensity behind his blue, very blue eyes. It wasn't until he removed his hat to reveal blond, very blond, curly hair streaked with silver that she snuffed her flash of hope. No chance he was her father. Still, there might be something to be learned about Clara from this older gentleman, this man who knew Clara.

"You took quite a tumble," he said. "Would you like to join me for a cup of tea?"

Kate smiled. A kindly man. Not her father but perhaps a father-figure. She missed Kevin, the loving man she had known as her father. She missed caring for him and his caring for her and her worrying about him every time he set foot out of the house. *Don't go near the ocean, Daddy. The ocean will sweep you away.* Kate wanted that companionship back. There was opportunity in this meeting today on Duckworth Street, not only for a possible father-figure but opportunity to get back at Clara who would be beside herself at the idea of Kate spending time with a much older man, a man who was a friend of Clara's. Would serve Clara right. All her lies. Perhaps Kate could learn the truth about her own paternity through this man. "I'm Kate," she said.

"Pleased to meet you, Kate," he said, looping an arm into hers and leading her to a tearoom.

Inside, all faded into the background as Kate eyed only Patrick. He placed his newspaper on the table. He did not reach for a cigarette. There was no scent of the drink or smoke on him at all when she had quite deliberately leaned into him. There was no danger here. Quite safe indeed. And, if Kate had her way, Clara would never find out about this meeting.

"I was just out for a stroll when I happened into you," he said. "I like to walk, in all kinds of weather." He paused then. "You look like your Aunt Clara."

"So I'm told." Kate dropped her voice to a whisper. "I'm thinking it would be better if you didn't tell Aunt Clara that you met me."

He raised his eyebrows, a question. Unasked. "As you wish, mademoiselle."

CHAPTER 21

A FEW DAYS LATER, AFTER school, Kate returned to the boarding house, dumped her book bag and shrugged off her coat, placing both at the foot of the stairs to be picked up on her way up. She set her boots upright on the mat beside the door. Chilled and ready for tea, Kate scurried toward the kitchen, stopping short when she detected voices from within. Dulcie, she expected that, but what was Nanny doing here? In sock-footed silence, Kate edged into the room.

Dulcie looked up. "And here she is now, Kathleen. My goodness, Kate, the wind has put apples in your cheeks."

"Nanny!" Surprised, then concerned, Kate felt her heart hammer. "Is something wrong?"

"Can't a grandmother come see her grandchild without there being trouble?" Nanny stood, arms wide and Kate fell in. She could have held back, after all Nanny had lied to her too. But Kate could forgive Nanny anything. She didn't know why. Just the way it was. The chill in Kate's bones vanished in the warmth of the hug, one that Kate felt reluctant to release but gradually did. The comfort remained. "I'm delighted, of course I am. Just that the sight of you made me wonder." She tilted her head. "You're not going to try to make me go back, are you? I haven't the slightest intention of going back."

"I don't expect any such thing."

"Good enough then. How did you get here?"

"Same way you do. The train."

"And I'm some glad for it," Dulcie said. Haven't had such a good chin wag in a long time. Enjoyed it more than I can say. But I'm sure ye've lots to talk about so I'll leave ye to it. I'm only going to ask that you move into the parlour so I can get on with supper."

"I'll help, Dulcie." Kate jumped to her feet.

"Never mind that now at all. Izzie will be home in a jiffy. She and Rosemary will help."

When Nanny raised her eyebrows in a curious look, Kate offered an explanation. "Both are boarders here."

Nanny nodded.

"Izzie has her own job but volunteers here sometimes," added Dulcie. "As for Rosemary, she has a daughter, Teresa, in third grade. She needed a job. I needed a helpmate. And that's that. And now, off with the two of you." Dulcie shooed Kathleen and Kate toward the door.

Once seated in the parlour, Kate tuned out the clatter from the kitchen and tuned in to Nanny. "More tea, Nanny?"

"Had enough time with the teacup, child," Nanny said, her tone fixed with purpose.

Kate wasted no time on small talk. "You worried about me, Nanny?"

"You did leave home in a bit of a huff in the summer."

"I'll grant you that. But you don't need to check up on me. I'm fine."

"I got eyes on me, child. But there are all kinds in this town, in this boarding house too, some hard tickets among the bunch." She leaned in. "You being careful?"

Kate nodded.

Nanny sat back again. "And how is school going?"

"Grand. The Sisters of Mercy are strict, but I have no problems. I like studying. Memorizing comes easily. And you? How are you? You're getting on in years, you know."

"I can count, young lady. Yes, I'm coming upon sixty. And strong as an ox."

The front door creaked: an arrival. Kate and Kathleen turned toward the sound. "Hello!" called a voice. *Izzie.* A thump of one boot to the floor, followed by another. Kate pictured Izzie placing the boots on the mat. "Hi, Kate," said Izzie as she entered the parlour and then stopped dead. "Didn't know you had a visitor."

"This is my nanny, Kathleen Kerrigan," Kate said.

"Nice to meet you, missus," said Izzie, shifting her gaze between Kate and Kathleen. "Sorry to interrupt. I'll go and let you have your visit." Without another word, Izzie scurried into the kitchen, closing the door behind her.

"What on earth is the matter with that one?" asked Kathleen.

"You mean the strange stares? I have no idea."

"I mean the looks you two were giving each other. Something going on between you and that young man?"

Laughter burst from Kate, and she gave Nanny's hand a reassuring pat before she proceeded with explanation. "That young man is a woman, Nanny. Her name is Izzie."

"Are you sure? She looks for all the world like that scrawny Joseph R. Smallwood."

Kate nodded. "Izzie poses as a man so she can earn more money." A touched amused, a tad curious, she awaited Nanny's reaction.

Nanny sniffed. "World is made by men, for men, with women at their whim. Women must get in their licks and get on with their lives however they can."

Pride surged through Kate and emerged as a smile. Neutral in nothing, her nanny.

After a glance at the kitchen door, Nanny looked back at Kate. "Actually, Clara told me about Izzie, about how you ran to help her during the fire. She must be a good friend."

Kate nodded, an effortless response which rang with truth, no words required. *Izzie is my very good friend.* The thought brought comfort and she hugged it for an instant before turning her attention back to Nanny.

A flicker of a smile appeared at the edges of Nanny's mouth. "I just assumed that Izzie, based on appearance, was a man. Makes me want to laugh at myself. I'm the one who lectured you on making assumptions about people when you were in Freshwater, and now I'm the one making the assumption."

Kate offered a weak smile. She dared not say a word. Heaven forbid the whole "things are not always what they seem" lecture make a second appearance. Just then, the tap of a cane announced Reggie's entry into the parlour. The two women looked at him. He gave them a glance and then proceeded to his wingback chair. In seconds, the radio blared. A relieved Kate brushed a relaxed hand through the air. "Reggie loves his radio," she said to Nanny.

Nanny leaned close, her lips inches from Kate's ear, her whispers clear despite radio blare. "Just remember that first appearances can deceive," said Nanny. "Few notice what is hidden in a corner, be that in a person's appearance, a person's mind, or a person's hiding place." She tilted her head toward the wingback chair. "Think on that when you judge Clara. Perhaps Clara is not hiding something *from* you, perhaps she is hiding something *for* you."

Kate was saved from a response by the ringing of the supper bell.

During the meal, Kate noted the deepening of concern on Nanny's face. Nanny glared at Reggie who, with the aid of his cane, took his place, ate quietly, and retreated to his wingback chair beside the radio for the news. Nanny appeared curious and watchful for the duration of the visit, three full days in which Nanny sat beside Kate and Izzie at meals, visited them when they were in a room by themselves, asked repeatedly about Izzie's life in Nova Scotia. Curious, this interest of Nanny's in Izzie. Was there rhyme or reason to it?

Kate was still puzzling over this after Nanny left.

CLARA

CHAPTER 22

Clara could do nothing about Kate who was away in St. John's of her own accord and who didn't even come home for Christmas. It was with relief that Clara saw December end. As for the new year? She sighed as she hung the 1944 calendar in the kitchen. Back to a workaday world for her.

Bundled against the January wind, Clara trudged through a foot of snow toward the base, her mind trundling through a myriad of worries. *Kate. Kate. Kate.* What would happen when Kate came back? *Will Kate come back?* At the rumble of a vehicle, Clara turned. A motorcar stopped; the window opened a crack.

"Mrs. Caulins, you want a ride?"

"Peter McGraw? What on earth?"A raw ocean gust clipped Clara's throat. Coughing, she plodded toward the passenger side of the car, yanked open the door, and clambered aboard. Instant relief from the cut of the wind. "So kind of you. Thank you. But what are you doing here? I thought you lived—" she broke into another coughing fit. "Excuse me, I thought you lived on the naval base." The wind blasted the door which struggled in response to Clara's tug. "Oh, for heaven's sake!" She planted both hands on the door handle and executed a sharp jerk. Slam. The door found home. Clara's relieved sigh aggravated her raw throat, the onset of another round of hacking.

"That's a bad cough you got there, missus. As for the base, not there anymore. I spent six months living on the *Richard Peck.* Six more in the barracks. Then the powers that be moved all local civilians off the base. I got me a room in Jerseyside now."

"All civilians, you say?" *Where is Patrick living?*

"Yes, missus. Pretty much." Peter put the car into gear and, alternating between clutch and gas, managed to get the car crawling. "Got to go easy on her at the start," he said. "Otherwise, we'll be spinning tires in snow, digging ourselves into a rut."

"So, you live in a boarding house?"

"Right. During the week anyway. On the weekend, I go home to visit my folks in Southeast, or I drive to St. John's."

St. John's? Is he visiting Kate? Clara bit her tongue. "How are you doing, Peter? You and your family getting on okay?"

"Well as can be expected. That is everyone except for my grandmother. Struggling with tuberculosis."

"That's a hard thing."

"Indeed it is," he said. 'One minute you're sledding with your friend in the Southeast, and the next you're leading a funeral carriage to the

church."

"I take it you did that?"

A brisk nod. "When I was young. It was a strange thing, marching down the Blockhouse Hill into Placentia in front of the funeral carriage of my friend. I shivered the whole time, wishing I had worn the woollen mitts that Mother had just knit for me. The brass cross I was carrying was taller than me and ice-cold. And I had to go so slowly. When a nudge from one of the carriage horses brought the warmth of his breath to the back of my neck, I slowed even more, hoping for more warmth. It worked. Until my father appeared beside me, lambasted me for fooling around."

"I bet you didn't slow down again."

"No, I didn't," said Peter. "TB was, is, scary for everyone. Strange that my family has been untouched until now."

"Why do you think that is?"

"All I knew was people got sick and were carted off to the san in St. John's and most of them never came back. When I was young, I thought the dole caused it," he laughed wryly. "According to the conversation I overheard between Father and Uncle John, it has something to do with the dole. 'Lazy arse sons of bitches sitting in their kitchens, living off the dole, that's what they are,' me father used to grumble. 'Can't be bothered to grow a vegetable for their children to eat and wonders why they're all dying in their beds.'"

"Well, your father may have had a point there, the one about gathering in the kitchen anyway. You and yours spent a lot of time working in fresh air. Apparently, consumption is transmitted in close quarters." She coughed again.

"You been in close quarters much lately? It's worrying, that cough." Peter cracked open a window.

Was all his talk about tuberculosis a reaction to her cough? Clara dug a handkerchief from her pocket and held it over her mouth. "Don't worry. I'm just getting over a cold," she said, words chosen to ease his concern and to dismiss her own. The cough had been hanging on for a while.

Peter shrugged as he stopped at the gate to the base where both flashed their identification to the guard in the booth. As they pulled into the Public Works area, Peter turned to Clara. "I can pick you up on a regular basis, missus. We're both going to the same place. No sense in you struggling through the snow."

"Thank you, Peter. Very kind of you." Clara assumed that this young man's kindness to her was all about impressing Kate. Well, for now, Clara could allow for that. No cause for worry there. In fact, it might lead Kate back to Clara as well.

She gave no further thought to the decision to accept Peter's offer of a regular ride to work, not until Saturday, when Kathleen was out of the house and Patrick McMurty was in it, repairing walls. There were several hands who could do repairs but the hands she wanted, for reasons other than repairs, were Patrick's.

Patrick wasn't long at her house on this day before questions poured out of him. "Who is this person I saw you with the other day? In a motorcar?"

"Oh, that would be Peter. A friend of Kate's. He offered to drive me to work. Very kind of him."

"Perhaps you shouldn't do that. Take rides from young men."

Is he jealous? Smugness filled her but she suppressed the urge to smile. "Peter is not a problem," she said. "He offers me rides and helps me out to get in good with Kate. I think he's in love with her."

"He visits her in St. John's?"

"Quite regularly, I think."

"Aren't you worried about her safety, a girl alone in the city with a young man pounding on her door?"

"Kate is safe. Dulcie sees to that."

"I'm sure she does." Patrick hammered the last nail into the wall stud. "Perhaps I should visit St. John's, check up on Kate."

"No need for that," Clara said.

Patrick shrugged. He twirled the hammer like a gunslinger and parked it in its holster on his tool belt. "That's done. You want me to spackle and paint?"

"I can manage that later." Clara tilted her head toward the bedroom. Patrick unbuckled his toolbelt. He locked eyes with hers. She offered a suggestive twinkle, then watched his eyes grow cold. "On second thought, I have to be off," he said as he buckled his belt and headed through the door, leaving Clara gaping in disbelief. She sat, rooted to her chair, attempting to make sense of Patrick's behaviour. The next thing she was aware of was the rattle of pots and pans in the kitchen. "Are you home, Clara?" Kathleen called.

Clara let out a sigh of relief. *Darn lucky Patrick left.* "I'm coming," Clara called and headed to the kitchen.

KATE

CHAPTER 23

On the cusp of summer in 1944, Kate was buoyed by the optimism in St. John's, a lightness that came in with offshore winds and with radio broadcasts bringing news about the success of D-Day. The beaches of Normandy had flooded with Allied troops who had overrun the Germans. How on earth, she pondered, had the Allies managed such an attack with nobody learning a thing about it? The participants were sworn to silence, now weren't they? Her thoughts turned to Clara who was sworn to silence about the one thing Kate wanted to know. *Who is my father?*

"What did you say, Peter?" Kate asked after she checked her cards. "Wait a minute." She planted an eight on the table and announced the suit. "Clubs," she said.

"You're not in the mood for Crazy Eights, are you?" said Peter. "I was telling you that your aunt Clara has quite a bad cough."

"You're right. Not in the mood for cards. Don't want to talk about Clara either." She discarded her hand and leaned back in her chair. Izzie walked in.

"What are you two playing? Can I join?"

"Nah. We're just giving up on it. Another time. But have a cup of tea with us before Peter leaves."

Peter looked at his watch. "Yep. Got to get on the road soon. Long ride home. And I have to pick up your Aunt Clara before work in the morning."

"*Aunt* Clara?" asked Izzie, raising her eyebrows at Kate who responded with a hard look.

Izzie retreated into silence.

"I'll get the tea," said Kate, heading off, leaving Izzie and Peter alone, then regretting that she had. What would they talk about? She hurried to put cups, plates, milk and sugar on a tray. While waiting for the kettle, she stood by the kitchen door, opening it a bit, her ear in the crack.

"Kate tells me you work in town," said Peter.

"I do. And you work on the Argentia base."

A muffled laugh came from Peter. "You don't waste words, do you?"

"I'm a friend to Kate and I'm nothing if not loyal."

"You'll have no objections to me, I'm sure."

"Perhaps not. But looks can be deceiving."

Kate jumped. Nanny had said repeatedly that things are not always what they seem. Now Izzie was saying the same. The kettle screamed and she jumped again. Tending to the tea, she called out. "Izzie, can ya put a few biscuits on a plate for me?"

There was the rumble of the front door opening and closing and another voice in the parlour before Izzie appeared in the kitchen.

"What was all that about?" said Kate. "Peter's a fine person."

Izzie laughed. "Eavesdropping, were you? Sorry. I'm sure you're right." She paused. "But if I were you, I'd get him out of here in short order. There's another man just come in and waiting to see you. Patrick somebody."

Sweet Lord Jesus! Kate's heart sped up and so did her feet. She was almost through the door when Izzie's singsong voice sounded behind her. "You forgot the tea tray."

"Damn it." Kate did an about face. "I'm not finished talking with you about the looks can be deceiving bit."

"Take it easy." Izzie plated the biscuits and added the plate to Kate's tray. Izzie held the door and made a generous sweeping motion with her hand. "M'lady," she said. Kate shot her a smirk and stepped through the door. Not ready to face the two men on the far side of the room, she stalled by taking time to greet the regular occupant of the wingback chair, Reggie. Strange that he was wearing an overcoat. A small, tan suitcase, its handle taped together, its body tied with twine, hugged the leg of his chair. "Going on a trip, Reggie?"

"Train," he said. "Visiting my sister for a week or two."

"Lovely. Have a good time." She took a deep breath and headed toward Peter and Patrick.

"Kate," said Peter, "this is Patrick McMurty, here to visit Dulcie. I met him on the base in Argentia."

"Nice to meet you, Kate,' said Patrick, a mischievous glint in his eye.

"Nice to meet you too," she said, puzzled but playing along. As she studied his eyes, she detected not mischief, but malice. A pang of guilt sliced through her. She had played at befriending him, this friend of Clara's, to spite Clara, perhaps to glean information about the identity of her father. But now the tables were turned, he was toying with her. A knot of discomfort arose and writhed in her gut. *Why is he here?*

"Happy to give you a ride back to Argentia, Patrick," said Peter. He pulled out his wallet, opened it, and returned it to his pocket.

"No need. I already have my train ticket, but perhaps you could give me a lift to the station?"

"Certainly," said Peter who then turned to Kate. "I was just telling Patrick that Dulcie is off to the shops today."

"Yes, Dulcie is shopping," said Kate, maintaining a calm surface despite rattled nerves. "Kind of you to stop by, Patrick. You can wait for Dulcie, if you choose. No telling what time she'll get back." She placed the tea tray on the table. "Tea for you?" she asked, not a hint of tremor in her voice. "I can get another cup."

"No need for tea," said Patrick. "I wouldn't want to keep Peter waiting."

"That's right," smiled Peter. "I better not have tea either. Time to get going."

Relief slid through Kate. She would be spared the awkwardness of further conversation. "If you must," she said. "Well then, I'll show you two out." She did exactly that, wishing Peter a safe journey, watching him get aboard the car. He rolled down the window. "I'll stop in next weekend if that's okay with you," he called out. She nodded and smiled and waved. As she was about to close the door, Reggie showed up at Peter's car window, suitcase in one hand, money in the other. *Strange.* She caught herself glancing at Reggie's wingback chair, empty now. Did he go through the rear door along the narrow fire path to the front of the house? Must have. She paused, eyes and ears on the scene as Reggie asked Peter for a ride. She drew back a bit, continuing to watch the activity surrounding the shiny blue Nash. A smiling Peter took the money, and a nodding Reggie approached the passenger side. Patrick got out and Reggie slid into the middle of the front seat. Then Patrick reclaimed his seat by the window. Kate parsed the situation as best she could: Reggie, like Patrick, must want a ride to the train station. Kate shrugged and closed the door. She rested her hand on the doorknob. Something was odd but what? Struggling to loosen the pebble of bother in her mind, she returned to the parlour where, for the second time, she glanced at Reggie's wingback chair. *What?*

Hurried footsteps interrupted Kate's concern which vanished irretrievably, like a dream upon awakening.

"Where is Reggie off to?" said Izzie. "He swept past me as I was standing at the sink. Nearly gave me a heart attack. Even left the back door ajar."

"Reggie said he was taking the train today to visit family," Kate replied. "I guess he got a ride with Peter to the station."

She turned away from the conversation and turned inward, all her thoughts now focused on the mystery surrounding Patrick's presence here today. Unprepared to discuss it with Izzie, or anybody for that matter, she meandered toward the stairs.

"Oh, that's fine. I'll clean up the teacups," called Izzie, a playful sarcasm in her voice.

Kate stopped at the foot of the staircase, hand on the newel post. "So sorry Izzie. I forgot." She started back toward the parlour.

"No," said Izzie. "I was just kidding. You need to sit with whatever is clouding your mind. I'll handle the cleanup."

"Thanks," replied Kate, as she plodded up the stairs.

CHAPTER 24

THE NEXT DAY, KATE WAS itching to talk to Izzie but not about Patrick. Not yet. Perhaps she could lean into it a bit by addressing the looks-can-be-deceiving comment Izzie had made yesterday. Having finished with the dishes, Kate stepped up to the sturdy drop-leaf table in Dulcie's kitchen and swept her hand across the oilcloth cover, checking for flour dust or biscuit crumbs. With no graze of grit and no sign of flour on her palm, she moved on: *time to get Izzie.* Kate opened the kitchen door a crack and called down the hall.

In short order, Izzie was there. "What's up?" She paused and searched Kate's face. "Something wrong?"

Kate waved away the question. "No, not at all," she said. "Have a seat." She plopped into one chair and pointed to the other.

Izzie obliged.

"I'm still baffled by your words about Peter, Izzie. 'Looks can be deceiving.' What was that all about?"

"Oh, is that all?" Izzie shrugged. "I'm cautious about boyfriends, yours, mine, all boyfriends. I know what women are supposed to do: get a boyfriend, get married by the ripe old age of nineteen, then have children." A long sigh slid out of her. "I've had a lot of losses. Boyfriends, I mean."

"I know about the sailor here in St. John's. But you mentioned two in Nova Scotia. You never did tell me the details. If you don't mind my asking, what happened?"

"One worked in an apple orchard. Died after a fall from a tree. Other one worked for the light and power company. He got electrocuted on the job."

"Surely be to God, you're not serious," said Kate.

"I know. I know. But it's true. And then . . ."

"The fire at the Knights of Columbus Hostel."

"Yes. Seems the universe is telling me I'm not meant to live by the rules. You know—the husband, children. A spinster's life for me, I guess."

"I'm sorry, Izzie." Kate's voice was a mere whisper.

Izzie sighed. "Shouldn't have brought it up. Truth is maybe I'm a bit jealous. You're trying to decide between two men who are hanging off your every word."

Sympathy swelled within Kate. "I *am* truly sorry for your losses," she said as she for reached for Izzie's hand. Izzie responded, her grip strong, her eyes piercing, her look yearning.

Enveloped by uneasiness, no way to explain it, Kate winced. To put herself at a safe remove from whatever her discomfort was, Kate pulled her hand away and picked up a thread in the conversation. "Two men, you say. In case you didn't notice, Patrick is old enough to be my grandfather. He's just a friend of my mother's, and she doesn't even know that I met him. Why he showed up here today, I have no idea. Now Peter is lovely, and I am seeing him, sort of, but—"

"Why not?" Izzie interrupted.

"Why not what?"

"Why doesn't your mother know that you met her friend Patrick?"

"Not worth the telling. Only met him the one time, had tea with him. Not at all comfortable with him showing up here unannounced."

"Why not?" Izzie asked again, but this time Kate waved away the question. Despite efforts at distraction by changing the subject to Peter and Patrick, Kate had not managed to quell the feeling that flared when Izzie gripped her hand, a feeling Kate couldn't even identify. "I'm just not, that's all." Kate stood slowly and took a step back. *What the hell?* What was Izzie jealous of? Kate, who had two men showing up? Or the two men who had all of Kate's attention while Izzie wanted all of Kate's attention and had none of it?

Izzie lowered her head and with her finger traced flower patterns on the oilcloth. "Don't worry," she said. "It's fine. Take your time."

Face burning, Kate fled the kitchen, anxiety nipping at her heels, propelling her forward. She could easily put space between herself and Izzie, but she couldn't outrun whatever this feeling was. As Kate locked the door of her room and leaned against it, fear sliced her gut and exploded into a full body tremor. *What is going on?* What was that flash of emotion she had just experienced with Izzie? She didn't know but she sure as hell knew what was pouring on top of fear. Guilt. But guilt for what? She understood having guilt about encouraging attention from Peter, but this? Not a clue. Had she done anything wrong? If so, she couldn't name it. Perhaps she just wouldn't dare name it. She couldn't even look in that direction.

Kate avoided Izzie. And Izzie gave her space.

Just days later, Kate and Dulcie were upstairs, doing the weekend cleaning. "Reggie said he'd be away for a week or two, but let's give his room a clean so it's nice and proper for his return," Dulcie said. "Seems odd to me, seeing that wingback chair empty." She opened the door with her pass key. The cupboard contained shirts and pants and empty wire hangers. Curiously, socks and boxers dangled from splayed dresser drawers.

Izzie called from the bottom of the stairs. "Kate! Kate! There's someone here to see you."

"Oh," said Kate. "That'll likely be Peter."

Dulcie waved her away. "Go on with ya then. Can't let a dust mop stand in the way of young love."

Heat jumped to Kate's face, and she turned before Dulcie could see the blush. Was this young love? Doubtful. Questions pummelled as she descended the stairs. Was she being fair to Peter? What would she say to him? Would she, should she say anything when she wasn't sure about anything? On the bottom step, she stopped, one hand on the newel post, and looked at the young man, a stranger, in the hallway. *Who are you?*

KATHLEEN

CHAPTER 25

It is unmasked, the sea.

The North Atlantic discloses truth in a sluggish poke or a threatening blast, fretting the shores of communities large and small with evidence of its complicity in war. Remnants of hulls and fuselage and bodies have bounced from crest to trough and are sliding ashore or sinking in surf. Once landed, flotsam and jetsam become salvage that is legal to collect and to use in one's own house or on one's own boat. Bits and pieces of salvaged furniture land in some of the new houses in Freshwater.

Secrets of war are exposed with the return of worn and weary ships that deposit survivors, many of them emotionless, speechless, and staring into nothingness. Those who can speak tell tales of mass murder, starvation, rape, tales that are hard to hear, harder to believe until newsreels and newspapers deliver images that explain the hollow eyes of the survivors and expel remaining gullibility in those at home. During the Great War, many young Newfoundland men went to Europe seeking glory and died there. Sadly, the lesson was not learned. There is no glory in war.

Still, despite hope offered by the success of the D-Day invasion, war wages on.

For many families, the lag between the departure and return of loved ones too is much to bear. Telegrams announce casualties, unwelcome news but news nonetheless, news that closes a door. Grief follows. Families trudge on. Others hear nothing and are stuck at a crossroads between life and death, no closures in sight. The military do their best to account for their own, the dead, the missing in action. The merchant marine holds no such promise.

In addition to the disappearances abroad, there are homegrown mysteries, vanishings of a different kind. *What happened to so and so?* Not until the *so and so* is one young Peter McGraw, do I pay heed.

As I revisit the day on which Peter was last seen, a swirl of dust hurls me through the open window of a navy-blue car and flings me to the top of a rear seat where I mingle with the specks of dirt that flew in with me. I recognize this car. It is a 1934 Nash, the pride of Peter McGraw. That familiarity is accompanied by a sense of uneasiness. Curiosity too plays a role. Why am I here? Am I to witness something I don't want to see? I've kept company with that feeling before, when I pretended that the body of my son Kevin was just one of a pile of logs deposited on the shoreline of a river in war-torn Europe. But Kevin is gone. I couldn't change his fate. And what about Peter's fate here? The air shivers with dread.

Peter is at the wheel. He is not alone in this car. There are two other men on the front seat, a bench seat, one man wearing a fedora, the other a sod cap. Conversation is minimal until after one of them is dropped off at the train station.

"So why are you going to Argentia?" Peter asks his lone passenger now.

"Visiting my sister. Have been eyeing this car of yours every time you come to town. Been itching for a ride."

"Oh," says Peter. I can sense his pride soar. So easily taken in, this young man, not realizing that the praise is not what it seems. The road flows on, unspooling ahead of them, bumps barely noticeable at first. Silence resumes until they are well outside the city. The next words are those of the passenger. "Do you carry a weapon when you are on the road?"

"Excuse me?" Peter's demeanour shifts. His nervousness prickles the air.

"There's a war on. You never know who you'll come across. It will be dark soon."

Peter tightens his grip on the wheel. There is the thump and rumble of gears shifting and Peter pushes the accelerator to the floor through puddles and potholes galore. The car rushes forward, meeting ruts full on, lurching, resisting. Does Peter not know of the hazard in such haste or is he so driven by fear that he doesn't care? Time stutters on. No further words spoken.

In a blink, the car is motionless, the doors open, no person inside. The vehicle is parked on gravel. No, not gravel but sand and seaweed, the air heavy with the scent of the sea. I'm still here, blended into a drop of condensation on the windshield. Drawn by the repetitive sound of pounding surf, I turn my attention to the landwash. There they are, both men walking toward the surf. Where are they going? The report of a gun. The air flinches. Pink mist rolls toward me like fog. And dusk falls into darkness. There are no images but that of a black cigar shape on a black sea, both of which glint in the moonlight.

KATE

CHAPTER 26

TIME HICCUPPED AS KATE STOOD on the bottom step of the stairs, staring at the young man in the hallway. It was not Peter, but he resembled Peter, the eyes, maybe the hair. He clutched his cap and cleared his throat.

"Are you Kate Kerrigan?" he asked.

She nodded.

"I'm Nate McGraw, Peter's brother," he continued, "and I'm wondering if you have seen him recently."

"I saw him a few days ago," Kate said, her voice mumbled, her thoughts fuzzy.

Dulcie brushed past Kate on the stairs. "Come in, Nate, come in," she said.

"Thank you," said Nate.

"We can sit in here." Dulcie waved the young man along and disappeared with him through the parlour door. Kate didn't move. *What is going on? Is Peter missing?*

Suddenly, Dulcie was back, tugging on Kate's arm. Kate took a tentative step from stair to floor but could not withdraw her hand from the newel post. It was Izzie who lifted that hand, Izzie who propped her up on that side. Linked, the three entered the parlour and sat on a chesterfield near Nate who occupied the wingback chair by the radio.

"Peter didn't visit home as expected. Then yesterday, his car was found abandoned on the beach at the foot of Blockhouse Hill in Placentia. Me mother is beside herself with the worry of it. I've been to his boarding house, but they haven't seen him." He dropped his gaze to his cap.

Kate listened with a vague sense of unreality. She offered no comment until jolted by a jab from Dulcie's elbow. "Peter was here for a short visit on Wednesday," Kate said. "I walked him to the door and watched his car pull away." She paused. "It was such a dry day that dust kicked up from his tires as he took off." *Why am I telling him about dust?*

"Was anyone with him?" Nate was staring intently at her now. Nate, who had eyes like Peter's.

"Reggie," she replied quickly. "One of the boarders here. I think he asked Peter for a ride to the train station." She paused. *Do I want to bring Patrick's name into this?*

At this point, Izzie leaned forward in her chair, as if to offer information. Kate turned to her, glared at her. Izzie leaned back. Kate took a deep breath and added, "There was another man. Patrick McMurty. I think Peter offered him a lift to the train station too." After that, Kate sat still, eyes and ears closed, no room in her for negative news or rampant speculation. *Peter is fine. Peter is fine.* When voices stopped altogether, when all stood in a clump to lead Nate to the front door, Kate broke away and charged up the stairs into her room and locked the door behind her.

It was the next morning that she dared come down the stairs. The story spilled from the radio and newspaper, and Kate could no longer stick with denial. After Peter's precious 1934 Nash, its doors spread like wings on a gannet, not a soul inside, had been discovered, police and volunteers had combed through brush and sand and sea for signs of life. In a tangle of seaweed, the remains of a young man had been found. The body was that of Peter McGraw.

Truth shook Kate and shock shattered her, her life spinning as members of the Newfoundland Constabulary and military police—why in God's name the military were involved she didn't know—arrived at the boarding house.

Questioned by uniformed men, Kate repeated the same story: Peter left, a swirl of dust, a boarder grabbing a ride at the last minute. Authorities took it upon themselves to inspect the room occupied by that boarder. They found four shirts and two pairs of pants on wire hangers in the cupboard, nothing untoward there, but all of it was bundled and taken by the police. They weren't done looking, however; they banged at the walls and the door and the window and the chest of drawers. There was a loose board, a false bottom in the chest, a hiding place that was empty.

Nothing found. Nonetheless, the event was fodder for gossip. Stories abounded.

A week passed before the police visited the boarding house for the last time. Content that no one was spying on them, plying them with questions, Kate, Dulcie, Izzie and Rosemary sat, chopping vegetables for stew, the talk stuttering around to the whole situation. "Some man approached me at work," said Izzie. "'You live in Bakeapple Boarding House, don't you?'" he said. "'And how is Mrs. Mullins doing the poor thing? A spy right under her nose. Imagine that.'"

"Nobody's got no proof of spies," said Dulcie. "With a war still on, you think people would have enough sense to put a lid on the gossip."

"Did you hear about—?" began Rosemary who then stopped and looked at Dulcie, as if asking for permission.

Dulcie indicated toward Kate. "It's Kate here you should be asking, not me. She's been through the wringer."

"Sorry, Kate," offered Rosemary. "Dulcie's right. Don't know what I was thinking. We can talk about something else."

"I'm sorry too," said Izzie. "I'm the one who opened up this conversation."

"I'm fine," said Kate. "And I don't mind the talk as long as ye makes a promise that what's spoken won't leave this room."

Knives and vegetables thudded to the table while the women nodded heads and crossed hearts. They resumed peeling and chopping while Rosemary continued the telling. "Some particulars came from out around Placentia Bay. Something about a periscope sighting, water foaming around it and then pouring down the sides of a U-boat that rose up from the deep in the black of the night."

Dulcie snorted. "Where on earth did you hear that pile of malarkey?"

"Have to admit that it came from ne'er-do-well, an old fella named Gus, known for his love of the drink."

"There you have it. A pile of malarkey, just like I said."

"Dulcie's right. How could anybody see all that in the dark?" Izzie asked.

"A crescent of moonlight, enough to cause a glint on the sea and the submarine."

"Was that all there was to the story?"

"Hang on, Izzie. I'm getting to it." Rosemary chopped up a potato and dropped it into a bowl at the centre of the table. "That Gus, he told a fanciful story. A skiff rowed out to the U-boat, hitting the hull with a *clunk.* There was a rattle of dropped oars and the shadow of a figure boarding the submarine which then slid back into the deep. Then? Nothing. No sight, no sound at all. Just the roll of waves to shore."

"I don't know about all that," said Izzie. "Sounds a bit like a mystery novel, Rosemary."

"Some believed the lot of it," said Kate.

"And some took no notice," said Dulcie.

"All of it nonsense," said Izzie.

Kate caught Izzie's eye, saw concern, and offered her a tiny smile.

"I don't know what's what," said Kate. "Does it matter? Peter's gone."

Conversation stopped then. Nothing but the peel and chop and the occasional plop of a chunk of carrot or turnip or parsnip into the bowl of water on the table. Then Kate spoke again. "Did they find that skiff, Rosemary, the one that rowed out to the U-boat?"

Rosemary shrugged. "I never heard that bit."

A deep sigh slid out of Kate. "Peter was all for going to war, but his mother wouldn't hear of it. She didn't want to lose her son. But he died anyway. On home soil. And he died by violence. If all you say is true, then it was a war crime."

"Yes," said Dulcie, "and now Peter's family are just like all others who receive notices about the death of a loved one. There's no sense in any of it."

"All Peter did was take a few dollars, give someone a ride." Tears formed in Kate's eyes. "I'll never understand it." To herself she wondered in part if Peter had a hand in his own destruction. Always patting his wallet. It was Izzie who interpreted that habit as a love for money, the root of all evil. Was his want of a few dollars what got him killed? She lowered her head and looked at the people around her. *Was it Reggie who killed Peter? Could it have been Patrick?* That second thought chilled her. Although she didn't know the why of it, deep in her heart, Kate believed it possible. Fear tiptoed in and lingered.

CHAPTER 27

TIME STUMBLED ON AND KATE stumbled back into a routine, one foot in front of the other into summer green, fall fade, and winter white. In the spring of 1945, war was ending, and hope was blooming, bringing a sense of newness to everything. With blackout curtains banished and windowpanes gleaming, the light of day brightened the inside of the boarding house, and the lamps of night warmed the souls of passersby. A special year, no doubt, and extra effort was put into the spring cleaning.

Kate was hard at the cleaning chores: puttering and dusting and mopping and scouring. She liked the work; the busyness of it kept her from thinking too much. A big job, the boarding house. Every semblance of a rug aired on the clothesline and beaten to within an inch of its life. Every bit of furniture shoved this way or that so every blemish on floors could be attacked with a scrub brush. Rosemary worked the upper floors. Dulcie scoured the kitchen. Kate and Izzie had at the parlour.

"I'll clean behind the radio. I don't remember ever doing it, and it probably hides a lot of dust." Kate tried to move the large, heavy floor model, but it wouldn't budge. "Over here, Izzie," she said. Izzie popped up from behind a chesterfield and the two of them tugged at the monster, which eventually relinquished its pigheadedness and slid about twelve inches. Something behind it clattered to the floor.

"Whatever in heaven's name is that?" asked Izzie.

Kate squeezed her small frame behind the radio. "That," she said, retrieving the item and holding it up, "is Reggie's cane." Puzzled, she looked at Izzie. She tapped the cane on the floor a few times. "Remember him coming down the hallway, shoe slapping, cane tapping?"

"Of course I do. But why is it here?"

Kate widened her eyes. "When Reggie was at the door of Peter's car, he held a small suitcase in one hand and waved money at Peter with the other. He had no cane." She recalled him running around the car to get in on the other side. She let out a gasp. "He had no limp either."

"So we were right to suspect him." Izzie's voice took on an eerie quality. "He *was* a spy. The gall of him, acting lame and quiet and working at the railway."

"Things are not always what they seem." Kate shook her head. One sudden lucid thought came up and tumbled out. *Reggie killed Peter.*

A trembling Kate held the cane at arm's length. "Should we give this to the constabulary?"

"To what end?"

"I don't know. Peter's dead. Reggie's escaped, if that U-boat story is true, gone to Germany. There'll be no justice for Peter."

"It would break Dulcie's heart if the constabulary came charging through here again," said Kate.

"Not much point to telling anyone anything, is there?"

Kate sighed. A clomp of familiar footsteps had them both turning toward the hallway.

"Dulcie's coming," whispered Izzie.

In a sweeping motion, Kate hid the cane behind her back. Izzie edged toward her until the two were side by side.

Dulcie, dust mop in hand, entered the parlour.

"Well, I got the ceiling dusted in the kitchen. You should have seen cobwebs in the corner by the—." She looked at the two of them. "What in the love of God are ye up to? What you got there, behind your back, Kate?"

Izzie pointed to the radio. "Just managed to move that beast of a thing. Taking a breather before having at the wall and floor behind it."

Kate's breath slid out long and slow. Izzie had skilfully skirted a lie.

Dulcie paused. Was that a glimmer of suspicion Kate saw on Dulcie's face? "What are you hiding, Kate? Please don't make me ask you a third time."

Kate moved the cane to Dulcie's sight line.

"Sweet Heart of Jesus, Mary, and Joseph!" Dulcie found the nearest seat, the wingback chair, and plopped down. "You telling me Reggie made it to Peter's car without that thing?"

Kate nodded.

Dulcie fanned herself with a dust rag from her apron pocket. "I don't want any more hell to come down on the boarding house. When I found that radio hidden in his room, I had to tell the military. If only I'd spoken to them sooner . . ."

"What are you talking about, Dulcie?" said Kate.

Dulcie waved the question away. "Need to know basis," she said as she popped to her feet, in a hurry now. "I'm going to put me mop and dust rags away and get some navy beans into a cauldron for a soak. You two get the wall done and the radio back where it belongs. And get rid of that cane." With that she was gone.

"Let's get to it then." They scrubbed the wall and floor, pushed the radio back, and jammed the cane behind it. "Let's keep this hidden forever. Not a word about this to anyone else, Izzie."

"Not a word."

"Thanks." Kate reached for a quick hug. When Izzie lingered, a startled Kate caught herself leaning in. *What is this?* Guilt panged, doubt swirled, and Kate sighed as she pulled away. Disappointment tugged but she tamped it down. Kate Kerrigan was not ready to acknowledge the fact that she craved Izzie's presence like air. Not now. Maybe not ever.

KATHLEEN

CHAPTER 28

It is provoked, the sea.

During six long years of the Second World War, the North Atlantic ingests toxins from chemicals and oil from shipwrecks and, as a result, its multi-faceted ecosystems suffer irreversible damage. Still the sea remains steadfast in its support of war, its energy circulating in rolling waves and absorbing all detritus as the ocean awaits one side or the other to declare victory. At the same time, there are rebellions from the Atlantic. On a brooding day, if pushed hard enough and long enough, it will revolt. An encounter with a rebellious sea is not for the faint of heart. The sea always, eventually, wins out. Water knows no boundaries.

The ghost that is me has awareness of the significance of events to come, events I cannot name and cannot see. I am encased in shadows like a mime in glass. I fume with anger. Is there neither rhyme nor reason to this rage? Annoyance builds as I slide through doors on the collar of a coat, through chimneys on a curl of smoke, through windows on the cusp of a breeze that billows curtains and unsettles dust. I hang unnoticed, clawing, nudging, and poking the edges of progeny. As I look at the living version of myself, I am frustrated, exasperated. Provoked by what? I don't know but I am ready to act. To do what? That I don't know either. Just that I am barred from doing so. I bounce into the pocket of the bib of Kathleen's apron, the frantic rhythm of her heartbeat vibrating through me. *What ails you, Kathleen?* I want to say. *What ails you?* But I know what ails her. Life ails her. Her baby Jimmy murdered by her husband. Alphonse murdered by her own hand. Her son Kevin murdered by German soldiers. Is that the end of the bloodshed? Kate and Clara are all that's left.

Sick of waiting for God knows what, I am determined to communicate with my corporeal self. I slam at Kathleen, fly through her, smack against the stovepipe in her kitchen. But I have no power here other than to observe and what I observe, what the living version of me seems to be ignoring, is that Clara has been wiping tears, whispering prayers, and contemplating years spent without her daughter, without a thought for her husband who was never her husband at all.

In a blink, I am in the boarding house in St. John's, and it is the day of victory in Europe, when revellers are dancing in the streets. Can I make a difference here? Likely not, but I'm determined to stay, clinging to a neglected cobweb near the ceiling in the parlour, a good vantage point to keep track of Kate, to follow Kate.

My Kate hasn't had much to smile about in the aftermath of the death of Peter. But on this day, some much-needed cheer shows up at her door in the form of a familiar visitor, one she hasn't seen for a long, long time. When she greets him at the door, her sombre face surrenders to a smile.

Later, spirits lifted, Kate heads outside to join the VE Day revellers. Unused to going out now, she stumbles through preparation, giving extra time to rouge and lipstick and choice of outfit. She descends the stairs to the main floor, which all have vacated in favour of celebration in the streets.

Pocketbook in hand, Kate heads out alone, bouncing along toward the downtown crescendo of accordions and songs and laughter. She crinkles her nose at the stench of booze and threads through the sway of people that increases in density, all sorts and sizes until they surround her. Still she meanders, bumping into this one and that, receiving occasional celebratory pecks on the cheek from smiling young men in uniform, strangers all. One rough sailor grabs Kate by the shoulders, and plants a kiss on her mouth. Would that I could at least bellow an objection, but Kate shows her mettle when she jerks away and runs through the crowd.

There is a blip in time and she is running again, heading home, picking up speed, seemingly unaware of anything or anyone, certainly unaware that she is being followed. As she enters the boarding house, I beg the Atlantic wind to still itself, to stop shaking what little is left of my soul. I cannot allow my granddaughter to come to harm.

Desperate, I seek help. I find Izzie lying asleep in her bed, her face flushed with illness. Can I get through to her? I cannot linger on doubt because Izzie is my only hope. I moan and bubble and croak, calling Izzie's name, but my efforts are useless, thwarted by the invisible yet impenetrable wall between the living and the dead. Below, the front door creaks.

Suddenly I am on the first floor, witnessing the entrance of the beast. Watching, always watching. I have so long been resigned to my eternal penance of watching. How often have I, like Dickens' ghost Jacob Marley, longed to intervene? All in vain. But, useless ghost that I am, I must attempt to make a difference here and now. The boarding house has spilled its revelling residents into the streets. There is only me. And Izzie. I hurl back to her bedside.

I pull in air and expand like a bubble. The wave of air around me continues to build, the bubble of me growing until it can grow no more. Then I let it go. A blast of three shouts. The universal signal for distress is three of any sound—three blasts from a whistle, three shots from a gun, three flashes from a mirror. "IZZIE, IZZIE, IZZIE."

Izzie does not respond.

KATE

CHAPTER 29

ON THE MORNING OF WEDNESDAY, May 8th, 1945, Kate heard the siren that screamed from atop the Newfoundland Hotel. The very same siren that had sounded every Thursday morning to remind the people they were at war was now announcing victory in Europe, that it was time to celebrate peace. The air was filled with a celebration of voices and bells and horns. A frenzy of vehicles, covered in bright bunting and with horns continuously blaring, crowded the streets, and flags flew everywhere. Even the vessels in the harbour had their say, their whistles constantly sounding.

Everyone was pouring into the street, partying, everyone but Kate, and Izzie, who was ill and had taken to her bed. Kate sat staring blankly at the headline in *The Daily News* "GERMANY SURRENDERS UNCONDITIONALLY." There was joy in it somewhere she supposed, but Kate didn't have much room for happiness in her. Almost a year since Peter's remains had been found and she didn't go out much, and didn't want visitors at the boarding house.

When a knock came to the door of the boarding house on VE Day, she realized that there was no one to answer it, only herself. And she had no intention of doing it. Let them knock whoever they were. And they did. Repeatedly. *Oh, for the love of God.* "I'm coming," she called. She cracked the door, peeked out, and was instantly lit from within. She swung the door wide. "Uncle Robert? Is it really you?"

"Indeed it is," he replied. "That is, if the young lady asking is Kate Kerrigan? You've surely grown."

Kate had no doubt that the gaunt face in front of her was Uncle Robert. But he was not the robust, well-groomed man she once knew, the one whose carriage spoke authority, whose words carried weight. This Uncle Robert had rounded shoulders, a reedy voice, and a skeletal frame. "How on earth did you find me?" she asked, the reality of the cost of war seeping through her. It was war that had creased Uncle Robert's face and wilted his body.

"A letter from your grandmother. Well, may I come in?"

"Oh," she said, pulling the door wide and ushering him in. "Where's my manners? I'm staggered, is all."

As Robert limped over the threshold, Kate cringed. "You are injured!" She reached for his arm and led him to the parlour, still trying to mesh her memory of Uncle Robert, a tall man who walked proud, with this wretched man with the curved back and the injured leg. He had always exuded confidence but now? That was gone. Maybe temporarily. Maybe permanently. Something else was off too, something missing. It was the scent of pipe tobacco. Kate always associated Uncle Robert with a meerschaum pipe between his teeth, tamping tobacco, lighting it, all slow and deliberate movements. "We'll have a sit down and I'll get you a nice cup of tea."

"Let's not bother with the tea. I don't have much time," he said. "Business things to attend to before I head to Freshwater. Will be in St. John's for a couple of days."

"I'd offer you a room here at the boarding house but there are no vacancies."

"Kind of you to think of it, young Kate, but I've already made hotel arrangements."

"Oh." Kate didn't ask where. If he'd wanted to share that detail, he would have. "So, you're on your way home to Freshwater? Your new home, I mean." Guilt struck her. She may not have asked where he was staying in St. John's but now she was angling for information. Yes, he was a weakened man, but she was a determined girl, her need for details about Clara prioritized over her concern for him. *Guilt be damned.* She waited.

Robert cleared his throat, an attempt to strength his voice, she supposed, but when he spoke, his tone was feeble. "Yes, I'm on my way to see Clara and your grandmother." Kate eyed his face as it turned from pale to crimson. He fidgeted with his tie, his fingers trembling. She had obviously pricked him and promptly regretted it. Uncle Robert had been good to her.

"Kate, you need to know . . . I was already married when I met Clara."

Kate was stunned. *Already married?* She instantly thought about Rosemary and her husband and Teresa. "A bigamist man," little Teresa had said, innocently spilling her mother's secret. Rather than hiding, Rosemary admitted it. Her husband had shown his true self. Kate turned on Robert. "Bigamy? You're a bigamist? Why are you telling me this? Does Clara know?"

"I know that it seems wrong, that it is wrong. I thought I was on a rescue mission when I married Clara. At the time, I was trying to redeem myself. It's a long story." He dismissed the topic with a wave of his hand. "The important thing is, yes, Clara knows."

Kate sat back, shocked. Robert obliged her reaction with stillness.

When she leaned forward again, he reached into the side pocket of his jacket. "I really came here to bring you something from Kevin." Robert paused. "I'm so sorry about the loss of your father."

Something caught in Kate's throat. She didn't risk speaking. Not the time for tears. Not the time to pursue the Clara issue. Time to get to the heart of the meeting. She nodded briskly. She watched as he withdrew a fisted hand from his pocket. He uncurled his fingers. Resting on his palm was a white oval stone.

"A stone? That looks like the one I used to have."

"Used to?"

"Flung it over Jerseyside Hill when I was livid with Clara."

"About?"

Kate shrugged. "Doesn't matter. Why are you bringing me another stone?"

"It's not a stone, although Kevin thought it one at first. He found it on the floor of a safe house in France, and it reminded him of you. He wanted to keep it but didn't want to steal from the good people who were helping us, so he returned it to the lady of the house. But she gifted it to him with her blessing." He passed it to her. "Open it."

Kate looked at him quizzically.

"Like this." He retrieved the oval and twisted it. A miniature rosary fell out onto Kate's open palm.

A wide-eyed Kate fingered the tiny beads. "Things are not always what they seem," she whispered.

Robert offered a nod of acknowledgement. "Like you, Kevin was surprised when the rosary appeared from within. Not a praying man, Kevin, but he made an exception with these beads. He asked me to give you this because it reminded him of you. He prayed on this rosary, I think, with the hope that it might remind you of him."

"And it will." Kate's vision blurred as she considered the tiny treasure in her hand. She carefully returned the beads to their oval case. "It's so kind of you to travel all this way to bring this to me."

Robert nodded. "Truth be told, this stop is only part of my reason for being in Newfoundland. I must see Clara so I'm going to Freshwater." He sighed. "I doubt Clara and Kathleen will ever forgive me for the death of Kevin."

"Why was that your fault?"

"Kevin sacrificed himself to save my family." Tears filled his eyes. "He led the enemy away so we could escape."

"Was it his choice to help you?"

Robert nodded, his grief palpable in the air around him.

Kate reached a sympathetic hand to his. "Then not your fault. You can ask Clara and Nanny for forgiveness," she said, then winced at the twang of hypocrisy those words brought her. *The nerve of myself, talking about forgiveness.* Not as if she'd ever forgive Clara.

"That I can. And will." He lowered his head.

Uncomfortable with her unforgiving self, Kate changed the subject. "You must have been through hell, Uncle Robert," she said, deliberately choosing the moniker, seeing gratitude in his eyes at the choice.

Robert let out another sigh, this one so deep that it rumbled through Kate. "War was hard to look at. Harder to get away from. A search for freedom," he said. "That's all we thought about. Freedom. My family and I achieved it, thanks to Kevin." He was silent again, contemplating. "It surprised me that life seems more difficult now because there are more choices. I sometimes don't know what road to take myself." He managed a smile. "But the road to visiting you? That was easy."

"Thank you for coming here. Thank you for explaining and, thank you for this." She held up the rosary.

"You're so welcome." Robert struggled to his feet. "I have much to do."

Kate took his hand and squeezed. Robert kissed her gently on the cheek and smiled. Then he was gone.

CHAPTER 30

AFTER ROBERT'S DEPARTURE, KATE TOYED with the tiny container that Kevin had sent to her. An unexpected blessing, this tiny oval that resembled a stone, but opened to reveal an exquisite miniature rosary, beads that had passed over Kevin's fingers.

Kate had been livid when Kevin left, but now? Anger lingered but love softened its edges. Yes, she had loved Kevin, she still did. Kevin was her father, but not her father. Baffled by it all, yet bolstered by Robert's visit, she reasoned that perhaps it was time to get herself out of her shell and out into the world. It had been a year since Peter's death, two years since she learned about Kevin's. She stood at the window of her room, leaned into the sill, and pressed her face against the glass. People everywhere. Victory in Europe. This day was a once-in-a-lifetime opportunity to celebrate. She was going to do exactly that.

A glance at the rosary still clutched in her hand, a thought that she might lose this treasure in the crowds, had her returning it to its container, which she placed in a drawer under a scarf. Safe and secure. She allowed herself time for a touch of makeup and a choice of outfit and then off she went before she could change her mind. She locked the door and headed down the hill toward downtown, winding her way through swarms of people with warm, smiling faces.

So casually did she stroll that she almost tripped over the extended legs of a woman sitting on the doorstep of a house whose façade, like most along the route, kissed the side of the road. The woman took no notice of

Kate, just leaned against the door, singing "The Ode to Newfoundland" at the top of her drunken lungs. Kate caught herself humming along as she skirted the singer. By the time she got downtown, she had hummed and sung several snatches of songs that floated past her. She wound her way through hordes of military men, many of whom took it upon themselves to plant a peck on the cheek of women passersby, herself among them. It was no bother to her on this day of worldwide celebration, and she assured herself that she was none the worse for it until met by a sailor whose rough hands grabbed her shoulders. "You Newfie girls," he said, the stench of alcohol and cigarettes and aftershave pouring off him, assaulting her. He yanked her close, his lips lodged against hers, his tongue forcing her teeth apart and thrusting itself down her throat. Repulsed, Kate jerked away and ran, glancing back until she was certain he was not following. After scurrying for another block or two, she threaded her way into the centre of a swaying, toe-tapping crowd who were singing along to a group of fiddlers sawing Irish tunes. Here she stopped. A safe place, she reasoned. Soothing.

She stayed a while and sang a while, then strolled further along, quite at ease until the sense of a presence beside her sent her heart racing. Ready to run, she turned her head. And there, smiling his biggest smile, was Patrick McMurty. A relieved hello fell out of Kate, but a sea of shouts and songs drowned the sound of her voice. She looked around for a quieter space. Patrick pointed to an alcove in front of a hat shop with a closed sign on the window. Nodding, she stepped into the recess, her back to the door, his to the street. "Nice to see you," she blurted. "You've not been to visit us at the boarding house. I haven't seen many people this last year. I've been distraught for a long time. I lost—you remember my friend, Peter. He was murdered. But today, I decided to join the celebration." Suddenly aware that she was talking too much, that he surely knew about Peter, that she did not want Patrick stopping by the boarding house at all, she paused.

"I see," he said, not a word more.

She waited. Unexplained, this uneasiness that crept in like a rising tide and triggered childhood memories of standing on tiptoes at windows watching the sea, struggling to guess its next move. The recalled images squeezed the good out of her now, not an ounce of strength left for dealing with current distress. "I'll just be on my way then," she said and attempted to step out of the recessed entry way.

Patrick immediately raised his arms and braced his hands against the wall on each side of her head. "You haven't been to visit Clara and your Nanny in a very long time," he said.

Kate studied his face, witnessing the soft outlines of the smile he had arrived with harden like crevices in sea-swept stone. Was it always there, that cruel glint in his eyes? Had she imagined the sting in his statement?

He parted his lips, then closed them again. After a stalled moment during which he turned to eye the crowds in the street, he looked back at her and shook his head. "Maybe I should just walk you home, see that you get back to the boarding house safely."

At this point, the word NO screamed in Kate's mind. She remembered Patrick's last appearance at the boarding house, recalled images of Peter and Reggie and Patrick in Peter's car. And then Peter was gone. She summoned her loudest voice. "No, thank you. No need. I'll be fine," she said. She thrust herself forward, slid beneath an extended arm and went on her way, walking, then, fearing he might follow, running, as she retraced her route, past the Irish fiddlers, through the military masses, skirting around the drunk woman on the side of the road.

At the boarding house, panting, Kate came to a full stop, pulled the key from her pocket, thrust it, turned it, and twisted the doorknob. Inside, she slammed the door and plopped onto an oak armchair, a convenience chair for slipping on and off overshoes on rainy days. She huddled there, her body clenched, her knee jumping, and then she lurched forward, feet pummelling up the stairs to the safety of her own room. She went into her room and sat down heavily on her bed. During a break in the noise from the street, the floor below emitted a creak, a familiar creak, that of old boards under heft. She flinched. *Is someone else here? Did Patrick follow me home?* Heart pounding, she crept along to the landing and peered over the banister. No one in the corridor, no groan from the floor. Her heart slowed its pace. Street noise picked up again, filling the void. *Just an aging house having its say,* she assured herself. Still, she continued down, checked the front door, which was locked, its key sitting sedately on the oak armchair. *Did I leave that there?* Nerves thrumming, she looked into the parlour, the dining room. Finding no evidence of anyone else's presence, she sighed into the idea of a calming cup of tea.

The north-facing kitchen had only one tiny window, its blind down, making day into night. Kate stepped to the centre of the room and pulled the string to click on the light, instantly illuminating resident cockroaches that scurried into cracks and holes. What was it Dulcie had said about vermin? People coming and going all the time and bringing in vermin. Hard to keep them at bay, the vermin. Her focus shifted to the butter yellow walls and coal stove and picture of the Sacred Heart on the calendar. And the odour of alcohol and smoke and aftershave. Startled by it, she froze. She remembered that odour. Patrick hadn't followed her home. But the sailor had, the one with the rough hands, the unwanted kiss, and the probing tongue. And he was standing right behind her.

"What are you doing here?" She managed to turn around.

"Looking for you, Newfie girl" he said, grinning.

Kate stiffened. "You are not welcome here." Her voice forceful, its meaning clear, her nod abrupt. She fisted her hands, fingernails digging into her palms like talons. Seemingly of their own accord, her arms lifted and folded across her body.

"Oh, I believe I am," he said, his eyes sparking like struck flint.

"You are not," Kate said again, her tone weaker now.

"Let me refresh your memory. A while ago we met on the street."

Kate stood, stunned and helpless. An urge to apologize if she had misled him rose in her core but she quickly slammed it down. *What the hell?* What was it Nanny said about women taking the blame for everything? All she needed to do was stay still, wait, and his insistence would wane. He would leave. But he did nothing other than stand there, the gap between them stretching and shortening with her every breath until dizziness beset her. The particulars of the kitchen evaporated. A shiver flickered through her. Her gut churned. When she could speak, the calmness in her voice surprised her. "Why have you come here?" She let that calm filter through her. In the back of her mind, she strategized. *Can I dash around him and through the front door? What about the back door? Locked tight. Where is the key?* She looked at the ring of keys dangling from a hook on the cupboard beside the Sacred Heart calendar. Her heartbeat quickened.

As if in response to her last spoken question, he rooted into a pocket and retrieved a knife, its blade flashing silver with a flick of his hand. Was it real, that knife, the tip of the blade pointing at the middle of her chest? The shiver that before had flickered now flared. The threat was real. A different level of familiar. This was not her first encounter with potential undoing. The ocean had stolen her. The ocean had spewed her back. Could she, would she come back from this? Aware of her fear, unable to look at her fear, or listen to her pounding heart Kate tuned in to the background in hope of help. A sound. A footstep. Anything. Anyone. But she was stranded, her mind churning with *if onlys* and *should haves*, all of which led to herself, for there was only herself to blame. She had not asked him here on this day but, in essence, this was her own doing. She neglected caution; after her first encounter with this sailor, she had run right back past him without a thought for her own safety. And now, she was teetering, not on the edge of a cliff where a single step back would find safety, but on the tip of a spire where any step at all would topple her.

"We're going upstairs to your room," he said. So casual was he that he could have been telling her the time of day. Kate turned cold. No emotion. No motion either. Couldn't move even if she wanted to. Was she asleep? Yes, that was it. Any minute now, she would wake up. Why was she napping in the daytime anyway? Supper time was approaching. She must wake up for she had work to do. Where on earth had she put her apron? Why couldn't she remember?

"I have lots of time, Newfie girl. My ship doesn't leave harbour until tonight. There's no one coming to rescue you." He stepped closer. The menace of him, the closeness of him, snapped her out of her frozen state. She turned. She moved one foot, then the other, making her way to the stairs, then up. The point of a knife at her back. The act of gripping the banister and pulling herself to the next step took all the strength Kate could muster. She thought of the tiny rosary beads inside the oval that Uncle Robert had given her. There is hope in everything, he said. *Where is the hope in this?* If she kept her movements slow, dragged her toes on the stairs, would that smear hope onto each riser? The tremors in both arms and legs made slowing down easy. She paused, knuckles turning white on the banister, before hauling her foot up a step. She stumbled. Unplanned. She righted herself and kept going. Could she stumble again? How could this be happening? At the top of the stairs, she hesitated. The point of the knife urged her onward. Time stuttered, the presence of daylight calling into question her plight. Evil things only happened in the black of night, didn't they? Not real, this. In her room now. Sun streamed in and motes of dust dangled and settled. *She should get the dust cloth and whisk them away.* What a strange thought. The door closed behind her, gently, a whisper. He nudged her toward the bed. She turned, looked at his face, seeing only a fog where his features should be, a shock of blond hair covering his forehead. Should she be yelling? Would anyone come? Could she be heard over the roar of the rabble in the streets?

He toyed with the knife, tracing the outline of her face with the tip of the blade. Nothing was required of her here. She gave nothing.

"I let you go the first time, but then you ran past me again. My lucky day," he said, his words engulfing her like the strangling familiarity of a tidal wave. She struggled to breathe. She'd done that before, struggled to breathe in a tidal wave.

He paused the blade at her lips, flattened it, and pressed it against her closed mouth. He then pulled the knife from her face, leaned closer, and murmured, "Take your clothes off."

Nausea coursed through Kate. Weakness overtook her. She collapsed like a marionette with uncommitted strings, knees meeting the floor with a thump. A pinched hold on her elbow followed by a sharp jerk brought her back to her feet. He flung her toward the bed where she landed, plopped like a rag doll, like her Mrs. Fan doll that her mother had given her. Not her mother Mavis, who *wasn't* her mother. Clara was her mother.

He repeated his command, the cut of his tone piercing her core. *Dear Father in heaven, help me. Am I praying now? Where will that get me?*

"Get on with it." He waved the knife at her.

Kate couldn't reason anymore. Why had she asked him here? Wait a minute. She hadn't done that at all. She had encountered him and had run from him.

He stepped back, watching her, waiting. Shaking, she sat up and she removed her cardigan, the blue one with the little yellow flowers around the neckline, the one that Dulcie had knitted in her spare time. *When on earth does Dulcie have spare time?* Kate fumbled at the top button of her white blouse with the Peter Pan collar. Peter? Poor Peter. He came to no good end. Loved money too much. Accepted money, gave a ride, lost his life.

"My name's not Peter," her attacker smirked.

Had she said Peter's name aloud? Did it matter? Kate had somehow escaped her body and was coasting along the ceiling, watching a monster paw and pound. And then she heard someone screaming. Screaming with her voice. Would anyone hear her? Would anyone, any help walk through that door?

Another pounding, the pounding of footsteps brought Kate back to her senses. The monster raised his head. The bulk lifted from Kate, the shape headed for the door, pasting itself to the wall behind the door. A fist hammered the door. Izzie's voice sounded, calling and calling and calling Kate's name.

Izzie tumbled into the room, the shape slid out behind her.

"Kate, Kate, are you okay?"

Kate moaned.

The monster slipped through the open door. The beast was gone.

"Oh, thanks be to God." Izzie's voice gushed with relief. She grabbed a quilt and spread it over Kate. "You wait here," said Izzie. "I'll get the doctor, the constable."

The shock that stilled Kate's body instantly gave way to violent shivers. "No," she cried. "No doctor. No police. Please. Just stay here with me."

"I'll stay," says Izzie. She looked away, eyed the door.

Kate lurched to a sitting position. "Oh, my God. Is he still here?"

"No, no, no. You can rest easy, Kate. I'll take care of you." Izzie tucked the blanket around Kate. Modesty didn't matter to Kate. Naked or covered. She was done now, no longer pure in her own mind and in the eyes of God. An encounter with evil had left her battered, body and soul. *Mea culpa.* She hadn't seen this coming. Why was she not paying attention?

Izzie lay down beside Kate, dropping an arm around Kate, uttering words of reassurance. Kate stopped shivering. She was safe, for now. But shame had taken root. How stupid she had been. Not an inkling what leaving caution to the wind would do. On this, a day of world rejoicing, Kate Kerrigan lay curled in a quilt, a mound of shock. She would never, ever tell anyone. Nobody else saw, did they? Nobody else here but Izzie who was holding Kate close.

Kate owned that Izzie would hold this secret close too.

CLARA

CHAPTER 31

Just a couple of days after VE Day, Clara led Kathleen outside to see the new blood-red paint job Clara herself had given the door of the root cellar. It had been nearly three years since workers had carved that cellar into a knoll and encased it with rocks. A fine job of it they did too, except for the dirt floor and the painting of the door, a slipshod paint job, which the Atlantic wind sneered at and shred to ribbons. The two stepped inside. "I suppose we should have had a cement floor poured, but we can do that eventually. Or never." She shrugged. "May not need it at all."

Outside, someone called Clara's name. *Patrick?* Pain gouged her chest. *Why can't I tell that man that I am done with him?* Of course, she knew why. He had threatened to shame her, to shame Kate. That was the why of it. Shaking, knowing she would have to head him off, Clara summoned her strength but before she could get out of the cellar, Patrick was there, standing in the doorway, blocking it, arms raised gripping the top of the frame, the light aback of him. "No answer to my knock at the house," he said. "No wonder. Here you are!" Clara looked at Kathleen whose face caught the stream of light between the red frame of the door and the raised arm of Patrick. The shock on Kathleen's face could have knocked Clara over. Clara stared without seeing, unable to make sense out of her mother's reaction, as Kathleen propped herself against a wall, her hand over her heart. "What ails you, Mom?"

Kathleen waved her off. Clara bit her lip. Kathleen the warrior, as enduring as the sea, never let anything take the good out of her. Wait.

That wasn't completely true. When Clara was a child, Kathleen had fallen into despair over the death of baby Jimmy and had strayed from a solid path for a long time. Why was Kathleen faltering now? Was she frightened by the sight of a man at the door of her root cellar? "Mom?"

"I'm fine, I'm fine," muttered Kathleen.

You don't look fine. Regardless, Clara stumbled into introductions, saying Patrick was one of the workers who had helped the community and who was now was off to build elsewhere.

"Nice to meet you, Mrs. Kerrigan," said Patrick, calmly removing his cap and holding it in front of his chest. Clara recognized the display of manners, had witnessed it on many occasions, usually in the company of the well-heeled. Puzzling. What was Patrick doing?

"I've enjoyed the company of Clara here on many an occasion and now I can see where she gets her beauty. Isn't it a lovely day today, Mrs. Kerrigan?" A smile then, or was it a smirk? Whatever it was, it goaded Clara into action.

"I'll see you to the gate, Patrick," she said as she squeezed between him and the door frame. "Good day to you, Mrs. Kerrigan," he called. Then he laughed.

"What are you laughing at?" Clara asked.

"Nothing. Thought you might have been in St. John's on VE Day."

"Why would I be?"

"Celebrate. See Kate." He paused at the gate. "I saw Kate."

An alarm went off inside Clara. "You didn't tell her anything, did you?"

Patrick smiled, seeming pleased, saying nothing.

"You better not have. Get out of here now." she said, looking back toward the cellar. *What is Mom thinking about all this?*

Shrugging, Patrick strode away. Clara headed back to the cellar, expecting a conversation with Kathleen, a talk about the man or about Kathleen's response to him, but Kathleen went quiet and brusquely left the cellar. Clara took a step or two to toward her but halted, deciding she would give Kathleen time to come to terms with whatever had upset her.

Curiosity burned and Clara couldn't, didn't wait long. A few days later,

Kathleen was sitting on the back steps of the house. Was she ready to let out her feelings? Certainly seemed so. All Clara had to do was pry the lid off. A determined Clara marched up to her mother, sat beside her, and opened her mouth. "Mom," she said, and stopped. At the edge of her vision, she caught sight of a lone figure approaching the garden gate. Dear God, Patrick didn't have the gall to come back, did he? Clara squinted. Not Patrick, this man. Relief gushed and slid to the back of her, her attention focused on the man in front of her. A moneyed man, apparently, if suit, tie, and fedora were any indication. But the nearer the man got, the sharper the sheen on his suit. It had seen better days, well-worn, probably threadbare. Even his fedora was faded and drooping. From beneath its brim, he was looking straight at them. Instantly, Clara's mission to question her mother fled. She had no notion about anything other than the man who just showed up. "Mom," she said again, this time voice and limbs as weak as a kitten.

"Yes, I know who it is." Kathleen pressed her hands to her knees and stood. "Might as well invite the man in before chins start to wag."

Clara sniffed. "That man is a bit of driftwood the sea should have kept to herself." She barrelled into the house, leaving her mother to escort this visitor–Clara's not-husband Robert Caulins–through the gate, through the back door, and into the kitchen.

CHAPTER 32

CLARA HAD PARKED HERSELF AT the kitchen table, arms crossed. Kettle be damned. She would make no tea. It was Kathleen who pulled out a chair for Robert. "Injured in the war, Robert?" she asked as he limped toward the table.

"In a way," he replied, removing his wilted fedora. "Every minute in a war zone has decades in it. Body and soul withered before their time." He struggled into the chair. Hat in hand, he looked around the kitchen of their relatively new house. "You've landed well."

"No thanks to you," said Clara, eyeing him as he stared at the red door that he and Kevin had built.

"I'll give you that. Still, it's good to be here and see this. To see you both thriving."

"Again, no thanks to—"

"That's enough, Clara," said Kathleen. "Let the man speak his piece."

Clara sat back.

Robert sighed. "I've been all over Europe. A whole continent shivering in fear. Swastikas flying from the Eiffel Tower in Paris. I wondered if the war would ever end. So much poverty and want, people selling crows and hawks in markets. I can't tell you what it means to breathe free air again." He looked straight at Clara. "Your anger is well-justified."

Clara wouldn't afford him a glance at this point, but she knew he was watching her, his eyes locked on. "I don't need you telling me my fury has legs to it."

"Your purpose, please, Robert?" Kathleen said. "Let's have it."

"You got my letter?" he asked.

No response from Clara.

"Clara?" he said, his voice wistful.

Again, Kathleen intervened. "You know she did. You told us all about you and your wife and family. You got some cheek showing up here."

Thanks, Mom. Buoyed, Clara straightened her back. She looked at Robert then, his thinness and feebleness arousing her compassion. His eyes, which once twinkled like the sea in the sun, were dull grey now, the light absent, realms of sadness in its place. Still, sympathy did not mean forgiveness. Given the option, she would usher him straight to the devil's kingdom.

Robert sighed. "Sorry doesn't begin to express—"

"Humph." Unbidden, that snort from Clara, but the spite that trailed it was deliberate. "What the hell are you doing here?"

"You know the answer," he replied without a raise in his voice. "I promised Kevin, God rest his soul, that I would come to see all three of you."

"Kate's not here," said Kathleen. "You darn well know that because I sent you her address in St. John's."

"Yes, you did. Thank you. I've already seen Kate. On VE Day, at the boarding house." He sighed. "Too bad she moved away from here," he said with a gentle shaking of his head.

"The child had no school to go to here," said Kathleen.

Patrick sighed again, loud and long. "War displaces everyone, everything." He toyed with his felt hat, running his fingers around the brim.

Clara had had enough of his talk. Her anger coiled into a spring and her knee bounced uncontrollably, silently, beneath the table. She scowled. *Get out what you got to say and get out of this house.*

Robert appeared unhurried. "I have messages for you, from Kevin." Clara stared at him blankly. He continued. "I promised him, Clara. I must be here. I won't stay long, believe me."

Get on with it. Clara commanded her knee to be still. She wasn't just staring now, she was scowling.

"Kate always carried a little white stone," Robert said.

"She threw it away," Clara said. "Flung it over Jerseyside Hill one day when she was angry at the world." Seemingly from nowhere, a question fired through her and made its way out. "Did Kevin know who Kate's real father was?" Clara immediately shrank, fearing a disclosure, one that she herself had regrettably made to Patrick, one that would have caused more suffering to an already pained Kevin. But there was no such revelation. Robert's voice was kind as he said, "I hinted at it once, the question I mean. On a train, if I recall. But Kevin just looked bewildered. I never mentioned it again."

Comforted by that, Clara slumped back in her chair.

Robert reached into his pocket and produced a small tissue-wrapped item which he passed to Clara.

Clara, stoic, didn't raise a finger to accept it.

"I promised Kevin," said Robert. He placed the item on the table.

Still Clara stalled, refusal at the front of her. Robert didn't move. Nor did Kathleen. Clara placed a hand on the table, fingers inching toward the package, stopping just short of picking it up. An abrupt grab, during which she felt its shape and its weight, had her trembling. As memories flashed and flourished, defiance vanished. Clara removed the tissue paper from the tiny sewing kit, the one that Mavis had owned, the one that Kevin had snatched from Clara the last time she saw him. He had slapped her hand away and stormed off. Then he was gone, forever gone, and she would forever live with the penalty of having lied to him, letting him think that Kate was his daughter. How could he ever forgive her? She placed the kit on the table and stared at it.

"Kevin wanted me to bring this back to you, Clara. He specifically asked me to tell you that it's handy for mending things."

"Handy for mending things?" she echoed.

He nodded.

Clara herself had used those very words, Mavis' words, to Kevin the day he left, and, in his anger, he had spit them back at her. Now brimming with images of her brother, Clara picked up the tiny kit and folded it into her palm. Kevin had sent those words back to her again. But this time? There was no anger here. Kevin sent her the sewing kit, the words, as an act of mercy; he had forgiven her for years of lies.

Clara gripped the sewing kit tightly. Her hand warmed to it and comfort streamed from it, threading through her. *Handy for mending things.*

Robert folded the tissue paper and put it into his pocket. "Just one more thing: the *Elizabeth J*?"

"Sold it to the military for target practice," said Clara, instantly regretted her cruelty. It wasn't necessary to tell him the sad fate of the schooner, but spite owned the edge of her, and she had let it fly.

Robert appeared taken aback, then shrugged. "Fair enough, I suppose. I am in North America now to see my sons, for whom I arranged refuge in Canada during the bombing in London. I will soon be able to take them home, back to England where my wife and daughter are waiting. I made the trip from Canada to Newfoundland to keep my promise to Kevin. I owe him my life. He saved my family."

He then looked at Kathleen. "You gave your blessing to Kevin's travels when you gave him his birth certificate. I can never thank you enough for that."

"Your gratitude has no meaning when there's nothing left of Kevin." Kathleen cast her eyes away, stared at the ceiling. "I can neither bless you for coming here nor blame Kevin for going there," she said wistfully. "When I turned over the birth certificate, I sanctified his participation in war. Not the proper thing for a mother to do." She brought her glance back down to Robert and let out a sigh. "And now there is no evidence that he ever existed. No body to grieve over. No grave to kneel at. Nothing."

"You're wrong, Kathleen. The evidence lies in the existence of my family. They are alive because of Kevin."

Kathleen sniffed.

My family. Clara was riled. "Did you tell Kate about this family of yours?"

After a barely perceptible nod from Robert, silence fell like a cloak. Clara watched as he gradually leaned forward, resting one hand hard on the table. He pushed himself away from the table, the scrape of chair against floor violating the stillness. He stood, unfolding his body, pulling back his shoulders, denouncing their slump. With back straight, head high, he walked to the front door.

"Thank you for letting me in, letting me have my say." He put on his fedora, angled it just so, and left.

Clara and Kathleen remained at the table. "He wasn't limping anymore," said Clara.

"I'm thinking that he might be healing."

"How could that be?"

"He said it was time in the war zone that aged him. But things are not what they seem. I'm thinking guilt had a hand in it. Secrets can maim a man. He's let it all go now. His body will heal."

Clara was familiar with the cost of secrets. She attempted a deep sigh, a bit of a struggle for her lungs as they flared in discomfort.

Clara said no more that day, neither about Robert nor about Patrick, although curiosity about the latter burned her innards. The next morning, ready to broach the subject, she entered the kitchen. Instantly, her mother, without as much as a morning greeting, walked past her and through the back door.

An affronted Clara took up residence at the kitchen window, pushed the curtain aside, and spied on her mother who marched to the roadside, lifted her apron to create a carryall, and gathered lupines which were just coming into their own. Soon there'd be a rainbow of them with their purples and blues and pinks and whites, but now? Early days. *What the hell, Mom?* If there was any sense to be had here, Clara couldn't find it. Kathleen certainly wasn't going to display them in crockery. Her mother was not much for flowers in the house other than on oilcloth or wallpaper. Toxic, lupines. Dizziness and confusion were the least of the trouble lupines could cause. "What are you up to, Mom?" she muttered as she hurried outside to watch and wait.

Kathleen paused to pluck a dandelion, its golden glory gone, its white puff ball poised. A wishing flower now. She eyed it and obliged it with a gust of breath. As its seeds scattered, Clara wheedled into conversation. "Are you making a wish, Mom? You want concrete on the cellar floor? We'll get it done soon enough."

"No need to worry about that now at all," said Kathleen. "We've made do with a dirt floor for three years, we can make do for the time being." She batted at black flies and picked more lupines.

Clara dove deeper. "Remember when Patrick came by? It seemed like you knew him, Mom. Did you?"

"Humph. I knew him all right." She clenched her fist around a cluster of stems and yanked up plants, roots and all.

"How the hell do you know Patrick?" Clara blurted the question and instantly put her fingers to her lips in regret. She could see that her mother was fired right to the eyes. How much prodding would it take for Kathleen's anger to explode? Or implode as it did in the past? A shard of memory, that of her mother running naked on the landwash with Dulcie in pursuit, deepened Clara's regret. She backed off, hoping that Kathleen would just ignore the question. She needn't have worried, as without a word, Kathleen turned her back to Clara and went right on tugging and plucking. Still the question clawed at Clara. *How the hell does Mom know Patrick?*

Frustrated, Clara sagged against the fence. She was about to ask again but one look at Kathleen stopped her. Her mother was a machine now, marching and plucking with military precision. Clara was ill-equipped to handle that exacting aspect of Kathleen. Not today. Perhaps in another day, maybe a couple, when Kathleen had calmed, Clara would approach her again.

Yes, that would have to do. Clara returned to the kitchen where there were dirty dishes in the sink, waiting for a wash. She tended to them and let Kathleen be.

CHAPTER 33

Another dawn broke and a sleepless Clara crept again toward the kitchen, leaned into the door jamb, and eyed Kathleen Kerrigan. Mom was seated at the table, head down, hands busy with the polishing of the tea caddy, the mahogany caddy Clara had bought in St. John's on the day of the fire at the Knights of Columbus Hostel. *What are you up to, Mom?* No doubt in Clara's mind that there was a plan in place.

Kathleen set the glossy tea caddy on the table, gave it a nod of approval, and then removed its two slotted partitions. A red-and-white striped dish cloth leapt into service, banishing dust from both the slats of wood and the caddy's innards. Clara contemplated. *Should I interrupt?* Kathleen appeared deep in thought. Perhaps Kathleen hadn't heard Clara enter. Perhaps Kathleen needed time to process whatever was going on inside her. No doubt about it, she would interrupt her mother. Not abruptly though. She sidled to the cupboard and claimed a china teacup. *Click* went the cup onto a saucer. The cup shimmied, an unintended clatter. Clara clamped her free hand on top of it.

"Remember the day you showed me the new paint job on the cellar door?" said Kathleen, her voice otherworldly, as if she were talking to anyone, or no one.

A shiver crept through Clara. She turned.

"Remember the man who came to the door and stood, arms up, the light aback of him?"

"Yes, of course I remember," said Clara, her heart jumping from patter to pound. *Here it comes. How does Mom know Patrick?* Not wanting to deter or distract, Clara stood still, barely a breath out of her.

"That's a bad one, you got there, Clara, that man."

What? The saucer slipped through Clara's fingers. She shot out a hand, catching the saucer in mid drop. She froze, knees bent.

"I know you married Robert against your will, Clara," Kathleen said, her eerie tone grating Clara's nerves. "I know you surrendered your child to Mavis against your will, and I know you've been seeing that man, that Patrick. Only I didn't know who he was until that day in the cellar."

Clara jerked into an upright position. "So who is he then?" she snapped, her tone so uppity it staggered her.

Kathleen mimicked both question and tone. "So who is he then?" She shook her head, as if ridding herself of those words "I'll tell you who he was. That Patrick of yours . . ."

"What?" Clara practically shouted. "That Patrick of yours, what?"

"Many years ago, that Patrick of yours interfered with me."

Clara fell back against the sideboard. Her fingers faltered. The china cup and saucer met their fate on the kitchen floor. Smithereens, the both of them.

"Leave that mess right where it's to. Sit down, Clara, before you fall down."

Clara stumbled through shards of china to a chair and plopped, elbows on table, head in hands. "That's a hell of an accusation to make against someone," she muttered.

Kathleen grunted. "I didn't know his name. But I know what he did, what he's capable of doing. You think I'd lie to you about this?"

While Clara examined Kathleen's face, she rummaged her own mind, looking for some semblance of sense. Words filtered in, slowly at first, then in a rush, a gathering storm. She bit her tongue as long as she could. "How? How the hell could that have happened? You never even set eyes on the man until—"

"Oh, I knew you were seeing someone," said Kathleen. "Didn't know who. Heard his name but it rang no bells. Wasn't until, as you were about to say, that day in the cellar . . ." Her voice faded. She closed the lid of the tea caddy and gave the exterior an extra wipe with the dishcloth.

"What about it?" said Clara.

Kathleen did not respond.

Clara flung her hands in the air. "You can't just leave me hanging." She clapped her palms into a praying position and held them firm. Clara Kerrigan was a beggar now, desperation having usurped her pride. She didn't care. "Please, Mom, please."

Kathleen tossed the cloth onto the table, pushed her chair back and planked her hands on her thighs, a precursor to standing. When she was on her feet, Clara tried again, grabbing at the daffodil pattern on Kathleen's apron. A clutch of yellow in her hand, Clara tossed one more appeal. "Please."

Kathleen sighed. A relieved Clara released a wrinkle of daffodils from her fist and uncurled her fingers. Kathleen reclaimed her seat. "If you must know . . ."

Clara nodded vigorously.

Kathleen leaned back. "That day in the cellar dug up a memory," she said. "Years ago, when you were six, when I told you it wasn't safe for you in the dory, you went anyway, hiding your tiny self under Kevin's oilskins in the stern of the boat. Almost served you right that you went into the drink that day. Still, I realized later that it was better that you weren't home. Heaven knows what . . ."

A subdued Clara leaned in.

"It was your Patrick," Kathleen continued, "your Patrick, a young man then, who planted his frame in the doorway of the storeroom while I was there, putting up strawberry preserves."

Clara recoiled, drawing her arms around her body like a shield. Disbelief floated at the fringe of her and she eyed Kathleen, hoping for a retraction, knowing it wouldn't come. Yes, Clara had begged to know but hadn't expected the violence of knowing. Struck, fearing that the slightest movement might dispel shock and instill reality, she froze. Clara Kerrigan would rather die than deal with the brutality of truth.

In stillness, she sat, no idea how long. If time was moving at all, it wasn't in a way she could track. Eventually sounds filtered in—the shriek of a gull, the yip of a dog, the growl of a car in the road. As Clara's breathing stuttered, her notion of time still in question, a story hurtled into her mind and lodged itself there. Kathleen's story about strawberry jam. Kathleen's tale of the brutality of rape, couched for consumption in a metaphor of the theft of the strawberry jam from the storeroom. "No," Clara whispered, watching her own hand brush denial through the air. She stopped her hand, stared at it, pulled it back.

"Yes," said Kathleen. Her thin hands, veined like leaves, fingers trembling, put the partitions back into the mahogany tea caddy.

"No. Both of us? It can't be." Clara shook her head side to side, slowly, gently so as not to disrupt the protective bubble of shock that surrounded her. Shame lingered nearby, seeking entry. Clara Kerrigan remembered shame, escaping shame by fleeing Argentia to birth her daughter in Burin. And now? Not a sliver of space inside her for shame.

"It can be, and it is. That man is a predator. And we are his prey."

"Predator? Prey?" Clara echoed the words but could find no meaning in them.

"You better sit with that for a while. When you think you're ready for it, I'll tell you the rest." With that, Kathleen got up and headed to the door.

Clara found her voice. "The rest of what, Mom? The rest of what?"

Kathleen kept walking.

"Mom!" Clara screamed. She jumped to her feet and stopped Kathleen in the porch. Staring, begging yet again, "The rest of what, Mom?"

With a sigh, Kathleen yielded. "Your brother Jimmy was the child of that man Patrick." With that, she left the house.

Clara tried to follow but only got a couple of steps before a spate of coughing racked her body. She doubled over. As soon as she could straighten, she started toward the door again. Had to get away, away from Kathleen's words which hung like a storm cloud, had to run but the storm cloud claimed her. There was no getting away from the words raging inside her head. "Mom? Mom!" she called, pulling the door open, tearing through it. The coughing returned, throttling her. She yanked her handkerchief from her pocket and hawked a glob of spittle into it. When she raised the white square into her sight line, it was spotted with red. At that instant, life brought her to her knees, from there to the ground where she curled up and whimpered like a wounded animal. She couldn't stop the sound, couldn't move her body.

After a while, Kathleen returned, sidestepping Clara on her way to the house. "When you're ready," she said. Nothing more.

Clara lay still. Drops of rain spat at her, then a torrent poured over her. She felt nothing, stayed there feeling nothing until Kathleen came out and helped her to her feet.

Arms entwined, the two shuffled into the house.

CHAPTER 34

YEARS AGO, WHEN A DRENCHED six-year-old Clara had shivered her way home after a fall from the dory, she had perched limply on a straight-backed wooden chair beside the stove as Kathleen peeled off her wet clothes, towelled her dry, and redressed her. Today, in an eerie repeat of that scene, a sodden grown-up Clara occupied the same chair while Kathleen supplied the same care. Clara allowed the attention. When her body stopped quaking, while Kathleen combed fingers through Clara's wet hair, Clara came up with the strength to speak. "Mom, I have to tell you . . ." She lost the power of speech then. How could she tell?"

"Out with it," said Kathleen.

Clara took a deep breath and spit out the chunk of information lodged in her throat. "Patrick said if I stopped seeing him, he would shame Kate; he would tell her and anyone who would listen that Alphonse was her father." She gasped then, tears formed, and she waited for words from her mother who was suddenly still, ghostly still. No words came. Clara let out another gasp. "What are we going to do, Mom?" The question posed, her body set to coughing again, her fingers flying to her throat.

The response came from Kathleen in a string of words. "Well, I won't be washing the feet of the man who interfered with us, I'll tell you that much."

Clara's cough was active throughout the answer. Had she heard it right? "What did you just say, Mom?"

"I said that Jesus can keep his forgiveness to himself."

"Oh." Not the same words that Clara thought she had heard during her spate of coughing, but the same message. "Are you going to turn him in to the constabulary, Mom?"

Kathleen let out a snort. "Not likely. Right now, now that the rain has stopped, I'm going to pick me some flowers," said Kathleen.

"Flowers? What the hell are you talking about, Mom? You're not making any sense."

Kathleen opened the front door, the red door, pushed at the screen door and stuck one foot in it to keep it cracked. With a white-knuckled grip on its handle, she turned. "Oh, indeed I am making sense, Clara. The one time in my life that I didn't see what was in front of me was the time that Jimmy died. I waited too long then. I won't be waiting around while that Patrick threatens to shame my granddaughter. If he doesn't get his way, what will he threaten next? Is she safe? I don't think so." She curled her lip. "I didn't see what was coming with Jimmy, but I saw it with Kate and I didn't allow my husband to kill my granddaughter. I'm sure as hell not going to sit on my arse waiting for that slime Patrick to threaten her or harm her." She left, pulling the red door to, letting the screen door slam. Suddenly, she marched back in. "No, I'm not turning him into the constabulary. The only thing I'm going to turn that Patrick into is his own grave."

With that she was through the door again and gone.

KATHLEEN

CHAPTER 35

IT IS UNLEASHED, THE SEA.

The North Atlantic chooses its mission and muscles its path, demolishing vessels, engulfing shorelines, tossing boulders or crushing them to sand. Whatever it aims to do, it does. The sea wins. Always.

Such level of commitment is a scarcity among humankind. People talk of missions and maybe start out. Many yield. A rare few, like the living Kathleen, set sights and push through. It is in this that Kathleen Kerrigan is like water. She never gives up.

On a tassel of breeze, the ghost of me eases through the open kitchen window into the company of the corporeal version of myself. A commanding force, the living Kathleen, sitting ramrod straight opposite Clara whose posture is a mirror of her mother's. The round table between them holds at its centre a mound of dried lupines. I hover on the catch of the window's sash, straining for every possible word, wishing that, like pipe smoke, or wood smoke, or even cigarette smoke, I could slide inside Kathleen or Clara and indicate my presence with a tickle of a throat, a sting of a nostril, or a slight irritation of a lung. But no. Frustration arises, and the phrase "useless phantom" crosses my path for the umpteenth time. Yes, I know everything, yet I know nothing for I never know exactly what's coming or where I'm going. Sometimes I see the story through the eyes of Clara or Kate or even Kevin, rest his soul. Sometimes I land in scenes with Peter or Patrick or Robert, even the priest. Penance dictates that I narrate this journey as it unspools before me like some fitful dream and that, despite occasional flashes of foreshadowing, I reveal nothing before its time.

Dizzying pictures of the past ring around me now, images of a murdered baby, a shell-shocked killer, an unresponsive mother who couldn't save her son. It was when Alphonse schemed to kill her granddaughter that Kathleen pounced. And from that time on, at any cost, Kathleen would protect her family from any threat.

But protection requires proximity, and, on the day of the assault against Kate, the living Kathleen was miles away. In her absence, the phantom me tried to intervene, a futile endeavour and stabbing reminder of my place: outside, looking in. I hover in this kitchen, waiting for whispered words, but silence reigns.

At this point, the living Kathleen knows nothing about the boarding-house assault on Kate; she and Clara are focusing their energy on the destruction of someone who might bring Kate to harm. Patrick.

The still air between the two women is resolute, a full Amen.

CLARA

CHAPTER 36

Clara sat across from Kathleen at the table in the kitchen, a mound of dried lupines jacketing the middle of the oilcloth. The two were silent, settling in.

During the three days prior to this table meeting, a dazed Clara had repeatedly approached Kathleen. "Mom? Can you tell me once more?" she'd say, and Kathleen would oblige. When Clara couldn't make sense of the answers, she kept up the investigation, questioning her mother again and again, hoping each time for a different response. One too many queries, perhaps, because Kathleen finally flung her hands in the air and walked away. But Clara followed.

Kathleen swerved and locked gaze with Clara. "He wasn't, isn't, what he seems. He is a predator and stalker who invaded our lives, yours, mine, and has threatened to shame Kate," she said, her voice nail hard. "That's the truth of it, Clara." Kathleen's rigid stance held for an instant, then softened. Her next words came in a whisper. "I'm so sorry, Clara."

Clara sucked in a deep breath. She wanted to say something, anything, but nothing was available to her, so she ran, to her room, to her bed, and stayed there with only the swish of sea and the screech of gulls clawing at her walled-in disbelief. While light ceded to dark and back to light, Clara remained there, stunned. Eventually, the truth writhed its way in, bit by bit until it owned her. Clara could neither opt out of it nor stop the agony and anger accompanying it. Patrick's betrayal had been thorough, a clean cut. An obsessed man, he interfered with her mother and threatened her daughter.

Clara was often told she looked like her mother. *The face and eyes. The face and eyes. The face and eyes.* How many times had she heard that phrase? And now, it was not only in appearance, but also in experience, that they resembled each other. Victims, both. There should be consequences for Patrick.

Kathleen Kerrigan was no stranger to creating consequence. With Patrick's evil evident, and whatever the plan, Clara would stand alongside her mother. Clara would help, her pace poking and plodding, one foot, the other foot, banishing emotion as any allowance for it would spike misery in body and soul. She would do what needed to be done. The covenant Clara forged with her mother was unspoken.

Now, at the table with dried lupines at the ready, Clara placed a folded tea towel on the table and passed a second one to her mother. She sucked in a wheezing breath, ignoring the thrust of pain in her chest. "I'm sure Dulcie and Izzie will keep eyes on Kate."

A single nod. "I take it you now know what kind of man he is?"

"Yes."

"A long time, you were seeing him. Had you no clue at all about who you were tangled up with?" In concert, they spread the tea towels on the table.

Clara fisted a bunch of flowers and held them so tightly that her fingers blanched. She uncurled her fingers one at a time, dropping flowers onto her tea towel, scraping stubborn bits from her palm with the blade of a butter knife. Her heart picked up pace as images of Patrick flashed in her head. He had always been there, hadn't he? After the rum-running episode in St. Pierre, he showed up, again and again—in the doorway of her house in Argentia, near a lamppost on Duckworth in St. John's, in the ballroom of the Newfoundland Hotel.

"Are you after hearing me at all, Clara?" Kathleen's voice interrupted Clara's thoughts. "Did you ever notice what he was doing?"

Clara shook her head. She shuddered as she contemplated past concerns about Patrick. Specifically, about his loyalty. Not to *her*. Never that. About loyalty to his country. "I wondered, at times, if he was a saboteur. I mean, he showed up at the at the Knights of Columbus fire in St. John's, at the USS *Prairie* fire in Argentia." Clara stopped there. Truth was, she never cared if he supported the Allies or the Axis, only that he warmed her bed.

"Didn't it occur to you that he had showed up repeatedly, not because he was spying, but because he was stalking? He a feral cat, you an unsuspecting sparrow. And Kate? When he saw Kate, what did he say about Kate?"

Clara didn't have to dig far for the memory. "She's the image of you." Those were his exact words, curious then, crushing now. *How could he have threatened to shame Kate?* Tears formed in Clara's eyes, and she hauled her sleeve across her face. She sniffed. Pointless to dwell. "He had the gall to stop by work today," she said.

"He doesn't know that you're on to him?"

"Not an inkling."

"Saturday will be heavy with fog."

"You're predicting the weather now?"

"I think you should invite him over to help dig the cellar."

"Already dug, isn't it?" Clara asked the question and knew the answer before her words met air.

Kathleen nodded. "Used the pickaxe to create a hole. Got the stubborn rocks out and refilled the hole with loose dirt."

"To make digging easier for him?"

"To make killing easier for us."

Clara shifted uncomfortably in her chair. "But he has already seen the finished cellar. How can I justify needing to dig it up?"

Kathleen picked up a handful of seeds and dumped them onto her tea towel. "Just say that we women did a bad job of it. It needs a man's hand. Ego will win out." She sighed. "Too bad it's not winter. Easy to break an ice candle from the roof. Very sharp, ice candles."

The implication shivered through Clara. She didn't dwell. "Lupines taste bitter, don't they?"

Kathleen pointed at the sugar bowl on the sideboard. "Does he like his tea sweet?"

"Very."

"Good enough." From the chair beside her Kathleen picked up two rounded rocks, each the size of a baking potato, and passed one to Clara. The two set to work, dropping a fistful of dried flowers onto a tea towel, folding the towel, and pounding. Then they held the towels open in a V shape and shook gently, watching as fine powder snowed into a mixing bowl already half-filled with tealeaves. In silence they repeated the procedure. Fisting, pulverizing, and sprinkling.

The mahogany tea caddy sat on the daybed, its lid yawning in wait.

CHAPTER 37

When Clara spotted Patrick on the base, she buried her rage and aimed toward him, normality wrapped around her like a winter coat. So determined was she to present a blank expression that she had practised her chosen mien in a mirror for hours. That man could scrutinize her from now until the second coming. He would find nothing amiss.

After making eye contact, she dispensed the usual pleasantries about health and weather. A break in the conversation afforded an opportunity and Clara pounced. "You want to stop by the house tomorrow?" she asked. "Mom and I need help digging the cellar."

A quizzical look came over him. He raised his eyebrows. "Come to your senses, have you?"

Couldn't blame him for the doubt he was blinking at her. But without a hiccup, Clara continued. "Yes, I guess I have. The truth is that Mom and I need help with the cellar. It was finished, but there's dampness in there, mould on the vegetables. Needs redoing. My mother is nothing if not stubborn. Tried to do the job herself but sprained an ankle. Limping now."

Line baited, Clara waited. She'd never asked him for help before. He'd offered to do some wall repairs—more insisted than offered—and he had handled a hammer with the ease of a hired gun. But she had never asked.

Patrick stared at her for a few seconds more. He raised his shoulders to his ears and dropped them. "Tomorrow's Saturday. I can hike that way. Sure. Why not?"

"Lovely. Thank you." Clara stared as he adjusted his sod cap to cover his eyes. He turned, waved, went off to wherever. Seemed to her that he was always in some type of get up, a disguise perhaps—fisherman, longshoreman, chauffeur. Interesting that the tables had turned, that now she was the one in disguise.

The day, as foretold by her mother, was heavy with fog. Easy to predict, Clara knew, in a place that had fog most of the year. On days like this, you couldn't see your hand in front of your face for the fog.

Clara waited beside the house until a crunch of gravel announced Patrick's approach. On tiptoe, she edged toward him, all the while remembering winter mornings as a child when the floors were freezing, when she flitted on butterfly toes from bed to dresser. There he was, the shape of him blurred by the blessing of fog. She watched him knock at the front door and wait to be admitted, the action of one who lived *in* the community but was not *of* the community. Locals would just crack the back door and call, "Anybody in?" A true come-from-away, Patrick. The only time he did charge through the door was on the day of the USS *Prairie* fire. All man then, rescuing her. Runnels of disdain dripped inside her as she watched him now, she the stalker, he the prey. The corner of her lip tugged in contempt. She caught it, stopped it. No time for betrayal of intent. She scooped up a fistful of dirt and spread it on her apron. A few strands of hair drifted over her face. Satisfied that surface met scheme, she spoke. "Patrick!"

He recoiled. "You scared me."

Clara concealed a smirk, masked it with a smile. "We've started already," she said, waving the shovel she was holding. "Happy to get you a cup of tea. Fog brings a chill. Need to warm up your bones."

He descended the front steps and joined her. "Always a cup of tea at the ready on this island," he said.

"Ready and waiting," said Clara. "Mom just made tea, and I'll get you some." She dropped her shovel and headed for the house. In the kitchen, she looked at the teapots on the table. Brown Bettys. One large, one small. "Use the small one," Mom had said, twice. Clara hedged for a minute, staring at the tea caddy, her gift to her mother. She lifted the mahogany lid. The compartments, all but one, overflowed with tea leaves. The one was empty, its leaves having been steeped. She closed the lid of the caddy and patted the top affectionately. She loved mahogany, the richness of it, the colour of it, and now the purpose of it. With a sigh and using the small teapot, she poured the piping hot tea, added a splash of milk and three teaspoons of sugar, then an extra dash, an afterthought, for good measure. *Was she ready?* She thought so but when she lifted the tea, the cup danced against the saucer. No choice but to set it back down. A few deep breaths calmed her hammering heart. She held her hand up, into her line of vision and splayed her trembling fingers. Only when the shaking subsided, did she head toward the root cellar to meet up with Patrick. "Not a drop spilled," she said as she passed him his cup.

"Where is your tea?" he asked.

"Had some just before you arrived," she said quickly, calmly. But she was on tenterhooks. *Just drink it, damn you!* How she wanted to heave words from the rough side of her tongue, but she snapped her mouth closed and opened door of the cellar. "Mom," she called, "Patrick is here."

"Give the man a cup of tea before you puts him to work," called Kathleen.

"Already done, Mrs. Kerrigan," said Patrick. "And a lovely cup of tea it is."

A relieved Clara reclaimed her shovel. "You better drain that cup so we can get a move on."

He nodded and obliged. "I'll just visit your outhouse first."

"Put the cup down there," Clara said, pointing to protruding stone with a flat surface. Patrick positioned the cup.

And Clara waited, the enormity of the upcoming deed rolled in a ball of sweat down her back. Certainly, she was slicing a chunk out of her soul. Would she ever regain it? *Do I even care?*

He returned, wiping his brow with the sleeve of his shirt. "Warm, all of a sudden," he said. He approached the cellar. A long-handled shovel sat in the doorway. Waving away flies, he picked up the shovel.

The day was grey, and the cellar was dark but a thin rectangular bar of light from the door extended across the dirt floor. Inside Kathleen, who was sitting on a stool, got stiffly to her feet. Around her three kerosene lamps blazed and Clara carried in a fourth she'd retrieved from outside the cellar.

Patrick stepped up to where Kathleen was working. "Don't know how you managed to get this digging started, Mrs. Kerrigan. How did you get hurt?"

"Doesn't take much when you get to be my age." Kathleen leaned heavily to one side, rounding her shoulders as she did so. "A slip of the foot and a fall from the porch."

"They say aging is not for the faint of heart."

"They got that right," said Kathleen.

Clara fussed over her lantern, a deliberate stall, turning the knob again and again under the guise of lengthening the wick for easier lighting. With Kathleen on one side and Clara on the other, Patrick leaned over, began to dig. Clara lit her lamp. Kathleen put down her cane, picked up a shovel. Minutes later, Patrick faltered.

"You doing okay?" asked Clara. He righted himself and, with a wave of a hand, protested weakness. Then he wiped drool from the corner of his mouth. Clara offered no more concern. *All man for sure, this one.* He continued shovelling for quite some time. Six feet worth of time. A mound of dirt grew beside the hole. He climbed out and then clutched his stomach. "Queasy," he said. "Dizzy too." He turned to Clara. "Damn. What was in that tea, Clara?" His tone was jocular but when she held up the lantern to make her every facial detail perceptible to him, she revealed the sneer that she had managed to conceal until this very moment. Confusion filled his face and, on its heels, came clarity. Just a moment of clarity, one in which he had no time to act. The air whooshed as Kathleen swung a shovel that struck Patrick in the back of the head. He dropped to his knees beside the mound of dirt. "Clara?" he uttered. She leaned down, lamp in hand, and stared into his usually proud eyes that were now wide with fear. Something else in them too, a pleading look. He had never begged her for anything before. Probably never begged anyone for anything. She sniffed and stepped back.

Hand on his head, Patrick struggled to get from kneeling to standing. The effort felled him. He lay, helpless, cushioned by a mound of dirt. With a practised move, Kathleen wrenched a knife from a nearby bin, the handle of which she had wrapped in a cabbage leaf. She raised it, plunged it, and Patrick let out a gasp. She pulled the knife back and was about to repeat the action, but Clara gripped her arm. "There's no need, Mom."

Kathleen pulled free, plunged the knife to the hilt and withdrew it. She fell back, panting, blood dripping onto her apron.

No movement from Patrick now.

"That's enough, Mom." Clara stooped to pry the knife from her mother's hand.

"I had to be sure," said Kathleen as she relinquished the weapon. "Help me get him into the hole."

They dropped to their knees and pushed at the dead weight until it gave way and rolled in. Eerily satisfied, Clara sat back on her heels.

"Get the lye," said Kathleen, still panting.

Clara scrambled to her feet. She reached for the lye, one bag, then the other, and plopped them beside the grave. With the bloodied knife, she slit them and slid the weapon back to Kathleen. Hefting one bag, then the other, Clara tipped until lye powdered the body and clouded the air. She sneezed. "Burns the throat, that stuff." The scraping of shovels was the only sound as they returned the mound of dirt to the hole Patrick had dug for himself.

"Knife to the sea?" asked Clara a little while later. She'd done that once before, fed a murder weapon to the Atlantic.

"Goes without saying," replied Kathleen, tossing aside the bloodied knife.

As they stood in the light of the doorway, Clara caught sight of blood spatter on her mother's apron. "You'll have to burn that apron, Mom," said Clara. "Likely the dress too."

Kathleen nodded. "Let's go stoke the stove."

CHAPTER 38

A FULL WEEK PASSED, DURING which Kathleen and Clara leaned ears to the community, checking the wind for rumours that they themselves had set in motion, rumours about Patrick McMurty being a spy, rumours that they intended to spread. One strategy would be to drop an earful to the telephone operator, a well-known repeater of everything she overheard. Another to Father Mahony, who had gossiped to Clara about his wayward curate. Today they would enlist his help.

Although it was customary to attend confession on Saturday before taking part in the sacrament of communion at Sunday Mass, Clara and Kathleen ignored the Saturday bit and attended Sunday Mass anyway. Throughout the hour-long service, they recited their Latin prayers and lined up for communion like everybody else. Once the service was over, they lingered at the back of the church. "I'm not sure about this, Mom," whispered Clara.

"In for a penny, in for a pound," replied Kathleen, elbowing Clara in the ribs. "There's Father Mahony ." Kathleen lifted her hand and beckoned him. He looked at them and then glanced over his shoulder, ostensibly to see who it was Kathleen was waggling a finger at.

"He's not going to like it one little bit, you bidding him," whispered Clara.

"Ssh." Kathleen gestured to the priest again.

Father Mahony put his hands on his hips and gave them a disapproving stare. Then he shrugged and ambled down the aisle toward them. "The likes of ye, summoning the priest," he said, wearing a grin that told Clara she need not concern herself. "How are ye doing today, ladies?"

"We're doing fine, Father, just fine," said Kathleen. "Trouble with the cellar when the damp had at it. Recently re-dug it and got the floor flattened and gravelled. It's about time too. Last year we had a time of it what with the critters tunneling up through the dirt. Isn't that right, Clara?"

"Indeed it is. Couldn't find enough rat traps. No end to the cabbages gnawed to shreds." Clara cleared her throat as planned. Before she could get out the prearranged cough, Father Mahony jumped in.

"Why don't I have some of the b'ys come and cement yer cellar for ye?" he said. "Won't have to worry about the rodents then."

Taken aback by the offer, Clara stood silent. Kathleen would handle this.

Sure enough, Kathleen did. "Lovely of you to say, Father, but we don't need builders coming around. Wouldn't mind a couple of bags of cement though. Clara and I can manage mixing and spreading. We'll find a two-by-four to level the floor, won't we, Clara?"

A wide-eyed Clara nodded. Kathleen nudged her in the ribs, a cue. Clara let a cough claw its way out of her chest. She pulled a handkerchief from her pocket and hacked into it.

Father Mahony took a step back. "That cough doesn't sound good, my child," he said. "Perhaps you're just brewing a cold, but you can't be too careful these days. You need to get yourself over to the Placentia hospital for a chest X-ray. Tuberculosis is everywhere."

Clara nodded. The cough persisted. The priest continued."Cement will be at your back door later today. Anything else I can do for you this fine morning?"

"Yes, Father," said Kathleen, her voice calm, "I was wondering if we need to still be worried about spies? Just the other day, I heard that a man was taken away when the powers that be discovered a radio hidden in his bedroom wall? In St. John's, mind you!" Clara's skin tingled in amazement at her mom's ability to intone a proper amount of shock.

"Yes, yes," said Father Mahony. "I heard that very thing, from our very own telephone operator, herself as good a soul as ever walked the earth. If there was a spy, and he's on the run, you won't see him again. He'd better be long gone before the military has at him. They shoot spies, you know." Father Mahony folded his arms.

Clara let her gaze wander as she absorbed her contentment. The telephone operator had done what they had expected.

"I heard it was that Patrick McMurty, Father," said Kathleen. "I haven't seen any sign of him this long while."

Clara caught her second cue and stopped her cough. "Patrick McMurty, Mom?" said Clara. "But I saw him myself on the base a few weeks back. Surely be to goodness, there's been a mistake!"

The priest shook his head slowly. "A mistake? Maybe. Hard to know. I haven't seen hide nor hair of him lately."

"Some shockin'," said Kathleen. Clara offered a slow nod.

"Not surprising to me, sadly enough," said the priest. "Born in a workhouse in England, Patrick was. A dreadful place where few youngsters lived past the age of four. Amazing he made it out of there at all, pour soul."

Clara winced. *Poor soul, my arse.* Patrick had threatened Kate. Pain gored Clara like barbed wire, compounding as she thought of her part in all of it. Father Mahony stared her in the face and her nerves danced. Was he on the edge of recall? Was he remembering the long-ago riot in St. John's, the day when she lied to him about her presence in the unruly crowd? Had he seen her with Patrick that day?

Father Mahony cleared his throat. He shrugged as he moved past the moment. Perhaps he hadn't grasped the memory after all. Relieved, Clara took deep breath and glanced at Kathleen, instantly mirroring her mother's stone face.

"Anyway," the priest continued, "I met Patrick when I said Mass at His Majesty's Penitentiary. A pleasant front, he put on. Voice of a gentleman. After his stint in prison, he showed up at my door in Argentia, young then, looking for a handout, maybe a fresh start. Didn't do much, a come-day-go-day-God-send-Sunday fellow. Came back years later. Not lazy this time though. As good as gold to the people of the parish." He let out a long sigh.

"Either he's back in His Majesty's Penitentiary or on his way to England. If he is a spy, well, he backed the wrong side."

"A sad state of affairs," said Kathleen.

"To be sure." The priest nodded. "Maybe you can light a candle for Patrick while you are lighting one for your dear, departed Alphonse then, Kathleen?"

"Yes, Father, I'll do just that. Right this minute. After that, we're off home for a bit of bread-making."

"Wouldn't happen to be making raisin bread, would you now?" He patted his stomach. "I'm partial to a bit of homemade raisin bread with a pat or two of butter."

"Well, we'll make that very thing for you. Cement at our door, and raisin bread at yours!" Kathleen said.

"You're a grand woman, Kathleen Kerrigan," said Father Mahony with a smile.

"Happy to oblige," responded Kathleen as she took her leave. With Clara on her heels, she headed down the aisle of the church and stopped in front of the votive candles. As she dropped pennies into the donation box, she turned and smiled at Clara. Clara smiled back. They were in the clear. The deed done and buried. Literally.

Clara recalled the Argentia church where she first met Patrick, where she had lit a candle to cover her deeds. And now? At the Freshwater church, at the strike of a match, after a series of sins, she'd come full circle. "Do you think that Patrick could have been a spy, Mom?" she said in a respectful whisper.

"We talked about this. No evidence. But he spied on the women in this family, no doubt about that, stalking and luring."

Clara shuddered as she lit a candle, her breath stuttered, the flame flickered in response. The pat of her mother's hand on her own then. Comforting. "Best leave well enough alone there," whispered Kathleen. "The world belongs to the men, the warmongers, Clara. Women just live in it. Whether he was a spy or not doesn't matter now. What does matter is that the possibility suits our purpose."

"That being that Kate is safe."

"Kate's safety being my purpose in life."

Clara sensed an opportunity and rose to it. "Shouldn't we go to town right away to check on her?"

Kathleen shook her head. "Not yet, my darlin'. We need to lay the cement in the cellar, to let it settle, to let things settle. With the demon done in, Kate's safety is guaranteed. Dulcie will care for her. Better for us to bide time here for a while."

"I've been biding time for nearly twenty years," said Clara. Disappointment owned her, emerging as a groan.

"Clara, nobody's denying you here. We'll go to visit when the time is right." With a softer tone, she added, "If you were faking that cough back there, fine. If not, you need a chest X-Ray just like Father Mahony said."

Clara, her throat on fire, nodded. She stifled the urge to cough.

KATE

CHAPTER 39

IT TOOK A LONG TIME for Kate to come back to herself. She couldn't consider the truth, couldn't allow for it at all. What she could allow for was vigilance, her ears tuned for a squeak in a floorboard or footfall in the hallway. *What if he comes back?* Time passed in a nervous blur, everything a threat—rain knocking at her window, shadows sliding past her door. When she recognized footsteps and murmurings in the hallway as those of Dulcie, Izzie, and Rosemary, she allowed herself a bit of ease: they were here; she was safe. Occasionally, the doorknob whined as one of the three twisted it, but Kate kept the door locked the door against all good intentions. When footsteps receded, she crept from the bed and cracked open the door to retrieve her meal trays. Other than that, she wasn't ready to surface, not with facts jabbing her, taunting her. Shame crept like body lice. Dirty all over.

For unending hours, she burrowed into bed hugging her pillow while details of the attack ran on a loop—an unstoppable hammering accompanied by a heft of shame. The shock of physical assault was a deep wound, clinging like a scab which a single negative thought would shred so it bled anew. Shackled to shame: why hadn't she paid attention to her environment, to potential danger in her environment?

Day after day, Kate lay in bed, staring at the ceiling, fingering the tiny beads left to her by Kevin, reciting the rosary, not so much as praying but keeping her mind busy, preventing it from going into the dark and taking her soul along with it. Whenever she dared crack open the door and peek down the hallway, anxiety rattled her. A necessity, trips to the bathroom, but not until the hall was all clear. She would advance then, in sock-footed silence, her eyes cast low, her soul clinging to the goal of invisibility.

After a while, she got braver. Still, it was plodding, her re-entrance to the world. A walk downstairs, a trip downtown, and chores at the boarding house when no one was around. A slow-motion summer, the height of which was Victory in Japan Day on August 15.

On that very morning, on her way to the bathroom, her drawstring bag of toiletries in hand, Kate passed Granny Grace in the hallway. Kate tried to shuffle past without interaction, but Granny Grace had other ideas.

"Haven't seen you in a dog's age," she said. "Need to get out and about a bit more, you do." She eyed Kate up and down and offered another unsolicited opinion. "You'll never get a husband if you keep putting on weight," she said and then tutted her way down the stairs.

Kate took umbrage to the comment about her weight. She hadn't gained weight, had she? She paused and pondered. In a lightbulb moment, she hightailed it back to her room and headed straight for the calendar. Toiletries thumped to the floor as she flicked calendar pages back and forth. *Sweet Heart of Jesus, Mary, and Joseph.* She heard a voice from the hallway. Izzie was calling her. Kate wanted to call back. *Please come in. Please come in.* Try as she might, Kate could not get those thoughts into words. But then . . . a tap on the door, a jangle of keys, and a bounce in Izzie's step as she entered. "Good morning," she said. "It's a blustery day today, Kate."

Kate sighed in relief that Izzie was here. But she couldn't match Izzie's cheerfulness: there was no today, only one long yesterday that started on VE Day, a yesterday that gripped her thoughts and seared her soul. The bruises that had bloomed on her arms, a bouquet of purple fingerprints, were long gone, faded to red and yellow and then to nothingness, just like the colours of his handprint on her face. But ever present was the guilt that bore down, locking her shoulders into a slump: there was no lifting them. Izzie nattered on but Kate didn't, couldn't, catch the gist of it, overwhelmed as she was with thoughts of an unbearably long summer and raw wounds. A sudden fear cropped up. "Izzie," she said, slicing into Izzie's rambling.

Instantly silenced, Izzie removed her glasses, pulled up a chair, the only chair, and leaned in. "I'm here."

"I'm scared, Izzie."

Izzie slid her glasses into her apron pocket. "You're safe now," she said, a puzzled look on her face. "He's never coming back, you know."

"I know that. At least, I think I do."

"Well, what then?" Izzie crinkled her nose and placed a hand on Kate's wrist.

Kate registered the concerned look, the gentle touch. "I just saw Granny Grace . . ." She couldn't complete the sentence.

"What about her?" said Izzie.

Kate shook her head and shook off Izzie's hand.

Izzie yielded, hands up, palms out. "Whenever you're ready. I'll wait."

After a time, Kate pushed at the silence, her voice a whisper. "Izzie..."

"Yes?" Izzie wiped her hands on her apron.

The subdued sound of Westminster Chimes rose from the first floor, the grandfather clock marking the quarter hour. Sighing, Kate dropped her head into her free hand. She sat like that until the clock chimed again, the full melody this time. She counted as it marked the hour, waited until the last chime faded. Ten o'clock. She looked up. "Izzie," she said," I haven't had my visitor since before that day."

Izzie, face baffled, then aware, let out a breath and with it the words, "Jesus God!" She sat motionless.

Kate waited.

Izzie pulled away, got up, paced the room, sat, and repeated the procedure. "Have you told anyone else?"

"Only occurred to me this morning, when Granny Grace told me I was gaining weight, to count the days," Kate said. "I had no intention of telling anyone, but now I don't have much of a choice. God help me, I have to tell Clara, Nanny too. I haven't seen hide nor hair of them in so long, but I have to tell them."

Izzie put her glasses on, straightened her bowtie, and took to pacing again. "Not yet you don't. You've got time." She stopped and counted on her fingers. "June, July, August." She was back to pacing. "Not a lot of time before it becomes too obvious though." Then she halted, still as a statue.

Kate lifted her head. *Does Izzie have an idea, a solution?*

Izzie pivoted in slow motion. Her eyes, lit with care, met Kate's. "Maybe you want to tell Dulcie?" Izzie said, her voice almost a whisper.

When Kate teared up, Izzie rushed to her, sat gingerly beside her. "Oh, don't cry, Katie." Izzie brushed her fingers through Kate's hair. "We can figure this out ourselves if that's what you want."

Kate reached for Izzie's hand. "I don't know, Izzie," she said, lacing her fingers with Izzie's, clinging tightly.

"I know it's hard. I just thought that, since Dulcie's loved you your whole life . . ."

"She certainly has." Kate sucked in a deep breath and pushed it out bit by bit. A brisk nod marked her decision. "Can you get Dulcie here now before I change my mind?"

"Dulcie will fly up the stairs if you need her. But you don't have to do this right now. You can bide your time."

"Until time runs out?" Kate released Izzie's hand, sat upright and swung her legs over the side of the bed. Izzie stepped aside and Kate stood. "Nothing gets by Dulcie," said Kate. "I wouldn't be surprised if she knows already." In a second, Kate was at the door and through the door and on the stairs at full tilt. She caught sight of Dulcie, climbing. Kate halted, then resumed at a slow pace, coming face to face with Dulcie on the landing. Dulcie's eyes questioned. Kate's responded with tears.

"Whatever it is, me darlin', I'm here," said Dulcie as she took Kate's arm and led her back up the stairs to her room.

Izzie was still standing beside the bed. "I'm guessing you two want some privacy."

Dulcie looked to Kate who shook her head. "No such thing now at all, Izzie," said Dulcie. "Get a chair from across the hall."

With everyone seated, Dulcie began. "Some things you hangs out in the wind, some things you doesn't. I'm guessing it's time for you to release what ails you."

So Kate released what she knew to be true.

Dulcie leaned back in her chair. "Your family will have to know about this," she said, her voice strained, no sign of its usual lilt.

Kate shook her head vehemently. "I don't want to think about it, but I know you're right."

"Would you like me to tell Clara and Kathleen?" Dulcie asked

"You?" A single word, loaded with anticipation. Kate held her breath.

Dulcie nodded. "Yes, me."

Kate jumped up, wrapped her arms around Dulcie and dispensed a cascade of thank-yous.

"It's fine, me darlin'," said Dulcie. A long hug and heartfelt reassurances from Dulcie were salve to Kate's soul. "I'm long overdue for a visit anyway," continued Dulcie, "so I will go to Freshwater, just for a day. I needs to see for myself how the people in the parish are managing things. In the meantime, you two can stay here and help Rosemary with the running of the place."

Izzie looked like a bubble about to burst. "Absolutely. Whatever it takes."

"You're a good one, Izzie," said Dulcie with a relieved sigh. "The both of ye just make sure the chores are done—dishes, dusting, mopping and the like. And for the love of the Lord, if I'm not back in time, see to it that Granny Grace has whisky in her teacup. If she unsnaps that brown handbag of hers and starts pulling out rosary beads and holy cards, pay heed. She'll be bringing out a silver hip flask too and setting it down in front of you. That's a cue for a refill."

Despite a swirl of shock and confusion, Kate managed a hint of a smile. She was still here. And she was not alone.

CLARA

CHAPTER 40

Clara adjusted the kitchen curtains. The screen door whined, the doorknob squeaked, and a voice called out. "Anybody in?"

Clara bounded across the kitchen, arms and smile wide, ready to greet Dulcie in the porch. "Dulcie! So good to see you." She reached for a hug, but Dulcie brushed past her.

"Where's Kathleen?" Dulcie asked. "In the kitchen? I needs to see the both of ye." She hurried off.

Concerned, Clara took a step back. Something was off here. Something was definitely off. When Dulcie winged toward the kitchen, Clara trailed her. When Dulcie hugged the daylights out of Kathleen, Clara waited. When Kathleen waved her away, Clara wilted. Muttering something about work to do outside, she headed through the back door, which she left ajar, hoping Mom or Dulcie would call her back at any second. Or that at least she could eavesdrop.

"I'm sorry to bring this to you, Kathleen, but—" Abruptly, Dulcie stopped talking. "Where the hell did Clara get off too?" She went to the door.

Included again, Clara slid past Dulcie into the house, happy to eliminate the noise aback of her—the thump of the clothes on the line in the wind and the scream of the gulls that rose up from the shore. She wouldn't have been able to hear a word.

Dulcie paused at the door and a blast of wind whipped her hair into loose spirals. With a brush of her hand, she stuck a strand behind her ear. "Great day on clothes," she said.

The phrase ripped open a curtain in Clara's memory. Years ago, on a windy day in Argentia, Dulcie had used that phrase. She had overheard Clara's secret in the confessional and had then vowed not to hang Clara's secret out for everyone to hear. "You going to hang something out in the wind today, Dulcie?"

Dulcie made eye contact. "Some things you do," she said and shrugged.

Clara grabbed Dulcie's arm. "What's going on, Dulcie?"

"Not for me to say to you alone." Dulcie dropped her eyes to Clara's hand. "The words I've got are for you and Kathleen."

Clara didn't move.

Dulcie met her glance again. "In the name of all that's holy, will ya let go of me arm?"

Clara released her grip but still stood there.

"Clara," said Dulcie, "follow me into the kitchen." When Clara still didn't move, Dulcie grabbed her by the elbow and pulled her along.

Seated at the kitchen table, a place for telling secrets and launching plans, Dulcie hung out the laundry, all the details of Kate's situation, the sailor, forever gone, the consequences, ever present. At the end of the revealing, Clara and her mom sat there stunned, exchanging knowing glances. They had done what they had felt necessary to protect Kate but while they were looking in one direction, evil showed up in another. Devasting to Clara, the idea that, as much as they tried, they could not shelter Kate forever.

Kathleen spoke. "You got the results of your X-ray yet, Clara?"

"All good," said Clara, the lie blackening the very heart and soul of herself. When the X-ray revealed a spot on her lung, Clara denied the truth in it, even through times when fatigue felled her and breathing failed her. She reassured herself with the knowledge that tuberculosis was difficult to spread. She would take no risks; she would not get too close Kate. But she'd be damned if she would lose an opportunity to see her.

"We're going to St. John's," said Kathleen.

"Indeed we are," Clara responded, her thoughts turning to filling her suitcase with extra underclothes that could provide bulk to her thinning body.

KATE

CHAPTER 41

Kate lay in her bed face to the wall, staring at the faded pink flowers on the wallpaper. Wind walloped the boarding house which responded in a cacophony of creaks and groans and judders. *No shortage of wind on this godforsaken island.* Certainly gave a ghostly quality to this old house.

The door to her room opened. Not a sound to it, its usual whine muted by bluster of wind. It was the accompanying draught that cued Kate, shivered through her. She turned.

"Your grandmother is here," said Izzie.

Nanny?

Izzie tugged at the quilt that enveloped Kate. "Get yourself up."

Before Kate could comply, the door to her room flew open, and Nanny strode in and sat on her bed. "I'm here, child."

In a spurt of energy, Kate threw her arms around Nanny and held tight. Tears came, a stockpile of them tumbling down her face. The salt tang on her lips triggered sobs.

"Get her a handkerchief," Kathleen said, waving a hand in Izzie's direction.

Izzie obliged, retrieving not one, but two crisply ironed handkerchiefs from the top drawer of Kate's dresser. "There you go," Izzie said as she deposited the handkerchiefs on the bed and headed toward the door.

"Don't leave, Izzie," said Kathleen. "What I have to say here today is for your ears too."

"Shouldn't I go downstairs to check on—" Izzie indicated the door.

"No need."

Shrugging, Izzie pulled the only chair in the room up to the bed and waited alongside Kathleen while Kate bawled through two handkerchiefs. Izzie repeated the trip to the dresser, bringing two more. Kate blubbered on and halted with a hiccup.

"Are you ready to talk now?" Kathleen asked. "Or at least to hear me out?"

Kate nodded. "I'll listen."

"Good enough then. Dulcie came to see us in Freshwater. She told everything. I suppose I would have known as soon as I set eyes on you that you had something under your apron. As for the situation, I'm giving you my two cents about all of this. Schooled, I am, having lived through this myself. First, you need to know that your Aunt Clara—"

"I don't want to be knowing nothing about *Aunt* Clara. Her and her lies. I got enough to worry about." Kate sniffled, stopping when Nanny placed a hand on her arm.

"Understandable that you feel that way but maybe you'll come to see differently. Time tends to heal all troubles."

The door to the room suddenly opened a crack. Kate flinched. "Is there somebody in the hallway?"

"No," said Nanny who immediately turned to Izzie. "Please close the door."

Izzie obliged and returned to her chair. Quiet until now, she reached her hand and brushed a strand of hair from Kate's face. Kate melted into the gesture. "Don't be too kind to me, Izzie," she said, eyes brimming.

"How can I be anything but?" Izzie replied, leaning closer.

Kate, prickled by the scrutiny of Nanny's gaze, pulled back. What words of explanation could she offer Nanny here? There were none. It was too new. It was too sacred. She was too scared.

"I got no judgement about what's going on here," Nanny said, looking from Kate to Izzie. She pointed a finger, wagged it back and forth between them. "I have to say you're not making life easy for yourself, but you two should do what you want, whether or not the world agrees." Another pause.

Kate's response was to touch Izzie's hand, a gentle pat. "Izzie is my friend."

"Oh, she's more than that now, isn't she? As I said, it's up to the two of you what you do."

How the hell did Nanny know what Kate herself was not sure of? More puzzling, how was her nanny so accepting? Staggered, Kate blinked at Izzie who merely shrugged.

"I'm on the declining side of life now," said Nanny, "and God knows I've committed my share of sins against the Church. Who am I to judge what's what?"

This stilled Kate. Should she pry into Nanny's 'sins against the Church'? Kate shrugged that idea off. It was Clara she wanted to lay into, not Nanny. But in the absence of Clara, Nanny would have to do. "Clara lied to me my whole life." She dropped the statement calmly enough, but when silence descended around it, and loitered, her fury flamed like a tinderbox. "Do you have any idea what it's like to find out your mother is not your mother, that your real mother lied to you your whole life?"

"Sometimes lies have their place," said Nanny, no hesitation this time. She immediately sucked in a breath. "Her name was Kathleen, just like you."

Kate fell back, defeated. "Oh, for the love of Christ! Settle in, Izzie," she said, voice sodden with scorn.

"Settle in for what?" Izzie crinkled her nose, and her glasses slid. She adjusted them.

"We're about to hear a story and there's no getting out of it. Isn't that right, Nanny?"

"Her name was Kathleen, just like you," said Nanny.

"See?" said Kate to Izzie. "Told you."

Nanny cleared her throat. "And she had a secret, just like you." Then Nanny told a story of the darkness of a storeroom and the theft of strawberry jam, a story which Kate had heard before, the memory of the telling as easy to retrieve as a word from a dictionary. A mere child at the time, Kate had asked if Nanny got her strawberry jam back and Nanny had replied that some things you lose you never get back. Kate took the story for what it was, the tale of a stranger stealing all the jam in the storeroom. But that was then. When she was little. When she knew only of the sweetness of jam, nothing of the criminal in man. Now in the depths of recall, she longed to cling to her childhood understanding. Might as well try to grasp the wind. The crux of the story hit like a slap. She cringed. *Nanny's story is my story too.* She waited until Nanny's words fell away. She leaned in, her hands on Nanny's arms. "It happened to me, Nanny. The same story you told about the strawberry jam. It happened to me and there's no getting myself back."

"It's not your fault, Kate. Life is awash with monsters and one of them, a soulless predator, showed up here. It is not your fault."

Kate nodded because that was what was expected, not because she felt blameless.

"So, you know that what you and I have in common is far more than the theft."

Kate nodded again. "Yes," she said, patting her stomach. "Another life."

Kathleen reached a hand, held Kate's chin, and stared directly into her eyes. "You have to know that it doesn't matter how that life is created. A child is innocent and deserves love."

"Love?" said Kate, shaking her head. "How can I?"

"The love will come. And—" Nanny stopped.

Kate searched her grandmother's face which glowed like that of the Virgin Mary on a prayer card. "Is there something else you want to tell me, Nanny? Something you need to tell me about loving a child?" she asked, just that, nothing more. Nanny remained quiet. Kate waited.

Izzie sat there in the hush until Nanny turned to her and gave her a quick nod. Out of the corner of her eye, Kate watched Izzie return her chair to its place and then pad across the floor. The door opened. The door closed. A slight breeze. No click of the lock.

It was as silent as snow until Nanny released a perceptible sigh. "No, darlin'. There's nothing else," she whispered. "I'm so sorry, Kate."

Kate drew Nanny close again. The years between them collapsed like the folds of an accordion as the oneness of their fates filtered in, a linking which lingered. Kate, cushioned from pain at least temporarily, was content to hold and be held forever. But this forever was short-lived.

The door flung open, banging into the wall behind it. Their embrace broken, Kate and Kathleen spun toward a fuming Clara, standing in the doorway, using her well-placed, black-laced shoe to stop the door from slamming back at her.

"How dare you?" Clara eyed Nanny. "After all this time telling me to lie to her, you told her? Why couldn't you leave well enough alone?"

"Clara, there's no need—"

"Yes, there is need, Mom," Clara said, arms flailing. "I'm not having it anymore. My whole life I've lived with lies. Lies from Alphonse, lies from Robert, lies from Patrick. 'Don't tell her,' you said." She pointed an accusing finger.

Nanny scrambled to her feet. Kate watched, bewildered, as Nanny paced, sat, rose, and paced again.

"I told her nothing," said Nanny, head down, eyes to the floor, still walking.

Clara drew closer. "Mom, I heard her ask. I heard you whispering. You told her."

Kathleen shook her head.

Kate stared from one to the other. "For heaven's sake. Whatever it is, out with it. One of ye!"

Nanny sat. Grasping Kate's hand, staring deep into her eyes, she said, "Yes, you and I were both robbed, both left with child." Nanny's eyes flickered with uncertainty. "But Clara . . ." she said and paused.

"Nanny?" Kate prompted but got no further.

Clara abruptly heaved her whole body toward them, landing on her knees at Kathleen's side, coming down with a force that shifted the bed and rattled Kate whose flight instinct kicked in. But there was no time to flee, no way off this bed before the storm broke.

"Dear God in heaven, Mom," Clara said. Kate watched Clara place her hands on Nanny's arm. "Pleeeease, Mom," implored Clara.

But Nanny brushed her off like a house fly and ploughed onward. "Clara was robbed too. By her own father. By Alphonse." She nodded.

Clara dropped her head into her hands.

Nanny wasn't finished. "Alphonse is your father too, Kate."

Kate couldn't move. Her heart had snagged like a sweater stopped by a nail. She would fall if she could, but paralysis owned her. She couldn't breathe. She wanted to stay here, in a vacuum devoid of pain, but a forceful thump, the fist of her grandmother between her shoulder blades, jump-started her heart. Kate's breathing followed suit. As she gulped in air, her heart rate accelerated and intensified until it boomed. Light pierced her eyes, pained her eyes, and she squeezed them shut. Then she was spinning, spinning, her whole body tossed like a lump of driftwood in a raging sea. Memories flashed and sea salt stung her nose. And the air Kate was trying to gulp wasn't air at all but sea water. Kate was drowning, swept up in a wave of icy dark water. Her hand banged against something. She gasped for air, she called for Mommy.

The slam of a cold cloth onto the nape of her neck jolted Kate, broke through the shock, and brought her back to the boarding house. To her room in the boarding house. Clara was there, holding the cloth. Kate's thoughts tumbling, she uttered one word. "Mommy?"

Clara sobbed, dropped the cloth, and ran from the room, feet like thunder on the staircase.

Nanny opened her arms to Kate and Kate leaned in, the images of the last few minutes splayed in her mind like shards of shattered china. Difficult to pick up, impossible to mend. Was there sense to any of it? *Leave well enough alone.* Did she think that? Did Clara just say that? Didn't matter. What had Nanny told her? *Alphonse? Clara's father? My father too?* Kate couldn't comprehend the words. Slivers and splinters. She stopped thinking, just slipped back to nothingness. Safe here.

Her nose twitched at the smell of whisky. Who had placed the drink in front of her? Izzie? matter. Didn't matter. Encouraged by Nanny's voice, Kate sipped. Eventually, despite the thunder of footsteps on the stairs and the roars of anger from the parlour, she slipped off to sleep.

CLARA

CHAPTER 42

Clara stormed into the parlour, muttering to herself. "Why couldn't she leave well enough alone?" When Dulcie and Izzie trailed her into the room, Clara scowled. "The two of ye better find yourselves a safe port." They did an about-face and scarpered down the hallway toward the kitchen. Clara marched into the hall and hollered after them. "Mind yer own damn business. And ye better be closing that kitchen door too." The door slammed, as did several doors, one after another like series of gunshots. Clara jerked her head back. *Do all the boarders think I'm talking to them?* Not a soul in the hallway other than herself. She shrugged. "They're all better off keeping away from me today," she muttered. But then footsteps sounded on the stairs. Clara didn't need to turn to know who it was. "What do you want now?"

"Park your tongue for a second, will you?" Kathleen steered Clara back into the parlour. Clara slumped onto a lumpy maroon chesterfield, curled her feet under her, and hurled a blameless needlepoint pillow across the room. She ran a hand along the raised edges of brocade on the arm of the chesterfield and picked at a frayed thread. No intention of looking up. Not giving Kathleen Kerrigan the time of day. At the stomp of Kathleen's footsteps, Clara nodded. *Good. She's leaving.* Clara raised her head. *Damn it!* Her mother was not leaving. She was just closing the door. A stubborn door, unaccustomed to push and pull, it complained but conceded to the force that was Kathleen. *Didn't everything and everyone, eventually?* At the click of the latch, Kathleen swung around and let loose her fury. "Are you out of your ever-lovin' mind? Yelling like a longshoreman?"

Clara met the rage and matched it. "Am *I* out of my ever-lovin' mind? Me? It's *you* who stepped over the line. Why the hell did you tell her? The three of us carrying unwanted children, all victims." The door rattled and Clara growled. No doubt Izzie and Dulcie had their ears to the keyhole. Probably Rosemary too. Clara was beyond caring. "Answer me, Mom. Why did you do that?"

"Because that's exactly what you wanted me to do."

"Me?" Clara exploded from her seat, planted herself in front of Kathleen, and fired denial. "I most certainly did not!"

"Indeed you did, Clara. Indeed you did."

"What in God's name are you talking about?"

"Sit your arse down, Clara."

"Don't you dare be thinking you're going to tell me a story because I just won't have it."

"No story. I promise." Kathleen sighed her way to the chesterfield, sat on the far end, and patted the cushion beside her. "Sit with me."

Clara didn't move.

"Please," Kathleen added.

With a huff, Clara obliged. "Well, what is it?"

"The truth about her parentage is a shock, but she'll deal with it. She will truly understand that you had her best interests at heart, that you lied to her because you love her. She will understand that once she has a child of her own to think about."

Clara sat in disbelief. Her anger resurfaced and she hurled words at her mother. "But there was no need for her to know about Alphonse. And didn't it occur to you that the hand you just dealt could stop a life before it starts? Desperate women have been known to seek solutions with coat hangers in back alleys, Mom." Quick as a snap of a shirt on the line in the wind, Clara knew that she had gone too far.

Kathleen wilted.

The door rattled and the trio of Dulcie, Izzie, and Rosemary tumbled into the room. Dulcie whispered something to Izzie who spun on her heels and headed for the stairs.

"Izzie will watch Kate," announced Dulcie who then commandeered Clara's place beside Kathleen on the chesterfield. "It'll be all right, me darlin'," Dulcie was saying into Kathleen's ear. "Everything will turn out grand. You just wait and see. Rosemary will sit with you while Clara and I make us some tea." She gave Kathleen a one-sided hug and then slid away.

Make tea? A baffled Clara watched Rosemary plop beside Kathleen. *Who the hell does Dulcie think she is, appointing guardian angels all over the place?*

Dulcie grabbed Clara's arm and pulled her through the door. In a harsh whisper, she said, "Izzie will keep an eye on Kate. It falls to you to keep an eye on that mudder of yours. What you just said to her may well be right, but what difference does right make if it breaks her? Wouldn't want to see her dancin' off with the fairies again like she did all them years ago. Do you remember that?"

Clara flinched. "Holy Heart of Jesus." How stupid was she at all, spitting venom at her mother? Why hadn't she just walked away? Too late now. God only knows what injuries she had resurrected in her mother's psyche. Clara only knew that her own past was wide awake and that the memories burned. All those years alone while Mom was at the mental hospital. All those years alone with Daddy in the house in Argentia. Humiliation still owned her.

Until this very minute, Clara had been confident she could battle the tuberculosis invading her own body. But now she was temporarily felled, leaning against the wall, sinking to the floor outside the kitchen door, her body shaking with a mixture of coughing and crying. Between sobs, she spilled the truth about her ailing body, warning Dulcie not to get too close. She longed for home, where she could curl up and hide.

But there would be no going home to Freshwater for her. Within hours, she was shepherded to the sanatorium overlooking Bowring Park on Topsail Road. Maybe for a long stay.

And what about her promise to Kathleen? A long ago promise. "As long as I got breath in me, you will never know want," Clara had said, meaning every syllable. But now, Clara was struggling for that very breath. Kathleen would be alone.

KATHLEEN

CHAPTER 43

It is traumatized, the sea.

Showing no partiality, the North Atlantic complies with combat and bombs and smoke. Until it doesn't. Then it rages and roars, reducing rocks to sand, ships to splinters, and flesh to frame.

Peace has been attained, the planet settles into a hopeful lull. Will it last? Perhaps. At least until the rise of the next tyrant, the next armed conflict when greed will again troll the sea to extract populations of fish and fill the water with bits of detritus that threaten what remains of its injured ecosystem.

The military leave St. John's, dispersing slowly. Young Newfoundland women marry soldiers and sailors and leave too, taking their culture with them. Daunted by brash and all-knowing Americans, traumatized by cultural difference in their new country and determined to fit in, they forsake their own history, art, music, literature, and particularly their accents. Effectively killing their very souls. The soul of Newfoundland itself is in question. Will it become a part of Canada? Will it be lost to the bitter wind of change, emptied drop by drop until nothing is left? It is yet to be determined.

Another war, that of the living Kathleen against those who threatened her family, is also won. With the help of her daughter Clara, she has banished the new demon Patrick to the soil, as she had Alphonse to the sea. But it is not without cost: Clara's health, Peter's life, Kate's innocence. And for the living Kathleen herself?

Like many cradle Catholics for whom guilt is iron in the soul, the living Kathleen, before she has even left the boarding house, starts in on herself. *You're a stupid old woman, Kathleen Kerrigan, saying too much too soon to Kate.* "Clara was right," she tells herself as she heaves her brown suitcase onto the bed of her allotted room and whips its lid open. "If Kate seeks solutions in shadows, it will be my doing." She flings clothes into the suitcase, slams it shut, and buckles its straps. "I'm no good to Kate now. What's the point of me at all?" With head down and not a word of goodbye, Kathleen tramps to the train station. Once seated for the rocky ride home, she sets to whispering, "Clara will recover. Clara will return." This she repeats like a mantra, its tempo a match for the steady clack of wheels against rails.

Back at home, Kathleen lives her habits: rises at dawn, stokes the stove, and fills the kettle for the inevitable tea. She measures flour, sugar, and yeast into a large bowl, adds water, stirs, and kneads dough into a smooth ball. A clean tea towel goes over the dough and the daybed converts into a proving place where the bowl sits waiting for its contents to rest and rise. Yesterday's bread comes into play as Kathleen planks a half loaf on the cutting board. She opens the cutlery drawer and pauses. It's the bread knife she needs but it's the butcher knife she selects. She holds it, stares at it. She is reliving events. The knife clatters back into the drawer. She replaces it with the serrated one and starts in on her task. She's about to cut a third slice but stops. "Sure, there's only myself here now." After a sigh, she resurrects her mantra. "Clara will recover. Clara will return."

This is the living Kathleen's life now, days with chores, nights without sleep, and jolts of violent memories. It's near the end of the summer when the priest shows up at the gate. "Good morning, Kathleen," he calls, unlatching the gate, escorting himself through like he owns the place.

A mute Kathleen stands beside the cellar door where she has been storing cabbages. Aware of her unseemly appearance, she raises a hand to her head and pats her mess of hair. When the priest looks at her from top to bottom, she follows his glance to a ragged strip of her full slip which dangles beneath her dress. Her face reddens and she turns slightly, an attempt to conceal her slovenly state.

"Let me have a look into the cellar." Father Mahony holds open the door and remarks on the floor. "You and Clara did a grand job of pouring the cement. Looks pretty level."

Kathleen finds her voice. "Thank you, Father. And what can I do for you this lovely morning?" She eases him from the door and closes it. She walks away. He follows.

"Well, I know that you're on your own here, with Clara in the san and Kate in the boarding house. Anyway, I wonder if you need help, or company. Or perhaps if you would like to rent a room in another house so someone can tend to you. You've worked hard all your life; it's time for you to rest on your oars for a bit. The parish is full of good people, you know. Love to help, the lot of them."

"Father, thank you. I'm here to stay until Clara comes back from the san." She heads toward her little garden plot, then plods back and faces him full on. "I'm sure you remember, Father Mahony, that I abandoned my daughter once when she was a child. I won't do it again. Clara will need me when she comes home."

Father Mahony nods. "If you change your mind . . ."

Kathleen turns away. She has gardening to do. Behind her, the sound of the gate latch, opening, clicking shut. A tremor sets up in Kathleen's gut, spreads to her limbs. She reaches for her wheelbarrow, but her unsteady hands tell her she's done in. For today anyway. A glance at the sky. The threat of rain. She turns the wheelbarrow upside down. Wouldn't do to have rust in its innards. She slaps at its wheel, leaving it spinning and clicking as she walks into the house.

In the kitchen, she grabs an apron from its kitchen hook and examines its pockets. She shakes her head and chooses another apron. "This will do," she says, then takes her sewing basket to her rocking chair. From the basket, she retrieves tools: thread, needle and thimble. One would assume that she was about to repair the dangling edge of her slip. But in a curious turn, with needle in hand, thread through eye, thimble on finger, she instead begins, reinforcing apron pockets that are without flaw, not a hole, not a rip, not a single raggedy edge.

Once finished, she carefully hangs the apron on a hook near the stove, within easy reach. With a firm nod, she walks away. Will she use that apron? Maybe, maybe not.

Something for the ghost of me to glean here perhaps but the discomfort of possibilities pushes me away and my spirit flits to check the lives of my daughter Clara, my granddaughter Kate.

CLARA

CHAPTER 44

In the sanitorium, on a women's ward with three other tuberculosis patients, Clara was ordered to stay in bed for the first two months as bed rest was essential for recovery. She offered no objection to leading the life of a log here. How could object she when all the good was gone out of her? Her body weakened, her soul blackened, not enough strength to raise her head.

Muttering voices filled the ward like radio static, the occasional patch of conversation filtering through. The nurses spoke in whispers about twenty-year-old and thirty-year-old patients succumbing to sickness. The women spoke of embarrassments—bedpans, sponge baths. With death prowling the wards, were these women really concerned about bedpans? Amusement tinged Clara. Bedpans and sponge baths. *Foolishness.*

Time sighed in and out, delineated by moan of patients, pulse of footfalls, and swish of floor mops. *Will I ever come back myself? How is Mom doing all by herself in Freshwater? And Kate? Will my daughter ever forgive me?*

Thoughts of Kate caused Clara's chest to spasm. She placed a weakened hand over her chest to curb the physical reaction. It came as a spate of coughing that rattled her every bone in her body. She wheezed and puffed, then paused while her heart rate slowed. Was her ailing body God's punishment for her flailing soul? If so, He was making a good job of it.

Flat on her back, feet raised to force her organs to block the movement of her lungs so as to give lungs a chance to rest, windows flung wide regardless of freezing weather so as to supply lungs with so-called healing air. Maybe she *was* being punished. She had ignored her body when it signalled her that she was ill. The arrogance of herself. Had she really thought she was immune to the disease that ran rampant on the island?

Perhaps the disease had crept into her lungs as God's punishment, Old Testament punishment, a scourge born from her own words which were infested with lies and secrets. Perhaps it had lain inert for years before bubbling up. Perhaps it foreshadowed her eventual outcome. Had she destroyed her own soul by abetting a murder? Was there a place in hell awaiting her arrival? In a constant state of anxiety, she looked for solace. All around were nurses and doctors in white, the only standout was a black cassock. A priest. She began to take note of his visits to the wards, especially the days he stood beside a bed and donned a purple stole. The stole meant the priest was there to give Last Rites, the sacrament of Extreme Unction. That thought brought an eerie comfort. The time would come for the priest to approach her bed, and she would divulge her sins, and he would bestow the forgiveness she needed to avoid the gates of hell. Clara would utter every syllable of the penance the priest would dole out. In fact, she would begin now with a confession now. "Father?" She croaked out the word. Yes, she would confess. That and a heartfelt Act of Contrition should do the trick. *O my God, I am heartily sorry for having offended Thee . . .* She paused. Was she truly sorry? Could she be absolved? Maybe not. But the round-bodied, bald priest was already shuffling toward her, his face red and his breathing laboured. *Sure he's on death's door himself. A wonder he can move at all.* She bid him good morning, asked for a blessing, but shelved the confession. When she could be 'heartily sorry,' she would tell her sins to a priest, perhaps this priest if he lived long enough.

For now, Clara, her existence of the cusp of collapse, would search her soul for the strength to recover. Not an easy task, that, but not easily defeated, Clara; certainly not when she had the hope of communicating with Kate, a vision of meeting her future grandchild, and a promise of caring for her mom. "As long as I have breath in me," Clara had said years ago. The sigh she let out was punctuated with a hissing sound; it was the very breath of Clara that was compromised.

KATE

CHAPTER 45

KATE KERRIGAN KNEW WHAT DENIAL was and she was content to stay in it, sealed in her room, swaddled in quilts. She had craved information about her father. Now that she had it, she didn't want it. *My mother and I have the same father?* The knowing was violent, ravaging her brain and gnawing her gut.

The words she had heard, thundering from the parlour, replayed in her mind again and again. Was Clara right? Could Kate now rid herself of the problem inside her? Would she? Kate slammed the door on that. Perhaps this was all a dream, a bad dream.

Day blended into night, night into day until time folded in on itself altogether. One day, she didn't know which, the click of the lock, the whine of the door, and the clump of sensible shoes alerted her to the presence of Dulcie.

Kate tightened her fists on the covers, but Dulcie, all grit now, was at the bed, grasping at quilts, wrenching them off. *Where the hell did Dulcie get this quickness? This strength?* Kate was having none of it. "Leave me the hell alone." The demand went unheeded. Kate made a stab at regaining her covers. Dulcie intervened, grabbing Kate's shoulders, shaking her. "Look at me," she said, her tone like a slap. Kate snapped her head up.

Dulcie brushed the hair from Kate's eyes. "Look at me," she repeated, her voice not wavering.

Kate obliged, the gaze between them taut as piano wire.

The tension remained until Dulcie trembled. She stood, walked to the other side of the room. *Is she leaving?* Kate resisted the urge to call her back. But Dulcie turned. "I won't push you, child," she said," but it breaks my heart to see you like this." With a helpless wave of her hand, Dulcie continued. "We can talk about things, when you're up for even a little bit of it."

The concern on Dulcie's face shattered Kate's resistance and she released a single sob. "It's easier to pretend nothing happened, Dulcie."

Before Kate could draw another breath, Dulcie was at her side. "Yes, but it did happen, my love. And you know as well as I do that staying here, living here in St. John's will do you no good. People are a nasty lot."

"But what else can I do? I can't go back to Freshwater—it wouldn't be kind either, that's for sure."

"Look around you at the young women here in St. John's who are left with babies when their military men were done with them. Poor young girls. Yes, those fellows could smile with their gleaming teeth as they worked their way into those young women's lives. It was their underpants those soldiers and sailors were interested in. Sure the first thing those fellas took off was their wedding ring and now—"

"I know, I know. But I can stay here, in the boarding house with you, can't I? You know I'll work."

Dulcie cleared her throat. "That's not going to take eyes off you, a young woman with a baby and no man to claim it. Die-hard Catholics and Protestants from here to Freshwater will deal out harsh words and condemning looks, and you know I'm right about that." After a pause, Dulcie whispered, "It's not just you they'll be judging, Kate. It's the little one too."

". . . the little one too," Kate echoed. She sat motionless, her mind seeking significance. Didn't take long before she found it. Actually, it found her and it dazed her.

"Tell you what," said Dulcie, "I'm going to the cathedral for the Saturday confessions."

Kate widened her eyes, said not a word.

Dulcie raised a calming hand. "Not you. You don't need to confess anything. But me?" She fisted her palm and placed it over her heart. "I need make a clean breast of things every once in a while." She bowed her head and pounded her fist against her chest. "Mea culpa," she whispered.

Still no words from Kate. Her shoulders could barely carry the weight of her own worries; she had nothing to offer Dulcie.

"Stay here if you want," continued Dulcie, "but I was thinking you might like a soothing spot to sit and sift through things. No place like a church pew for that. Take this chance to go to the cathedral. Not confession. You've done nothing wrong."

Oh, yes, I have. Did she say that out loud? No. She wanted to though, to speak truth to Dulcie. Kate had indeed done something wrong. She lowered her head.

"Might as well go to church now," added Dulcie. "You won't be able to later."

Puzzled, Kate looked up. "Won't be able?" Then she understood. A visibly pregnant woman in church? The disapproving stares from all the good Catholics would slash her to ribbons. But she couldn't think that far ahead. What troubled her now was guilt about Clara, guilt that hung like a yoke on her shoulders. "Have you seen Clara?"

"Of course not. You know there are no visitors allowed at the sanatorium."

Kate nodded. "My fault," she said.

"Whatever are you on about, child? Clara's being sick is no fault of yours."

"If I hadn't been so angry with her. If I hadn't stayed away for so long, I would have seen the signs. Forced her to take care of herself." She dropped her voice to a whisper. "Is she going to be okay? Is my mother going to be okay?"

Dulcie wrapped her arms around Kate. "I really don't know, me darlin'. It's in God's hands now. People all over dying from the consumption. You could possibly write to her, maybe pray for her."

Write to her, pray for her. "What about Nanny? How is Nanny?" Kate asked.

"I'll be going to visit, will check on her once in a while. No need for you to worry about your nanny, just add her to your letters and prayers."

Write to her. Pray for her. The words floated through Kate's mind like dandelion seeds in the wind. Kate sighed. "For now, I'll just go with you to the cathedral."

Kate and Dulcie climbed the hill, arms linked against the taunt of wind and rain. Kate looked up at the cathedral, a daunting stone giant on the uppermost ridge overlooking the city, the first building visible to ships entering the bowl of St. John's harbour. Prominent and dominant. No accident, the location, the size, the intention. A statement of the significance of the Catholic Church here. It owned the city and the island, as much a part of its soul as the sea.

Kate opened the heavy centre door of the church and the two stepped inside. A nudge from Dulcie edged Kate forward toward the font of holy water where she dipped her fingers and made the sign of the cross. Onward then to the nave, every footfall reverberating and every inhalation fragrant with incense and candle wax. Genuflecting at the High Altar, moving to a side aisle, they slipped side by side into a pew. The wool of their coats, sodden from the rain and steaming in the heat of the church, added a wet-sheep odour into the mix. Kate glanced at the profusion of lit candles at the front, a reassuring indication that war had gone and had taken blackout regulations with it.

She considered the confessional. Should she go in? Could she? The dilemma sat like an unwanted guest. When Dulcie left their pew and headed to the confessional, Kate lowered the kneeler, placed her hands on the pew in front of her and pulled herself forward. On her knees, about to fold her hands in prayer, she reached into her coat pocket, searching, fumbling. Where was the tiny oval with the rosary beads? Her fingers landed on it and relief slid in. She palmed it. Opening the oval, she removed the beads and wove them through her fingers. Now she folded her hands. She prayed while time stuttered on. When her knees had had enough of the unforgiving wooden kneeler, she sat back in the pew.

Dulcie exited the confessional, approached the altar, and genuflected.

Then she was on her knees and bowing her head and praying her penance. *Is there ever such a thing as enough penance?* Kate sighed. Perhaps if confession was good enough for Dulcie, it was good enough for her. She stood and made her way to the confessional.

"Bless me, Father, for I have sinned," she said, shivering like a first-timer. She remembered it well, her first time in confession when she made up a list of sins. Dulcie had bristled at the shock of it, Kate lying to the priest. Nanny had instantly elbowed Dulcie, silencing her, then returned to basting the hem of Kate's First Communion dress. Nanny told Kate that she should not confess if she had done nothing wrong. But here and now? Kate heaved a sigh. She made her confession, muttering her way through all of it, clutching her stomach, waiting for judgement.

The priest gave it: Kate was an evil woman who had tempted a man and deserved what she got. Shrouded in humiliation, Kate could barely raise her head. She was aware that the depth of shame would endure for as long as she stayed in Newfoundland. Worse still, it would condemn her child.

Dulcie was right. Kate would have to leave. But where would she go? How would she get there?

CHAPTER 46

Days passed as days will, no holding them back, the movement of time a tormentor for Kate who was all too aware of time's impending cruelty. She spent most of that time in her room. When stale air stifled, she stumbled to the window, clawing at it in a futile attempt to open it. It was as stuck as she was. She stared through it. The September wind made a show of itself, rattling rafters inside and spinning dirt devils outside. A longing for a breath of fresh air came over her and lingered until it overwhelmed her. She yielded, sneaking from her room and creeping undetected down the stairs, wrapping her cardigan around her and stumbling over the newspaper on the stoop as she exited the house. A gentle push from the Atlantic wind aided her downhill scurry. At the bottom of the hill, she paused, took a deep breath, held it, and released it. *Yes, this is what I need.* Felt so good she did it again. Relief was there until she looked behind her. It was a short trip down that hill but now she would have to climb it, and it seemed steep, so very steep. What the hell was she doing out here anyway? She couldn't run from her problems. Time would catch up to her. She began the slog up the hill.

The newspaper still lay at the doorstep of the boarding house. When she leaned to pick it up, her fitted skirt strained against her expanding belly. In that instant, it came home to her that time was already catching up with her. Tears came and she wiped her eyes with the sleeve of her sweater. It was four months since VE Day already, four months during which smiles abounded around town, indeed around the continent. And yes, her stomach was tightening, and her breasts were swelling and now her heart was pounding in panic. What was she going to do?

Inside the boarding house, she entered the parlour, her purpose being to place the paper on a table. But the far end of the room was alive with the chatter of women and the clatter of knitting, all of which suddenly stopped. *Damn.* Kate didn't want to be seen at all. But here she was. *Exposed.* She dropped the newspaper and faced Dulcie, Rosemary, and Izzie, who were sitting at a card table placed in a corner. One empty chair. "What are you doing?" she asked,

"Knittin' and talkin' and waitin'," replied Dulcie.

"All knitting and talking stopped when I walked in. I assume ye are waiting for me?" said Kate.

"Right as rain," said Dulcie.

"Come sit," said Rosemary.

Kate hedged, staring at the chair. "Not interested in pity."

"Good," said Dulcie, "because we got none." She put her knitting down on the table. The other ladies followed suit. "We have answers."

Rosemary patted the seat of the chair. Kate slumped onto it.

"You can come with me," Izzie said.

"There you have it," said Dulcie. "You and Izzie can go away."

A bewildered Kate looked at Izzie who nodded. "Go where?" asked Kate. "And what will people say? And what if that sailor comes looking for me?" The thought still haunted Kate.

"You can go to Canada with Izzie, say you're going to work like many young women before you," said Dulcie. "Clothesline gossips can't say nothing if they don't know nothing. And, as for that sailor. Long gone." All the while Dulcie was talking, she was fidgeting, poking hair behind her ear, eyes darting all over. Was Dulcie hiding something? Kate didn't dare ask. "There's no need for you or Izzie to tell nothing to no one." Dulcie looked at Rosemary. "Your turn."

"First of all, I'm grateful to the lot of ye that I can live here and have a life for me and my daughter," Rosemary said, stumbling over the words. She rummaged through her apron pocket and produced a gold ring. "I won't be needing this." She placed it on the table in front of Kate.

"What am I supposed to do with that?" Kate said, recognizing the very ring that had showed up on her plate, in her pancake, on Shrove Tuesday. She had returned it then. What possible use could she have for it now?

"I would very much like to help those who helped me. Let's put that piece of gold to good use."

Kate stared blankly.

"Okay then, I'll lay it all out for you," continued Rosemary. "You could say you had a husband. Perhaps he was in the merchant marine. Perhaps he joined up. Perhaps he died in the war." She sat back, her eyes filling with tears, which she dabbed at with the corner of her apron.

Kate opened her mouth to respond. The rattle of the doorknob stopped her. All eyes turned as the door whined open to reveal Granny Grace, her cheeks rouged, her knitting bag in hand. She took a good look at the group. "Well, any fool can see that this is a private knittin' session. Guess I'll have to wait a while for me special teacup." She caught sight of the newspaper Kate had deposited and moved further into the room to claim it. "This'll keep me busy for a while," she said as she shoved the paper into her knitting bag. "No need to be worrying about me. Ye can take yer good, sweet time." She waved a hand as she turned to leave.

Granny exited, closing the door behind her.

"Will bring a spot of tea to your room later, Granny," Dulcie called.

The door reopened and Granny poked her head in. "Lovely," she said.

The click of the door again, then total silence in the room. Kate picked up the wedding ring. Could it be this easy? Her mind went back to their brief stay at a boarding house in Placentia when the landlady, Mrs. Wittier, berated the men for leaving for war, all kinds of them, regardless of there being work in Argentia, regardless of there being no conscription. They just up and joined the service. The story that Kate married, that her husband died . . . completely believable.

"You're all of nineteen now," said Dulcie. "No one in Canada would question you if you said that your husband joined up and never came home."

Dulcie was right. No one would question Kate. The solution offered by the group was well within the mandate of society: any girl not married by nineteen, twenty-one at the latest, could expect labels like "old maid" and "spinster" flung at them or whispered behind them. Yes, the idea would work. Kate sighed, almost settling with this course of action, but then wondering if she had other options. Clara had had her sister-in-law, Mavis. Kate had no Mavis, no siblings at all, and she certainly couldn't go home to Nanny. "What does Nanny think of all this?" she asked.

"Saw her just the other day in Freshwater. Your nan is holding her own," Dulcie said.

Not an answer that, but an evasion. When Kate opened her mouth to ask another question, Dulcie sat bolt upright in her chair, arms folded, lips tight. Kate winced, regrouped. She turned to Rosemary and held up the ring. "Are you sure?"

Rosemary waved a hand through the air. "I'm long past it. Use it. Keep your secrets. Truth is unnecessary."

With the plan unfolded like a map, Kate leaned back and pondered. A simple solution, wasn't it? Yes, she would have to go away, but would it be a wrench to leave Newfoundland? Could she do that? This island was her birthplace, but she was not in thrall. The sea had battered her family, the war had ousted them, and the men? No words for the cruelty of men. As the women waited, Kate turned to Izzie.

Izzie adjusted her glasses. Her eyes wide and brimming, she whispered, "Whatever satisfies the soul is truth."

"Walt Whitman," said Kate, remembering, naming, and owning the quote. She pulled back slightly and closed her eyes to shut out influence. *Her* choice, this. Motionless, Kate wondered what would satisfy her soul. *But it's not one soul now, it's two, isn't it?* The words flickered across her mind like candle flames in a breeze. *Not one soul, but two.* Her eyes fluttering, then wide, she searched Izzie's face. "You're sure, Izzie?"

"I am, Kate. You know that."

Kate, no response at the ready, remained mute.

Dulcie spoke up, talking to everyone in general, to Kate in particular. "A cycle it seems," she said, her tone melancholy, "men's taking advantage of the Kerrigan women. First your nanny, then Clara, now you, Kate.

When Clara carried you, she fled to the Burin Peninsula where she birthed you and entrusted your care to Mavis. Clara did what she had to, and she did it for you, all for her child Kate."

The monologue ended. Silence gaped. Kate blushed in the face of well-meaning scrutiny as the three women stared at her, waiting for her. Even the air around them seemed to be holding its breath in anticipation. Kate lowered her head, unconsciously placing a hand on her abdomen. Something inside her fluttered. She instantly lifted her hand and let out a tiny gasp. Eyes wide, she looked from Dulcie to Rosemary, both of whom wore knowing smiles. Izzie tilted her head, curiosity shining through.

Kate didn't quite know what she had just experienced: the movement had been slight, her reaction disbelief, so she placed her hand on her abdomen again. The quickening came, this time followed by a rush of certainty. This was real, this life inside her. Yes, real. But there was something else niggling. Kate, heart hammering, eyes tearing, waited for the knowing. When an image of Clara flashed before and an agony of emotions assaulted her, Kate knew. She was understanding, experiencing, owning Clara's pain. An upsurge of emotion ripped through Kate, stopping at her throat like a logjam. Seconds later the clog broke, and Kate's long-cultivated glut of anger toward Clara gushed. Gone. Forever gone. With the heel of her hand, Kate wiped tears from her face. A handkerchief emerged from a dress pocket and made its way, hand over hand, to Kate.

"If we go to Toronto," Izzie was saying, "you won't even have to change your surname, but, if you want, I will change mine."

"Ontario?" questioned Kate. "But you're from Nova Scotia."

"Yes. And I know people there, people who might want explanations, but Toronto is big, lots of comings and goings. No one will pay attention to us."

"Tell her about working there," prodded Dulcie.

Izzie placed a hand over Dulcie's. "I'm getting to it," she said and then turned back to Kate. "Women can still get clerical work, even with the men back from war. I can type and file with the best of them. No one will question us, Kate. We can keep your secret, our secret, in plain sight."

The conversation had begun to blur in Kate's mind, the speed of it too quick. She had missed something. "What did you say about changing your name, Izzie?" she asked.

"Just thought it would be easier if people thought I was your sister-in-law."

A sister-in-law, like Mavis across the bay who covered for Clara and cared for Kate. Izzie's offering sat while Kate's soul stirred. "You would do that for me?" Kate whispered.

Izzie, her face shining like sunlight, said, "Together, we will take care of the little one."

Kate smiled in recognition of the significance in Izzie's words. No need to speak that meaning aloud. *Some things you hangs out in the wind, some things you doesn't.* Izzie knew. That was enough. Right from the start, Kate had had such ease with Izzie, such curiosity about Izzie. "Thank you, Izzie." She nodded slowly as the puzzle pieces slid home.

Dulcie brushed her hands together. "There it is. All tied up with a bow."

"Amen to that," said Rosemary.

Relief oozed through Kate. One problem solved. But another nagged. "I need to see Clara," she said. "Clara is my mother, and I need to see her."

"Surely be to goodness, Kate, you know you can't do that," Dulcie said as she touched Kate's hand. "No visitors allowed at the san."

A disappointed Kate nodded.

"Maybe she'll pull through and someday, you can see her again. But for now, write a letter?" added Dulcie.

"Yes," said Kate. "A letter."

CLARA

CHAPTER 47

FRESH AIR WAS A PART of the treatment for tuberculosis at the sanatorium, all windows flung wide to beckon the Atlantic wind. Clara clasped her covers and shivered nonstop. There was nothing as fresh as the smell of the sea and nothing as bitter as the blast of its blow. There were never enough blankets.

Occasionally, Clara's bed, like the others, was wheeled onto a balcony into the sunshine for part of the day, allowing relatives and friends to wave from the street below. And wave they did, Dulcie and Rosemary. Not Kathleen nor Kate. *Is Mom all right?* She hadn't heard from her mother for a while. What if Kathleen had gone dancin' off with the fairies again like she did when baby Jimmy died? Dulcie had mentioned that it could happen. *Dear God in heaven, please don't let that come to pass.* Clara sniffed at her own audacity: the likes of herself, daring to utter a prayer. *Some good that's going to do me now.*

She shook off thoughts of Kathleen, and turned her fretful mind to Kate. *Is she still angry with me?* Tears rushed Clara's eyes, but she didn't let them spill. All her life had been for Kate. All for Kate.

Rosemary and Dulcie gone, Clara retreated from the balcony to the ward. The arrival of a nurse, holding a letter, raised her hope and her spirit. *So kind of Dulcie or Rosemary to remember her. Maybe it's from Mom?* But a closer look at the letter showed not Dulcie's or Kathleen's or Rosemary's penmanship. The flowing cursive on this letter was Kate's. A disbelieving Clara gaped at the envelope. A dream she had longed for, hearing from

Kate. She ran her fingers along the envelope's edges and jabbed her fingertips with its corners, little prods to prove that this longed-for thing was real. When truth sank into her bones, Clara sank into her pillow, still staring at the letter. It was with trepidation that she opened the envelope and unfolded the pages. *What if Kate has written to me just to condemn?* But then the words were there, right in front of her face. "Dear Mom," she read.

Overwhelmed, Clara dropped the letter. It took the better part of five minutes for her to convince herself to pick it up. Having done that, she read a line or two and then set it down again. This she did repeatedly until she reached the forgiveness part. After all the years and all the lies, Kate was forgiving her. At last. These were the words Clara wanted to see. Awash with relief, then with gratitude, Clara paused her reading. *Is there a future in which I can be with my daughter and with my grandchild?* She allowed herself to dwell in the light of possibility for a time, but then . . . "I am leaving Newfoundland," Kate's words, a simple sentence. Disappointment swept through Clara but didn't linger because she wouldn't allow it to. An expected outcome this. Clara understood this type of leaving all too well. She would waste no time wishing it could be different.

The next day Clara, having absorbed every facet of Kate's letter, set about responding, expressing her love, writing her hope that she would see Kate again soon. And, the very next sunny day, Kate stood among the crowd below the balcony. It was through smiles and tears that Clara waved to her daughter that day: Kate was leaving Newfoundland.

It was a sad Clara who then began an epistolary journal, which the nurses mailed on her behalf to Kate almost daily. A long time, Clara's lifetime, it seemed, as she recalled event after event. She wrote about her near drowning at six, about Kevin leaving at sixteen, about her mother being at the mental, about her father being at home, about herself giving birth on the Burin Peninsula and leaving her daughter in the care of Mavis. She wrote about the sudden marriage to Robert, the rum running with Robert, and the adulterous affair with Patrick. She wrote daily, breaking when too ill, too tired, or too disheartened.

Will I ever be able to go home?

Month in and month out in the sanitorium turned into year in and year out, manifested in a blur of images of rain or snow or fog bordered by the window frame and accompanied by a cacophony of beeps and moans and hacking coughs. The quantity of daylight decreased a minute or two at a time until all seemed to be going dark forever. At that point the process reversed itself until daylight prevailed again. When Kate's little one was born, Clara had been in the san for half a year. The thought of her granddaughter, Kathy, warmed her heart as she bided her time in the cold on the balcony, in the boredom of cards and Bingo, hoping for the best, wanting for the health of her lungs to return. She couldn't stay in this state; couldn't let it end her. Over and over, Clara's promise to her mother scrolled across her mind. *As long as I got breath in me, you will never know want.* With that very breath compromised, a walled-in Clara willed herself to get better.

It came as a surprise to her that, early the following year, in 1947, "better" at last showed up. A tall, tired-looking grey-haired doctor, his tie askew, his white coat wrinkled, stood beside her bed, medical chart in hand. "Mrs. Caulins, I'm happy to report that you have had a clear X-ray."

Clara's hope soared. "I'm going home?"

His fingers tapping the chart, he looked from it to her and let out a sigh. "I'm thinking I should caution you that, if we release you, you must be careful, you must continue your regimen of rest. You, and your immune system, are not strong."

"But I'm going home?"

The doctor nodded.

KATHLEEN

CHAPTER 48

It is liberated, the sea.

The North Atlantic, released from the burden of ferrying young soldiers to war, completes its duty by ferrying tired warriors back. The demobilized, some hardened, some broken, hunger for home yet wrestle with return: a difficult transition, that from controlled military to unrestricted civilian. By 1947, the sea is free, the soldiers are free, and my island, Newfoundland, is also free from war. Hovering beneath the joy of peace among islanders is the concern that freedom is temporary, that Newfoundland may return to the prison of pre-war poverty.

The liberated North Atlantic, Newfoundland's original architect, now becomes liberator, for, in carving this island near the mouth of the St. Lawrence Seaway, it has given Newfoundland options. Newfoundland is a British Dominion, but British influence is waning, Canadian influence is rising, and American influence is holding strong. Both Canada and the United States have a vested interest in controlling the St. Lawrence Seaway. The Newfoundland National Convention is established to decide the future of Newfoundland. Will Newfoundland remain a British dominion? Will it become a footnote to Canada? To the United States? Will the independence of citizens be usurped? Who will own Newfoundland?

Will Newfoundland lose its very soul?

As Newfoundland makes tentative steps toward the freedom of continued prosperity, I watch the living Kathleen who, once she has heard the news of Clara's healing, removes a certain apron from its hook in the kitchen, the apron whose pockets she had carefully reinforced. Down to the bedroom she strides and buries that apron under clothes at the bottom of a dresser drawer. She smiles. Clara is coming home.

Clara's initial steps from her confinement are cautious: it could be temporary, this remission. Clara stops at the boarding house. Not for a long stay, just for a careful chat with Dulcie wherein Clara shares her soul in the form of plans for Kathleen and hopes for Kate and Kathy. "I need to put my affairs in order," she tells Dulcie.

"Proper thing, for a dutiful daughter like yourself, Clara," says Dulcie. "And you knows in your own heart and soul that Kathleen is more than welcome at the boarding house if the work of the Freshwater house ever gets too much."

Clara lets out a deep sigh, a sign of freedom from worry. It is no surprise to Clara that Dulcie will 'do' for the corporeal Kathleen: no end to Dulcie's willingness to clean, cook, care. Maybe Clara just needs to hear the words. Her smile beams. "Thank you, Dulcie," she says.

The very next day, Clara heads home.

The arrival of Clara brings the light back to the eyes of the living Kathleen who hurries to her chores, renewed hope in every kettle boiled and potato peeled. Together they sit at the table and set about paperwork that will move the title of the house to Kate. "You do realize that Kate will never live here," says Kathleen.

"Wouldn't want her to," replies Clara, no explanation given, none needed. "We just need to ensure that, in the event of the property being sold, the proceeds have a direct line to her. Most sales are informal around here, people negotiating for themselves. I know you don't like to hear it, but I could relapse. If that happens, if you happen to move to Dulcie's boarding house, we're going to need local help with all this."

"Father Mahony offered help from parishioners with the care of the place. I'm sure that, if we stuff the collection plate, he'll help with the sale of it too."

"And the rich get richer," says Clara, her tone one of acceptance. She visits the rectory and makes the plans.

With paperwork done and dusted, Clara, despite medical warnings, turns to chores of gardening and upkeep. All the while, she yammers on about her hopes to go to Ontario.

"That's all very well and fine," says Kathleen, "your wanting to see Kate and meet the little one, but if you think you're going to do that soon, then you got another think coming." She pulls Clara away from her current task of repairing a window latch. "Sit your arse down and rest. It takes a long time to recuperate from what your body's been through. Take it slow."

Clara hears but doesn't always heed. Yes, she concedes to a slight cough one day, stays in bed, but as soon as the cough abates, she's up and on the go again. The ease with which she tires, however, reminds her that her immune system is still weak, and she must slow down.

As the circle of day and night continues, Clara exchanges letters with Kate and rejoices at replies from her daughter. Christmas shows up and Clara attends Midnight Mass with her mother in a packed church, no end to the coughs and sneezes, no wonder that she comes down with a cold out of it. The cold passes as colds do but a cough lingers into spring, through spring and into summer. She ignores it. She plans on attending the annual August Garden Party, pulls a dress from her closet for the occasion, and tries it on. When its shoulder seams slip down to her biceps and its pencil skirt billows around her hips, tears cloud her eyes. Clara stares at herself in the bedroom mirror, her face gaunt. It saddens me thatI can do nothing but watch as she lets gathered tears fall. Even sadder to me is the slump on the shoulders of the living Kathleen as Clara is escorted back to the sanitorium.

The ghost of me follows her, hovers near the foot of Clara's bed, her pained existence manifesting in an ailing body. In no time at all, blankets pitched aside, she's tossing and turning and dripping sweat, bones sticking like daggers through sagging skin.

The air here is raw with cold, the agony of witnessing is brutal. Clara is the last of my three children. The corporeal me suffered through Jimmy's death, the phantom me witnessed Kevin's. Neither in spirit nor in body can I observe this a third time. Yet, death is coming. How can it not be? I fear for the fate of her soul. Will she, like me, be forced to live in limbo and observe her life?

All I hear now is the rasp of Clara's struggling lungs. My spirit craves a way out, out of this story, out of this moment in this story. A gust of wind rattles the raised window. Sea air sweeps the room, filling it, lifting me, an offer of an exit strategy. In a soundless wave, I flit toward the window, clinging to it, a foggy splotch on the pane above the latch. Within seconds, I slip downward, through the open window, and into the night.

KATE

CHAPTER 49

SEATED AT HER DESK IN the living room of her rented Victorian house near the Scarborough Bluffs in Toronto, Kate stared through lavish loops in the lace curtains on the bay window. Her pencil and paper and typewriter were waiting, but Kate was watching her little girl skipping through grass like a lamb in springtime. Kate had had high hopes for this spring, hopes that her mother would come and visit. But Clara had relapsed in the fall last year and was back in the sanitorium. Little hope left. Kathy was three now. She would likely never know her grandmother. Kate sighed.

For a long time after Kate left Newfoundland, long after the shock of assault had subsided, Kate's gut roared like the blast of a furnace. A buffer between herself and the world, this fury which held, no letup. None, until after her daughter was born when Kate stared at tiny fingers which curled around one of her own. "My baby," Kate whispered, the puff of her breath enough to snuff the anger lodged within. She debated the baby's name, Kathleen or Clara, and although the birth had given her empathy for Clara's plight and Clara's choices, she decided on Kathleen who had intervened in Alphonse's plan to dispose of Kate herself. This she knew from Clara. "You will be Kathy," Kate whispered to her little one.

Kathy was a bright button of a child, blond-haired and blue-eyed, smiles never far off. Not at all the 'face and eyes' of her mother, a phrase that had held true for both Kate and Clara. No, Kathy resembled her father as did Kathleen's baby Jimmy many years ago. A shudder darted through Kate, ushering in a mental image of the unnamed man in uniform, an image that snagged her breath. She paused then, stopping all thoughts; let continue, they could strangle her altogether. In a practised move, Kate raised and lowered her shoulders, a deliberate shrug. *Let it go.* Kate had tried pushing negative thoughts down but came to see that they pushed back. Harder. A slow process, learning to nurture the art of dismissal, but it worked.

When her breathing calmed, Kate returned her attention to Kathy who was blowing her a kiss. Kate played at grabbing the kiss and putting it into her pocket, in the process almost knocking Kathy's collection of tiny white stones from the windowsill. As she realigned the stones, she kept an eye on Kathy who, with Aunt Izzie on her heels, made her way to the swing and hopped on. When Kathy pumped her pudgy legs to no avail, Izzie supplied a push, propelling Kathy into the blue. The little girl's laughter rang through the air, infectious. Kate caught the joy.

"Oh, how I love to go up in a swing," called Izzie, the care in her voice warming Kate's heart. How fortunate was Kate at all, having a partner like Izzie in her life. The word gratitude couldn't describe her appreciation for this woman who had upended her own life for the benefit of the three of them. No longer did Izzie have to pretend to be a man for salary purposes as she had done in Newfoundland. Pretense was still there, different now, subtle, adorned in shoulder-length curls and cat's-eye spectacles. Izzie had ousted her button-down shirts and bow ties in favour of twin sets and pearls. She was all in as Aunt Izzie, Aunt Izzie who worked as a file clerk to support their little family while Kate worked at night classes with the goal of becoming a teacher. As soon as Kathy started school, Kate would start a teaching career. All that possible due to Izzie.

A ripple of a fable ran across Kate's mind, an Aesop's fable about breadsticks: one alone is easily broken, a bundle not so. If not for the women in her life, Kate would be alone, a young unwed mother shamed constantly by scathing looks and acerbic remarks. Yes, if it hadn't been for Rosemary and Dulcie and Clara and Nanny and Izzie . . . Kate smiled.

Her very own bundle of breadsticks.

CLARA

CHAPTER 50

CLARA LAY IN A BED on a ward at the Sanatorium, the whole place a waiting room for the decrepit and dying. Laboriously, she lifted a hand and stared at it. Were those gnarled fingers hers? She tugged at her hair and a few strands came away, white, brittle slivers among the brown. Grey hair? Was she that old? She had recently seen her fortieth birthday, and, with burden of disease abetted by a lifetime of deceit, she doubted she would get much past that. She emitted a sigh of acceptance. A breeze brushed past. She shivered. The windows were still open all hours. She had grown accustomed. On this night, the scent of the sea wafted in, summoning her. Would she accept the invitation? Her spirit screamed yes, her body grumbled at first, but then surged to the challenge. This could be her last chance. She would go.

Careful lest she jar patients from sleep or alert wardens in white, she slid from her bed and leaned against it while she gained her footing. The meeting of bare feet with cold floor reminded her of childhood, the morning after Kevin left home, the morning she flitted on butterfly toes across the icy floors of her room. The memory gifted her with a giggle. She adjusted her flannel gown, eased into the hallway, and slipped past another ward where rattle and rasp ricocheted against walls and slid through a partly open door into Clara's reluctant ears. Her heart sped up and she picked up her pace, hurrying past death's silhouettes, dodging death itself. She reached the exit door, pushed it, and it yawned. She stepped into the night. The darkness embraced her. Relief settled in. And now to the sea. Was her schooner waiting?

A clamp of a hand on her shoulder stopped her in her path. All hope of sea and schooner dropped away, and Clara turned to face a plump nurse in a white uniform, a crisp white hat atop netted brown hair. Clara's next breath was a sigh of surrender. Her demise was coming, and she had nothing to do but wait.

Day and night cycled twice before death marched to the foot of Clara's bed. Fear rose and she grappled, struggling to make her shroud of a blanket rise and fall. The priest, purple stole against black cassock, stood beside her muttering prayers and anointing her forehead with oil while she clawed her chest with one hand and thrashed the air with the other. Was she stunned enough to try to scrape off death? Did she think she could outwit this gatherer of souls? Every breath grated and her breathing slowed, then stalled. No fight left. She dropped her flailing hand to the bed. The priest began the prayers for the departure of the soul. Then came the inhalation that fell deep into her body, deep enough to collect the very soul of her which she ejected with her last breath.

KATE

CHAPTER 51

KATE STARED AT THE RINGING phone on her kitchen wall. She knew what was coming and she was ready for it, or so she thought. But the shrillness of the phone shot needles through her and set her to shaking. She managed to answer, to ascertain that Clara was on the verge, and to hang up the phone. Did she remember to thank the caller? Did it matter? Her mother was dying. Her mind throbbing with grief, Kate sighed her way into a chair and eyed her suitcase sitting, waiting, beside the front door. *Clara is dying.* Tears sprang and flowed, unchecked. It was okay for now, this crying. Then, despite sorrow rolling through her like billows on the sea, she would have to shore herself up. According to custom, the funeral would occur three days after death. Kate had a long journey ahead of her, hours on trains and hours on a ferry, to get from Toronto to St. John's for the funeral. It was time to go.

"Should we all go together?" she had whispered one night to Izzie. "I don't want to leave little Kathy."

"Kate, my love, don't you think it better that I stay here with her? You and I both know what we'd be facing if we went back there together, a child in tow." She pointed at the gold wedding band that Kate always wore. "That ring will only take you so far. Practical here. But there?"

"Should I leave the ring at home?"

Izzie shrugged. "Up to you."

Kate sighed away her silly notion, that of taking Kathy to Newfoundland. Conversations would be whispered, not directly to Kathy but around her, a word here and there would be picked up by this little-pitcher-with-big-ears child. Kathy would sense the judgement, not knowing the why of it. "I can't expose Kathy to that kind of scrutiny," she said.

"I agree. She's safest here. When I'm at work, Mrs. Jenson will tend to Kathy. She's right across the road, and you can't get a better caregiver." Izzie yawned. She said no more, just fell into a gentle snore.

Kate envied Izzie's ability to slumber through storm or shine. Sleep did not come easily to Kate. Even after all this time, Kate's past lurked, especially at night when a vigilant Kate would roam the house. On this night, she crept downstairs, treading lightly, hand on the banister, avoiding the step with the creak in the middle of the stairs and then sliding her fingers over spines of books on hallway shelves. She circled the first floor twice before stopping in front of the oak curio cabinet with curved glass walls and mirrored back. The light of the full moon through the bay window opposite afforded Kate clear visibility of keepsakes on the middle shelf: at centre was her grandmother's mahogany tea caddy, flanked on the right by the rosary from Kevin, on the left by the sewing kit from Mavis via Clara. Izzie's copy of Walt Whitman's *Leaves of Grass*, the book that satisfied both their souls, was on the far left and, on the right, an empty space for Mrs. Fan, the doll that was now weathering its third generation of love in Kathy's arms.

Kate brushed a hand along the top of the cabinet and meandered to the bathroom where she flicked on the light and caught a glimpse of herself in the mirror. The face of Clara stared back at her. Brown hair, brown eyes, narrow shoulders. She cringed. Would she ever fully be able to stand the sight of herself? No answers came. Would she ever again want to be looked at by men? Not hardly.

Kate meandered to the doorway of the small nursery to watch her sleeping child. Held in Kathy's chubby hand was the *Little Golden Book of Poetry* by Robert Louis Stevenson, open to a page with an illustration of a child playing on a swing. Mrs. Fan was in her usual position, hugged tightly to Kathy's chest. Kate slipped onto the edge of the bed, seeking the soothing sound of Kathy's steady breathing. The thought of leaving her, even for a few days, was painful. A memory slipped in, herself a sleeping child, her daddy sitting on her bed, concerned about leaving her for a few days. Perhaps a part of life's circle, this experience. With a sigh, then a smile, Kate stood to leave the bedroom. Kathy would be safe at home with Aunt Izzie and Mrs. Jenson who would recite the rhymes, read the story books, tend to Kathy's needs. Decision made, Kate returned to the bedroom she shared with Izzie, to the comfort in Izzie's presence. Kate's heart skipped a beat every time she heard Izzie's key in the door at the end of a day. A secret life, Izzie and Kate. No hand holding in public. Just sitting side by side at church, at the movies seemed daring enough. Kathy was their focus. A secret life and a happy one.

CHAPTER 52

Kate had taken a window seat on the train from Toronto to North Sydney. She would watch scenery. Perhaps she would find conversation with one of her fellow passengers in this train carriage, or on the ferry or on the next train from Port Aux Basques to St. John's. Kate caught her reflection in the window. There it was again, her face, her mother's face, her grandmother's face. It didn't matter. She was a stranger to all on this journey. She could be anyone here. Free to talk. Free to invent a name.

At a thump on the bench seat, she turned her head. Beside her sat an angular woman wearing a red sweater set and a black, pleated skirt. Her shoulder-length brown curls showed flecks of grey, and her manicured nails matched both sweater and lipstick. Perhaps a chat? But no, the woman pulled a book from her capacious purse and turned to a marked page, ignoring Kate's glance. No chance for Kate to invent herself for a stranger.

In Nova Scotia, Kate boarded a ferry to cross the Cabot Strait. The sea was in a mood and stayed that way, pitching and tossing for the entire sixteen hours of the journey. Kate was still swaying when she stepped ashore in Port Aux Basques, but in short order regained her land legs and clomped her way to the train station to check for a possible telegram from Izzie. No surprise to Kate that it was there, this notification of Clara's passing. She swallowed the lump that emerged in her throat: at least she would arrive in time for the funeral.

On a train again, she chose a window seat and scanned the car as passengers rambled in, not a hurry in any of them. A thirty-ish brunette with her hair in a bun, a snag in her stocking, and a baby in her arms plopped down beside Kate and smiled.

"Don't worry about sitting next to a screaming baby. My little one here could sleep through anything."

"What a little lamb," offered Kate.

The woman's eyes lit up. "I use that expression too," she said. "My little lamb. Sort of goes with her name–Mary. I'm Doris by the way."

"Kate. I'm Kate." No last names needed. "Very pleased to meet you." Kate twirled the wedding ring on her left hand, Rosemary's wedding ring.

Doris caught the action. "You married long?" she asked. Pleasant enough.

Kate took a deep breath and exhaled her well-rehearsed lie. "Four years ago. My husband got called up to the navy and, shortly after that, I got a telegram."

"So sorry for your loss." Doris shifted in her seat. "I remember my wedding. It rained that day." She smiled. "I love rain, you know. It curls my hair." A long sigh came then. "Lovely man, my husband. Bought me flowers every week." She wiped tears from her cheeks with the back of her hand. "I'm a widow myself."

The words plunged Kate into sadness. "I'm sorry," she whispered.

Doris continued. "At least I think I am a widow. My husband piloted Hurricanes. His plane was shot down over Germany in the last throes of the war."

"I'm sorry," Kate said again. She sat still for a minute, looking at the baby who couldn't have been more than a few months old. Little lamb Mary was not the child of the Hurricane pilot husband.

Doris sighed. "I'm beyond caring how others decide the fate of my soul."

Heat crept into Kate's cheeks, and she swallowed uncomfortably. Had Doris read her mind? She couldn't say "I'm sorry" a third time. "My apologies," she muttered.

Doris shrugged. "The truth is I don't want another husband. No man could measure up. You know, my husband used to go to bed before me and get into my side just so it would be warm for me."

"Lovely," said Kate, grateful for another word.

"Lovely indeed. No, no other husband for me. But I did want a baby." She held her child close. "And now I have Mary."

Doris' honesty prompted a tug of remorse in Kate whose tangle of deceit unravelled like defective knitting. Suddenly, she felt an urgent need to release her truth. "The ring is a lie, Doris. Just for show. Not married at all. On VE Day when everyone was out partying, a man . . ." A shudder struck her gut and snaked through her body. She took a deep breath. "Still can't say it out loud. I have a three-year-old daughter, my little Kathy. The ring eases things, allows me to raise my daughter without raising eyebrows."

"Do you love her?" Doris asked, not missing a beat. "Your daughter?"

Kate stiffened. "Of course!"

With her free arm, Doris patted Kate's hand. "Take it easy, darlin'. I knew the answer to that question, but I thought you might like to hear yourself say it."

"Oh," said Kate, her anger erased, replaced by nothingness, no feeling or thought or word. It was Doris who spoke, who moved Kate forward.

"I needed to escape judgmental eyes too," said Doris, "but I'm going to face the lot of them now. On my way home to Gander," she said, her tone gentle. "Scary, isn't it? The pain of bringing a little one into the world, then raising her on your own. It's all bluster on the outside, shivering on the inside. That was me anyway. Common sense gave me a kick. I need help and my little Mary needs her grandmother. The rest of the community can go to hell in a handcart for all I care. But my mom? Mary's grandmother? Now there's a woman who never leans over clothes lines, casting judgements."

Kate sighed out a memory. "I was three-and-a-half when I set eyes on my grandmother." She paused. "My father and I escaped the tidal wave, and I was petrified of everything until the moment I met Nanny."

"Burin? The tidal wave in Burin years ago?"

Kate nodded. "It took my whole family except for Dad and me."

"God rest their souls." A whisper. Sufficient.

"Nanny told me that the ocean had spit me back, that if it wanted me, it would have kept me, that I was safe with her. Said she would see to that for the rest of her days."

"And has she?"

"Always there for me, my nan."

"You going for a visit?"

"Yes, and no. I'm going to a funeral. My Aunt Clara died. TB ravaged her. The funeral is in St. John's. Nanny will be there."

"May Clara rest in peace." The sign of the cross.

"Doris," Kate began, then stopped. *How can I put this?*

"Out with it," prompted Doris.

"Are you going to tell her? Mary, I mean. Are you going to tell her who her father is?"

"A good question. I'm thinkin' on that one. I'm going to Gander and I'm going to talk to Mom. I'm sure she'll help me get things sorted." She nodded. "I think I will tell Mary though. Secrets can sear the soul right out of you. Some say that your children know something's wrong even if they don't know what it is."

"How long will it be before you tell her?"

"How long is a bit of twine?" Doris shrugged. "When she asks about her daddy, I guess. A few years before that happens."

"The truth? Will you tell her the truth?"

Doris turned and stared into Kate's eyes. "Like to think I would. People need to know where they come from. Besides, it doesn't matter how a child starts off life, it only matters how they end up, and that comes down to the choices they make."

Kate shook her head. "I'm not sure," she said. "I spend so much time arranging the furniture in my little one's life, trying to protect her from sharp corners and edges. How could I ever tell her?"

"Seems impossible now. And it is. No need tormenting yourself over it. Put it at the back of your mind. Let it sit, percolate. You will know when you're ready, you will know when she's ready. Then you can choose to tell. Or to ignore."

Kate let out a long sigh. "Yes," she said, "I suppose you're right." Something in Kate gelled, a temporary settling. She had time on her side. The worry fell away. Kate drifted, vaguely aware of clacking of rails and shunting of trains.

Kate said goodbye to Doris in Gander and settled in for the trip to St. John's. As expected, the Avalon Peninsula was socked in with fog and the train rolled into and through the grey. A void in time, her mind blank until the train ventured deeper into the peninsula and the fog became intermittent, allowing for scenes of scrubland, gnarled trees, and jagged rock. A harsh environment. When the train screeched to a halt in Riverhead Station in St. John's, Kate was more than happy to see the end of her journey. Would Nanny meet her? Dulcie?

Kate stepped onto the platform and into the station, staring, searching the crowds. No sign of Dulcie. No sign of Nanny.

"Kate. Kate." A familiar voice. Kate turned.

There was Rosemary, rain dripping from her nose and hair plastered to her head. Her trench coat was unbuttoned, its belt undone and dragging through footprints and cigarette butts and God knows what else on the station floor. Slightly disconcerted, Kate managed to smile. "So good to see you, Rosemary," she said as she retrieved the soiled end of the wayward belt and threaded it through its waiting loop. She leaned in for a hug. "Terrible day for you to be out and about. Here, take my handkerchief. Where is Nanny? Dulcie?"

"We'll get to that, my love." Rosemary dabbed her eyes and blew her nose. She shoved the handkerchief into a pocket.

Something was off. "Where are they?" Kate asked again. "Is everything okay?"

Rosemary tugged at Kate's arm. "Let's get home first. I barely remembered to turn off the stove. Thank goodness for eggs on the boil clicking against the pot. I got to them right quick."

Alarmed now, Kate locked her stance. "No, Rosemary," she said, her tone battle-ready. "I'm not going anywhere until you tell me what's going on."

The two stood taut in the centre of a crowded station with veterans limping, babies crying, and porters hauling. Around them chatter swirled, words about Newfoundland remaining independent or becoming a tenth province in Canada. Political concerns for political times. Occasional announcements about arrivals and departures and delays cut into the jumble. The look between Kate and Rosemary did not break until a thin man in a pin-striped suit, grey hair and beard walked between them. A peripheral glance at the two women had him stepping back from them, walking around them. "Please do excuse me," he said, his tone so kind that it melted the standoff between Rosemary and Kate.

Both women sighed. "You're pushing at an open door, Kate," offered Rosemary. "I'm not trying to keep secrets here." She pointed at a wooden bench in the heart of the station and aimed toward it. Kate followed.

"Where's Dulcie?" Kate said as soon they had taken a seat.

Rosemary took her time, let out a slow breath. "Long story, that."

"Shorten it."

"Good enough. Dulcie . . . well, Dulcie has not been herself recently. Forgets what she's doing and why she's doing it. Went for a walk in the middle of getting the dinner the other week. And yesterday, she got herself in a bit of trouble."

Kate blinked. "I'm going to need details."

"Shoplifting."

"Dulcie? Stealing? Why in heaven's name would Dulcie take anything that wasn't hers?"

Rosemary shrugged. "She muttered something about being old, therefore invisible to the clerks at the store. Anyway, she took the stuff she wanted, just marched out of the Bon Marché with three pairs of socks on her hands and a pair of nylons in each coat pocket." Rosemary held her hands up and looked from one to the other, comic disbelief on her face. "Just this morning she said she was going off to the constabulary to turn herself in. Against my better judgement to let her go but, as I said, the eggs were on the boil."

"This morning? But Clara's funeral is today."

"Said she'd be there in time if she's not in His Majesty's Penitentiary."

"We have to get her." Kate lurched to her feet but couldn't convince those feet to take a single step. "Wait a minute." She slowly pivoted back to Rosemary. "Where's Nanny?" she said.

"As far as I know, your nan will be at the funeral. Father Mahony said he would give her a ride to the funeral." Tears flooded Rosemary's eyes. "It's been a bit of a worry lately, your nan. Hopefully, she'll move into the boarding house after today. We have room and would love to have her. I don't really know what's going on with her."

Kate caught curious eyes around her, people pausing, pointing fingers before moving on. She dismissed them outright. Her only concern was her grandmother. "Rosemary," she said tentatively, "do you remember Dulcie warning Clara to keep an eye on Nanny?"

Rosemary nodded. "All too well. And Clara did her best. But Clara was ill."

"I know. I know." Agitated, Kate looked around, taking in all the people for a second time, searching for some sign of the two she wanted to see. No joy there. What to do next? "We'll see Nanny at the funeral then," she said. Kate moved into action. "Right now, we must find Dulcie." With Rosemary on her heels, Kate tore past people and baggage and benches, through the doors and then stopped, stymied. Rosemary, breathless, caught up.

"Where first, Rosemary?" said Kate. "The constabulary? The boarding house?"

"You looking for me?" The approaching Dulcie wore a slump and walked with a limp.

Kate reached and gathered Dulcie in, hugging her, then holding her at arm's length to take in the grey hair scraped into a bun and the deep lines etched onto her face. "Whatever are you doing, Dulcie? Stealing? And you a saint of a woman."

Dulcie pulled out of Kate's grasp. "Saint, my arse. Most of my saintly life is like the wake of a ship. Behind me now. Aging is not for the weak, let me tell you. Tried to get the shop people to serve me but they don't pay no never mind to old people. They looked right past me to the painted floozy at the back of me. I don't know what came over me, but I helped myself to stockings and socks and sailed right out the door. They didn't notice me coming and they didn't notice me going."

"So you really didn't get caught?" said Kate.

"No, but the guilt of it had at me and I wanted to be free of the deed before the funeral. This morning, a young constable took both my confession and the merchandise, offering to return it himself. 'You look just like my granny,' he said as he patted my arm and sent me on my way." She reached into her pocket. "Sweet Heart of Jesus!" She withdrew a pair of nylons and held them up for the others to see. "I'm going to hell now for sure."

"Put them away." Rosemary shoved the nylons back into Dulcie's pocket.

Dulcie was having none of it. She retrieved them and dropped them into a nearby garbage can. Returning, she brushed her hands together. "Don't need no stolen stockings." She turned to Kate. "Where's Kathleen?"

"We think Father Mahony is bringing her to the church," said Kate.

"Think?"

"We don't know for sure, Dulcie," said Rosemary. "We just don't know."

"Oh," said Dulcie, the one syllable sagging with disappointment. She swallowed hard. "It's difficult to believe Clara's gone, isn't it?"

Back at the boarding house, with the kettle on the boil and two hours on their hands, they shared their grief in stories and tears. A pause in the talk came with tea and toast, obligatory fuel, traditional comfort. Spoons clinked cups, knives scraped butter, and Kate scanned faces. Only three at the table. There was a time when there were six, Nanny and Clara and Izzie too. The table teetered. Rosemary grabbed a matchbook from her pocket and stuck it under the wobbly leg. Balance achieved. Rosemary was good at that, finding balance. Kate gave her a grateful smile.

CHAPTER 53

At the funeral Mass for Clara in the Cathedral of Notre Dame, *Pater Noster, Dominus vobiscum,* and *Requiescat in Pace* wafted to the heavens on tendrils of incense, the fragrance serving to lock in the memory of the day, its silence, its sadness. Throughout the service a puzzled, an anxious Kate looked for her grandmother. *Where are you, Nanny?* Kathleen was nowhere to be seen.After the burial, back at the boarding house, Dulcie took charge.

"We need to know what's going on with Kathleen," she said as she took off her coat and hat. "Why has she missed her own daughter's funeral? We must call Father Mahony. Kate, would you right away?"

"Of course, I'll do it." Kate dialled the operator and in minutes had reached the rectory in Freshwater. Kate cut short the obligatory greetings and condolences, and got to the meat of the matter.

Hanging up the phone, she turned to the others. "Father Mahony stopped in at Nanny's to collect her for the drive here. She refused, saying she would take the train. He'll go back again, to check on her, he promised. He'll get back to us as soon as he's been to her house."

Throughout the evening, into the night, the phone on the wall in the hall of the boarding house refused to ring. Occasionally, Dulcie or Rosemary or Kate would walk past it, willing it into action or checking for the dial tone. No news came. The baffled residents of the boarding house caved to fatigue.

"Tomorrow is another day," offered Dulcie as they all trudged off to bed.

"Tomorrow," echoed Kate who would have headed to Freshwater that night if she could, but there was no train or taxi available until the morning.

On that tomorrow, she boarded the first train to Freshwater to find things out for herself. At the station in St. John's, Kate pocketed her wedding ring: different lies required now, lies in which she would be single, working as a receptionist, and living in a boarding house in Toronto.

In Freshwater, Kate walked into a deserted house, its walls bleeding loneliness. She remembered the time she asked Kevin if houses get lonely, and the memory brought a glacial pang. Now she saw the answer. Sadness sank her and she sat, staring at walls, then broke into sobs. *Where are you, Nanny?* After she had cried herself out, Kate headed for the rectory, knowing that the best option for help was through the priest from the pulpit on Sunday morning. Unable to sit still with the worry for the rest of Saturday, she opted to stop in at one house after another, calling "anybody in?" Questions asked, no answers, tea offered, none taken. When neighbours offered to continue the door-to-door search, an exhausted Kate nodded gratefully and headed back to Nanny's house and lay down; sleep instantly took her into blackness.

The next morning after Mass, Kate stood on the steps of the church, where many members of the congregation stopped to express sympathy over Clara and hope about Kathleen. Unfortunately, some had more to say.

"I'm Bridget, dear. Sure you don't remember me," said one woman, "but I must say to you that your grandmother got pretty good at keeping to herself. Haven't seen her in a dog's age." Kate nodded. When Bridget stepped back and cleared her throat, Kate leaned in. *Is there something more?*

"And how is it that a young woman like yourself is living in Toronto?" Bridget asked, edging closer, so close that Kate could peer into every wrinkle in the battlefield on the woman's face. Kate shuffled her feet and lied her lies and watched disapproval rise in the eyes of the overly concerned Bridget. "Such a sad thing, a spinster like yourself with no future to look forward to." Bridget pursed her lips and patted Kate's shoulder before sidling away.

Kate caught herself being amused by this simple encounter, one which affirmed that there was indeed no future to look forward to . . . not here anyway. Gossip about her spinster state would spread like weeds throughout this community. How right she was about leaving her little one out of this situation.

A week passed, with no word or sight of Nanny. Reluctantly, Kate left her family house, locking the door, dropping the key off at the rectory into the reliable hands of Father Mahony, whom Clara had named executor. She could handle any required paperwork from St. John's, or if need be, from Ontario. She went back to the boarding house, planning to stay at least another week.

One morning near the end of that week, she awakened to the scent of bacon and the swish of a dust mop, its strands of yarn poking into the space between door and floor as it fluttered past her room. Familiar this place and its daily routine. Helping with cleaning and cooking used to be Kate's job. Now it was Teresa's.

Kate tossed the blankets and took time stretching. No sense of urgency. If news about Nanny had come overnight, it would have found its way through her door. She allowed herself the comfort of momentary reprieve from worry about her grandmother. Images of Izzie and Kathy drifted in, stirring up love and longing.

As she switched to thoughts of Clara and her funeral, a wave of sadness descended. Heavy with loss, she struggled to sit upright, hoping that the heft would slip away. But no. She sighed into the certainty that she would carry it for a while. No sense struggling against it when the way out of it was through it. Yes, Nanny would have said that, and Nanny would be right as rain. *Where are you, Nanny?* With the need to know came the need to move, to get out of this room. She swung her legs over the side of the bed.

In the kitchen, Kate found Dulcie at the kitchen table and staring at the calendar on the wall.

"Any news?"

"Not a word." Dulcie set her spoon at a lean and stomped toward the calendar where she stabbed a finger at the date. "June 9, 1949. They'll be swearing in the first provincial cabinet. There's no going back now. We're all Canadian and that's all there is to it." A deep sigh fell from her. "Maybe Clara is better off. The soul of Newfoundland might not survive the likes of this."

"The soul of Newfoundland? Dulcie, I haven't given enough thought to the soul of Clara, never mind that of Newfoundland. Right now, my only concern is the whereabouts of Nanny."

"Well, me darlin', there's likely no need to worry about the soul of Clara anyway. I'm sure she found whatever peace she was after in the sacrament of Confession. There was a priest there at the end, you know. But as for your grandmother?" She let out a sniff. "We don't know where Kathleen Kerrigan is, but we do know she did not seek solace from her parish priest."

Kate paused. "Do you suppose . . ." she said.

"Suppose what? Out with it, Kate, whatever it is."

Kate plunged. "Do you suppose she did herself in, Dulcie?"

Dulcie crossed herself. She shuddered. "All we know is no one has seen her since Father Mahony stopped by to offer her a ride to the funeral."

"That doesn't answer my question, Dulcie," Kate whispered. "You used to say that one time she had gone off 'with the fairies.' I know she was at the mental hospital then."

Dulcie looked Kate straight in the eyes. "I hates to say it, but the truth is I'm scared out of my wits thinking she just took herself into the sea."

The words coiled painfully into Kate's innards. Served her right, asking such a question when she didn't want to hear tell of a truthful answer. She plopped into a chair and pushed against the hurt. "Why would she do that to us?"

"It would be herself she'd be doing it to, not us, not you, Kate. Sometimes life bends us to the point where it breaks us. Sometimes there's no coming back from it. Maybe the loss of Clara was just too much."

"But she came back before, didn't she? A long time ago? When Clara was a little girl?"

Dulcie patted Kate's hand. "A long time ago," she said. A long sigh followed. "We can only hope, just take each moment as it comes. I'll grant you that the hardest part of any hard situation is the waiting." Pushing her hands against the table, Dulcie hefted the weight of herself to her feet.

"Don't be bothering yourself with trying to unravel the mystery that is Kathleen Kerrigan," Dulcie said. "Some stories she told you, others Clara has put on paper for you. I know she sent you some letters, but Clara said there were enough stories to last a lifetime. The rest are stored in a well-worn brown suitcase."

Kate uttered a gasp. "What suitcase? Where?"

"Arrived from the sanitorium just this morning. Don't know what the holdup was, but Teresa is putting it in your room as we speak. It'll be there for you after you have your breakfast."

Curiosity pricked Kate but courtesy restrained her. She made her way through the tea and toast Dulcie made for her and even cleared the table. Then she bolted.

CHAPTER 54

Kate grabbed the suitcase from the floor in her room. She grappled with locks, lifted the lid, and dumped the contents onto the bed. For a long time, a longed-for time, she combed through notebooks and letters. Clara had written everything she knew, everything she thought, every opinion she had formed. Kate read until her eyes ached.

Strand upon strand of stories lay in front of her. Stories about Nanny, Clara, Kevin, Robert, and Dulcie. What, if anything, should she do with all these stories? Clara, bless her heart and rest her soul, had penned all this to show her love for Kate, to explain her choices to Kate. A younger Kate, a naïve Kate would have needed this explanation. But Kate was a mother herself now. The mere thought of having to give up her Kathy? Kate shuddered. Yet, Clara had done that. Clara had sacrificed motherhood for Kate.

What about Nanny, who was still nowhere to be found? Kate expected grief to rise again, but what cropped up in its stead was gratitude. Surprising, at first. But then its appropriateness sang: Nanny had saved her life, had loved her, and cared for her. She tightened her fingers around her teacup and stumbled into her next breath. Without Nanny, all that was left now of her bloodline was little Kathy and Kate herself. All the rest dead or faded away, all kith and kin. Had Nanny chosen to disappear forever?

"Her name was Kathleen, just like me," she said into the mirror above the dresser. Her reflection, that of a young Kathleen or a young Clara, offered her a quizzical look. "Are you coming back, Nanny?" asked Kate.

The 'no' that she sensed caused tears to spring. A blurry-eyed Kate looked at the bits of stories scattered on the bed like pearls from a broken string. If not shared, the stories would vanish like Nanny. Should Kate let that happen? *Would Nanny want me to tell these stories to Kathy? Would Clara?*

The image of her smiling three-year-old, blond-haired, blue-eyed daughter dispelled the idea of sharing the stories. In a flurry, Kate clawed up letters, shoved them into the suitcase, and slammed the lid. Her child could be hurt by these stories, these *weapons.* She wouldn't hide these papers; she would destroy them. *The kitchen stove? The parlour fireplace? Which would be the funeral pyre?*

She reached a hand to the doorknob, the cold of which met her resolve and splintered it. Her mind returned to an image of Doris from the train, Doris with the baby, Doris with the issue: would she tell her own child the truth? What was it Doris had said? "People need to know where they come from." Kate could have sworn that Doris' voice had sounded in her ear.

Sighing, Kate walked backward from the door, bumped into the bed, and plopped onto it. She dropped the suitcase and, on pause now, reconsidered the situation. *Perhaps Doris is right.* Kate could not destroy the stories, not today. She could save them. She could hide them. Perhaps, at some point, she *would* destroy them. Perhaps not. Perhaps Kathy would come across them in the attic, the way the Kate had come across letters on the schooner. Letters that wove the truth about the life of Kate Kerrigan, about Clara's willingness to sacrifice motherhood to protect Kate, about Kathleen's willingness to sacrifice her own soul to protect Kate. And Kate, due to their good graces, despite her own mistakes, had found what she needed in life: the joy of motherhood and the love of Izzie.

It was time for Kate to go home.

KATHLEEN

CHAPTER 55

IT IS STILLED, THE SEA.

The North Atlantic is hushed, its surface stripped of warships, its depths of warheads. Allied victory ushers in global change: the United States and the Union of Soviet Socialist Republics emerge as superpowers.

The Second World War conquerors pay heed to lessons learned at the end of the Great War when, in 1918, no recovery assistance was offered to the aggressor Germany. That lack of compassion led to starvation and desperation and escalation of a man called Hitler. Now, it is determined that the US will fund the economic revival of Japan and Germany, and that the USSR will do the same for the East European countries. In this, the two powers can agree, but their differing ideologies lead to political hostility: a Cold War looms.

In 1949, Newfoundland walks into the arms of Canada. Many disappointed citizens of St. John's had wished to be an independent country again. On Confederation Day, they lambast the people of outport communities for their foolishness in following the brash Joey Smallwood into Confederation. On the day that Newfoundland becomes the tenth province in Canada, its tricolour flag—pink for the rose of England, green for the Emerald Isle, a white band separating the two—flies at half-mast in St. John's. The grief-stricken singing of "The Ode to Newfoundland" fills the air.

The spirit of me flies low, also stricken with grief. I too need repose. But I must finish this telling. Almost done. Certainly done in.

Among things told is that my daughter, my Clara, has succumbed to tuberculosis.

Among things told is that my granddaughter Kate has left the island again, to be with Izzie to raise their little girl.

Among things to be told is the fate of the disappeared: the corporeal Kathleen . . .

For a long time, Kathleen holds hope that Clara will come home. Indeed, for a short time, Clara re-appears, but then illness reclaims her. After Clara's return to the sanitorium, every crunch of gravel in the lane spurs Kathleen through the door to the garden gate where she searches in vain, hoping to see her daughter again. An everyday event this, after which she trudges to the cellar door and stops, shoulders slumped, nostrils flared, and sniffs the air, perhaps looking for a telltale odour of what lies within. Then she retires to her rocking chair with her knitting. Despair seems imminent but she holds on as days dissolve, one into the next, on and on.

One day in 1949, Father Mahony arrives at Kathleen's door for the second time in recent days. He marches straight into the kitchen and states his purpose: announcing Clara's demise, offering Kathleen condolences and blessings and a lift to the funeral.

Kathleen blinks in silence at the news. Suddenly, she scowls. "Do you think I'm daft? Last time you gave me a ride to town, Father, you dropped me off at the mental hospital. I'll be making my way on the train, thank you very much." His face reddens and he scurries away. She remains sitting, thinking.

Her catalogue of memories, locked down for decades, splits its seams and streams images of death across Kathleen's mind: the innocent Jimmy, the demented Alphonse—*Thou shalt not kill.* The heartbroken Kevin, and the evil Patrick. *Thou shalt not kill.* The Commandment repeats in her mind now, unbidden, gathering speed like a runaway train on a downhill slope, her a mere passenger accruing guilt.

In her bedroom, Kathleen rummages through a drawer, pulls out the apron with the reinforced pockets, and dons it. She heads through the front door, leaving it ajar. Her pace slow and determined, she walks from Freshwater toward Jerseyside Hill. Fog appears on the horizon and rolls toward her, a welcoming cloak.

On the shoreline, Kathleen spends time looking longingly at the sea. Then she collects beach rocks, medium size, all colours—sand, brown, reddish, white. She palms them, she pockets them.

A quivering wisp of ghost, I glide through the grey haze that covers the side of this hill and slide alongside the corporeal Kathleen as she stares toward the sea. Her breath pours in and out, a surprisingly steady rhythm. I slip into a rock-filled pocket of her apron, for I know her intent.

"Our Father who art in heaven," she says aloud. Kathleen has come here with a purpose. She knows there is no forgiveness for what she is about to do. Nonetheless, a litany of prayers spews from deep within her.

As her ghost, I am privy to her swirl of thoughts, or perhaps I recall them, her going over and over them—Alphonse, Jimmy, Kevin, Patrick. Kate. And Clara whose childhood innocence Kathleen couldn't protect. Thoughts spinning and spinning until Kathleen's mind is crowded, then stilled, catatonic. This is a familiar state for the corporeal Kathleen, the same one she was in when her child Jimmy died at the hands of her husband. Thoughts hurtled then too. She couldn't rein them. She had sprinted from the house, scratching her skin and shedding her clothes as she ran. It was Dulcie who saved her, shielded her, and sent for the priest. But now? Dulcie is nowhere in sight. As for me?

I, the ghost, am mere observer as the living Kathleen stands alone, staring at the sea near the former location of the pontoon bridge. "Won't last jig time," the old salts had said of that bridge. And ultimately, the ocean proved them right.

The wind is still, the sea is calm, and the haze hangs, a silent curtain. Any sound, a simple cough, could be carried across the Gut, caught in Placentia on the other side. The Atlantic nudges Kathleen, sliding a small beckoning wave over her feet and drawing it back. Then it idles in wait.

Kathleen remains motionless while two gulls drift in and land on a nearby rock. When they scream warning calls, she erupts, spitting at them.

"Ye mind yer own damn business," she says. "As if the likes of ye are going to stop me doing what I got to do." She waves a hand at them. "Be off with ye!" The gulls comply and whatever ties fastened Kathleen to the earthly world begin to snap, thread by thread. As it did many years ago, on the night she fed Alphonse to the waves, the ocean stirs in compliance. A groan emanates from Kathleen's core, trailed by manic muttering and wringing of hands.

The living Kathleen is done with living. In her careworn heart and beleaguered soul, she knows the finality of this choice allows no opportunity for a breast-beating *mea culpa* in a confession box. But that holds no sway. For Kathleen, the saddest thing in the world is to lose a child and she has lost all three, one to murder, one to war, one to disease. But her granddaughter Kate and great-granddaughter Kathy are safe. With Izzie.

Kathleen sees nothing left for herself, no purpose to her at all.

As ghost, I see nothing left for me here either. Unable to extricate myself from the stones in Kathleen's apron pocket, I move with her as she moves forward, the stones clacking with her every step. Nothing for me to do but to wait and narrate. Like the Ancient Mariner, burdened to tell and tell and tell again.

The last strand of Kathleen's thin moorings snaps. As Newfoundland walks into the arms of Canada, Kathleen Kerrigan walks into the arms of the sea. With her steps certain on slick stones, her body impervious to icy water, she edges forward, the sea wrapping her ankles, her shins, her knees. When the water climbs to her thighs, she leans and tumbles. The sea welcomes her into the same rough current that had once vanquished the pontoon bridge. Will she re-surface?

No. The ocean is granting her what she needs, to be swept away, her remains unattainable. That is for the best. A body found with rock-filled pockets leaves no doubt about intent. If her body were to be recovered, would there be forgiveness? The very existence of me, the phantom, on an eternal journey of penance is evidence to the contrary. Not in this time, not in this place, not with this Church, not with her God.

And I, the ghost, confined to watching, am left with nothing to see, nothing but the sea, as it swishes still water into waves and ushers the corporeal Kathleen to its depths. Gently into the dark she goes, ready for it, no quarrel about it. The instant her heart stops, her soul leaves. And I, a grey wraith, soar to the surface. I have weathered another telling. But there is no reward for it, no rest in it.

I sweep through time and space and come to an abrupt halt, a speck of dust in the wind on the shore of Argentia, a small fishing community in the summer of 1915. Eyes on the sky, I follow the blinding-white underbelly of a seagull to an offshore dory rowed by a teenage boy whose eyes go wide at the sight of a little stowaway—his six-year-old sister—emerging from beneath the oilskins in the bow.

That's the cue. Once again, I start my story . . .

"It begins, and ends, with the sea."

QUESTIONS AND TOPICS FOR DISCUSSION

- In each book of this trilogy, Daylon has given a starring role to one character: Book I, *Of Sea and Seed,* focuses on the journey of Clara; Book II, *Of Sea and Sand,* on the journey of Kevin; Book III, *Of Sea and Soul,* on the journey of Kate. The umbrella character is Kathleen Kerrigan whose story runs the entire length of the series. There is one more character, the sea. How is the sea a mirror for Kathleen?
- One of the themes of Book III is "things are not always what they seem." What are examples or instances of this?
- At the heart of Of Sea and Soul lies the journey to the soul. Kate, at the beginning of Book III thinks she knows who "knit her," then learns that her "aunt" Clara has lied. Yes, she knows who her mother is, but who is her father? Why won't Clara tell her? What steps does Kate take in pursuit of the answer?
- What gifts from Kevin does Robert bring to Clara and Kate? What is the meaning of these gifts?
- Kate wants to live the truth of her soul but is mired in religious and cultural beliefs about the role of women. Eventually she comes to her own conclusions. Would she, if not in a dire situation, have chosen the life partner she did?
- Clara keeps secrets from her daughter Kate. Will Kate follow the same path by lying to her own daughter? Kate could destroy all evidence, reasoning that her child Kathy need never know the pain of the truth. Under what circumstances, if any, would Kate reveal the story of Kathy's beginnings?
- In Book I, Daylon says, "There's no accounting for the mood of the sea. It rocks you into a state of trust and then steals your soul." How does that apply in Book III?

READING/VIEWING LIST

THE KERRIGAN CHRONICLES TRILOGY

Andrieux, J. P. 2009. *Rumrunners.* St. John's, NL: Flanker Press.

Anonymous. 2003. *Eine Frau in Berlin (A Woman in Berlin, Eight Weeks in the Conquered City).* Germany: Eichborn AG, Frankfurt am Main

Argentia 282 Coastal Defence Battery Municipal Heritage Site. Canada's Historic Sites. https://www.historicplaces.ca/en/rep-reg/place-lieu.aspx?id=6122

Barrett, Heather. 2021. "The Mill Girls." CBC Radio Documentary https://newsinteractives.cbc.ca/longform/the-mill-girls/

"Behind Enemy Lines, Story of British Commandos in WWII." 2001. Netflix Documentaries. https://www.netflix.com/ca/title/80114588

Bond's Path and Southeast Come Home Year Committee. 2006. *An Armful of Memories.* Placentia, NL: Transcontinental.

Bedard, John. 2017. *Thetford Park (Halifax to Liverpool on a coal burning ship stuffed with ammo).* Canada: Independently Published.

Berman, Kathryn. n.d. "Hidden Children in France during the Holocaust." The World Holocaust Remembrance Center.
https://www.yadvashem.org/articles/general/hidden-children.html

Cashin, Peter. 2012. *My Fight for Newfoundland.* St. John's, NL: Flanker Press.

Collier, Keith. 2011. A Trip to the San: TB Patient Experiences in Newfoundland in the 20th Century. Newfoundland and Labrador Heritage Website.
https://www.heritage.nf.ca/articles/society/tuberculosis-experience.php

—. 2011. Cottage Hospitals and Health Care in Newfoundland. Newfoundland and Labrador Heritage Website. https://www.heritage.nf.ca/articles/society/cottage-hospitals.php

—. 2011. History of Tuberculosis and Its Prevalence in Newfoundland. Newfoundland and Labrador Heritage Website.
https://www.heritagenf.ca/articles/society/tuberculosis-newfoundland.php

Collins, Gary. 2013. *The Gale of 1929.* St. John's, NL: Flanker Press.

Collins, Gerard. 2011. *Finton Moon.* St. John's, NL: Killick Press.

Crook, Flight Lieutenant David, DFC. 2015. *Spitfire Pilot: A Personal Account of the Battle of Britain.* Amazon Digital Services LLC.

Davies, Christine. 2015. "Sounds of Victory: St. John's Celebrated VE-Day 70 Years Ago." CBC News. https://www.cbc.ca/news/canada/newfoundland-labrador/sounds-of-victory-st-john-s-celebrated-ve-day-70-years-ago-1.3053991 Accessed January 29, 2023

Dohey, Larry. 2019. "Celebrations in the Streets, VE Day." http://archivalmoments.ca/2019/05/06/celebrations-in-the-streets-ve-day/ Accessed August 3, 2021

Duke, Darrell. 2013. *Thursday's Storm: The August Gale of 1927.* St. John's, NL: Flanker Press.

–. 2018. *An Irish Tale of Leaving*. Newfoundland: Stagehead Publications.

–. 2021. *The Garden Gate: Argentia's Sacrifice for WWII.* Newfoundland: Stagehead Publications.

Duley, Margaret. 1941. *Highway to Valour.* New York: The MacMillan Company.

Evans, Calvin. 2014. *Master Shipbuilders of Newfoundland and Labrador, Volume 2.* St. John's, Newfoundland: Breakwater Books.

Everts, Lee K. M. 2016. *The Placentia Area: A Changing Mosaic.* Placentia: Lulu.com.

Fitzgerald, Jack. 2005. *Newfoundland Disasters.* St. John's, NL: Creative Publishers.

–. 1989. *Strange but True Newfoundland Stories.* St. John's, NL: Creative Publishers.

Freshwater Come Home Year Book Committee. 2002. *Freshwater Come Home Year.* Freshwater, NL: Robinson-Blackmore.

Goodall, Scott. "The Freedom Trail (Chemin de la Liberté): WWII Escape Route to Spain." https://www.ariege.com/en/discover-ariege/occupation-and-resistance/freedom-trail. Accessed June 25, 2018.

Gooley, Tristan. 2016. *How to Read Water: Clues and Patterns from Puddles to the Sea.* North America: The Experiment, LLC.

Halliwell, Sarah and Cooke, Tim. 1995. *Eyewitness War: Personal Accounts of World War II.* London: Marshal Cavendish Books.

Hanrahan, Moira. 2006. *Tsunami: The Newfoundland Tidal Wave Disaster.* St. John's, NL: Flanker Press.

Hershco, Dr. Tsilla. 2007. "The Jewish Resistance in France During WWII: The Gap between History and Memory." http://jcpa.org/article/the-jewish-resistance-in-france-during-world-war-ii-the-gap-between-history-and-memory. Accessed Aug 2, 2018.

Higgins, Jenny. 2007. "Great Depression—Impacts on the Working Class." Newfoundland and Labrador Heritage Website. https://www.heritage.nf.ca/articles/politics/depression-impacts.php

–. 2006. "Royal Navy." Newfoundland and Labrador Heritage Website. https://www.heritage.nf.ca/articles/politics/royal-navy.php

–. 2006. "Argentia." Newfoundland and Labrador Heritage Website. https://www.heritage.nf.ca/articles/politics/argentia-base.php

High, Steven, Ed. 2016. *Occupied St. John's: A Social History of a City at War, 1939–1945.* Montreal: McGill-Queens University Press.

Hisscock, Phillip. 1999. Newfoundland and Labrador Customs. Newfoundland and Labrador Heritage Website.
https://www.heritage.nf.ca/articles/society/newfoundland-labrador-customs

Holocaust Encyclopedia. Kristallnacht. USA: United States Holocaust Memorial Museum. https://encyclopedia.ushmm.org/content/en/article/kristallnacht

Houlihan, Eileen. 1992. *Uprooted! The Argentia Story.* St. John's NL: Creative Publishers.

Johnston, Wayne. 1999. *The Colony of Unrequited Dreams.* Toronto, Ontario: Vintage Canada.

Kitts, Kathy H. 2013. *The Minesweeper's Letters.* USA: Kitts Family Publications

Lannon, Alice, and McCarthy, Mike. 1991. *Fables, Fairies, & Folklore of Newfoundland.* St. John's, NL: Jesperson Press Ltd.

"Life in the Shadows: Hidden Children and the Holocaust." USA: United States Holocaust Memorial Museum. https://www.ushmm.org/exhibition/hidden-children/insideX/

Major, Kevin. 2001. *As Near to Heaven by Sea: A History of Newfoundland and Labrador.* Toronto, Ontario: Penguin Books Canada Ltd.

"Mildred Quilty's story: Surviving the deadly K of C Hostel fire of 1942." CBC Archives. Posted: Dec 12, 2014 https://www.cbc.ca/news/canada/newfoundland-labrador/mildred-quilty-s-story-surviving-the-deadly-k-of-c-hostel-fire-of-1942-1.2869438

"Navy ship named after Margaret Brooke, 'naval hero' in SS Caribou sinking." CBC Archives. Posted: Apr 13, 2015 https://www.cbc.ca/news/canada/newfoundland-labrador/navy-ship-named-after-margaret-brooke-naval-hero-in-ss-caribou-sinking-1.3031254

Neary, Peter. 1988. *Newfoundland in the North Atlantic World 1929-1949.* Kingston and Montreal: McGill-Queen's University Press.

–, ed. 1996. *White Tie and Decorations: Sir John and Lady Hope Simpson in Newfoundland,* 1934-1936. Toronto: University of Toronto Press.

McKenna, Brian. Director. 2016. "Newfoundland at Armageddon." CBC Documentary. Gala Film Productions. Morag Loves Armageddon Inc. https://www.cbc.ca/documentaries/specials/newfoundland-at-armageddon-1.5092119

"No Price Too High: Canadians and the Second World War." Morningstar Entertainment. 2004.

O'Connor, Joe. 2016. "The Myth of Beaumont Hamel: How Newfoundland's tragic death march became a noble advance." Canada: The National Post. https://nationalpost.com/news/canada/newfoundland-beaumont-hamel

Phyne, John. On a Hillside North of the Harbour: Changes to the Centre of St. John's, 1942–1987.St. Francis Xavier University. https://journals.lib.unb.ca/index.php/nflds/article/view/22414/26068 Accessed October 4, 2023.

Power, C. Olive, ed. 2012. *Bridging Places & People from Big Barasway to Ship Harbour.* Placentia: Placentia Intertown 2012 Come Home Year Book Committee.

Raley, James. 2013. *I Fell four Miles and Lived: Missing in Action–WWII.* USA: Jamesgate Press LLC.

Rasky, Frank.(Page contributed by Chris Shelley, March 2000.) "Newfoundland's Furious Fire by Sabotage: The Knights Of Columbus Hostel Disaster of 1942." Newfoundland Grand Banks Website. http://ngb.chebucto.org/Articles/dis-knights-of-columbus-1942.shtml

Romkey, Bill, ed. 2009. *St. John's and the Battle of the Atlantic.* ST. John's, NL: Flanker Press.

Rosbottom, Ronald C. *The City of Light under German Occupation, 1940-1944.* New York: Little, Brown and Company, 2014.

Simon, Marie Jalowicz. 2014. Underground in Berlin: A young woman's extraordinary tale of survival in the heart of Nazi Germany. Canada: Alfred A. Knopf.

Strowbridge, Nellie P. 1988. *The Newfoundland Tongue.* St. John's NL: Flanker Press.

"Survivor of 1942 SS Caribou sinking recalls ordeal." CBC Archives. Posted October 4, 2012. https://www.cbc.ca/news/canada/newfoundland-labrador/survivor-of-1942 ss-caribou-sinking-recalls-ordeal-1.1287401

"The Placentia Area." Decks Awash: The Placentia Area Volume 17, No. 3. St. John's, NL: Memorial University of Newfoundland, May-June.

"Underfire: The Untold Story of Pfc Tony Vaccaro." 2016. HBO Documentary. Max Lewkowicz, Director.

Walsh, Barbara. 2013. *August Gale.* USA: Globe Pequot Press.

"War Junk: Juno Beach." 2015. Season 3, Episode 1. https://www.history.ca/shows/war-junk/video/juno-beach/561452611642/

"When I was in the San. "2020. Season 55, Episode 14. CBC Television: *Land and Sea.* https://gem.cbc.ca/land-and-sea-nfld/s55e14

"World War II Great Escapes: Freedom Trails, The Pyrenees." 2017. CBC Documentary Channel.

Yardley, Jonathan. 2014. "A History of Paris during Nazi Occupation." Date accessed August 2, 2018. https://www.washingtonpost.com/opinions/a-history-of-paris-during-nazi-occupation/2014/08/29/fce9e112-222c-11e4-958c-268a320a60ce_story.html?utm_term=.e792b4fee2b1:/

Young, Ron. 2006. *Dictionary of Newfoundland and Labrador.* St. John's NL: Downhome Publishing Inc.

–. 2005. *Downhome Memories.* St. John's, NL: Downhome Publishing Inc.

ACKNOWLEDGEMENTS

FIRST AND FOREMOST, I AM grateful to my father, Andrew Lannon (1922–2019) who sparked this particular writing journey when he told me a true story about a little girl who survived the 1929 Newfoundland tsunami. Subsequently, he told me many tales about life in Newfoundland during the Depression and Second World War.

Thank you to my mother, Mary (Shea) Lannon (1922–2000) who encouraged my interest in language by teaching me to recite Latin vesper hymns when I was in first grade. That ability earned me a place in the church choir where Gregorian Chant was the order of the day. I still love Latin, I still love to sing, and I still remember those hymns.

Thank you to "Tea & Critique" partners, Fran Brown and Mary Keane, for their invaluable input. Great writers, great friends, greatly appreciated.

Thank you to: Ron Young, founding editor of Newfoundland's *Downhome* magazine; Paul Butler, author of *The Good Docto*r; Nellie Strowbridge, author of *Ghost of the Southern Cross*; and Darrell Duke, author of *Thursday's Storm* for their generosity in taking time to read and endorse the first book of this trilogy. An extra thank you to Darrell Duke who is writing about the same area during the same era and who is gracious in sharing his knowledge of the time.

Thank you to Brian Rodda at www.roddawrites.com for creating the inset map of the Avalon and Burin Peninsulas of Newfoundland.

Thank you to Kilmeny Jane Denny for her superb editorial skills, excellent advice, and overall support throughout the publishing process of Books II and III of this trilogy

Thank you to the Newfoundland Archives Department of The Rooms Museum in St. John's, Newfoundland, for taking the time to respond both by email and phone to my concerns regarding the publication of the evacuation letter sent to all Argentia residents.

Thank you to *Downhome* magazine to which I subscribed for years. Throughout the writing, this monthly magazine was a constant source of information, entertainment, and inspiration.

Thank you to *Land and Sea*, the TV series from the CBC whose episodes, too numerous to detail, have inspired me.

Thank you to Argentia Facebook Group members Donald Lannon and Gerry Dollmont for taking time to respond to my research questions.

Thank you to the teachers at St. Edward's Elementary School, Sacred Heart High School, and Laval High School in Placentia, Newfoundland, for their skill, dedication, and high standards. The rules of grammar taught in English, and reinforced in Latin and French, have served the teacher and writer in me well. A particular nod to Grade 8 teacher Mrs. Annie Murphy for her habit of quoting lines from Shakespeare and for her insistence that poetry be committed to memory. It was in these formative school years that I learned to love the history, craft, and poetry of the English language.

Thank you to the Writers' Alliance of Newfoundland and Labrador for advice and support.

Thank you to the Federation of British Columbia Writers for information and support, in particular to past president Ben Nuttall-Smith, author of *Secrets Kept, Secrets Told*, for his ongoing encouragement.

Thank you M.T. Lannon for pointing me in the direction of the Basilica Heritage Foundation in St. John's, Newfoundland for information on the use of Latin in the Catholic Church in 1942, and thank you to John FitzGerald, Ph.D., Executive Director of the Basilica Heritage Foundation, for promptly supplying that information.

Thank you to British Columbia's Chilliwack/Abbotsford bookstore The Book Man (www.bookman.ca) for its enthusiastic support of local authors.

Thank you to my husband David for his love, support, and encouragement throughout all my creative endeavours. It takes perseverance to write novels; David has modelled that in his own life, having persevered though a long haul of cancer treatment which, twenty years ago, culminated in a stem cell transplant. He is my inspiration, my soulmate, my joy, my rock.

About the Author

Annie Daylon was born and raised in Newfoundland. She studied music at Mount Allison University and education at both the University of Manitoba and the University of British Columbia (M.Ed.). After many years teaching, she delved into her passion for writing. Annie lives in the British Columbia Fraser Valley with her husband, David. You can find out more about Annie at www.anniedaylon.com.

Dear Reader,

Thank you for taking the time to read *The Kerrigan Chronicles Trilogy: Of Sea and Seed, Of Sea and Sand,* and *Of Sea and Soul.* If you enjoyed these books, please consider telling your friends or posting a short review. Word of mouth is an author's best friend and is greatly appreciated.

My best to you,

Manufactured by Amazon.ca
Bolton, ON

50931342R00210